PETER Ralph

WHITE COLLAR
BLACKMAIL

ISBN: 978-0-6480514-3-5
Copyright © 2016 Peter Ralph

Typesetting and layout by WorkingType Design

BOOK 1

Prologue

The discovery of Richard Frampton's bound, blindfolded, and gagged body in a seedy Oakland hotel shocked the business community of San Francisco. Thought to be staid and conservative, Frampton had been a director of five public companies. Police were unable to determine whether he had been murdered or whether an S & M adventure had gone horribly wrong. Frampton had been found naked on his stomach, expertly bound in nearly one hundred feet of ropes. He had died of asphyxiation when one of the ropes had blocked his airways. Friends and business associates were shocked to find out about Frampton's clandestine life and were of no help to the police. He had been well known in the S & M community, but no one knew who he had been with the night he died.

Valerie Gibson had been PA to the CEO of a Miami-based high-tech public company, Xenex Inc., which provided customized cloud solutions to major corporations. She was a loner addicted to heroin and yet somehow had managed to hide her habit from her bosses. It was only when police found her body with a syringe next to it that her secret was revealed. Infection around countless puncture marks and bruises on her upper arms, told her sorry story. Police had no idea whether she had been murdered or died from an accidental overdose.

Les Carroll was a thirty-eight-year-old Philadelphia bachelor who was the financial controller of a medium-sized public company producing components for the airline industry. Carroll loved the poker machines and the booze. On Saturday nights, he would take a cab to 30th Street Station and a train to Atlantic City. He was a regular at Star City Casino and one night, when he left his billfold at home they were more than happy to provide him with credit. He hadn't intended it, but slowly the amount of credit increased until he owed so much he could no longer sleep. Strangely, the casino never sought or demanded payment from him, and he was lulled into a false sense of security. It was only when the Star City sold his debt that he realized the extent of his problems. The buyer immediately demanded payment in full, and when Carroll couldn't pay, he was told not to worry, that he could pay the debt off by providing financial information about his employer. He was outraged, and at first refused, but the buyer's employees were intimidating and very persuasive. Eventually, he caved in but was racked with guilt and the only solace he found was in a bottle.

One night, after a heavier than usual night's drinking, Carroll was standing on the Atlantic City rail platform waiting for a train back to 30th Street. Suddenly, he appeared to stumble, lose his balance and fall in front of the train. The station was crowded, but CCTV picked up a small, old man wearing a low-sitting hat, and a black overcoat, collar pulled up around his neck, standing directly behind Carroll. In the pandemonium that followed, the man remained at the back of the crowd for a few minutes before hobbling off the station. Atlantic City Police interviewed other witnesses who had been near Carroll, but all attempts to locate the old man failed. Police were not overly concerned as it was obvious that Carroll had been very drunk and accidentally stumbled off the platform into the path of the train.

Nothing connected the three deaths and after preliminary investigations, police put them in their cold case files and they gradually drifted off the radar.

FBI investigator, Chas Grinich, had stumbled upon the death of company director, Richard Frampton, when he had been investigating share transactions in companies in which Frampton had been a director. Grinich was a twenty-year veteran, and as soon as he became aware of Frampton's double life, he knew that he may have been subject to extortion. And that perhaps he was being blackmailed into releasing confidential, corporate information. Large, but not over-the-top long positions had been taken in the stocks of two companies that Frampton had been a director of immediately prior to the release of favorable, market sensitive information. The stocks had been immediately sold, and significant profits were realized. When Grinich checked the larger transactions, he found brokerage accounts in the names of homeless people that were closed after the stocks were sold. One account was in the name of someone who had been dead for more than a year. The bank accounts had been cleaned out, the funds disappearing into a merry go round of accounts controlled by lawyers and accountants. Grinich's gut told him that he was on to something big and sophisticated.

While investigating stock transactions in Xenex Inc., Grinich became aware of Valerie Gibson's death and her addiction to heroin. The stock dealings mirrored those that had occurred in the companies associated with Richard Frampton.

Grinich, motivated by his findings, searched the FBI's database looking for corporations where senior executives had met their deaths in suspicious circumstances. Les Carroll's name was one of those that appeared. Carroll had been an addicted gambler with large debts. Another easy mark. When Grinich checked the stock transactions in the company in which Carroll had been the financial controller, he saw the familiar pattern.

Grinich knew there had been stock manipulation and also suspected murder. If he was going to find those responsible, he would need help. He picked up his phone and called Aaron Lord, a good friend and the SEC's hardnosed, star investigator.

Chapter 1

The cab ride from the Carnegie Center to Chatham Square in Lower Manhattan along FDR Drive took just twenty minutes. Todd Hansen directed the taxi driver to a small pawn shop on the outskirts of Chinatown and told him to wait. He strode to the back of the shop, pushed a large black curtain out of the way and took the stairs to the basement. Facing him was a door with a small panel in the middle. It was about five foot from the floor. He was 5' 9" so he put his face to the panel and knocked impatiently. It slid away and behind it was an opaque glass window. He heard a whirring sound and knew the electronics to open the door had been activated.

Two doormen who might have been defensive linemen in another lifetime nodded as Todd entered the room. One of them said, "You're here an awful lot lately, Red. Maybe you should bring a bed." Todd ignored him. The smell of stale smoke assaulted his nostrils and yells of exultation were punctuated by groans and cursing. Television monitors showing horse races, basketball games, baseball, and the fights hung from every wall. Large boards flashed the odds of sporting events all over the US, the UK, and Australia. Half a dozen tables and chairs were spread around the room on clean but well-worn dark brown carpet. There were maybe twenty-five to thirty patrons, mainly men lining up at windows at the rear of the room. Todd joined one of the lines and when he reached the window said, "Santa Anita, race three, ten thousand the win, number seven, on my tab."

The teller looked up. "Yes, Mr. Hansen," she said, handing him his ticket. "Good luck."

The middle-aged, Armani-suited man who'd been behind Todd left the line without placing a bet and instead ordered two coffees from one of the waitresses. Most of the other patrons were imbibing drinks far stronger than coffee.

Todd took a seat at a vacant table, removed his iPad and was soon absorbed inputting details of other races. After about ten minutes he pushed the iPad to one side, glanced at his watch and then at the monitors. He heard the caller say, "Cozy Babe goes into gate five, and they're ready to jump in the third." He didn't believe in omens, but a warm feeling coursed through him at the mention of his horse's name. In less than sixty seconds, the race was over, and while there had been a lot of screaming and shouting, anyone looking at Todd would not have known whether he'd won or lost. The iPad was back in front of him, and he was inserting details of times, margins and anything else relevant for every horse in the race. Before the day was over, he would repeat the exercise for every horse in every race across the major North American meets. He felt the presence of someone standing next to him. When he looked up, a man holding two cups of coffee said, "Congratulations, young feller. It's not every day you win sixty thousand. Do you mind if I join you?"

Before Todd could answer, the man had taken a seat. "Here," he said, pushing a cup of coffee toward Todd. "I was behind you at the window and was sure you'd need this after the race. I backed Brazen Warrior and thought it was a certainty. I think it's still running." He laughed.

Todd wanted to tell him to get lost but instead found himself taking the coffee and saying, "Thanks. That's bad luck."

"You mean bad choice," the man said extending his hand. "Jack Elliot's the name and who might I be talking to?"

Elliot had a genial face, but Todd was an astute observer of human behavior and noticed that his eyes didn't smile. They were dark blue, unblinking, and there was scar tissue over them. "Todd Hansen," he replied. "Jack, I don't want to be rude, but I've got a cab waiting for me. I have to get back to work."

"What do you do?"

"I'm an accountant," Todd said, standing up. "Sorry, I have to fly."

"Before you go," Elliot said, "do you have a tip in the fourth? I've gotta get my money back. My wife will kill me."

"I wish I could help, but I don't even know the names of the horses in that race. After I've inputted the fields in all races, my system throws up the horses I should bet on. It only threw up one today."

"Incredible. Is your system foolproof?"

Elliot seemed friendly enough, but something about him made Todd uncomfortable. Perhaps it was the way his heavyset body destroyed the cut of his suit. Todd already regretted saying as much as he had. "Sorry, I have to go," he said, pulling his overcoat up around his neck and making a beeline for the door.

Elliot remained sitting at the table for a few more minutes. He hadn't learned anything that he hadn't already known about Todd Hansen, but that was hardly surprising. He already knew Todd's life history from kindergarten right up until his current employment as an audit manager with Montgomery Hastings & Pierce, accountants and tax consultants to the rich and famous. He finished his coffee before ambling over to a door next to the tellers' windows. The nearest teller pressed a button on the counter, and the door to a short corridor opened. There were two offices at the end of it, and Elliot entered the first and sat down opposite a weasel-faced little man.

"Ronny, how much credit are you giving the red-haired kid?" he asked.

"I already told you. Fifty thousand. He's never used a cent, and he's taken nearly three hundred thousand out of here in the past six months. He's got this system that's nearly infallible. A win rate of close to fifty percent. I ain't ever seen anything like it." Ronny groaned.

"Christ, you've been around for a hundred years and haven't fucking learned anything." Elliot snarled. "It's a flash in the pan, a hot streak, and it's gonna come to a sad end soon. I've never seen a system work in the long term, and when it fails, I want to be there to pick up the pieces. I want you to praise him, massage his ego, and encourage him to make bigger bets. He bet ten grand today and won sixty – tell him it could've been six hundred if he'd had bigger balls and bet a hundred grand. Once he starts losing, I want you to extend his credit to half a million. Don't worry, when the time is right, we'll buy his marker off you."

Chapter 2

The unobtrusive but luxurious offices of the privately owned ACME Investments Inc. were on the fiftieth floor of the Truman Building. There were no more than a hundred employees. Mainly accountants, lawyers and debt collectors employed to protect ACME's assets and ensure that rentals, dividends, and other income were collected and promptly banked. ACME had assets and investments in the billions, but its capital was only one hundred dollars with its funds coming indirectly from loans made by a Bermuda-based company, Vulture Inc.

A private elevator, exclusively for directors, whisked them from the underground parking garage to a small lobby adjoining the board-room. The floor to ceiling glass windows in the large room provided magnificent, unimpeded views of Central Park. The boardroom table had been carved from one enormous piece of Huon pine, and there were half a dozen leather chairs around it even though there could've been double that. The wall directly opposite the windows concealed a well-stocked bar. Like the offices, the boardroom was both luxurious and Spartan. There were no paintings or prints adorning the walls and there was not an artifact to be seen. Two distinct board meetings were held every month, the first formally considered and reviewed the operations of ACME. The second was of the board of Vulture Inc., the ultimate owner of Acme. The board meeting scheduled for today was of the latter variety and due to commence at 2 P.M. Minutes of these meetings were never taken, and each director was expected to take notes on matters that he or she was responsible for. Five blank pads and pens were on the boardroom table.

New York-based chairman, Dermott Becker, was the first to arrive. The urbane, tall, silver-haired, sixty-something Becker had been disbarred from practicing law for witness tampering while still in his early thirties. He had never looked back and had never sought readmission. Instead, he had amassed a small fortune. He took the chair at the head of the table.

A few minutes later, Becker was joined by the slightly younger Arthur Ridgeway, a former accountant who had signed off on a false prospectus that had cost investors millions of dollars. Becker had used all his brilliance to defend Ridgeway, but despite his efforts, the accountant had been imprisoned in Bonemount Penitentiary for five years. He'd lost all of his hair in jail and, being young and weedy, had suffered terribly at the hands of the other inmates. After his release, Ridgeway had shifted to Los Angeles and put the past behind him. He may have been small, but he was mentally tough and had somehow managed to block out the memories of Bonemount. Looking after ACME's interests in California, Arizona and Nevada had been his salvation and most likely saved his life. He shook Becker's hand and took the chair to the right of him.

The third director to arrive was engineer, Harry O'Brien, who was only in his mid-forties. He had made the mistake of under-engineering a small steel bridge to save costs. A family of five had died when the bridge collapsed, and it was only Becker's brilliance that had resulted in a hung jury and no jail time. Later, there had been rumors of witness and jury tampering that eventually resulted in Becker's disbarment. O'Brien lived in Columbia and handled South Carolina, Georgia, Alabama, and Florida. "How long is this going to take?" he asked, glancing at his watch.

"Harry, if you don't like making money you can always resign," Becker said, stifling a yawn.

O'Brien was about to respond when the Prada-clad Lydia Coe made her entrance right on time. She was the only woman on the board and the only director not guilty of negligence or a misdemeanor. A forty-year-old former actuary, she'd been framed by one of her superiors to take the fall for a mistake that had cost her employer millions. She had been summarily dismissed and with that black mark on her record found employment impossible to attain – until she had met Arthur Ridgeway at a party in L.A. and explained her woes to him. She had been bitter, hate-filled and spiteful, but Ridgeway had provided the leg-up that she needed, and she had proved to be an invaluable asset. No one else on the board had her ability to assess risk quickly and accurately. She had shifted from New York to Dallas and oversaw ACME's operations in Texas, Arkansas, Kansas and New Mexico.

It was 2:05 when Ridgeway said, "I don't know why we put up with this shit. Borchard's late for every meeting. It's disrespectful, that's what it is. Are you going to say anything to him, Dermott?"

"What's a few minutes between friends?" Becker responded. "He'll be here soon enough, and you're not flying out until tomorrow morning, so it's not as if he's holding you up, is it?"

"I think you're scared of hi–"

"Scared of who?" Brock Borchard asked as he took the chair at the opposite end of the table to Becker. He was thirty-five and the only director without academic qualifications. He had approached Becker about joining ACME after he found them sniffing around a business in Chicago that he too was interested in buying. It had been difficult and cost tens of thousands of dollars to get a handle on Borchard. Even now the unknowns far outweighed the knowns. Born Bratislav Bozovic on a small farm on the outskirts of Belgrade, his mother had died bearing him. Serbia was experiencing severe economic problems as a result of its history of wars and skirmishes. His father was a brute of a man with a violent temper who, despite severe food shortages, could always find a drink. Raised by his uncles and his father's male friends, young Bratislav rarely saw or spoke to a woman while he was growing up. He later made up for it in a prolific way. Little was known about how he entered the U.S., but private investigators had discovered the foundation of his wealth was collecting debts and pimping in Chicago while still in his mid-teens. It had provided him with the seed capital to get into drugs, illegal gambling, loan sharking, and the construction of high-rise buildings. He was the only builder in Chicago without union problems. He employed three compatriots as bodyguards, union organizers and standover men, who along with him were known as the Serbian Mafia.

"Hello, Brock," Becker said, eyeing the younger man. His jet-black hair was pushed back in the style of the old-time Chicago gangsters, and his eyes were cold and expressionless. His lips were thin and cruel and a fine almost perfectly straight scar ran from the right side of his forehead to his jaw. "Arthur was just saying that he thought I was scared of the newly appointed police chief. I was about to disagree, but only a fool underestimates his enemies. I'm wary of him but so long as he stays away from our businesses he can do what he likes."

"Is the bum on our payroll?" Borchard asked.

"Not yet. We still don't know if he's receptive," Becker replied.

"Christ, everyone's fuckin' receptive," Borchard replied. "Ya just gotta get the size of the bribe right. Don't haggle or penny pinch. I can tell ya from firsthand experience that having the police chief in our back pocket is worth a shitload. We'll get back what we pay him a hundredfold."

"I thought this meeting was about new projects," Harry O'Brien interrupted. "Can we get on with it?"

"Harry's got a hot date." Becker laughed. "Lydia, do you have anything new on the drawing board?"

Five years earlier, she had been a dorky actuary, wearing horn-rimmed glasses and clothes from the Victorian era. Laser-eye surgery and the skills of the best plastic surgeon in New York had enhanced her face, upper deck, and confidence. Add a designer wardrobe and visits from a personal trainer every other day and you had a hot, assertive woman in her prime. "Nothing new," she said, "but I'm expecting to foreclose on those three new exploration wells in the next ten days."

"How'd they perform?" Arthur Ridgeway asked.

"The first two are gushers, and they're drilling the third now. Because of their success, they're going to expect us to extend the finance package. They're going to be in for a shock," Lydia responded.

"You lent them just enough to ensure they'd fail," Ridgeway said.

"Exactly, and I didn't release the loan monies until after they'd drilled the first well and struck pay dirt," Lydia said.

"Well done, Lydia," Becker said. "Those wells will add nicely to our energy portfolio. Okay, Harry, you're in such a hurry, you're up next."

"I'm making sure that our transport business wins a major tender for the delivery of milk in the south." O'Brien grinned, pushing his chair back so that the table didn't confine his ample girth.

"And how are you doing that?" Becker followed up.

"The current contractor, Webb Transport, is having all sorts of difficulties." O'Brien laughed and his jowls jiggled. "Their drivers are blowing up engines, backing into loading docks and smashing rear tail lights not to say anything of delivering late and leaving retailers stranded. They'll be lucky to survive, let alone be competitive with the current tender."

"What's it costin' and what are we gettin' out of it?" Borchard asked.

"About two million to our friends at the Transport Employees Union to ensure their drivers wreck Webb's tractors and trailers. The contract's worth a hundred mil and will add ten mil to the bottom line," O'Brien replied.

"Good stuff," Borchard said. "Well done, Harry."

Murmured congratulations went around the board table before Becker asked Arthur Ridgeway if he had anything new to report.

"Nothing new, but as you know our spare parts business, Trailer Parts, has been incurring losses because it's under severe pricing pressure from Superior Spares. I've got one of our people into Superior's head office. He's an accountant. We'll soon have their price lists, costs and know where they're buying their parts. If I find our suppliers have been supplying them at better prices than us, there'll be hell to pay."

"How long's our spy been on the job?" Becker asked.

"Two weeks. It'll be a month or so before we have anything. I told him to be careful. He's no good to us if he gets caught," Ridgeway said.

"I like it," Borchard said. "I've got nothin' new, but I'll have something juicy to report at our next meeting. I can report that that fuckin' weirdo, Frampton, is no longer a problem."

"Did you have to kill him?" Ridgeway asked.

"Fuck, Arty, you were at the last meetin' when I was told to fix the problem. Once he found out that he had incurable cancer there was nothin' to stop him blowin' the whistle. Do ya think he was still worried about us tellin' the world he was a fuckin' sicko? He was about to come outta the closet and confess that he'd been leakin' inside information. Jeez, he only had six months to live."

"I don't like it," Ridgeway said. "We're not murderers."

"Really? Dermott, why don't ya tell Arty about Valerie Gibson?" Borchard said.

"Unfortunately the drugs have got her. It's only a matter of time before she's outed and then we won't have any hold on her," Becker replied. "She'll soon blab to the SEC that she leaked inside information about her employer."

"Yeah, she's a crackhead," Borchard said, "and when she's outed she's gonna sing like a canary."

"You-you're gonna kill her too?" Ridgeway said, shaking his head.

"We're gonna give her one final shot." Borchard smirked. "She'll die happy."

"It has to be done, Arthur," Lydia Coe said. "If she talks, the SEC will be all over those stock transactions."

"Dermott, I know you're busting to tell us about your latest convert," O'Brien interjected. "He'll more than replace Frampton and Gibson."

"We've had our eye on a young accountant who's an audit manager with Montgomery Hastings & Pierce. He gambles on the horses at one of the betting parlors on the edge of Chinatown. He's been having an incredible run using some convoluted, self-designed betting system," Becker said.

"He'll end up losin'," Borchard said, "they always do."

"Yeah, you're right, so we've made sure that his credit's been extended to half a mil. When he starts losing we'll own him," Becker said.

"Half a mil's not much," Ridgeway said, "surely he'll be able to get the money from somewhere. Is his family poor or something?"

"On the contrary, and that's the beauty of it." Becker smiled. "His father's a surgeon; his mother's a doctor, and he has a sister and brother who are both surgeons. He's the black sheep, the failure of the family. He went to the best schools, the same ones his siblings went to and ended up as an accountant and major disappointment to his father. The betting system is his way of proving that he's as smart as, and can make as much money as anyone else in the family. He'll never ask them to cover a gambling debt. Can you imagine the shame?"

"Yeah, yeah, that's all very interestin'," Borchard said. "Whatta we get out of it?"

"I'm getting to it," Becker responded. "Montgomery Hastings & Pierce is a very prestigious firm, and the big four have been trying to take them over for years without success. But what's most appealing about them is that they audit forty public companies listed on the NYSE and NASDAQ."

"What's the big four?" Borchard interrupted.

"The four biggest accounting firms in the world," Becker said. "Can you save your questions until I'm finished? This guy will have access to the sales and profits of those companies before they're reported to the market. When he's in our pocket, we'll also have that information. It'll be like reading tomorrow's newspapers today."

"Fantastic," Ridgeway said.

"Brilliant," Lydia Coe chimed in.

"I'll ask ya again. Whatta we get out of it?" Borchard said.

"The return could be north of fifty mil for an outlay of two," Becker replied.

"It sure makes my milk deal look puny," O'Brien said.

"Yeah, looks okay, Dermott, but so did that deal ya had Elliot do with the Italian stockbroker. The prick who fed us bullshit inside information," Borchard said. "Didn't we end up payin' him and losin' millions?"

"We paid Giovani a million dollars for the information, and he invested it in the same stocks he recommended to us," Becker said. "This is different. We'll be dealing in facts, not rumors, and if it works, we'll be able to infiltrate other accounting firms using the same or similar methods."

"For a fifty mil return it's worth a try," Borchard said. "Whatta ya gonna to do about Giovani?"

"Do? I'm not going to do anything. What do you expect me to do?" Becker replied.

"We lost millions, and you paid him a mil for bullshit! Did ya at least get that back? Because if ya didn't, it sends a terrible message to others who deal with us. It says we're soft, we can be ripped off, and we're gonna do nothin' about it. It's a bad message. Next thing you know we'll have stooges linin' up at the door to feed us bullshit," Borchard said. "Dermott, you've got a good man in Jack Elliot workin' for you. Get him to take care of it."

"He can't pay us back. Didn't you hear me? He put the million into the same stocks he recommended to us. I told you when you joined us that the only people we prematurely terminate are those who might pose a threat. Giovani's not a dying weirdo or an out of control drug addict. He's no threat to us. We're not the Mafia, you know." Becker laughed. "And, unlike the weirdo and the addict, he has a large family. If anything happens to him, there'll be a lot of questions asked."

Borchard sat at the end of the table massaging his goatee with his thumb and forefinger. He was an intimidating presence, lean as a greyhound with a swarthy complexion and piercing black eyes. "Prematurely terminate! You fuckin' silver tongues make me laugh. Why don't ya call it what it is? Murder. If ya don't do something about Giovani, I will," he said.

"Whoa, right there. Brock, we're not Murder Incorporated," Ridgeway said. "Giovani can't and won't hurt us. His killing would be pointless."

"I'll second that," O'Brien said.

"Perhaps Brock's right," Becker said to the astonishment of the others. "Leave it with me. I'll need a month or so, but I'll take care of our little Italian friend."

Borchard stood up and walked to the door. Becker thought the bastard hadn't smiled once, but that wasn't unusual. He never smiled. "I gotta get back to Chicago," Borchard said. "Gentlemen and lady, you have a fucked up enforcement policy. I'm relyin' on you to fix it, Dermott. Don't let me down."

As Borchard closed the door behind him, Ridgeway said, "Who the fuck does he think he is? Why do you put up with that shit, Dermott?"

"He's just flexing his muscles," Becker said. "Don't worry about him, Arthur. He's a big man in Chicago. He's nothing here. He just doesn't know it."

Chapter 3

Montgomery Hastings & Pierce had offices all around the world with each national firm being a separate legal entity. With more than fifty thousand employees, it was large but not a behemoth like PWC or EY. The US arm of Montgomery Hastings & Pierce had offices in every state and was overseen nationally by a democratically elected eleven partner committee. Two members of that committee came from the New York office. The firm was highly respected, private and abhorred any form of publicity. It had been held up to ridicule after the committee declined the audit of Enron and annual fees exceeding fifty million. After Enron collapsed and took huge accounting firm Arthur Andersen with it, the wisdom of the committee's decision was recognized.

Todd Hansen was glad to see that he hadn't been missed when he got back to the office. He had three supervisors who reported to him. Two were out on audits, but the third, Wendy Abbott, whom he'd asked to cover for him, gave him the thumbs up as he entered his tiny, eighty square foot cubicle. It had taken six years to achieve this status, and he'd previously occupied one seat at a long desk that would accommodate thirty. He could see the rows of desks from his cubicle, and they reminded him of the production lines of the many factories he'd tromped through. To say that he hated accounting and audit was an understatement, but with good luck and good horses he'd soon be saying farewell to this environment.

He had barely sat down when the intercom buzzed and his boss and one of the national partners, Doug Lechte, asked him to come down to his office. When Todd entered the large corner office, Vanessa Hodge, another audit manager, was sitting opposite Lechte enjoying a joke. "Grab a seat, Todd," he said, unbuttoning the top button of his shirt and removing his tie. "I was just talking to Vanessa about a reassignment of audit clients between you two."

As Todd sat down, Vanessa crossed her slender legs and gave him a brilliant smile.

"There'll be a little bit of interchange between members of our teams," she said. "It might be fun."

Todd looked at her and thought *I'd kill to have some physical interchange with you.* He had dreamed about asking her out but had always become over-awed and chickened out. Besides, as far as he knew, she was so determined to make partner, she didn't have time to date. It crossed his mind that she might be gay, and he thought *what a waste.* She was African-American with the looks and body of a supermodel. Her wavy, shoulder length hair glistened. If that wasn't enough, she had been blessed with a humongous IQ and was as smart as a whip. "Sounds good," he said. "When's it going to happen, Doug?"

Lechte rolled his sleeves up exposing his brawny arms and ran his hands through his cropped gray hair. He was naturally untidy. Some of the partners didn't like it but dared not say anything. He was the firm's rainmaker and could converse with cleaners and senators with equal ease. Never one to talk about himself, it was rumored that he had been a champion college football player who could have played NFL had he not torn his ACL. Todd thought himself lucky to work for Lechte. "I think we should aim for the first of December. That'll give you a few weeks to organize things between yourselves. Does that work for you, Vanessa?"

"That'll be fine," she responded. "Todd will have no trouble picking up the status of the audits from my client files."

Todd had no doubt that was true but wondered how Vanessa and her team would do working on his client files. His work had been deteriorating for over a year, ever since he had started developing his betting system. He wasn't worried, though. If all went well, the life of being a boring auditor would soon be behind him.

"I'll leave it with you two to organize, but, Todd, I want you to handle the Marks & Spender and the Hallstrom audits, and Vanessa you'll handle Crisco and Homewares. You'll need to coordinate and work together during the overlap period," Lechte said. "Now get out of here, I've got an appointment downtown, and I'm running late."

As Todd strolled back to his cubicle, he smiled. Doug Lechte was a great guy, but he could be tough, too, and was certainly no one's fool. There were six audit managers, and Lechte could have selected any one of them to switch assignments with, but he'd chosen the brilliant Vanessa Hodge. Todd suspected that this wasn't the interchange and reassignment that Lechte had said it was, but rather an internal review by Vanessa of his work and working papers. When he'd entered Lechte's office, Vanessa had been laughing. Maybe the joke had been about him.

Still, it wasn't unexpected. He had been devoting more and more time to horses and less to work. Now the chickens were coming home to roost. He had hoped to have a stake of a million before quitting work and becoming a full-time gambler. He hated that description, though, and saw himself a systems analyst exploiting the foibles of bookmaking that others hadn't been smart enough to decipher. If he had to make a start with just under three hundred thousand, then so be it. He'd proven that his system worked, and now it was time to increase the stakes. If all went well, he'd have a mil within six months.

Todd spent the rest of the day mulling over his future. At exactly five o'clock, he left his cubicle and headed for the elevators. It was the official finishing time of Montgomery Hastings & Pierce, but no one left at that time, well not anyone who wanted to progress, that was. The main office was abuzz, and the long desks were crammed with recently qualified graduates trying to impress their immediate superiors. Managers aspiring to make partner would not leave before eight o'clock, and some of the more ambitious would still be toiling away at midnight. The street lights were already on when Todd left the building, and he walked briskly toward Park Street, little clouds of condensation forming in front of his face.

His fully furnished one-bedroom apartment was on the second level of an old four level building on East 60th Street. The rent set him back more than five thousand a month and was way more than he could afford. However, the burning desire to impress his parents and family overrode more sensible and less expensive options. Despite it being more than he could afford, he loved the lofty ceilings, the king-sized bed and the open kitchen with every conceivable stainless steel appliance. It was only a fifteen-minute walk from the Carnegie Center, but it was dark when Todd opened the door and entered the spacious living room. He flicked the lights on and went to the recently renovated bathroom and splashed water on his face. He could have had a doorman and concierge in one of the high-rises, but it would've been half the size.

Todd turned the heat on full blast and grabbed a Budweiser from the fridge. He made himself comfortable on his suede sofa and settled down to do some hard, enjoyable work. With his iPad in hand, he entered the results of today's race results. It was slow, methodical work and he listed details of positions, track conditions, jockeys, trainers, weights, times, odds, distances and margins. Each category had a simple numerical weighting assigned to it. Once the database was complete, he inputted fields for tomorrow's races. Then he got to the fun part and ran a scan that produced the forecast results for every race. The results were listed in order of probability, and a numeric rating between 1 and a 100 was assigned to each horse. Todd's success had come from forecast winners with a rating of 95 or higher.

Chapter 4

Brock Borchard eased into his first class seat and accepted a glass of orange juice from the flight attendant. As the jet departed La Guardia, he mused about how easy it was to become rich in America. He had only known poverty in Bosnia but had learned the lessons of fear and violence well. Killings in Bosnia were an everyday occurrence, so New York held no fears for him when he disembarked from a merchant ship, alone at the tender age of sixteen. By the time, he was twenty-one he had murdered five men and attempted to murder another. New York became too hot for him, and he took off for Chicago, the best decision he would ever make. He had no education or qualifications, but he was a smart man who sucked up knowledge like a sponge.

It was by chance that Borchard found out about Vulture Inc., and he'd only been a shareholder and director for two years. He was still getting to know his co-directors. Arthur Ridgeway had been doing diligence on a transport company in Chicago that Borchard also wanted to acquire. In normal circumstances when Borchard was bidding against another party, he'd instruct his men to persuade that party that they shouldn't be bidding. The usual tools of persuasion were baseball bats, but there were no limits to what Borchard would do to win. For some reason, he decided to have dinner with Ridgeway before he broke his kneecaps. At the dinner, Borchard found out about Ridgeway's record and the business he had built with tainted lawyer, Dermott Becker. Borchard may not have been educated, but he knew what villains were. As he listened to Ridgeway, he realized he was talking to a master, legal crook. Someone who knew enough about business and law to walk the tightrope, and sometimes fall, but with enough know-how and contacts to pick himself up and recover unscathed. By the time dinner was over, baseball bats had been forgotten, and Borchard had agreed to withdraw his bid, subject to meeting Dermott Becker.

Two days later Becker flew into O'Hare for what he thought would be a short meeting with Borchard. He returned to New York seven days later, having reluctantly entered into an in-principle agreement with Borchard to sell him fifteen percent of Vulture Inc. Part of the consideration was Borchard's cocaine business and his Colombian contacts. Vulture was running cocaine in New York, but the quality and purity was vastly inferior to what Borchard was running in Chicago. Borchard knew his investment was going to be extremely profitable and would've been prepared to accept less than fifteen percent. What he wanted to see was how these white collar criminals operated. Once he'd learned all they could teach him, he would buy them out. Should they be disinclined to sell, he would remove them.

He hadn't been disappointed and had come a long way in a comparatively short time. He remembered his first board meeting when Dermott Becker had said there were a hundred companies interposed between Vulture and ACME. Borchard had no idea what interposed meant, but he wasn't shy about asking. He'd sat in many meetings where the participants were too embarrassed to ask what they saw as dumb questions for fear of being ridiculed. Brock Borchard had no such reservations and asked any question that came to his mind. Only the brave and the stupid laughed. He'd always known that the mega-rich had international bank accounts but had no idea of their intricacies. Now he could differentiate the pros and cons of Liechtenstein, Hong Kong, the Caymans, Swiss and Irish banks. His businesses now operated under complex corporate and tax structures and Ridgeway had shown him ways to launder cash that defied belief. ACME owned legitimate retail chains comprising more than a thousand outlets and banked large amounts of cash daily. A perfect cover to launder drug monies. When Borchard had asked about the taxes the retail businesses paid on the drug monies, Dermott Becker had said, "We don't mind paying our fair share of taxes. No one around this table is going to meet the same fate as Al Capone."

When Borchard got off the plane, he was greeted by a gigantic man with scraggly black hair and a swarthy complexion not dissimilar to his own. "Did ya have a successful trip, boss?"

"It was fine, Farik," Borchard replied. "We have little time to waste? Where's the limo?"

"At the front of the terminal with the engine running. I knew you'd be running short of time, so I brought Ahmet with me."

The limo was in a no parking area, and the rear door was being held open by a man only slightly less monstrous than Farik. "Ahmet, take me to my penthouse and wait while I get changed," Borchard said. "I'm havin' dinner with Joe Brereton of the Federated Laborers Union, and I don't want to be late. Did you get the cash, Farik?"

"Of course, boss," Farik replied, "fifty thousand in a plain envelope just as you said."

"Good, and, in case I forget to tell ya later, I want ya to pick me up at five in the mornin'. I'll need a run, some cool air, and a hard work-out after puttin' up with Brereton's bullshit tonight."

It was a bleak morning; the wind was howling, and it was bitterly cold when Farik pulled up at the front of the Rialto Towers in exclusive North Wabash Avenue. Sitting next to him was the third member of the Serbian Mafia, a wiry little man who had changed his name from Dragan Voinovich to Dirk Vaughan shortly after coming to America. A master of disguise, he was the smallest and most deadly of the trio. They saw their boss coming out of the revolving doors wearing a white t-shirt, black tracksuit pants, and Nikes. He immediately started running at a rapid rate, enjoying the feel of the icy wind cutting through his lean body. He lengthened his stride and increased his pace as he turned hard right onto East Ohio Street. A few minutes later he was on North Lake Shore Drive heading to North Beach. It was pitch black, but he could hear the lake's water lapping up against the shore. He looked down at the stopwatch on his right wrist before glancing at the heart rate monitor on his left. It was reading 185. His doctor had told him that his maximum safe heart rate was 150 beats per minute, but still he pushed harder. He'd completed two miles and knowing that he only had another mile to go, he again increased the pace. His lungs were burning and despite the cold, sweat from his forehead dripped into eyes and blurred his vision. His legs ached but still he drove himself. He was one of that rare breed who loved pain. He knew that he was within range of breaking his personal best time, but the shrill beep from his heart rate monitor warned him that he'd just gone through 190. All it did was drive him harder.

The two men in the limousine following fifty yards behind him wore thick overcoats, and the heat was turned up to the max. Every second morning they watched their boss go through this ritual and on the other mornings he sparred six rounds with a former contender for the light heavyweight title. In the winter when there was heavy snow and the lake was frozen he was forced onto a treadmill. He hated it and on those days his men did everything they could to avoid him rather than feel his wrath.

"He'll be in a great mood today." Farik smiled. "I might ask for a raise."

"Stupid is as stupid does," Dirk replied.

Farik didn't respond. There were only two men in the world that he was wary of, and they were both within range.

With four hundred yards to go, Borchard demanded that his body and legs give more. His face was contorted, and the heart rate monitor began emitting a constant beep. He disregarded it and instead focused on his stopwatch, breaking into a full sprint knowing he was about to break seventeen minutes for the first time in years. As his feet touched the sand, he came to an abrupt halt and hit the red button on his stopwatch. Seventeen minutes and three seconds, an outstanding time for a man his age. As he bent over, hands on knees, gasping for breath, he scowled and wondered whether he'd started his stopwatch a few seconds too early. Dirk got out of the limo, the collar of his overcoat turned up around his neck. "Great run, boss. Do ya wanna drink?" he asked, handing Borchard a bottle of water.

"I broke seventeen minutes. There are very few men in the world my age who could come even close to that." He took a swig from the bottle, dropped to the damp sand, and in one motion did the first of two hundred push-ups. He followed with two hundred sit-ups and then in push-up position, held himself for five minutes. It was five degrees, but the wind chill factor made it closer to minus ten when he kicked his Nikes off, dispensed with his tracksuit pants and threw his t-shirt on the sand. He was wearing a black pair of Speedos, and his body was ripped. His long, sinewy muscles rippled, and his six pack was cut to the max. The scars on his body told a story; one ran across his left arm, another about four inches long crossed his left pectoral, and the largest and ugliest sat just below his Adam's apple.

He pulled his goggles down before striding into the near freezing water. Without pausing he dived in and surfaced freestyling strongly, churning through the water with smooth rhythmic strokes. When he was about three hundred yards from the shore, he turned, took a deep breath and started back, pulling the water through his powerful hands.

As Borchard neared the shore, Farik climbed out of the limo carrying a large towel, a thick white dressing gown, and small bag. "Make sure the heat's turned off before I get in, Farik," Borchard shouted.

"It's done, boss. When have I ever forgot?" Farik shouted back as he picked up the damp and sandy t-shirt, the tracksuit pants, and Nikes. As he bent down, his overcoat opened at the top, and a gust of wind cut through his chest like a knife. He silently cursed his boss's eccentricity.

Borchard strode from the lake, hands locked behind his head, breathing deeply.

"Good swim, boss?"

"Yeah," Borchard replied, taking the towel and rubbing his body vigorously. After a few minutes, he dropped his goggles, Speedos and towel on the sand and fully naked, held his arms out so Farik could put his dressing gown on him. "Is that okay, boss?"

"Yeah," Borchard grunted, striding toward the car with Farik waddling close behind.

Dirk was holding the rear door of the limo open, a small hand towel over his arm. Borchard climbed in and swung his legs out of the car so that Dirk could clean the sand from his feet.

"They're clean," he said, slipping into the slippers that were waiting for him. His water was on the console and the newspapers were sitting next to him on the adjoining rear seat. He picked up the *Tribune* and turned to the sports section. "Let's go, Farik. I've got a lot to get through today."

Chapter 5

It was unusual for the partners of Montgomery Hastings & Pierce to ever brawl in public, but loud voices coming from Doug Lechte's office belied that convention. Managing partner and the firm's other representative on the national committee, Phillip Cromwell, was laying down the law. He was everything that Lechte despised. Cromwell had done everything to convince the committee to accept the Enron audit, and it was only Lechte's astute presentation of the case against that had thwarted him. He was pompous and overbearing and even after Enron collapsed hadn't had the good grace to apologize to Lechte. Cromwell's white shirt was immaculately pressed, and gold cuff links protruded from under his Zegna suit's sleeves. He was tall, slim with an aquiline nose and receding dark hair. For him, the perfect weekend was an evening at the opera followed by a day yachting around the Hamptons. In contrast, a great weekend for Lechte would start with a day at the baseball field or basketball with a few close friends, a can of beer and a hot dog. Making it perfect would be spending a day fishing the following day.

"Your vote's killed her twice," Lechte shouted.

"She's not ready for partnership." Cromwell sniffed.

"Is it because she's black or is it because she's a woman?"

"That's a cheap shot. If you haven't noticed, Martin Lawrence is an African American and we have six female partners. Face it, she's too young, too inexperienced and hasn't put in enough hours."

"Jesus, I'm sorry, Phillip. It's not because she's black, and it's not because she's a woman. It's because she's both. Now, understand this. The firm's never had a smarter employee and that includes you," Lechte yelled, thumping his fist on the desk. "If we don't admit her as a partner, another firm soon will. It may have escaped you, but we don't have a monopoly on talent."

"You know, Doug, there's only one thing wrong with that little summary. It's your opinion, and that's all it is. If you want to nominate and vote for her, be my guest. She'll not get my vote or the votes of my bloc."

"You're making a mistake, and you're as closed-minded as you were with Enron. Didn't you learn anything?"

Cromwell turned bright red and momentarily lost control before he smiled. "How's your other star, Todd Hansen, performing? I've been getting some poor reports from some of the other partners about him. Seems he's away from the office quite frequently and yet he's not with clients. Where's he going? What's happening?"

Lechte silently cursed. Todd had called to say that he was feeling ill and wouldn't be in today. It was a regular occurrence, and Lechte wondered whether the wheels were falling off. "I haven't seen those reports, and he's responsible to me! Why are the partners complaining to you?"

"Maybe because I'm managing partner." Cromwell yawned as he stood up. "Don't embarrass yourself again by nominating her, Doug. She doesn't have the numbers."

"Asshole!"

Cromwell swung around as he reached the door. "What did you say?" he demanded.

"You heard," Lechte said dismissively.

Todd Hansen hadn't planned on taking the day off but, when his system threw up three winners all rating higher than 95, he had no choice but to head to the betting parlor. He was confident and when he saw the four to one odds on offer for Dancing Girl in the second at Turfway Park he struggled to maintain his calm demeanor. She had rated 99, the equal highest rating that had ever come up on his system. The two other horses who had rated that highly had won easily and Todd had had some nice collects.

The teller looked up abruptly at the words 'fifty thousand for the win on my tab,' and asked Todd to wait while he disappeared out the back. When he returned, he said, "That will be fine, Mr. Hansen," and handed him his ticket. It was twenty minutes to start time, and

Todd ordered a mineral water and sat down at a vacant table. It was the biggest bet he had ever made, but he gave no thought to losing, and had already worked out how much he'd have in the bank at the end of the day. He looked up at the monitor and saw the horses being pushed into their gates.

A few minutes later, the commentator shouted, "They're racing," and then "oh no, Dancing Girl was slow out and lost four lengths at the start." Todd watched in horror. After two furlongs, Dancing Girl was still last and fifteen lengths from the leader. With a furlong and a half to go, the jockey let her go, and she surged around the field, and Todd's hopes surged with her. Her run was short lived and by the time she drew up to the leaders she was spent. The jockey on the leading horse gave it two cuts with the whip and it shot four lengths clear of its nearest rival. Todd had had losers before and knew his system wasn't foolproof, but he'd never lost fifty thousand, and it was the first time a horse ranked 98 or higher had been beaten. His face was white, and he was finding it hard to focus. He called a waitress over and ordered a black coffee.

Todd struggled to get clarity of thought. He had planned to have thirty thousand on Viking Flyer in the fifth at Belmont Park. Now he was confused. Viking Flyer ranked 96, but he'd just watched a horse ranked 99 lose. His painstakingly crafted plan was in tatters. He saw a hard-faced blonde with a cigarette hanging out of the corner of her mouth reading the Belmont Park form guide and asked if he could borrow it. He ran his eyes down the starters in the fifth race and studied their recent form. He'd never done this before and had always relied on his system, but yet again, he'd never bet sixty thousand dollars before. Satisfied that Viking Flyer was the best horse in the field, Todd made his way to the betting window, but the confidence he'd felt two hours earlier had disappeared. It was only thirty minutes to start time but for Todd time seemed to stand still. As the minutes dragged on, he again felt himself losing control. Perhaps after Viking Flyer won, the calm would return. As the starter called the horses into the gates, Todd prayed for Viking Flyer to make a fast start.

"They're racing," the commentator shouted, "and Viking Flyer went straight to the lead." Todd felt himself relaxing, the chestnut colt in the distinct black and yellow colors was two lengths in front, and there was no chance he'd be buffeted. A minute later the commentator screamed, "Viking Flyer's clear at the top of the stretch but here comes The Phoenician." Todd's eyes were glued to the monitor as he watched the big black horse in the red and blue colors edge closer and closer to Viking Flyer.

"Use the whip, use the whip," he screamed at the monitor.

"It's a photo," the commentator yelled, and then, "it's The Phoenician who gets the money by the shortest of margins. What a race. What a great pair of horses."

Todd couldn't move. He was in a state of shock. The blonde asked if she could have her form guide back, but he didn't hear her. He had lost a hundred and ten thousand in less than two hours. What had happened to his system? The Phoenician's ranking was only 74, and he had been expected to finish eighth. How could he have won?

Todd looked up to see Ronny Conroy, the owner of the betting parlor standing in front of him. Todd didn't know Ronny, but they had had a few meetings when he set up his account and Ronny had allowed him to bet on credit. "You're having a rough time," he said.

The last thing Todd wanted was false sympathy from this scrawny little man. "I don't want to be rude," he said, "but I've got one more bet, and I need to focus."

Ronny laughed. "I won't hold you up. You're a top client, your credit's good with me. If you need more to keep your head above water, that's fine with me."

"I thought you'd be pleased I'm losing," Todd said.

"You know that I make a book. When I get big bets like yours today, I don't take the other side, I lay them off. If I get my book right, I win, irrespective of which horse wins."

"Yeah, I know," Todd replied, "that was a stupid thing to say. Thanks for offering to help. Hopefully, I won't have to take you up on your offer."

"Todd, one last word. Everyone in this game goes through losing streaks and suffers setbacks. Your system's been working fine so whatever you do, don't dump it. Tweak it, refine it, and perhaps make a few adjustments, but you know the guts of it are robust. And remember, don't judge it by what's happened today, judge it on your success over a year. I want you to keep betting and to keep winning."

"Thanks, Ronny. I feel a little better."

Todd's last bet was meant to be twenty thousand the win on Brown Sugar in the last at Lone Star Park. At three to one, it wouldn't recover what he'd already lost unless he increased his bet to forty thousand and if he wanted to walk out winning he'd have to outlay sixty thousand. Brown Sugar's ranking was 96 and the projected second place getter in the race was Texas Beau with a ranking of only 82. On the face of it and based on his system, Brown Sugar was a certainty. The race was over one mile, a distance at which she had never experienced defeat. A little of his confidence returned, and he wondered what the odds were on three horses, one ranked 99, and the other two ranked 96, all being beaten in one afternoon.

Highly improbable!

He waited until five minutes before the race and then placed sixty thousand on Brown Sugar to win. After she won he would be up seventy thousand for the afternoon, but he never wanted to go through another day like this. He knew what he had to do to tweak his system. He had to make sure that the first bet he placed was a winner because the pressure of a first bet loser destroyed his plan. Coping with a loser after having already backed a winner carried far less stress than starting with a loser.

The commentator said, "They're being led into the gates for the last at Lone Star, folks. Hi-Jinx moves in next to The Matador, and Texas Beau is the last to go in. They're set. Racing! They jumped as one and Debt Collector went straight to the front and took up the running. Eddie Bates has got the favorite, Brown Sugar, four back on the fence in perfect position to make her run for home."

Todd took a sip of mineral water and breathed a sigh of relief. Finally, a race was going to plan.

"They're at the top of the stretch, and Brown Sugar's cruising and just needs a way out," the commentator shouted. "Bates sees a gap on the inside and drives her toward it...but wait, Hi-Jinx has leaned in, and the gap has closed. Bates is trying to pull Brown Sugar to the outside, but I think it's too late. The Matador's set sail for the wire, and they won't catch him. If you backed the favorite, you were desperately unlucky. She had a dream run until she was severely checked by Hi-Jinx a furlong and a half from home. Stewards will look at the riding of Bill Hunter on Hi-Jinx and determine whether he intentionally blocked Brown Sugar."

Todd couldn't believe it. He had lost one hundred and seventy thousand. He was shattered, confused and knew that his dream of following the horses full-time was just that, a dream. When he'd left his apartment for the betting parlor this morning, he was unconcerned about what might happen with his job. Now, he couldn't afford to lose it.

Chapter 6

Englewood's Astor Motel located in southwest Chicago had seen far better days. The brass handles on the large double front doors were tarnished; the glass was grimy, and the carpet in the foyer leading to the reception desk was threadbare. Its owners were just waiting for the economy and locality to improve before tearing it down and replacing it with a skyscraper.

The reception clerk was in his late thirties, dirty, unshaven with thin brown strands of hair combed over in a fruitless attempt to hide his bald patch. Despite the no-smoking signs, he held a cigarette between his nicotine-stained fingers. His teeth were green, his eyes were red, and his skin was blotchy. He was absorbed in the current edition of *Playboy* that was spread out in front of him. Andy Prowse was a sleaze and a loser and the world held little in the way of hope for him.

The rap on the reception counter startled him, but he made no attempt to close or conceal the magazine that was opened at a pic of a voluptuous bunny revealing all of her assets and then some. The young man in front of him was wearing opaque oversized sunglasses and a beanie that concealed his hair. He was well over six foot. Despite his feeble attempt at disguise, Andy recognized him instantly. Devlin Cooper, the Cougars gun quarterback and superstar. "I'm looking for a room. Can you help me?" he asked nervously.

"Here, fill this in," Andy said, pushing a registration card toward him. "How long will you be with us Mr…"

"Brown, Corey Brown and just one-night thanks. How much will it be?" Cooper replied, pulling out his wallet. "I just want to catch up on some sleep. I'll be pushing off early in the morning so I'll pay now."

I bet you want to catch up on some sleep Andy thought. "It's a one hundred and ten bucks. How will you be paying?"

"Cash."

As Andy picked up the notes, he said, "You're in 712," and passed Cooper the key.

"Please make sure I'm not disturbed."

"Certainly, Mr. Brown."

For the first time in weeks, Andy was sharp and alert. Less than twenty minutes later the foyer door opened. A woman wearing a large silk scarf, sunglasses, and a fleecy collared jacket pulled up around her chin made her way to the elevators. Andy watched the elevator stop on level seven and smiled. It was his lucky day. He knew who she was the minute he set eyes on her. Coach Tom Deacon's wife.

Andy waited five minutes, grabbed one of the hair conditioning sachets that were for guest's rooms and took the elevator to level seven. He let himself into 714, opened a cupboard and activated a sophisticated set of cameras before putting his eye up to a small peephole. Karen Deacon was naked, spread-eagled on the bed and Devlin was kneeling on the floor licking her shaven pussy. She was writhing in pleasure and gasping "Oh, that's good. It's so good."

Devlin Cooper sat up abruptly. "Enjoy." He grinned.

Karen rested on one elbow, took his hand and put his forefinger on her clit then moved it in a slow circular motion. She dropped her elbow and laid back down. "Slowly, slowly," she groaned.

Devlin leaned forward, keeping his finger circling while driving his tongue deep inside her.

"You're such a fast learner," Karen gasped.

Andy yanked his zipper down and covered his hand in hair conditioner. It was the best sex he'd seen, and he'd recorded hundreds of couples and groups doing things to each other that he hadn't believed possible. Every CD was labeled and when Andy got sick of *Playboy* and wanted to relive an experience he just played the CD. He hadn't watched them all live, but this was Devlin Cooper and Karen Deacon. Perhaps they were turning him on because they were so famous. Yes, that was it. Andy guessed that Karen was anywhere between twelve and twenty years older than Devlin. She was only a little over five feet with a tiny waist and fabulous, (no doubt surgically-enhanced) tits.

Her long black hair cascaded down over them, and she said, "That's enough foreplay, put it in."

Devlin got up off his knees, and Andy's left hand shot up to his mouth to muzzle the "Oh fuck!" Devlin was gigantic, and his angry knob was nearly purple. Andy stopped masturbating, fascinated by how Karen was going to accommodate such a monstrous weapon.

"Slowly, big boy, slowly," she said. "I like to feel every bit of you sliding into me. Oh, that's good. That's so good. Do me, do me hard."

Andy was wiping himself clean as he watched Devlin thrust himself in and out of Karen with long strokes while she moaned in ecstasy. In no time at all, Devlin let out a deafening yell and rolled off her. They lay motionless for a few minutes and then they both burst out laughing.

"That was so good," Karen said.

"Fucking fantastic, more like it." Devlin grinned, sitting up and throwing his legs over the side of the bed. "I love seeing you naked, Karen."

Andy had watched countless couples fuck, but Karen and Devlin were the sexiest he'd ever seen. He was tempted to stay perving and masturbating for the rest of the day but knew what he'd just seen was worth a fortune. He'd make a phone call and then come back up to the room. As Andy was contemplating this, he watched Karen shimmy down Devlin's cock and wrap her legs around him. Devlin stood up and laughed. "No hands," he said, and then his face turned serious as he put his hands under her ass and pushed her up against the wall. Andy found it nearly impossible to tear himself away; his eyes glued to Karen's passion-filled face as Devlin pounded her into the wall. Two things eased Andy's concern about what he was going to miss. The first was that he was recording the action and the second was that he knew they'd still be hard at it when he got back. They couldn't get enough of each other.

Andy was flushed when he got back down to reception and anxious to get upstairs again. He hurriedly thumbed through his Teledex under B and grabbed the motel's old handset and dialed.

"Dirk Vaughan, speaking."

"Dirk, it's Andy from the Astor Motel. I need to talk to Brock. It's urgent."

One of Vaughan's main jobs was to keep time-wasters and shit-kickers away from Brock Borchard. "Why don't you let me know what it's about, Andy? Then I'll let you know whether he wants to talk to you."

"It's private," Andy said. "I can't. I can tell you that what I have is gold, and if Brock doesn't want to talk to me, I'll phone Nick Gianelli. I know he'll be interested."

"Listen you slimy turd, don't threaten me. Brock's a busy man. He's got more important things to do than talk to assholes like you. Now tell me what it is you think you have."

Andy didn't reply but heard raised voices.

"Andy, it's Brock. Anything you have to tell me, you can tell Dirk. Do you understand?"

"I don't think you'll say that after you hear what I've got," Andy said. He related what he'd seen.

"Who'd believe it?" Borchard said. "The golden boy and little Miss Prim and Proper."

"The *Tribune* will pay me two hundred thousand for the CD," Andy said.

"You've talked to them?"

"Not yet, but that's what it's worth. Brock, I'm giving you first option. Are you interested?"

"I'll give you for four hundred thousand in cash for the original, but there are to be no copies. Do you understand? If a copy ever surfaces after I've paid you, you're dead."

"Can I keep one for personal use?" Andy whined.

"Personal use? What the fuck is personal use, you sicko? Anyhow, the answer's no. There'll be the original, and that's all. If I need copies, I'll have them made. Oh, and Andy, how'd you know to record that room?"

There was a long pause. "I've got a room permanently set up. When a hot looking couple checks in, I always put 'em in that room. The equipment's in the adjoining room, and there's a little peephole so I know when to activate the cameras. No one's gonna check into this dive to sleep or stay. They come here for one thing, and that's to fuck discreetly and on the cheap. I just record a little memento of their visit." Andy laughed.

"Jesus. What do you do with the CDs?"

"Nothing. They're for personal use."

Borchard scratched his head. He'd have never thought of what Andy was doing. He smiled when he thought about the peephole and wondered how much time Andy wasted with his eye up against it. "I'll send Dirk over with the cash and you can give him the CD."

"No, no," Andy said. "They're still at it, and I'm recording. Besides, I want to make sure the CD is perfect before I hand it over."

"I bet you do." Borchard laughed. "Phone me tomorrow after you've checked it. And remember, Andy, don't keep a copy."

"I won't Thanks, Brock. I'll be seeing you," Andy hung up and raced toward the elevators.

Borchard looked at Dirk and said, "Fuck, there are some sick bastards in the world. Have a listen to what that sleazy prick's been doing. I wonder how many others there are like him and what they get up to?"

Chapter 7

The door to Doug Lechte's office was always open, so when he summoned Todd to his office and told him to close the door, the young man knew he was in trouble. "Todd, twelve months ago I thought you were partner material. Now I'm fighting off demands for your head. You disappear during the day, and you phone in ill at least once a month. More importantly, the supervisors who report to you are taking more responsibility for corporate audits than you are. What's wrong? Are you sick of working here?" Lechte asked, a scowl crossing his usually friendly face.

Todd was glad he hadn't been hauled before Lechte two days earlier because he would've told him to stick his job where the sun didn't shine. That was before he lost the one hundred and seventy big ones. "I'm sorry, Doug. I've had some family problems. I never knew they'd drag on for so long."

The scowl on Lechte's face evaporated and was replaced by a look of concern. "What's wrong? Your mother and father are pillars of the community. Is there anything I can do to help? They're not ill are they?"

"No, nothing like that, they're fine. It's a private family matter. I'm pleased to say it was resolved yesterday."

"So you won't be disappearing anymore or taking sick days?"

"Doug, I can get back to putting in a minimum of sixty hours a week. I feel bad about letting my supervisors down. I intend to mend those relationships and get back on top of my assignments."

"I'm pleased to hear that. I wasn't sure you'd still be with us by the end of the day. Don't waste too much time on your old assignments. Vanessa will take care of them. You concentrate on the portfolio of clients you're inheriting from her."

"I feel stupid. I thought you were giving her my assignments so you could check up on me."

"Why would you think that?"

"I'd rather not say. It's nothing," Todd replied.

"No, tell me."

"Well, you and Vanessa were laughing that day we discussed re-assigning clients. When I came into your office, you stopped. I thought you were laughing at my expense."

Lechte shook his head. "I never put you down as being paranoid, Todd. The problems with your family have obviously impacted your psyche. If it eases your mind, I told Vanessa a Warren Buffet joke. Why did the twenty-two-year-old beauty queen marry the seventy-year-old billionaire? Because he told her he was ninety." Lechte laughed.

Todd grinned. "That's a good one."

"Todd, I'm going to level with you. I wanted Vanessa to become familiar with your clients because I wasn't sure how long you'd still be with us. I'm glad I didn't have to fire you. Now get out of here and get your head back on the job," Lechte said, putting his hand on Todd's shoulder.

Todd walked out of Lechte's office knowing he had dodged a bullet. He didn't intend to give up the horses, but his visits to the betting parlor would have to be on Saturdays. When he got back to his cubicle, there was a note from Vanessa on his desk asking if she could see him. It was initialed VH with a smiley face. Her cubicle was just a little further along the wall, and Todd kept on walking. She was on the phone but pointed to the chair opposite her desk.

"Mom, I know," she said, "but I can't get home for dinner tonight. I have a job to complete and won't get away from the office before ten."

"Yes, yes, I know it Mikey's birthday. I'll make it up to him."

There was a pause before Vanessa said, "Yes, I know he'll only be fourteen once. Why are you trying to make me feel guilty?"

Vanessa smiled at Todd and shook her head. "You love boasting to your friends about how successful I am. Don't you understand? I'll never make partner unless I put in the hours."

Vanessa sighed. "That's not true. I come home every Thursday night for the family dinner. I never miss. Why can't we have Mikey's party then?"

"Yes, yes, I know it isn't his birthday on Thursday night. Mom, I have someone waiting for me. I have to go. Love you. Bye." Vanessa put the phone down.

"Problems at home?" Todd asked.

"It's my youngest brother's birthday, but I promised Doug I'd complete the Hubble audit and have it on his desk first thing in the morning. I can't let him down."

"I've got some time. Is there anything I can do?"

"That's sweet of you, Todd." Vanessa smiled. "But you know what it's like. It'd take me as long to bring you up to speed as what it'd take to finish it myself. Thanks for asking, though."

"Anytime," Todd said, trying not to stare. She was so natural and unassuming. *Surely she knows the effect she has on men,* Todd thought. He found it hard to focus when he was in her presence. "What is it you wanted to see me about?"

"I've organized for us to go out to Hallstrom's on Monday morning. You can meet their financial controller and their accounts people. It's a very straightforward audit, and you've audited major retailers' before. You won't have any problems but if you do, just give me a call."

"Sounds good. Have you been checking up on me?" Todd asked, pointing to the Homewares executive summary file on her desk.

"Why would you say that?" she asked, looking puzzled. "Don't you remember? Homewares is one of the clients I'm taking over from you. I'm just looking for a starting point. I'm not going to review what you've already done. Why would I?"

Todd felt the color rush to his face. "I'm sorry. I just thought…it doesn't matter what I thought. Sorry."

"Todd, this isn't a points scoring exercise. Even if by chance I found something, I'd come and see you. Hopefully we'd fix it between ourselves. That's what I would expect you to do for me in the same circumstances." Vanessa frowned.

"Of course."

"Good. Jot your address down. I'll grab a cab on Monday morning and pick you up. Be on the sidewalk by eight o'clock."

"Where will you be coming from?"

"The office. I've got to leave a plan for my supervisors before heading off."

"Christ, what time are you going start?" Todd asked.

"Six-thirty," Vanessa laughed and stood up. "It's going to be fun working together."

"I'm looking forward to it," Todd responded, trying to hold her eyes. The few beautiful women he knew wouldn't give him the time of day. Vanessa was stunning but unaffected. She was also very ambitious. Even the thought of starting at 6:30 was too much for him. He knew the fourteen hour days she was working were all about her quest to make partner.

The Homan Ave location that Borchard owned and ran his empire out of was in one of the roughest areas of Chicago. He'd been renting the 40,000 square foot warehouse during the GFC when he found the landlord was having trouble paying his bills. Ever the opportunist, Borchard instructed his lawyers to approach the mortgagor with a low ball offer. It was an old tin shed with cool rooms that served Borchard's needs to store contraband and stolen goods. He'd spent big dollars modernizing and soundproofing the offices. The warehouse was still the same as the day he bought it except for the signage that bore the name, Refrigerated, Chilled & General Storage Inc. In the early days, there had been a few break-ins but the Serbians had been quick to unleash viciously on the gangs. It hadn't taken long for them to get the message, and Borchard's warehouse was the only off-limit premises in the area for the local crims.

When Vaughan got back from the Astor with the disk, Borchard was in the theater that he'd added to the modified offices. He was watching the football game on a huge screen.

"What do you want me to do with this, boss?" he asked.

Borchard hit rewind on the remote. "Take a seat. You've never shown any interest in football. I want to bring ya up to speed. After the Hawks kickoff, the Cougars offense will take over. Our friend Cooper is the quarterback; he'll be the guy two back from the line of scrimmage on the right. He'll throw, handoff, or, if he gets into trouble, run. The guys on the other side, the Hawks, they're gonna try and kill him. I don't understand everything, but it's a great game." Borchard laughed. "Oh, and see the fair-haired guy with the headphones on the sidelines, that's Coach Deacon. The woman's husband."

It's Chad Bennet coming to you from Brook Field. It's a full house, folks, and Devlin Cooper's Cougars are taking on the unbeaten Hawks. The Hawks won the toss and deferred so they'll be kicking off from the South End Zone. The kick is short. Eddie Dalton fields it at the 16. He takes it up across the 20 to the 25, zig-zagging his way back into open field before he's brought down at the 34 where the Cougars offense will take over.

The Cougars break the huddle and Cooper will take his position behind center for the first time today. Cooper sets the offense, spreads Patterson out wide right. Rogers is in the slot. He goes in motion...the snap...Cooper pitches to Rogers, who takes it to the outside for about 8 yards before getting run out of bounds.

"Dirk, keep your eye on Cooper," Borchard said. "You're soon gonna be havin' a lot to do with him, so ya should know as much about him as what you can.

It's Second and 2. Cougars set in a single back formation. Here's the snap. Cooper fakes the pitch left, and he keeps it himself on a naked bootleg. He's got some daylight. He's at the 40, 45, 50 and out of bounds at the Hawks 47. A great Start for the Cougars

"He's something, isn't he?" Borchard said.

"This isn't football," Vaughan said. "They handle the ball and throw it."

"Fuck! I thought you knew the basics. Just watch Cooper."

First and seven on the Hawks 47. Rogers in motion again, the snap... play action...Cooper drops back and delivers a bullet to Patterson at the 25, who takes it all the way inside the Hawks 10, to the 8. This guy's arm is something else!!

First and Goal. Cooper pitches to Jordan, who bobbles the pitch, regains control, cuts inside and dives into the end zone. Touchdown Cougars!!!

Devlin Cooper strode from the field and removed his helmet.

"He looks more like a film star than a football player, doesn't he?" Borchard said.

"Yeah, he's a pretty boy all right."

And here comes the Hawks' defense.

"We don't wanna watch this shit," Borchard said, fast forwarding until he saw Cooper leading the Cougars offense back on the field.

"What's this about, boss?"

"Devlin Cooper just turned twenty-three, and he's the hottest property in football. If he stays fit and healthy, he could play until he's forty. The Packers quarterback just negotiated a deal that'll see him drag in a hundred and ten mil in the next five years. Cooper's contract is up for negotiation at the end of next season. He's worth more."

"Yeah, but what do you want me to do?"

"It's a test, Dirk. I want ya to watch the rest of the game. Don't worry about watchin' the Hawks' offense, just Cooper. I wanna see what you learn about him. Ya can learn a lot about a man by how he reacts on a sportin' field. The Cougars play the Pirates in seven weeks. The sportswriters say that the Pirates are the worst team in football history. There's gonna be some juicy odds on offer," Borchard said. "I want you to persuade Cooper to help us."

"Ah, now I understand." Dirk grinned.

"After you've finished watching the football, I want you to watch the disk?"

"Are you going to watch it?"

"Nah, porn doesn't do anything for me. It just makes me think of that sicko, Andy. I know what's on it, but you might learn a little more about Cooper. Oh, and Dirk, cut two more copies and put them in safe places.

"I'll do better. I'll store it on my computer."

"No! What happens if it falls into the wrong hands or the cops seize it? Just do the copies and hide them."

"Okay, boss."

"Dirk, remember there are three things that could fuck this up. If you push him too hard, and he suicides. Make sure you don't. If he talks to the woman, and she leaves her husband and moves in with him. It devalues the adultery and porn and in some folks' eyes makes it romance. Make sure he doesn't talk to her. And thirdly, he double-crosses us on game day. If that happens, you'll have to kill him."

Chapter 8

The week had dragged for Todd. The earliest he had left the office on any day was seven o'clock, and he'd worked to ten on Monday night. His near death experience with Lechte had refocused him, but he still hated his job. Despite the long hours, he had tweaked his system by factoring in a new variable. Bad luck. He knew it was ridiculous, but the experience with Dancing Girl, when she'd been slow to start after the gates opened, had burned him badly. He reasoned that there were horses that seemed to find a way to get beaten, no matter what. The habitual second-place getters were the worst. They always offered hope the next time they raced. His newly tweaked system had thrown up three winners all ranking above 96, and he resolved to have ten thousand on each. He wouldn't get his recent losses back, but it would restore his confidence and faith in his system.

The betting parlor was far busier and noisier on Saturday than on weekdays and punters were at every table. Todd waited patiently in line and when he reached the window said, "Saratoga, Race two, ten thousand the win, number five, on my tab." He took his ticket, ordered a mineral water, and found a place on the wall where he was directly in front of the monitors. The horses came out on the track, and Todd felt a surge of confidence rush through him. Gunbarrel was a huge chestnut colt with a white diamond in the middle of his head. Five minutes later the commentator was screaming, "Gunbarrel's kicked six lengths clear at the top of the stretch and is cantering to the easiest of wins." Todd was elated and then disappointed. If only he'd had sixty thousand on Gunbarrel. He would have recovered his losses and then some. As he was pondering this, Jack Elliot sauntered up to him.

"Good to be winning again, kid," he said.

What the fuck does that mean? How does he know I backed the winner? How does he know I lost? Maybe I'm overreacting. He's only ever seen me win. Maybe that's why he said again? "How do you know I won?"

"Come on. I was watching you. I thought you were going to burst out cheering at the furlong." Elliot grinned. "You did back the winner, didn't you?"

The only time Todd could remember displaying emotion was when he'd lost the hundred and seventy, but maybe he'd let his guard down with Gunbarrel. "Yeah, I did."

"I lost. Maybe I should buy that system of yours. It seems you're always collecting. If I had your system, I'd be making some big bets."

"And what's a big bet for you?" Todd asked, expecting the answer to be a few thousand dollars.

"A hundred thousand. That's a big bet for me, but I've made bigger. I've got this motto, if you want to win big, you bet big. Anyhow, I'll leave you to it. I've got a sure thing in the third at Sacramento. Are you interested?"

"Thanks, but no thanks," Todd replied, thinking this was the guy who was worried about his wife finding out about his losses. Bullshit!

"Of course." Elliot grinned, as he turned to go to the betting windows. "You've got a foolproof system. Why would you listen to my tips?"

Todd was glad to see the back of Elliot, but he had said two things that resonated. It was a good system, and if you wanted to win big, you had to bet big. Hadn't that just been proved with Gunbarrel? Todd's next bet was going to be Gala Supreme in the fourth at Santa Anita, which would add another forty thousand to his kitty. However, the more he thought about what Elliot had said, the more inclined he was to increase the size of his bet. A bet of fifty thousand would net him two hundred and a bet of a hundred thousand would recover all his losses and make him no longer dependent on Montgomery Hastings & Pierce. The more he did the sums, the more logical it was to increase the size of his bet. Besides, Gala Supreme was ranked at 98 which made his decision even more compelling. By the time they jumped at Santa Anita, Todd had bet eighty thousand on Gala

Supreme to win three hundred and twenty. Gala Supreme didn't have any history of bad luck so how could Todd have factored in his heels getting clipped by Monterey at the turn. The ensuing spill brought down three horses, including Gala Supreme. After the race the commentator said, "I'm pleased to say that the jockeys and horses are okay. Monterey came down very hard, and I feared they might have to destroy him. All's well that ends well."

All's well that ends well. Those words echoed in Todd's head. He hadn't thought of the welfare of the horses. He was too busy wallowing in misery. But he still had one bet to go and perhaps the race caller's comment was prophetic. If Todd's one remaining bet won, and he had enough on it, all would end well.

Thirty minutes later, he put on his overcoat and stumbled toward the door. He had lost one and fifty thousand. Jack Elliot was at the door talking to one of the heavies. "How'd you go, kid?"

Todd could hardly speak. His chest was constricted, and the weight of the world was burying him. "Not so good," he muttered.

"That's a pity," Elliot said, doing his best to look concerned. "That tip I gave you came in at six to one. I won three hundred thousand. You should have been on it."

"Yeah, yeah."

Todd didn't usually drink spirits but on the way back to his apartment he picked up a bottle of Johnny Walker. It was futile, and he drank the bottle in less than three hours, but the misery remained. He toyed with going out to get another bottle before deciding to turn in. The whiskey didn't help. He tossed and turned for hours, unable to fall asleep. Why was the system that had been so successful failing? What was he doing that was different? What had changed at the race tracks? He owed Ronny over three hundred thousand and had less than two hundred in the bank. Eventually, he fell into a fitful sleep.

He awoke on Sunday morning still feeling like shit. The sleep had done nothing for him. He was positive that the only way he'd get his money back was the way that he'd lost it. His heart wasn't in it, but he forced himself to bring his system data up to date by entering details of all of the prior day's races. By midday, the data was entered, and he was again studying his system looking for ways to tweak it. He pulled out an old form guide and compared the information in it with what he had on his iPad. The information he had was far more extensive and detailed than the form guide. No, there was nothing wrong with the system. He had made numerous bets of ten thousand or less, and more than sixty percent had been winners. The problem was the five big bets that he'd made which had all been losers. The answer was simple – bad luck. He would persist with his system knowing that this temporary run of bad luck would soon end. The haze that had enveloped him since his last bet was starting to lift.

The traffic was heavy, and the cab was a few minutes late when it pulled up in front of Todd's apartment building. Vanessa was sitting in the back wearing a stylish gray pin-striped pencil skirt and a four button V-neckline blazer, together with classic black suede stiletto pumps. She had dressed carefully, confident and capable, professional yet feminine. Todd climbed in next to her and caught the trace of an intoxicating perfume.

"Good morning, Todd. What were you up to over the weekend?"

"Hi, Vanessa. Nothing much."

"What? You didn't get together with friends or family. You must have done something." She laughed.

Todd hadn't given much thought to friends lately. He used to have a lot until he had become obsessed with his betting system. "Oh, I had dinner with a few friends on Saturday night. What about you? Did you do anything exciting?"

"I worked on Saturday and spent Sunday afternoon with my family as penance for missing my brother's birthday. It was fun."

"Do you have any other brothers or sisters?"

"I have three brothers and three sisters. I'm the oldest. My nickname's Bossy." She smiled.

"You work long hours. What do you do to relax?"

"I do kickboxing classes with a girlfriend from my apartments on Monday and Wednesday nights. I never miss them. They keep me sane."

"Besides kickboxing and family, how do you spend your time? Do you have a boyfriend?"

"That's a very nosy question. I don't have a boyfriend. I'm too busy. If I did, when would I ever see him? There'll be plenty of time for boyfriends after."

"After?"

"Yes, after I've made partner. Isn't that what you want too, Todd?"

Todd could think of nothing worse. Even as a junior partner he knew the money would be enormous but the last thing he wanted was a life of drudgery. He wanted freedom and the respect of his family. That would only come via success with the betting system he'd spent thousands of hours on. Once he'd grown his stake, he'd buy properties and stocks and live off the rent and dividends. "I'll never make partner." He laughed. "I'd be up against you. I wouldn't stand a chance."

"Hmm, I'm not sure that's true but if I made partner, I'd support you. Don't sell your chances short. You're too good for that, and it's a characteristic I can't stand. There is nothing worse than wasted talent. I don't want to look back in twenty years' time and regret that I didn't do everything possible to make it to the top." She burst out laughing. "God, that was a sermon, wasn't it? Sometimes I get carried away."

She laughed a lot, was fun, had a brilliant mind and was drop dead gorgeous. She was another reason Todd had to get out of the firm. He knew she would never jeopardize her chances of making partner by dating him while he was still working at Montgomery Hastings & Pierce. However, maybe that wouldn't be the case if he could build up the courage to ask her out after he left. They pulled up at the front of a Wall Street high-rise, and Todd held the door open. Vanessa brushed past him, and a trace of her perfume tantalized his nostrils.

He thought it ironic, perhaps fateful that the betting parlor was only a brisk fifteen-minute walk away.

As Vanessa had suggested, Hallstrom's was a typical retail chain that wouldn't present any problems for Todd and his team. He decided to spend the rest of the day preparing the audit plan while Vanessa went back to the office at midday. The financial controller had only been able to give them fifteen minutes, so Todd had organized to meet with him tomorrow morning. Just after 5:30 P.M he hailed a cab to take him home. It would be his first early night since his epiphany about the importance of his job. He told the taxi driver to wait for him while he ordered two hamburgers. He was a junk food fanatic and hated cooking.

After Todd had eaten and watched the news, he performed his daily ritual of inputting the results of the day's major North American races into his iPad. Once he'd completed this, he entered the fields for tomorrow's races and ran his scan. He wasn't sure why. The only day he could bet was Saturday. Checking the results, even though he wasn't betting, gave him some comfort, particularly when they indicated his system was finding winners. Of course, he was disappointed that he hadn't been able to bet on them. He checked the scan and was staggered to see Londonderry, in the second at Belmont, ranked 100. It had never occurred before, and he knew that Londonderry was unbeaten over the past year and had won five consecutive races. There was no other way a horse could rank 100 and even then, substantially more criteria had to be met. When he checked the form, he found that Londonderry had only had five starts. He didn't usually read the form guide, but the commentary said, "Brilliant unbeaten colt. Moving up a class but should win." He knew the odds wouldn't be good, probably two to one and perhaps as bad as six to four. Still, what difference did that make? A certain winner was a certain winner! Better still, the planets seem to be aligned in his favor. Hallstrom's was close to the betting parlor, and the race was at 1:30 so he could place his bet during the lunch break. It was perfect.

Todd found it hard to concentrate on Tuesday morning but convincingly winged his way through the meeting with Hallstrom's financial controller. The work that he was doing was easy, and he'd prepared countless audit plans before. At 1 P.M., he went out for lunch. At 1:20, he entered the betting parlor after a head-clearing walk in crisp air. Londonderry was the two to one favorite and Todd made the largest bet of his lifetime. Such was the size of his bet, the teller asked him to wait while she got an answer on whether they would accept it. Compared to Saturday the betting parlor was quiet, and Todd sat at a table directly in front of the monitors. "They're moving up nicely for the second at Belmont Park, a five-furlong sprint," the commentator said. "Londonderry goes in, and we're only waiting on the Lone Ranger. He's in. They're set. Racing!"

Chapter 9

"Londonderry's four lengths clear at the top of the stretch and drawing away. He's a mighty colt."

Todd thought *fantastic* but didn't let his emotions show. Then he heard the race caller scream, "Something's spooked Londonderry. He almost stopped. Danny Ryan's got him going again, but Red Diver's finishing fast. Red Diver and Londonderry are neck and neck, heads bobbing. Red Diver gets to the front. Red Diver wins. What a sensational race. I don't know what happened to Londonderry."

Todd thought he was going to vomit. What had gone wrong? Why had Londonderry almost stopped? Had the jockey gone to sleep? Whatever the reason, Todd knew he was deep in the mire. The television channel was replaying the last furlong of the race in slow motion. They froze it just before Londonderry went up in the air, and it showed a distinctive, large, black bird flying in front of the horse's head. "Have you ever seen a horse get beaten like that before, Bob?" one of the commentators asked. "He was spooked by a bird."

"Never, Ted, but I have heard of seagulls spooking horses, but I've never heard of a bird costing a horse a race. We might just have witnessed a first."

"He was a very short priced favorite. It's a shame for the connections that his unbeaten run is over."

A shame for the connections? What about me, Todd thought? He felt his legs go out from under him as he stood up, and he put his hand on the table for support. It hurt to think, and when he got out on the sidewalk, he struggled to work out which direction he should be walking.

In the week and a half since Vaughan had watched the CD, he'd had Devlin Cooper followed. Cooper had had two more sessions with

Karen in sleazy motels, but that wasn't the reason Vaughan was having him watched. The CD was more than enough. Vaughan wanted to know what Cooper did with his days. He spent most of his time at football training. On two Friday nights, he'd gone nightclubbing but had left the club to go home by 11 P.M. He hardly touched alcohol and had only gone to the club to mix with friends. He knew and socialized with many girls but didn't have a girlfriend. To the public and those who knew him, he was the fresh-faced all-American boy with the bionic arm. He spent a lot of money hiring limousines, and that seemed to be his favored mode of transport even though he had a Ferrari and Lamborghini in his garage. The same driver drove him everywhere irrespective of the time of day. What was most interesting for Vaughan was that on both Mondays, a limousine had turned up at Cooper's home at precisely 7:30 A.M. to take him to training. Vaughan knew nothing about football but it didn't take him long to learn that a typical Monday for the Cougars involved treating players for injuries and going through their first weightlifting session of the week. If Cooper was picked up by limousine for a third consecutive Monday at 7:30 A.M., Vaughan would implement the first part of the plan that he'd worked out with Borchard.

Todd had his head down and was shuffling along Water Street when his cell phone rang. He was reluctant to even look at it but when he saw it was Doug Lechte he had no choice but to answer. "Hello, Doug."

"Where are you?"

"Just getting some lunch. I'll be back at Hallstrom's in about five minutes. Is there a problem?"

"Are you nearly finished?"

"I have about an hour left to complete the audit plan."

"You can do that in the office. I want you to get back here pronto. Max Lustig is coming in, and I want you to sit in on the meeting."

Ten minutes later Todd was in a cab. He felt like shit and was dreading the meeting but knew he had to focus. His job had just become essential. He wondered if Ronny Conroy would let him have more credit. If anything Londonderry had proved that his system was robust, and it was only freakish bad luck that had cost him a big win. More worryingly, what was he going to do if Ronny called in his debt? He tried to block that thought out knowing that he needed to be sharp in front of Lechte.

Todd knocked and entered Lechte's office. He hadn't seen the other man for years and doubted that Max Lustig would remember him. He was a national identity who ran and owned a huge transport fleet. Rumors abounded that as a young man, he had smashed the knee-caps of those who had stood between him and winning a contact. Now in his early fifties he still cut an imposing figure. He was about 6' and 230 pounds with a shiny bald head and intense green eyes. He'd come a long way and was famous for his philanthropy and the media loved him because he was always good for a one-liner. The bones in Todd's right hand screamed as the trucking tycoon held it in a vice like grip. "Good to see you again, Todd," he said, in a booming voice.

"Max is looking to add a small New Jersey outfit to his fleet, but he's not happy with his accountant's due diligence. He suspects the figures aren't kosher and wants us to have a second look at them. You did the work on the Dexon Transport merger, so you're a natural for the job," Lechte said.

"What makes you think the numbers are wrong, Max?" Todd asked.

"Simple," the big man replied. "They cart refrigerated and chilled produce as do many of my operations. That's why it should be a good fit. Anyhow, the ratio of fuel costs to sales is way out of kilter. It's way less than I've ever achieved which makes me think they're inflating sales or not showing all their costs. It's the type of thing sellers do when they're trying to pump up the price of their businesses. Christ, I used to do it when I was selling dud divisions of my business."

"What did they say when you confronted them?" Todd followed up.

"Their fleet's more modern than mine, and their drivers don't exceed the speed limits. Hell, I've got five thousand tractors on the road. I can tell you where every one of them is, the speed they're doing, the fuel consumption and, if need be, when the driver last took a leak. They must think I'm suffering from dementia." Lustig laughed.

"You know Max is more than a client, he's a friend, Todd. I want you to prioritize this assignment," Lechte said, passing Todd a large two ring binder. "Everything you need to know is in here. Head to New Jersey tomorrow. It shouldn't take you long to find out what's going on."

Chapter 10

Phillip Cromwell loved everything about St. Patrick's Cathedral, the beautiful architecture, the Monseigneur, the priests, the nuns, the organ music, the choir boys and the congregation. Many New York parishes secretly supported gay marriage, birth control and other abominations that sickened Cromwell to the core. Not the priests at St. Patrick's who preached within the confines of the edicts of the Vatican and the Pope.

Cromwell had been appointed parish treasurer when he was just twenty-one. Thirty-eight years later, he still held the same honorary position. He liked to claim that he'd hardly missed a Sunday morning mass in all that time, conveniently forgetting the numerous days spent at his yacht, tennis and golf clubs. Religion was very important, that is, providing it didn't impact on his social life. He knelt in the front row next to his wife, Mary. They'd married when he was twenty-four. They had had a son and daughter, both adults now, who'd been raised to be good Catholics. Mary had been the daughter of the managing partner of Montgomery Hastings & Pierce at a time when a prerequisite for admittance as a partner was being a Roman Catholic male from a wealthy family. Cromwell yearned for those days again but had been unable to stop the firm broadening its horizons and partners now included, Methodists, Baptists, Jews, Lutherans, Anglicans and even a Muslim in Dearborn. They also included women, African Americans and those who were openly gay. If that wasn't bad enough there were also the likes of Doug Lechte and his followers who did nothing for the dignity of the firm.

The priest finished the prayer, and the congregation rose. Cromwell assumed his duties as one of the ushers, smiling warmly, greeting parishioners as they dipped into their pockets. As he moved down the aisle, his thoughts turned to the fierce arguments he was having with Lechte. Lechte was nothing more than a salesman, and if it were not for his rapport and popularity with clients, he would never have made partner. Now Lechte was pushing for the admittance of his protégé as a partner and accusing him of being racist and anti-women. Cromwell would never admit to the truth of these comments, not even to himself, and besides, they were just two reasons why he would never vote in favor of admitting Vanessa Hodge to the partnership. He'd had her thoroughly investigated and found that her family had no social status and were dirt poor. She'd even had to get grants to get through college. No wonder she was trying to improve her station in life by working huge hours. It wouldn't help her though, because no one with a family background like hers was going to be admitted to the New York partnership while he was managing partner. He would do his best to ensure the national partnership adopted the same standards.

As far as Cromwell was concerned, future partners would be like him, religious, socially acceptable, from a wealthy family, honest, hardworking, heterosexual and with a strong moral fiber. Vanessa was diligent, but in his eyes she dismally failed most of the other criteria.

It was 7:25 A.M. on Monday and the limousine was only five minutes from Lincoln Park. The driver made the same trip every Monday morning at the same time. Traffic was medium to heavy, when without warning, a black SUV came flying out of a side street and slammed into the rear of the limo. Two tradesmen jumped out of the SUV and started waving their hands and verbally abusing the driver of the limo.

At the same time, Devlin Cooper answered his phone. "Mr. Cooper, it's Marty from Exclusive Limousines. I'm sorry to tell you, but John has had an accident on his way to pick you up. Don't worry, we have another vehicle in the area that we've reassigned to you. It should be there any time now. You'll still be at training on time."

"How's John. Is he all right?"

"It's just a fender bender. John's fine, Mr. Cooper."

Cooper was on the third level of his four-level mansion looking out the huge glass windows when he saw the limo pull up in the driveway, and the driver get out and hold the rear door open. "I'm glad to hear that. Your limo's just turned up. Thanks for that. Give John my best."

Cooper could've taken the elevator but instead took the stairs two at a time to the foyer. He felt fantastic as he opened the front doors and strode toward the limousine, his hand extended to the driver. "Devlin Cooper," he said. "That's bad news about John."

"Good morning, Mr. Cooper," said the driver, touching his over-sized chauffer's cap that together with his sunglasses concealed his upper face. "My name's George. You'll be pleased to know it was only a minor accident and that John was unharmed."

"Do you know where we're going, George?" Cooper asked.

"Of course, Mr. Cooper," the driver responded, glancing in the rearview mirror, as he reversed out of the driveway. He drove slowly down the street and turned left at the first intersection as John always did. Cooper was about to tell him to get a move on when he brought the limo to a halt near a heavily treed park.

"What the fuck are you stopping for?"

Two gigantic men ran from the park toward the limo and Cooper heard the rear door locks release as they got in on either side of him.

"What the–"

Cooper got a whiff of ether before everything became hazy, and he lost consciousness.

Farik looked at Ahmet and said, "Find his cell. Dirk said to get rid of it. I don't know why, but we better do it."

Cooper woke up in a dark room. He was tied to a chair, and his hands were handcuffed behind him. His throat was dry. "Whe-where am I?" he rasped.

A slightly accented voice from the darkness behind him said, "Don't worry, we're not going to hurt ya. We're going to show ya a movie and then we're going to let ya go. Would ya like a drink?"

"Who are you? What do you want with me?"

"All will be revealed after you've watched the movie," the voice said.

Cooper looked up. There was a man standing next to him with his head hidden by a hood, holding a blinding flashlight. He put his hand behind Cooper's head, tilted it back, and poured water into his mouth. The flashlight dimmed, and he saw a large white screen. The groan that he let out when he saw himself eating Karen echoed around the room. Two hours later he felt sick and wanted the world to swallow him.

"Wh-what do you wa-want?" he asked.

"With endorsements, we think you're going to earn three hundred million over the next fifteen years. We'd hate for ya to lose it all because of a little fling with a woman fourteen years older than you. And we'd hate your mom to see it. What's her name? Doreen, isn't it? What would she think of her little boy?"

"Fucking bastards! How much do you want?" Cooper said. "I'll pay anything you want."

"That's no way to talk to your friends, Devlin. We don't want your money. We just want you to do us a few favors when we ask. Now we're going to put a prepaid cell in the pocket of your jacket. Keep it with you at all times. When it rings, it will be us. Understand?"

"Wha-what do you want?"

"All will be answered in time. Just relax. You have nothing to fear from us. We're your friends. Oh, and don't waste time going back to the Astor. We could've filmed you at any number of locations. You've been very active."

"Fuck you."

"That's no way to talk, Devlin. A word of warning. We'll be watching you. If you talk to anyone, we'll know. If you're thinking about going to the police, don't! Half of them are on our payroll. Oh, and don't talk to the woman, not a word. We won't kill you, but she's worth nothing, so she's expendable. Get it?"

Before Cooper could respond, a cloth soaked in ether was held over his mouth and nose. His head slumped forward, and he drifted into darkness.

Dirk looked at Farik and Ahmet. "Carry him out to the limo and be careful not to hurt him. Drop him off at that park near his home. Just prop him up on one of the seats. It'll only be a few minutes before he wakes up. He'll be okay. Just remember, be careful. If you damage him, the boss will tear strips off you."

Todd knew that the only way out of the mess he'd got himself into was to get more credit from Ronny Conroy. He knew his system was robust and with this in mind he took a cab to Chinatown and the betting parlor just after midday.

"You better be here to pay me, Todd," Conroy said.

"No, no I'm not," Todd replied. "Ronny, I need more credit. You know that I'm only in trouble because of rotten luck. You know my system works. If you can just see your way clear to letting me have another two hundred, I'm sure I'll be able to clear my debt."

"You've got fucking big balls, I'll say that for you. You're in for five hundred, and you want to stiff me for another two."

Todd hung his head in despair. "Does that mean no?"

Conroy laughed. "To most people it would but obviously not to you. I've gotta talk to some people who I can't pay because of you. If they say they'll extend my credit, then I'll extend yours. Don't get your hopes up, though, because I don't think they're going to. Tell me, if they don't, how are you gonna pay me?"

"I-I don't know," Todd said. "I'll find a way."

"You better make damn sure you do. Now get out of here. I've got work to do," Conroy said.

As Todd stumbled out of the pawn shop, he didn't look up or notice Max Lustig enjoying a meal at the Chinese restaurant directly opposite.

Dermott Becker stared into the bathroom mirror. He was still a good-looking man, but the crow's feet had become condor's feet and his forehead resembled a cattle grid. *Too many late nights and too much sun when I was younger,* he thought as he splashed cold water on his face. Nadia, his wife, was twenty-five years his junior and had been pushing him hard to go and see her cosmetic surgeon but, so far, he'd resisted. She had an enormous influence on him, and it was only her persistence that had resulted in him buying the Hamptons house. "Thirty-eight million," the agent had said, "and don't miss it. It's a bargain."

He strolled back to his study and looked out of the window at

Nadia and her girlfriends playing tennis. She was a joy to behold and still as natural as the day she was born except for the Botox and fillers. He watched and smiled as her sports bra fought a losing battle against the bounce. Long legged, powerful and very fast, she was a fierce competitor. The phone rang, and Becker turned back to his desk overlooking the Atlantic and cursed. It was the Serbian.

"Dermott, it's Brock. What have you done about Giovani?"

It was the fourth time Borchard had called since the last board meeting. "As I've told you before, I am attending to it, Brock," Becker replied.

"Do you need any help? I can send one of my men. We cannot let anyone con us and make us look like fools. If we let him get away with it, we'll be seen as easy targets by others."

Becker sighed. The Serbian was ignorant on matters of finance. Did he think there was a clique of stockbrokers who sat around saying, *how can we fleece Jack Elliot today?* Borchard was applying the same principles that he applied to the poor souls who owed him money and didn't pay. Victims of his loan sharking operation. All Giovani had done was pass on inside information that hadn't worked out. Becker had given up trying to explain it to the Serbian and knew he would have to take some action. He didn't want to do it before Todd Hansen was on the hook though because if Giovani was cooperative then he could kill two birds with one stone.

Chapter 11

The week seemed like it was taking forever to end and every day Todd waited to hear from Ronny about the additional two hundred. By Friday, he hadn't heard a word and was incapable of concentrating on anything. He tried to convince himself that no news was good news but didn't believe it.

Just before midday his cell rang, and he didn't recognize the number when he answered.

"Todd, it's Ronny Conroy, they said no, and you're in the hole for five hundred and twenty thousand. When are you going to pay?"

Todd felt like he was going to puke. "Ronny, Ronny can you ask them again? I know I can win everything back if you give me a chance."

There was a long pause. "Ronny, are you still there?"

"Are you saying you don't have my money? Christ, I've got commitments to these guys. How would you feel if you'd won, and I couldn't pay you? You'd be pretty pissed off," Ronny said. "I need that money."

"I-I can't pay. Well, not right away anyhow."

"Bullshit? Your mom and dad are rolling in cash. Ask them to help you."

"I-I can't ask th-them. I can't!"

Again, there was another long pause. "Todd, I have to have the money by Monday. If I don't have it by then, I'll have to take recovery action."

"How will you do that?" Todd asked.

"Not the way your firm recovers the debts owing to it." Ronny laughed. "If you want to remain healthy, you'll get my money. I hope, for your sake, that I see you on Monday."

Todd was about to respond when he heard dial tone.

Todd cradled his head in his hands. He wanted to cry. *Where am I going to get the money? I don't have any friends I can ask to lend me that much. Dad won't lend it to me. Mom might but she won't without telling Dad, and once he knows he'll make sure she doesn't. My brother's tougher and meaner than Dad. My sister's my only chance, but she can't keep a secret. She'll tell everyone and Dad will tell me that I'm a loser and always have been. No, I can't ask the family. What am I going to do?*

The next call that Ronny Conroy made was to Jack Elliot who was elated. It had taken longer than his boss, Dermott Becker, had thought, but they finally had the accountant in the bag. Becker arranged for Elliot to pick up a briefcase containing five hundred and twenty thousand, together with an assignment of debt form. Becker knew enough about Todd Hansen to know that he wouldn't be able to pay.

Todd had had little social contact since his obsession had taken over. Now, on a bleak New York night, he wished he had a girlfriend or best friend with whom he could share his misery. He had many friends but no one close. He briefly thought of calling Vanessa Hodge but quickly changed his mind. He'd just be confessing that he was a loser. He couldn't believe that his life had come to this, and he wondered and worried about what Ronny would do on Monday.

Will he send thugs to break my legs? What would be the point of that? He'd never get his money.

Depressed, scared and sick Todd forced himself to make a toasted ham and tomato sandwich but then couldn't eat it. He had to do something to get rid of the black dog, so he flicked the television on. He heard the newsreader say that mob boss and murderer, Frankie Arturo, had been sentenced to two life terms in Castlebrough Penitentiary. The last thing he needed was bad news, so he turned the television off and settled down on the sofa to input the results of today's races. He then inputted the fields for tomorrow's races just as if it was a typical weekend. His scan produced two forecast winners ranking 97 and 98.

When Todd woke up the following morning for the first time in his life, he contemplated suicide. It wasn't the fear or the money he owed but the shame and dread of how his family would react when they found out. The minute he'd refused to study medicine his family had virtually disowned him. The thought of his father saying *I always told you, you were a deadbeat* was crushing.

To add to Todd's misery, the two horses that his system threw up both won at the very juicy odds of three to one and of six to one. If only Ronny had provided him with an additional two hundred thousand, he would've won enough to pay off his debt and be left with nearly three hundred thousand.

On Sunday, Todd moped around his apartment that he could no longer afford and wondered what was going to become of him. In the space of three short weeks, his life had fallen apart. He went to bed early but fought with the blankets and sheets until 5 A.M. before collapsing into a deep sleep. Two hours later he pulled the pillow over his head in a futile attempt to block out the clock radio.

On the short walk from his apartment to the office, Todd found himself continually looking over his shoulder. Ronny hadn't specifically said how he collected debts, but his inference had been unpleasant. Todd breathed a sigh of relief as he entered the elevator. He was safe. Well at least for the rest of the day because he had no intention of leaving the office. He didn't know how he was going to get any work done. He wanted to remain at work until midnight but didn't want to walk home in the dark. Todd didn't do much but, for once, the day flew when he wanted it to drag. It was still daylight when he left the office at 4:55 and he half ran half walked the short distance to his apartment. He opened the door and quickly closed it behind him, carefully locking it. He rested his forehead up against the door and let out an audible sigh of relief. *God, I can't live like this.*

When Todd heard the voice behind him, he jumped and nearly screamed.

"Hello, Todd, it's nice of you to come home early. We thought we might have to wait all night."

"How di-did you get in? Wh-what do you wa-want?" Todd said, eyeing the young man. He was thickset with narrow eyes and a shaven head.

"I think you know what we want." The man grinned through compressed, thin lips.

It was then that Todd noticed the other man sitting on the couch. He was wiry with sunken cheeks, neatly combed gray hair and looked to be about fifteen years older than his partner. He'd helped himself to coffee. "Who are you?"

"I'm Ferguson," the young man said, "and he's Fraser. We're facilitators."

"Facilitators?"

"Yeah, we smooth out our clients' problems," Fraser said. "Ronny Conroy's one of our clients and your failure to pay put him under a lot of pressure, so we organized to have your debt paid. You'll be pleased to know you don't owe Ronny anything, and if you don't want to, you never have to talk to him again."

"I don't understand," Todd said.

Fraser got up from the sofa and handed Todd a single page document. It was a discharge of debt form that had been signed by Ronny Conroy and witnessed. "Does this make it clear?"

Todd glanced at the document. "But why?"

"We have another client, and it took an assignment of your debt from Ronny. It's a corporation, and you might be tempted to find out who owns it. You'll be wasting your time. All you'll do is find other corporations and a huge loop that takes you nowhere. Here's a copy of the assignment."

"You haven't answered my question."

"We don't know," Fraser said, "other than one of the corporation's managers knows you and wanted to help."

"Who?" Todd asked.

"Mr. Elliot," Ferguson said.

"Who?"

"Jack Elliot."

"Why? I hardly know him," Todd said.

"We don't know. He did say to tell you not to worry about anything and that he's sure something can be worked out," Fraser said, joining Ferguson at the door. "Unless Mr. Elliot wants us to remain involved, our job is over."

As Todd was opening the door, Ferguson said, "Oh, and don't forget interest at ten percent is running on the debt."

"I never agreed to pay interest," Todd said. "Besides ten percent is outrageous. Six percent's the going rate."

Ferguson was in the corridor when he turned around and smirked. "Ten percent per month," he said. "You're playing in the big league now, kid."

Chapter 12

Devlin Cooper woke up sitting on a bench seat in a park. He shielded his eyes against the weak sun and took a few minutes to get his bearings before realizing he was less than a mile from home. He reached around for his cell phone but only found the one that the thugs had put in his jacket pocket. *Why would they have stolen my cell phone?* He checked his wallet. His cash and credit cards were intact. His Rolex was still on his wrist, and it was 12:20, five hours since his kidnapping. He needed to get to a phone and make contact with the club.

He took his time on the short walk, cursing himself. On reflection, it was easy to work out what had happened. It had been that sleazy, little weasel ogling the *Playboy* centerfold who'd set him up. He'd had a bad feeling about the sleazebag the minute he saw him and should've just walked out and found another place, but it was too late now. Complacency and lust had him on the rack, and he had no idea what he was going to do.

He and Karen had always been attracted to each other but never in his wildest dreams had he ever thought that he would end up in bed with her. The day that changed his life had started innocently enough. It was the offseason, late in the afternoon, and he'd finished doing some shopping and was enjoying a latte in a small coffee shop. She had walked in, saw him sitting in the corner and joined him. Perfectly natural, perfectly innocent. It was fun, and they were joking around. They ordered a second round and continued with the harmless banter. He'd said to Karen that he had to phone for a limo, but she had insisted on driving him home. By the time they left the coffee shop, it was dusk, and the weather had turned decidedly chilly.

He still didn't know who had made the first move. One minute they were sitting in front of his house with the engine still running and the next minute they'd been tearing at each other's clothes. They could've gone into his home and started that night, but they didn't. Sanity had prevailed before any real damage was done. The following day, Karen called to apologize and say she didn't know what had gotten into her, and it would never happen again. Devlin said that it was all his fault and that he was sorry. Deep down they both knew their lust was overwhelming and that it would only be a matter of time.

Three months later, the season was in full swing. It was Friday, the easiest training day of the week, and Devlin had an early morning dental appointment when Coach Deacon called. In his rush to get to training, the coach had forgotten some plans and asked Devlin to swing past his home and pick them up. Karen could have had them in her hand when he knocked at the door, but she didn't. Instead, she invited him in and within five minutes they were half-undressed and on the carpet of the living room floor. Devlin had had sex with young girls before but had never been with anyone who was into it more than him. It was different and exciting, almost as if it was his first sexual experience, and he couldn't get enough. They were both embarrassed after it was over and hurriedly put their clothes back on. Karen said she was sorry, that it was her fault, and that it must never happen again. Devlin was equally remorseful and insisted that he'd made the first move, but they both knew it had been spontaneous combustion. What they didn't say was that the sex had been spectacular, and they were both already lusting for their next encounter. Devlin's head was spinning when he climbed back into the limo, and he hoped that his driver, John, wouldn't notice the change in his demeanor.

Coach Deacon was forty-two, five years older than Karen and had been like a second father to Devlin. Devlin was racked with guilt when he handed the plans to the coach, who noticed the change in Devlin's manner and asked if anything was wrong. Devlin had mumbled something about the dental injection and Coach Deacon had laughed and told him to toughen up. That had been a year ago and as time went by and Devlin was more frequently with Karen, his conscience went on vacation.

Now it had returned along with a healthy dose of fear. He'd never expected their clandestine affair to last so long and in most of the novels he'd read, affairs were usually over after six months. That wasn't the case with him, and he thought about having sex with Karen nearly every waking moment. He'd arrived at training a few times unable to get out of the limo and had had to chat with John until his lust became less visible. As he reached his front door, the last thing he was thinking about was having sex with Karen, and there was no visible sign of arousal. The figurative cold spoon that had hit his manhood on the knob had removed all lustful thoughts. Last night, had he been asked, he would have said that lust was a far more powerful emotion than fear. He now knew that answer was wrong.

What would he do if the CD was shown to the public? His mother would die of shame. His dad loved to boast about his famous son. What would he think? What would his sisters and brothers think? What would his fans think, particularly the younger ones? What would Coach Deacon do? How would it impact on the Deacons' three children? Would the Cougars keep him as their quarterback? Most likely not. Would any other NFL team pick him up? No.

Fuck! Why didn't I keep my dick in my pants?

Devlin racked his brain to come up with someone who he could talk to. The only person who came to mind was Karen.

Dermott Becker hadn't seen or heard from Harry O'Brien since the last board meeting and presumed that the Transport Employees Union's assisted sabotage of Webb Transport's fleet was continuing as planned. When Becker picked up the phone, O'Brien could barely contain himself. "Dermott, how would you like to own Webb Transport rather than just stealing a milk contract from them?"

"Go on."

"Lou Gerrard, the president of the Transport Employees Union, called me last night and said that he's prepared to call a general strike and take all Webb's drivers out. It'll just about break them and make them ripe to be taken over. It would've cost close to a billion to buy them a year ago. I reckon we might be able to pick them up for two hundred mil. It's the deal of the century," O'Brien gushed.

"How much does Gerrard want?"

"Ten million paid into a Liechtenstein bank account. He also wants a guarantee that the payment will be untraceable."

"I'm not sure we want to do this deal. If we do, we can't give him a guarantee. Christ, how does he expect us to document a bribe to commit an illegal act? You can tell him that he can nominate the country from where he wants the payment to emanate. Hong Kong, Switzerland, Ireland, the Caymans, even Timbuctoo if he'd like. No one, not the IRS, not the SEC and not the Justice Department is ever going to trace the payment."

"I thought you'd be jumping to do the deal. I don't understand. What's wrong?"

"Webb's been losing contracts because their customers don't like this rolling industrial action. That prick, Max Lustig, has been knocking off their contracts, and I don't want to go up against him. It's only a good deal if there's still some meat on the bones. Christ, I don't want to buy them and find there are no cartage contracts. If you can buy them within five days of the drivers going out on strike, it's probably a deal. Any longer and they won't be worth buying."

"You're not interested," O'Brien whined.

"I didn't say that. Here's the deal you put to Lou Gerrard. We'll pay him his ten mil conditional on Webb accepting our offer for two hundred million within five days of the drivers going out on strike. Force Lou to work for his money. If he wants it, he'll make sure the deal gets done on our terms."

"You don't sound confident."

"I'm not. Max Lustig has as much union influence as us, and Lou Gerrard could be playing you off against him. Keep your wits about you, Harry. It's not as straightforward as Gerrard is making out," Becker said, putting the phone back in its cradle. He was disappointed. He was a thousand miles away from the action but still knew more about what was going on than O'Brien.

Chapter 13

Todd had no idea why Elliot had bought his debt but in some ways he was relieved. The guys who'd broken into his apartment had told him not to worry, and he was no longer concerned about his legs being broken. He knew he wouldn't have to wait long before being contacted by Elliot.

His cell phone rang at 6:30 on Tuesday morning and he slid his hand out from under the blankets. "Hello."

"Good morning, Todd. It's Jack. We need to meet today."

"Where?"

"If it's convenient for you at your apartment tonight."

"I don't know what time I'll be working to," Todd said.

"That's not a problem. I'll just let myself in. I'll have coffee and watch some television while I'm waiting." Elliot laughed.

"Listen, I might owe you a lot of money, but I don't want you or your thugs breaking into my apartment. I'll meet with you at a café or coffee shop."

"That's no good. Our conversation has to be private. I've got a suite at the Hyatt on East 42nd Street just down the road from your office. Phone me when you're leaving tonight and I'll buy you dinner."

"No thanks. I'll get my own dinner."

"What? Those greasy hamburgers you live on? Todd, unless you can come up with my money, we're gonna be working together for a long time. You can do it the hard way or the easy way. It's up to you."

"I'll see you tonight," Todd said, hitting the end button.

Phillip Cromwell was elated. At his insistence, the firm had made a large donation to the mayor's reelection campaign. A donation that Lechte had strenuously but unsuccessfully opposed. Now it was starting to pay off. The mayor's office had called to ask Cromwell to accept the position of honorary auditor of The Disabled Children's Fund, a charity set up and overseen by the mayor's wife. Fees were unimportant as this was a highly sought after prestigious appointment that would lead to more lucrative work in the future. Cromwell and his wife had also been invited to a fundraising dinner at the St. Regis on Friday night. It promised to be a glittering event and Cromwell was looking forward to mixing with the who's who of New York. With luck, he might even win some important, new clients. Not the rough and tumble nouveau rich clients that Doug Lechte had won, like Max Lustig and his ilk. Lustig might be a billionaire, but he was crude and crass. The clients Cromwell would win would be old money and not only rich but genteel. He saw it as a wonderful opportunity to bury the nonsense that Lechte was the firm's rainmaker and the only partner who could win influential, new clients.

At 8:30 P.M. Todd strode across the foyer of the Hyatt to the elevators. He was apprehensive about what Elliot might want. Elliot opened the door, and Todd entered a suite that contained a large leather sofa, a marble coffee table, and an inbuilt bar and television. At the other end of the room, there was a dining table surrounded by half a dozen chairs. Elliot was wearing a white T-shirt and jeans. His bicep danced when he pointed to a chair. "Take a seat."

"Where's your wife?" Todd asked.

"What are you talking about?"

"You know the wife who was gonna kill you after your losing bet."

"Oh, that one." Elliot smirked. "It was bullshit. I'm not married, but it seemed convenient to be at the time. I'm gonna order a steak. Do you want one?"

"I've eaten."

"Yeah, and I've got a wife. Come on, you must be starving. I promise I won't add it to your debt."

"No, thanks."

"Have it your way. Stand up, I need to pat you down before we talk. I hope for your sake that you're not stupid enough to be wearing a wire."

As Elliot frisked him, Todd said, "You've been watching too many

70

gangster movies. I'm not wearing a wire. Why would I? I don't like being threatened."

"And I don't like threatening you. All you've got to do is what I tell you, and we'll get on fine," Elliot said, putting the assignment of debt in front of Todd. "You remember this?"

"Yeah, I do. It's an assignment of my debt to Genesis Nominees. Who's Genesis Nominees and where do you fit in? How do I know you've got anything to do with Genesis?"

"Here's the deal, smartass. We bought your debt on a full recourse basis. That means we can hand it back to Ronny anytime we want. The people he hires to collect debts use baseball bats. If you continue to be a dickhead, you're gonna end up in a hospital, if you're lucky. The question you have to answer is, do you want to deal with Ronny's people or me?"

"Let's get to why I'm here. What do you want? Why did you buy the debt?"

"We want to help you," Elliot said, taking a bottle of mineral water from the fridge. "Want one?"

"No. Can you just get on with it?"

"Temper, temper, Todd. I want you to answer a few of my questions first. Your father's New York's finest neurosurgeon and by all accounts is worth a fortune. Why don't you just borrow the money from him?"

"Leave my family out of this. It's none of their business."

"That just halved my questions. Let's cut to the chase. Your firm audits some of the largest companies listed on the New York Stock Exchange and NASDAQ."

"Yes," Todd said, looking puzzled.

"And they report their results every three months."

"Yes."

"And your firm knows those results a day or two prior to their release to the market."

"Oh, fuck," Todd said. "You're kidding. No, I won't do it."

"I haven't asked you to do anything yet. Settle down."

"You're going to ask me to leak the results to you before their release to the market. Then you're either going to buy or short the stock. No,

I'm not doing it. If I get caught, they'll lock me up and throw the key away."

"It's a victimless crime. We're not going to buy or sell the stock. We'll buy derivatives offshore, and the SEC will be none the wiser. We'll make a couple of small killings, and then you're off the hook. Your debt's extinguished and no one need ever know. What could be fairer than that?"

"Victimless? When there are information leaks, it brings the whole integrity of the financial markets into question. That's why the penalties are so severe," Todd shouted.

"You're the last person who should be delivering a sermon about integrity. Let's face it. You're a two-bit gambler who lost half a million of someone else's money. How much integrity do you think you have?"

"It makes no difference. I can't help you. I couldn't even if I wanted to. We audit maybe fifty listed companies in North America but only thirty out of New York. There are five other audit managers besides me. I can't access their files."

"Yeah, I know that and a little more. Montgomery Hastings & Pierce's New York office audits thirty-two listed companies, and I can tell you who they are and which manager audits them. We employ former big four accountants and know exactly what you can access. We'll settle for the information on two companies. Virtex Software and Philco Laboratories. It should be easy. Your colleague, Vanessa Hodge, audits both of them."

Todd grimaced. Elliot had done his homework. The two stocks were incredibly volatile and sensitive to financial information. Anyone who had pre-release financial information on these companies could make some serious money. "I won't do it, and you can't force me to! You must think I'm stupid. If I did it, you'd have a hold over me for the rest on my life."

"Two companies, Todd. That's all we're asking. My boss is a man of his word. Do it and you'll never hear from us again. I promise."

"Who is this boss? When can I meet him? I want to hear him say that if I do it, you pricks will never trouble me again."

"Forget it. You aren't meeting him. Not ever. You deal with me."

"Then there's nothing to think about. I'm not doing it."

There was a knock on the door and a room service waiter entered wheeling a trolley. Elliot tipped him generously and removed the silver cloche covering the plate. The smell of steak and vegetables wafted around the room. Todd felt sick with hunger. "You're hungry," Elliot said. "I'm happy to share."

"I told you I'm not hungry."

"Have it your way," Elliot said, picking up the T-bone in his hands and taking a huge bite.

"I will."

With his mouth half-full and his fingers dripping with oil, Elliot said, "So you're happy for me to front up to your father. I'll tell him that his little weasel of a son lost half a mil gambling and can't pay. Or would you prefer it if I went to your mother? You know there's an old wives tale about redheads being fiery and courageous. You sure destroy that tale."

"Stay away from my family. Stay away from them."

"The mouse that roared." Elliot grinned. "What are you going to do to me if I approach your family?"

Todd leaped to his feet and opened the fridge and grabbed a bottle of mineral water. He gulped it down, wiping the drops from his chin. "You're a real bastard, aren't you?"

"You still don't get it, do you? I'm good cop. Ronny Conroy's bad cop. If I hadn't bought your debt, you'd already be in a hospital with your legs and arms broken. Not to say anything about how your head would look. I rescued you. All I'm asking in return is a little favor."

"Liar! You saw an opportunity where for a small outlay you could reap millions. You couldn't care less about me."

"You call half a mil a small outlay? And don't forget, it's increasing at ten percent a month. How are you ever gonna pay?"

"That's bullshit! I never agreed to that. It's outrageous. No court will ever enforce an interest rate like that."

Elliot leaned forward, flexing his muscles and began to wring his hands. He sneered. "You still don't get it, do you? We don't use the courts to collect our debts. I could have you killed for five thousand and your worthless body would never be found. Think about it, Todd. You're worth five thousand, and if something happens to you, I'll hand the debt back to Ronny. He'll give me back my cash, and that'll be that."

Todd picked up the empty bottle of water and sucked the last few drops from it. He folded his arms and stuck his jaw out. "I won't do it. If you approach my family you won't have to worry about the five thousand, I'll take my life."

Elliot burst out laughing. "I was waiting for you to come up with that bullshit. It's easy to say and fucking hard to do. Some say that you've got to have guts to do it. That's bullshit! It's the coward's way out. You're lots of things, Todd, but you wouldn't be sitting here if you were a coward. So let's just put that down as your first lie and move on."

Todd closed his eyes and massaged his temples. He could feel pressure on every part of his body. "I want to meet your boss."

"No way. It isn't gonna happen."

"Have it your way then, but for the last time, I won't do it."

"Okay, you won't do it." Elliot smiled with lifeless eyes. "How are you going to pay us?"

"I don't know. I need to think about it. I need time."

"I'm not an unreasonable man. You've got seven days to come up with the money. Oh, and don't try and run. You're being watched around the clock," Elliot said as he got to his feet. "It was nice of you to visit, Todd. I sure hope you can come up with our money."

"I bet you do," Todd said, ignoring Elliot's extended hand.

Within two minutes of Todd leaving, Elliot was on the phone to Dermott Becker. "It went exactly as we thought. He point blank refused to help, but he'll come around. He wants to meet you."

"That worked out well. What did you tell him?"

"I said it's not going to happen. It made him more determined. The next time he asks, I'll weaken."

"Perfect. Well done. How sure are you that he'll come through?" Becker asked.

"I'm certain. He was all bluster and bravado, but he'll cave in. The poor little bastard was starving but refused to eat with me. The kid's got grit. I like that.'

"Just so long as he doesn't have too much grit, Jack. It's the sweetest of sweet scams, but it's all reliant on him. Did you tell him that after he's given us the information he's off the hook?"

"Of course."

"Did he believe you?"

"That's why he wants to meet you. He wants to hear it from you."

"Fool! We'll own him for the rest of his life. Keep on top of him, Jack. If you can pull this off, you're going to earn yourself a big bonus."

It was late on Saturday afternoon, and Vanessa Hodge was, as per usual, the last one left in the office. She was anxious to finish the assignment she was working on and finally have a Sunday to herself. It was dark when Vanessa left the office, and she hoped she wasn't wasting her weekends for nothing. A few minutes later she was on a bus to her studio apartment in West Village. Three people got on after her, none of whom were conspicuous, especially not the slim, graying man in his early forties. When she got off the bus, the man followed her, never getting closer than fifty yards. He watched as she entered an old three-story building. Five minutes later the man entered the foyer and immediately went to the mailboxes. Many tenants had their names printed on their boxes including Vanessa Hodge.

Chapter 14

The transport strike in the southern states was now in its fourth
day and national news. Manufacturers' factories and warehouses
were overflowing, fruit and vegetables were rotting, milk supplies
were at a standstill, retailers were running out of stock and super-
markets had been rushed, and their shelves were empty. Irate call-
ers swamped talkback radio demanding the drivers return to work.
Others said that Webb Transport should be stripped of its contracts.
However, the vast majority wanted other transport companies to
come in and get goods moving again, even if only as in interim
measure.

There were three reasons this wouldn't happen. The drivers didn't
want to be labeled as scabs, the transport companies didn't want to
be blackballed by the unions, and the thousands of tractors and trailers needed to get goods moving again were not available. Transport
Employees Union boss, Lou Gerrard, blitzed radio and television
stations castigating Webb Transport's management for their bloody-
mindedness and intransigence. For their part, the management of
Webb described the TEU as a rogue union defying court orders.
After being asked why his large fleet couldn't help, Max Lustig said,
"We have great relationships with our drivers and the TEU. We don't
intend to do anything that might jeopardize those relationships."

Dermott Becker watched the saga unfolding on television from
his study in the Hamptons. A few more days and Webb wouldn't be
worth buying. If that was the case, O'Brien would have to move fast to
buy Webb's tractors and trailers instead. Whoever owned the equipment would win the contracts. Becker was nervous mainly because
of Max Lustig's presence in Alabama. He was a tough, wily bastard,
and Becker didn't fancy O'Brien's chances against him. Under
normal circumstances, a few well-directed threats would drive other

interested parties away but that tactic would never work with Lustig. He'd just return fire with more brutal threats and wouldn't hesitate to carry them out. The answer was simple. Lou Gerrard had to come through in the next twenty-four hours. He had ten million reasons to do so. Becker's real concern was that Lustig was paying Gerrard more to break Webb and that he'd already done a deal to buy the equipment.

Becker was about to turn the television off when the newsreader said, "We have breaking news from Castlebrough Penitentiary. Convicted murderer and mob boss Frankie Arturo has been charged with the murder of career criminal and fellow inmate Alexei Petracca. Arturo allegedly repeatedly smashed Petracca's head into the concrete floor."

It had been ten days since Devlin Cooper was picked up, and he hadn't heard a word from the thugs. He'd hardly slept during that time, and when Karen had called him at home, he'd been short with her. Nor had he given her the number of his new cell phone. He'd had a dreadful game against the Twenty-Niners. Three of his passes were deflected, and he'd been sacked twice. The commentators and newspapers had accused him of being asleep and suggested he was spending too much time in nightclubs.

When the dedicated cell phone finally rang, Cooper thought he would puke. It was the same voice. "You had a poor game on Saturday."

"What did you expect?"

"We didn't expect anything but your poor form was opportune. We want a repeat performance but even worse against the Pirates this Saturday."

"Do you know anything about the game? That won't guarantee a Pirates win. They have the worst offense in the NFL, and we have the best defense. The probability is that they won't score," Cooper said.

"Oh, they'll score all right. I can guarantee it."

Cooper took a deep breath. That could mean only one thing. One or more players on defense were also being blackmailed or bribed. "And what happens if I say no?"

"You know the answer, and if you double cross us, we'll make sure that every member of yours and Coach Deacon's families get copies of the CD."

Cooper hung his head. He'd known that it would come to this. "And you're going to keep blackmailing me, aren't you?"

"Yeah, get used to it, Devlin. We own you. Don't worry, though, we're not going to ask ya frequently. We're talking maybe one game a season. We know that it's not unusual for a quarterback to have one bad game a season. If ya last seventeen seasons, we're looking at about the same number of games. The last thing we want is for you to get caught."

"Who have you got on our defense?"

"You ask too many questions. Are you going to do what we want?"

"What choice do I have?"

"That's a wise decision," the voice said.

Phillip Cromwell couldn't believe his luck when he and Mary were seated next to Mayor Sam Johnson and his wife, Jill, at the charity function at the St Regis. Many prominent business luminaries extended their best wishes to the mayor, and he introduced Cromwell and Mary to them as his close friends. Cromwell didn't usually drink, but the mayor did and Cromwell, anxious not to offend him, let the waitress pour him a white wine. Three glasses later he was relaxed, lightheaded and in deep, one-on-one conversation with the mayor. The mayor was coarse and his jokes raunchy, and, had it been anyone else, Cromwell would have expressed his disgust. Instead, he laughed along with the mayor and patted him on the back. Unlike Lechte, who he envied, Cromwell had never been a man's man, and he was enjoying the attention of the mayor and his powerful friends. He glanced over at Mary and heard the mayor's wife invite her to morning tea at the Four Seasons next Tuesday. Cromwell was elated. Membership of the exclusive Hamptons Yacht Club had been his crowning social achievement, but now he was rubbing shoulders with New York royalty.

Chapter 15

After the meeting with Elliot, Todd had gone home and listed every friend and business contact he had. Then he'd gone over the list with a red pen in hand, asking himself two questions. Did they have access to five hundred thousand dollars? The first question eliminated three-quarters of the list. Of those remaining he asked himself the second question. Will they lend it to me? Five names were left.

He hadn't seen two of the people on the list for over two years and didn't know the other three all that well. What he did know was that they were loaded and the sum he was seeking was nothing for them. It was 2 A.M. when he turned the lights off but he couldn't sleep. He had no doubt that Elliot, Ferguson and Fraser were gangsters and that they had set him up. Elliot had mentioned that he had a boss, but he was probably lying. Elliot also claimed that he was good cop, but Todd knew that he was a nasty piece of work. Exhausted, he finally drifted off. All too soon the clock radio snapped him out of a deep sleep. He was tired, felt like shit and his throat was dry. The thought of jumping on a plane and disappearing was enticing, but he knew that he was being watched. After lying in bed for another ten minutes, he jumped out and wrote the three remaining names down. He was wasting time for the sake of wasting time and was unlikely to forget the names of the only three people in the world who could save him.

After arriving at the office, the first person he called was on business somewhere in Africa and not contactable. The second person he called was cold and aloof and the vibes that Todd got told him not to bother asking. He'd studied with the third person, Wendy Thomson, got along well with her, and knew that she received a seven figure trust distribution from her father's estate every year. She seemed genuinely pleased to hear from him, and they chatted about old times as he tried to build up the courage to pop the question. Surprisingly,

Wendy was not shocked or unreceptive to his request. "If you let me have a business plan and some cash flow projections, I'll see what I can do," she said.

Todd grimaced. How would Wendy feel about a business plan centered on a failed betting system? She had misunderstood his needs, and he just couldn't bring himself to tell her that he'd lost more than half a million betting.

Each night he came up with another person or way that he could pay off the debt. Each morning he woke up exhausted, stressed, depressed and without hope. One name that wouldn't go away was Doug Lechte. Todd role-played throwing himself on Lechte's mercy but wasn't confident about how he would react, and in a worst case scenario he might find himself fired. The last thing he could afford was to lose his job. It took an enormous effort to focus on work during the day when he was carrying the worries of the world on his shoulders.

The call that Todd had been sweating over came just before midday. "Todd, it's Jack Elliot. We've given you seven days and a few extra hours. Do you have our money?"

"I need more time."

There was a long pause. "Hello, hello, are you still there?" Todd asked.

"We'll always be here and you know we could give you five years, and it won't make any difference. You still won't be able to pay. I don't want to talk on the phone, but you know what you have to do. Two little chores and your world returns to normal. It's easy."

"Yeah, I bet its two chores. You pricks will never be satisfied."

"You have my word."

"That hardly reassures me. I want to meet the big man, your boss, and have him tell me," Todd said.

Again, there was a long pause. "All right. I'll pick you up tonight. Be out in front of your apartment at eight o'clock and don't give me any shit about having to work late. He's a busy and important man."

Todd was taken aback. He hadn't even been certain Elliot had a boss. "You didn't say that I'd agreed, did you? Because I didn't. If I think he's bullshitting about the two chores, I won't even think about doing what you're asking."

"He knows. You might even like him. He's a fun guy."

"Yeah, I bet," Todd said. "Where's he live?'

"Manhattan. Not all that far from you. Look for a black limo."

When Harry O'Brien got off the phone from Lou Gerrard, he was jubilant. The union boss had asked him to increase his offer to two hundred and fifty million, and the owners of Webb Transport would sell. However, O'Brien was surprised by Dermott Becker's reaction to the news. "Harry, can't you see what that little toad Lou Gerrard's up to?"

"It's a good deal, Dermott."

"Yes, it is a good deal but it could be better. Gerrard's gone to them and said, *guys, I can screw another fifty mil out of these pricks, but if I do, I want ten.* So now he's on ten from us and ten from them. It's as obvious as the nose on your face. You should have told him to fuck off when he asked, and we would've had the business by now for two hundred. Instead, you said you'll find out and get back to him. And you know what he did as soon as you said that. He went back to them and said, 'It's in the bag, I've got the extra fifty.' Fuck!"

O'Brien had expected congratulations and praise rather than getting a berating. "It's still a good deal. You said so yourself. We'll make a fortune. The union will be in our pocket. Think about it, Dermott. What's an extra fifty mil?"

Becker gripped the phone tightly. Harry had been a good operator but had become lazy. Physically he'd let himself go and was at least one hundred pounds overweight. Mentally, he was no longer sharp, and Becker pondered whether he ever had been. Perhaps O'Brien had outlived his usefulness? Becker hated being forced to make hard decisions as a result of the incompetence of others. He now had to throw the owners and Gerrard a bone, but it wasn't going to be fifty mil. "Tell Lou that we'll increase our offer to two hundred and twenty mil and that's it. And Harry, don't fucking call back with a counter offer. I'm not authorizing one cent more."

The black stretch limo came around the corner at exactly eight o'clock and Elliot rolled down his window and shouted out to Todd, who opened one of the rear doors and climbed in. The windows were dark from the outside and transparent on the inside. He was surprised to see Ferguson and Fraser sitting opposite Elliot. There were bulges under their suit coats. "What are your goons doing here?" he asked.

"That's not very friendly, Todd." Ferguson smirked.

"The boss likes to make sure he's got protection," Elliot said. "Frisk him, Ferguson."

"Do you think I'd be stupid enough to wear a wire?"

"He's not looking for a wire," Elliot said.

"You think I'm carrying a gun? You're watching too many gangster movies."

"The boss didn't get where he is by taking stupid risks. Desperate men do desperate things," Elliot said.

"I'm far from desperate."

Dark glass separated the front from the rear and Todd had no idea who was driving but guessed it was another of Elliot's thugs. The limo turned slowly into Madison Avenue and was crawling past a coffee shop when Elliot screamed, "Motherfucker! It's him. It's the stockbroker. Take the next left and go around the block."

"What's happening? What's wrong?" Todd asked.

"Shut up," Elliot said, snatching the limo phone.

"Boss," he said, "we just drove past a coffee shop and that little bastard Giovani was in there as large as life. What do you want me to do?"

There was a pause and then Elliot said, "Yeah, yeah, boss. I'm on it."

"Go around to the coffee shop," Elliot shouted at the driver. "Fraser, take Ferguson with you and make sure that slimy prick doesn't slip through your fingers. Call me when you've got him."

"What the hell's going on?" Todd yelled.

"Calm down, kid. A short, unavoidable delay," Elliot said as Fraser and Ferguson got out of the limo.

"Park around the corner and leave the engine running," Elliot said to the driver.

"I didn't buy into this. I'll get out and walk home. I'll meet your boss another time," Todd said, but the doors were locked.

"Just sit there and shut the fuck up," Elliot said, "this won't take long."

A few minutes later, Elliot's cell phone rang and he shouted at the driver, "Go, go."

Fraser and Ferguson were standing on either side of a squat, dark haired guy whose face was a sickly white. They hustled him into the limo and sat him between them. His hands were trembling, and Todd noticed two tiny tattoos on the inside of his wrists. Dollar bills.

"Hello, Giovani," Elliot said. "Longtime no see. Why have you been avoiding us?"

"I-I have-haven't."

"We haven't seen you for four months. Have you been vacationing in Italy?"

"No, no. I-I've jus-just been busy."

Elliot banged on the dark glass and shouted, "Head to Chinatown."

"What the hell is this? Let me out," Todd shouted.

Elliot glared at him. "Here's the deal, kid. You can keep your mouth shut or I'll get Ferguson to shut it for you. Doing it yourself will be a lot less painful."

Todd looked at Ferguson, and a cruel smirk crossed the thug's face.

"Have you got our money, Giovani? It's long overdue, and the interest is running."

"I-I'm get-getting it. I-I'll have it for you in a few weeks," Giovani replied, and a tear ran down his cheek.

Elliot's face turned bright red, and he screamed, "You're a fucking liar. You pissed off without paying. You didn't think we'd find you. Slimy bastard."

"No, no. I-I was jus-just put-putting it to-together."

"Is that right?" Elliot sneered. "If we drive to your place now, how much will you be able to give us?"

"I-I don't have any-anything at home, but I-I've got a few deals ab-about to come off. Then I-I'll be able to pay."

Elliot reached over and picked up the limo phone. "He's got nothing, boss."

Elliot listened intently and then said, "Nah, not a cent. He said he's waiting for a couple of deals to come off." Elliot laughed.

There was a pause before Elliot said, "Yeah, it's bullshit. What do you want me to do?"

There was a far longer pause and Elliot grinned. "Yeah, not a problem. You'll send the truck? Yeah, about twenty minutes."

Elliot looked at Giovani who was shaking, and dribble was running down his chin and onto his shirt. "The boss is not happy with you. Not happy at all. Give me your wallet. We're going to drop you off in Chinatown and you can make your way home with no money."

Todd watched as Fraser and Ferguson momentarily tensed up. Ferguson felt inside his suit coat, and his hand made the bulge even larger.

Ten minutes later the limo turned down a dark alley and stopped when it got to the end. "Get out, Giovani," Elliot said.

Fraser got out first and held the door open. As Giovani got out, Fraser grabbed him and pushed him in front of the limo and onto the ground. "On your knees," he shouted.

Ferguson got out the other side and withdrew his gun and screwed a round tube on the end of the barrel.

"What's going on?" Todd shouted. "What are you doing?"

Elliot reached over and grabbed Todd's neck and held his head firmly. "Watch," he said. "Watch what happens to non-payers."

Ferguson stood behind Giovani and pointed his gun at the back of his head. Todd heard *phut, phut* and saw two short yellow flashes. Giovani fell forward and didn't move.

"No," Todd screamed, diving for the open door. He vomited uncontrollably on the pavement and down the wall. "You-you didn't have to do that."

Ferguson pushed him back in the car and climbed in after him. The limo reversed down the alley, and as it reached the street, a truck loaded with forty-four-gallon drums pulled into the alley. Todd was shaking and couldn't stop crying.

"That's our clean-up truck," Elliot said. "By the time they're finished, there won't be a sign of blood and Giovani will be in one of the drums. It'll be full of quick setting cement within an hour, and two hours later it'll be on the bottom of the Hudson. Vale Giovani."

Elliot picked up the phone again. "It's done, boss."

He pushed the phone hard up against his ear so Todd couldn't hear the response.

"You don't think it'd be a good move to meet with the kid now? Sure, I understand, boss," Elliot said and hung up.

He rested his hand on Todd's knee and said, "Sorry about the diversion. The boss doesn't think it'd be healthy for you to meet with him given the circumstances. He said that if you saw his face now you might have to go the same way as Giovani. We don't want that, do we? You and I will sort out how you're going to pay us. Don't worry, we'd far rather get paid than do what we had to do tonight."

Todd was deep in shock. He looked over at Ferguson and Fraser, and they were grinning like Cheshire cats.

"You gonna have a beer when we get back?" Fraser asked.

"Sure," Ferguson said. "I'm hungry. We'll grab a steak."

Ten minutes later the limo pulled up in front of Todd's apartment building. "Try and forget about tonight," Elliot said. "Come up to my suite tomorrow night and we'll work out how you're going pay to us. Be there at eight. And Todd, go straight to bed. You look like you could use a good sleep."

Todd could barely hold his key let alone get it in the keyhole. He finally pushed the door open and collapsed on the sofa. He'd known that they were thugs, but he'd never thought they'd resort to murder. Worse, they were so cold and dispassionate. Five minutes after killing Giovani they were talking about drinking beer and eating steak. It was obvious that he hadn't been their first victim.

Chapter 16

Phillip Cromwell was euphoric. Sitting opposite him was Thomas Vanderbilt, a close friend of the mayor and senior partner of establishment stockbroker, Morgan & Vanderbilt. Their accounting, taxation and consulting work had been being handled by a big four firm for years, but Vanderbilt had decided that it was time to make a change. Cromwell knew that the fees wouldn't be large, but that was unimportant, the doors that Morgan & Vanderbilt could open for the firm were invaluable. Better still, Morgan & Vanderbilt had been around for a hundred and fifty years, and their money was old and blue. Cromwell could hardly wait for the next partners meeting when he would rub Lechte's face in it. Lechte was about to find out that the firm had a new rainmaker.

Cromwell had a small team auditing The Disabled Children's Fund, the mayor's wife's charity and had been staggered to find that annual donations and bequests exceeded one hundred million dollars. It might be an honorary audit, but it involved a significant amount of time. Cromwell wasn't worried, the prestige and recognition that came with auditing a major charity was pure gold.

Todd hadn't slept a wink but surprisingly wasn't tired. He'd been up drinking coffee all night and fretting. He'd known that he was in deep trouble after he'd lost the half mil but was staggered by what he'd witnessed the previous night. It had briefly crossed his mind to phone the police but knew that they'd find nothing in the alley. Besides, he was scared, really scared, and knew what Elliot would do if he found out that he'd contacted the police.

It had been nearly six weeks since the board of ACME Investments Inc. had met, and a formal meeting had been convened and held earlier in the day. The directors had then adjourned for lunch, and now they filed back into the boardroom for the Vulture Inc. meeting. The blank pads, pens, two pitchers of water and a dozen glasses were on the table. Dermott Becker had been noticeably testy at the earlier meeting. He took his seat at the head of the board table and eyeballed O'Brien saying, "We'll hear from you first, Harry."

"I have some great news," O'Brien said. "As you know with the help of our union friends we were sabotaging Webb Transport's fleet so that we could win the tender to distribute milk in the southern states. Well, it turned out far better than I expected. We bought Webb's business for two hundred and twenty million. It's a business that would've gone for a billion eighteen months ago."

O'Brien looked around the room and was surprised to see only blank faces. He didn't know what Becker had told his fellow directors when he'd convened the meeting.

"Yes, it's a good deal," Becker said, "but it should've been better. We paid twenty million too much because Harry got led up the garden path by that union weasel, Lou Gerrard."

"Yeah, it was poorly handled," Arthur Ridgeway said.

"Yes," Becker said. "So poorly that I think the twenty mil should come out of Harry's loan account. That way, he might exercise more care when he's next involved in a similar situation."

"Fuck!" O'Brien exclaimed. "That's bullshit. Where do you get off coming up with crap like that?"

"If you don't like it, you can always sell your stock and resign," Becker said. "Maybe it's time to put your feet up?"

"I'd be happy to buy ya out for a fair price and pay ya the balance of your loan account, Harry," Borchard said.

O'Brien's face was red, and his sweat-stained shirt was straining to contain his stomach. "I'm not selling," he said, "and no one's gonna stick me with a twenty mil charge."

Becker ignored him and looked around the table as he raised his hand. "All those in favor of charging Harry's loan account with twenty mil."

The other directors, excluding O'Brien, raised their hands. "Carried," Becker said. "You're up next, Arty."

O'Brien stared at Becker with hate-filled eyes.

"As you all know our trailer parts business has been under severe pricing pressure from a rapidly expanding new company, Superior Spares Inc. Mainly axles, suspensions, turntables and landing legs. High-value items. My spy found out that the manufacturer, Fillwell Axles Inc. is supplying Superior at the same price as us, but here's the rub; Fillwell Axles are providing Superior with a significant volume rebate and paying it into Superior's bank account at the end of every month. It's strange because we buy far more but don't get a rebate." Ridgeway grinned.

"Go on," Becker said, having already been briefed by Ridgeway.

"It took a lot of tracing but it turns out that Fillwell's major shareholder is the father-in-law of the guy behind Superior. Fillwell is either funding the son-in-law or setting him up to go into distribution. Either way we're getting screwed."

"I don't know what you're grinning about," Borchard said.

"You will after he finishes," Becker said. "Tell us how you retaliated, Arty."

"I gave them some bullshit about expanding into Canada and bought six months stock from them. They were rapt to win an order of that size. They're not gonna be so rapt when we don't pay 'em. It's gonna seriously stretch their cash flow."

"Go on." Becker smiled.

"We've got six months' supply; we've got Superior's price lists, their customer lists and copies of their sales invoices. I've told our sales guys to drop their prices to twenty percent less than cost," Arty said.

"Fuck!" Borchard said. "Where's the sense in that. I don't get it."

"You would if you could understand Fillwell's financials." Arty smirked. "In six months' time, they're going to be teetering on the edge of bankruptcy, and without Fillwell's funding Superior will be fucked. It's the deeper pockets strategy, and our pockets are far deeper than theirs. We'll own them both and be a near monopoly. It won't take long to get back what we lose, and we'll own two new businesses."

Borchard tapped his pen on his table and pondered what he'd just heard. They were smart bastards all right, and he knew he couldn't have come up with that scheme. It didn't worry him, though. He'd just employ devious bastards like Ridgeway, and they'd come up with the schemes and he'd fund them. "I like it, Arty," he said, "I like it."

"Well done, Arthur," Becker said, thinking it was a pity that O'Brien wasn't half as smart. "Brock, you wanted to hold the meeting. What do you have?"

Borchard explained in great detail how he had blackmailed Devlin Cooper and how they would make a huge killing on the Pirates game.

"You'll have to tone it down," Becker said. "Cooper having a bad game is going to be suspicious. The more money on the Pirates, the more suspicious it will look."

"You're right," Lydia said, "I wouldn't outlay more than two million."

"Fuck," Borchard said, "we'll only make ten to twelve mil. I thought we'd hit the bookies across the country and make a huge killing."

"Lydia's the risk assessor," Becker said. "Betting a larger amount is a recipe for trouble. It's a nice little earner, though. Once a season for fifteen years and we'll pick up a hundred and fifty mil. That's nothing to sneeze at. Oh, and we'll place all our bets with illegal bookies. They'll lay 'em off with the legal bookies, but if anything blows up, I don't want our payouts frozen."

Borchard crunched his knuckles. He looked angry. The Devlin Cooper collect was going to be far less than he had anticipated.

"Do you have anything new, Lydia?" Becker asked.

"No, but the falling oil price is sure to throw up some opportunities."

Still peeved, Borchard said, "What have you done about the Italian, Dermott?"

"I had him removed," Becker replied.

Gasps went around the table. In Vulture's first twenty-eight years, the company had undertaken some devious deeds but never murder. Now, in the space of two years since Borchard had joined the board they had the blood of three victims on their hands.

"What do you mean removed?" Obrien asked nervously.

"He's gone," Becker said. "Never to be seen again. I can't make it any clearer."

"I didn't think you'd have the balls," Borchard said. "You're full of surprises, Dermott. How are you progressing with the accountant?"

"He'll be onboard by tonight. We're setting up CFD accounts in different corporate names with different brokers in Switzerland. We're going to trade them actively with the aim of doing no worse than breaking even. When we make the insider trades they'll be of a similar size to our earlier ones. That way we shouldn't arouse the suspicions of the brokers or authorities. We could make fifty million."

"What's a CFD?" Borchard asked.

"It's a derivative. It stands for Contract for Difference. Using them to trade stocks in the US is illegal. However, they're legal in just about every other country, and you can trade CFDs over US stocks in those countries. Think of them as massively geared margin loans. I could buy twenty million dollars of Bank of America stock for an outlay of a million."

"Jesus," Borchard said, "but you said they're illegal for US companies."

"No, I didn't. They're illegal in the US," Becker said, "but as I just said, you can buy CFDs on US stocks in other countries."

"I don't understand," Borchard said.

"You don't need to," Becker replied. "Does anyone have anything else? No. Then we're adjourned."

It was 7:45 on Wednesday night when a white van pulled up on Hartnett Street adjacent to Vanessa's apartment building. Ferguson and Fraser were in the front dressed in dark gray uniforms embossed Pivot Electrical on the pockets. The peaks of the matching caps they wore were pulled down low over their foreheads. They didn't have long to wait before Vanessa Hodge and her girlfriend left the building to go to their kickboxing class only two blocks away.

"We've got an hour," Ferguson said, taking a tool box from the back.

"That's more than enough time," Fraser said. "Let's go."

Two minutes later they took the stairs to the third story and more particularly to apartment #36. Ferguson took a leather key holder from his pocket with a dozen metal picks inside and in less than thirty seconds they entered Vanessa's apartment.

"There's her purse," Fraser said pointing to the coffee table. "Make sure you don't make a mess."

"I know. I reckon her passport will be in the drawers next to her bed."

"You're right," Fraser replied, removing his iPhone to photo it.

"Ah, I've got her driver's license," Ferguson said, passing it to Fraser.

"Good, all we need is an invoice or receipt for rent or electricity. It looks like she keeps her unpaid bills attached to the fridge door. How easy is this?" Fraser laughed. "Is everything back in her purse as it was?"

"Yeah."

"Let's go."

Chapter 17

Todd knocked on Elliot's door, telling himself not to show fear, but it was easy to think and hard to pull off. Elliot answered wearing a T-shirt, jeans, and the hotel's white slippers. He had a Budweiser in one hand and a handful of mixed nuts in the other. "Come in, Todd," he said. "Just stand there while I pat you down. I'm watching the Soup Nazi. It has to be the best Seinfeld ever made. I must've watched it twenty times. It's got a few minutes to go. Take a seat. Can I get you a beer, soda, mineral water? Would you like something to eat? I haven't eaten yet."

"I want nothing from you! Not ever. You killed someone last night for a few lousy dollars, and it's like you've already forgotten about it. What type of callous bastard are you?"

"Whoa, right there. I didn't kill anyone. I have to hand it to you, kid. You've got real chutzpah. Look at you, you're shitting your pants and yet you're still accusing me. Was that your plan to prove you're not scared? If it was, you failed," Elliot said, stifling a yawn.

"Liar."

"Did I pull the trigger? I didn't want you to see what happened last night but since you did, can you imagine how easy it would be for the same fate to befall your parents or siblings or even you? That's the last thing I want."

"You leave my family out of this," Todd said, but as he listened to himself, he sounded like he was begging rather than threatening. It was hard, in the presence of a murderous thug, not to show fear.

"Have a look at that Newman." Elliot laughed. "He was the funniest character in the show."

"I don't want to stay here a minute longer than I have to," Todd said. "Tell me what you want."

"Don't be a smartass, kid. You already know what I want," Elliot said, putting his feet on the coffee table. His biceps bulged as he put his hands behind his head.

"You know that I don't audit those two companies. I can't get the information you're after."

"You're starting to make me angry. You work on the same floor as that woman, what's her name, Hodge? You can easily get what we're looking for."

"No, I can't. I can't access her computer. I don't have her login or password."

Elliot yawned. "You're starting to piss me off. She has to eat lunch, have morning and afternoon tea and go to the toilet. Don't tell me she logs off and on every time she moves. Besides, now that you're working with her, it'll be easy."

"How do you know that?"

"We know a lot about your firm. Keep that in mind before you lie to us."

"I still want to meet your boss."

"Are you fucking stupid? If you meet him after what you saw last night, we'll have no choice but to kill you. Do you want to meet him that much? Take my word, you'll be off the hook and owe us nothing after you give us the information on those two companies."

"Your word." Todd smirked. "Can I take it to the bank?"

"You're such a fucking smartass. You'd be wise to watch your mouth. You've got my word, and that's all you're getting."

Todd was sick of being in the presence of Elliot. He was scared but hoped that his fear wasn't palpable. His head was hurting, and he felt his heart racing. He needed to get out and fill his lungs with fresh air.

"I'm about to order salmon," Elliot said. "Do you want me to order for you?"

"Hell will freeze over before I ever eat with you," Todd said, standing up. "I'm out of here."

"Take this prepaid cell phone," Elliot said. "We'll use it to call you to set up meetings. No conversation will last longer than a minute, and we'll never talk business. Recording the calls will achieve nothing, and it'll be pointless trying to trace them. Don't think you can trick us. We've been doing this for a long time."

"Yeah," said Todd, opening the door.

Opening a Gmail address in the name of VanessaHodge007 presented no problems for Fraser. The woman with him was a master forger and completed the PS 1583 for a mailbox with UPS in Vanessa's name. Then she affixed her notary's stamp to the copies of Vanessa's driver's license and passport. After scanning them, Fraser attached them to an email to the local UPS office. The covering email supposedly sent by Vanessa said that she would pay for the mailbox at the same time she picked up the keys.

Passport photos are predominantly only of use to skilled and experienced immigration officials. The scanned copy of the photo of Vanessa's passport did not reflect her beauty and showed a grim-faced young woman. The woman who entered the UPS office on 77th Street had been made up to look like Vanessa and was carrying the original notarized copies of the documentation. She appeared to have hurt her right hand and had some difficulty when signing for the keys.

At first the illegal bookies were happy to take the bets for ten, twenty-five and fifty thousand on the Pirates. However, when the flood of money continued, they started laying off as fast as they could. In the space of thirty minutes, the Pirates firmed from six to one to the ridiculous odds of two to one. Television and radio sports commentators speculated about where the money had come from. They were unanimous in their opinion that the Pirates form had done nothing to warrant such a huge plunge.

When Karen called, she was crying uncontrollably and wanted to know what she had done. Cooper brushed her off as he had done the other times she had called. They had warned him not to talk to her, and he feared they might have bugged her phone. He felt sorry for her but was sure she wouldn't feel any better knowing the truth. He knew he'd feel better if she knew, and that she must be thinking that he'd dumped her.

On the way back from training, Cooper got the limo to stop at a phone store and bought himself a bright green, prepaid cell phone. He didn't want to run the risk of mixing it up with the one the hoodlums had said they'd use to contact him. His SMS was brief. *The first coffee shop. Same time as last. Tomorrow.* He didn't use his name but knew Karen would know it was him.

When Karen entered the coffee shop, Cooper was sitting in a dimly lit booth furthest from the door. He held his hand up. As she approached, he could see that her eyes were red and puffy. The waiter took her jacket, and she sat down. She was wearing a black coat, a white woolen sweater and designer jeans. "So you've finally decided to talk to me," she said. "Got sick of being a bastard, did you?"

Cooper raised his hands palms out. "Hear me out," he said, "and then judge me."

Ten minutes later she said, "My God, what are we going to do? I could leave Tom and take the kids with me, but he doesn't deserve that. I'm not sure it would help, though. Having a fling with a middle-aged woman and moving in with her are two vastly different things, aren't they?"

"If I had to I wou–"

"Devlin, I'm sure you've thought it through. You're only twenty-three. What would your parents think if you moved in with me? Your siblings? Your friends? Your teammates? God, why did I ever do it? You may not believe it, but I've never been unfaithful to Tom before. I could've been, many times. He just works so hard, and the romance in our marriage died long ago. Yes, we still have sex. The roll-on, roll-off variety. You pressed all my buttons the minute I laid eyes on you. Shit!"

"I'm just going to have to do what they want. I've worked out a plan. I'm going to have to let myself get sacked in the early plays. That way the media will put my bad game down to being dazed. I think it'll work, that is if I don't get hit so hard that I need to be carried off."

"You poor thing."

"If I do what they want, I think they'll stick to their word. After all, once it's out there for everyone to see, I'm of no value to them."

"Oh, my God," Karen said, turning bright red. "If it gets on the net, my parents will see it. My kids will see it. Their friends will see it. My girlfriends will see it. I'd be better off dead."

"Don't say that," Cooper said. The same thought had crossed his mind about himself.

Karen smiled wanly. "I have to say it's a real passion killer. I'm glad you told me, though. I knew we were never going to be together in the long term, but it hurt to get dumped and not know why."

"If I think of anything that might help, I'll text you," Cooper said. "You've got the number of my prepaid cell, so if you come up with anything, do the same."

"Thanks for letting me know," Karen said, signaling the waiter for her coat. "I'm going. We shouldn't run the risk of being seen together."

Chapter 18

Elliot had said they were going to buy and sell CFDs on international markets so it wouldn't impact the US markets. Todd knew that he was lying to himself, but perhaps Elliot was right. Maybe what he was about to do really was a victimless crime. This thought helped ease his troubled conscience.

On a deeper level, Todd knew that the international CFD providers would buy and sell stocks on the US markets to hedge their CFD positions. Not unlike bookmakers laying off big bets with other bookmakers. As much as he hated to admit it, he knew that the CFD providers would distort the US markets and that the distortions would come about as a result of the inside information he provided.

Elliot had also said that they would only buy or sell CFDs in volumes that would not flag anything untoward to the authorities. If he stuck to his word, Todd rationalized that the probability of getting caught was minimal. The only problem that he foresaw was gaining access to Vanessa's computer, but again Elliot had been right. There would be opportunities. Todd knew that if he was careful he could pull it off without anyone ever knowing or getting hurt.

If there was a plus to the dreadful mess that he found himself in, it was that his obsession with his racing system had disappeared. He hadn't inputted one race into his iPad since he'd come home to find Ferguson and Fraser in his living room. The thought of Ferguson cold-bloodedly killing the Italian guy sent a shiver through him. He knew that he'd wasted the past eighteen months and that gambling on horse races was not the answer to his hate for accounting.

It was a bitterly cold winter morning, with a light smattering of snow on the sidewalk. Todd had his overcoat buttoned to the neck, and wore a thick woolen scarf as he trudged along 50th Street. His mind churned over numerous plans about how he was going to get the information. In many ways, he thought that he'd been lucky when Lechte had reassigned clients between Vanessa and himself. He now had an excuse to be in her cubicle when she wasn't there. By the time he entered the offices, he had the bones of a firm plan.

He hung up his overcoat, went to the kitchen, made two cups of coffee and headed off to visit Vanessa. He sat down and pushed her cup across the desk toward her.

"Good morning and thank you." She smiled. "Did you put sugar in my coffee?"

"No way. Half a Truvia packet and a touch of soy milk, shaken, not stirred." Todd laughed.

"I had no idea that you were so observant. I'm impressed," Vanessa said, "but why the coffee and why the visit?"

"I just wanted to reconfirm the date for Hallstrom's results. I have four other companies that I have to sign off on in a very compressed period," Todd said, specifically going over the companies and reporting dates. "I know you're handling Crisco and Homewares, but if you need any help, I'll find the time."

Vanessa hit a key on her computer and scanned her diary. "They report on the 11th, so you'll need to be finished by the 9th," she said. Then just as Todd had hoped, she went over each of the companies that she handled. He was only interested in the dates for two. Virtex Software on the 18th and Philco Laboratories on the 20th. "I don't think I'll have any problems, but I appreciate you offering to help. If you have any trouble, particularly with the clients you're taking over from me, just buzz and I'll be there."

"Thanks, Vanessa," Todd said, standing up.

Arthur Ridgeway was an introvert who didn't like talking to people he didn't know. He was the perfect exemplar of a backroom string-puller. A master planner, manipulator, and tactician, adept at telling others what to do, but without the skills or personality to execute the tasks himself. Prison had hardened him, and he had an underlying cruel streak. It had been ninety-five days since Fillwell Inc. had supplied the huge order to Trailer Parts, and they hadn't been paid a cent. All other suppliers were being paid in thirty days or better. Ridgeway wanted to send a don't-fuck-with us-message. The CEO of Fillwell was angry and had demanded to speak to someone with the authority to authorize payment. It was one of the few calls that Ridgeway had been sweating over.

Fillwell's CEO was all bluster. "Mr. Ridgeway," he said, "your accounts people won't pay us and told our credit department that you're the only person who can authorize payment."

"That's true," Ridgeway replied. "I can authorize payment, but we're short on ready money. We've got a heap owed to us, and we've got a lot of stock out on consignment. When that gets sold, we'll be back on top and able to pay you."

"That's not my problem," Fillwell's CEO shouted. "You knew our terms when you bought those axles and suspensions. You've got seven days before we commence legal proceedings."

"I'm sorry to hear that. Naturally, we'll instruct our lawyers to vigorously defend the action. That will drag proceedings out. Are you sure you don't want to save yourself the legal hassle and stress? We'll probably be able to pay you in another month or so."

"What defense? You don't have any defense. We'll get judgement and execute on it." The CEO laughed derisively.

"Well, we've had complaints of cracks in the suspensions you supplied, and we're testing the hardness of the steel used in your axles. We're not unreasonable and could've overlooked these quality defects but from what you're saying, I should instruct our lawyers immediately. I doubt you're going to get judgement without fighting a long, drawn-out court battle."

"You bastard. You slimy bastard," the CEO shouted. "There's nothing wrong with our products. They go through the most rigorous quality control and testing. You're a lying bastard who's just trying to string payment out. Let me tell you why you have no cash and what your real problem is. Your sales people are selling our products at less than cost and rule number one, business 101, is that revenue has to exceed cost."

"Thanks for the information and advice," Ridgeway said. "I know what our selling prices are. I set them. We're using your products as loss leaders, but the losses are more than compensated for by the margins on the equipment that we're importing from China. By the way, how do you know what our selling prices are?"

There was a long pause. "Everyone in the market is talking about them."

"Really? I don't want that. Perhaps we should have supplied our customers at full list price and then banked a rebate into their accounts at the end of the month. You'd know all about that, though."

There was an even longer pause. "I don't know what you're playing at, but I'm instructing our lawyers this afternoon."

Ridgeway could sense the CEO trying to hide the desperation in his voice. "I'll see you in court," he said.

Five minutes after Ridgeway finished his conversation with Fillwell's CEO he was back on the phone to his chief rumor spreader. Ridgeway liked to call her his anti-public relations agent. "Fiona," he said, "I want it all over California this afternoon, that Fillwell Axles Inc. can't pay its debts and that anyone doing business with them should insist on cash. Be sure to warn against taking checks."

Arthur Ridgeway put the phone down. He didn't like talking to people, but sometimes it was cathartic.

Chapter 19

K aren Deacon turned on the television to see the Pirates run onto Daley Field before seventy thousand roaring fans. The commentator was saying:

The Cougars had a horrible game last week, and if they're going to improve, it has to start with their quarterback, Devlin Cooper. Coach Deacon defended him after his dismal performance against the Twenty-Niners.

It's Reggie Harper kicking for the Pirates. Bradbury's returning, and it's a good drive start across the 30 for the Cougars where Cooper will take over.

The Cougars break the huddle. Cooper sets the offense...the snap... Cooper feints to the left and then turns to the right...oh no! Two hundred and seventy pound Pirates linebacker Barry Drinan has blindsided Cooper and buried him in the turf. It's nasty, folks. Cooper's not moving, and his helmet's on the ground. That was as brutal hit as I've ever seen. Trainers are all around Cooper, but it's hard to see him playing on. I can see replacement quarterback Jeff Sweeny warming up. They're bringing out a stretcher, but wait, Cooper's getting to his feet and waving the trainers away. He looks groggy, but the Cougars fans are going crazy cheering.

Karen turned the television off. She couldn't watch. He'd done what he said he was going to do and nearly killed himself. She had seen the looks on the trainers' faces and knew they had feared for him. He had grinned when he got to his feet and waved the trainers away. It was the dopey grin of a boxer who had taken a brutal punch. Karen felt sick.

Three hours later Karen was stressed and worried about Devlin, so she turned the television back on. He was battered and dirty. She had never seen him like this before. The game was in its dying stages, and Karen prayed that Devlin would get through it without taking another hit. The crowd was roaring, and the commentator was screaming:

Cougars are down 13-7, no timeouts and less than a minute left in regulation. Devlin Cooper just can't seem to get it together out there. I don't think he's recovered from that huge hit in the first minute. He's fine between the twenties but once he gets into the red zone, he looks like an undrafted rookie. One costly mistake after another, not something we're used to seeing from an All-Pro. Cougars break the huddle as if they have a 6 point lead instead of a deficit. No urgency whatsoever. I don't understand. Cooper walks up to the line of scrimmage. It's second and goal and the clock's ticking…38 seconds. Cooper needs to get this into the end zone or hustle up to the line and stop the clock. Cooper takes the snap and drops back. Protection is good, but he's only got two receivers downfield as he's in a max protect package. Cooper rolls right, tucks the ball and takes off running. He makes a great move at the 15 and spins out of another tackle at the 10. There's only one man to beat, but no, no! Cooper's pounded at the 3 with 12 seconds left, and he's not getting up. He's down as his team rushes to the line of scrimmage to snap the ball and kill the clock for one last shot to get into the end zone. Too late, it's all over, folks. The referee calls timeout for the injury with 8 seconds left. The Cougars have no timeouts left, so that's an automatic 10 seconds run off the clock which means the ball game's over. An unbelievable finish for the Cougars, and especially for Cooper, who is finally up. He's walking off the field all alone, not a trainer or teammate in sight. Talk about a dead man walking! That's what Devlin Cooper, the Golden Boy of the NFL just one year ago, appears to be today.

Tears streamed down Karen's face. Then she felt a sudden buildup of bile in her throat and rushed to the toilet.

The mood in the locker rooms is never happy after a loss. Cooper's ribs were strapped, and his head swathed in tape, cotton wool, and bandages. Even with all of this padding, blood was still seeping from his wounds. The helmet had provided enough protection to save his life, but not enough to ensure he remained unscathed.

The coaches were in the corner of the room engaged in animated conversation. Occasionally they would glance at Cooper and then there would be head shaking and hand gestures.

The players were quiet, but a few of them commiserated with Cooper and told him he'd have a better game next week. Cooper looked up and giant, offensive lineman, Corey Wilson, was beckoning him. Cooper hobbled over to the other side of the room expecting that Wilson wanted to commiserate with him. Wilson glared at him and then in a menacing whisper said, "You motherfucker. You threw that game today. How much were you paid?"

"That's bullshit," Cooper replied, but couldn't hold the big man's eyes.

"You mighta fooled the coaches, and you mighta fooled the media, but you didn't fool us," Wilson said, glancing around the room.

Most of the players on the offensive line were staring at Cooper. None of them were smiling.

"If you ever do it again, we'll do the same," Wilson said. "We'll act like we're trying, just like you did today. We'll make sure we're brushed aside, and it won't be just one or two of the defense that sacks you like it was today. It'll be the whole defensive line. You'll be lucky to walk off the field alive."

"You've got it all wrong."

"Yeah, yeah," Wilson said turning his back on Cooper.

The mood in the rooms turned from unhappy to poisonous.

In the week prior to Virtex Software Inc. reporting, Todd kept a close eye on Vanessa's cubicle. The only time she left it for any amount of time was when she was at a client's. When she was out, Todd dropped memos and documents in her in-tray but her desktop was always turned off. When she went for coffee or to the bathroom, there was always someone hanging around her cubicle. Her supervisors and other subordinates would wait just outside for her to return while partners like Doug Lechte would take a seat in the visitor's chair. Todd worked as late as Vanessa, waiting for an opportunity to present itself. However, her team was very conscientious and, unfortunately, worked the same or similar hours to her. Elliot had been calling every night, pouring the pressure on, but being careful not to say anything incriminating.

By Friday morning, Todd still didn't have anything. Elliot was furious and called demanding to see him. "You've seen what we do to those who play us for fools. I'll send the limo to pick you up at the front of your apartment at 8 P.M.," he shouted.

Ferguson was in the back seat. He quickly frisked Todd, then put a black mask over his head.

"What's this about?" Todd asked.

"The boss doesn't want you to see where you're being taken. It's for your own safety." He laughed.

The limo seemed to drive around corners for about five minutes, and Todd knew this was to confuse him. Eventually, the limo got onto a long stretch of road and Todd sensed it was FDR and that he was being taken to Chinatown. The limo got off the main road and a few minutes later stopped.

"Don't touch the mask," Ferguson said, as he got out and opened Todd's door.

Todd heard a door open, and Ferguson pushed him inside. He could smell alcohol and food cooking and guessed that he was in a restaurant. He could hear an undercurrent of voices as Ferguson hustled him up some wooden stairs, and another door opened.

"You can take the mask off," Elliot said.

Todd rubbed his eyes and looked around the room before glancing at his watch. It had taken forty minutes, so he knew he wasn't in Chinatown. Elliot was sitting behind a large desk cluttered with cell phones, documents, and a desktop. The timber paneled walls were bare. As Todd's eyes adjusted to the lights, he looked around the office. It was plain with six visitors' chairs. In addition to the door that he'd entered by, there was another door to the left of Elliot's desk.

"Where am I?"

"If I'd wanted you to know I wouldn't have had you blindfolded. All you need to know is that it's my place of business."

"It's a restaurant," Todd said.

"Really? Are you hungry, kid? Would you like something to eat?"

"No, just tell me what it is you want? I don't want to be here a minute longer than I have to."

Elliot came around from behind his desk and pushed Todd in the chest with some force causing him to fall onto one of the chairs. "Do you think we're playing games?" he said, jabbing his forefinger hard into Todd's chest. "I want that information about Virtex and I want it now."

"I-I've tried," Todd said. "I haven't had an opportunity. I'm trying. You have to believe me."

Elliot dropped into the chair in front of Todd and stared into his eyes. "I've got people who are on my back. Not nice people. You better pull your finger out."

"She often works on Sundays," Todd said. "I'm going to the office this weekend. An opportunity might arise. If she's not there, she may have hidden her login and password in her desk." He knew this was a longshot. Worse, security would have him in the office but not Vanessa, so there was a strong probability that his unauthorized login might subsequently be detected. The one plus about Sunday was that if Vanessa was there, she'd almost certainly be working on Virtex Software.

Elliot was far from appeased. "I don't fucking care how you get the information. Just get it! Put the mask on him and take him back, Ferguson."

"I need to use the bathroom," Todd said.

Elliot nodded at the other door.

It was a small bathroom without windows and when Todd switched the light on an overhead extraction fan whirred noisily. He had hoped he might find something that would give him a clue to where he was. There was nothing.

It was 10 A.M. when Todd got to the office on Sunday morning, and he breathed a sigh of relief. The lights above Vanessa's cubicle were on, so he strolled over and said, "Good morning."

She looked up from the files on her desk. "What a shock this is. I never thought I'd see the day that Todd Hansen worked on a Sunday." She laughed. "You're not making a run for partner, are you?"

"Not likely," Todd replied. "I've got deadlines I have to meet. I can assure you, I'm not looking to make partner, and I'm not here by choice."

"I know what you mean. I'm struggling too. I'll be glad when this week is over."

"What time did you get in?"

"Oh, I've been here for a few hours," Vanessa said, glancing at her watch. "I'm just off to make myself a coffee. Can I get you a cup?"

Hallelujah! "Thanks, black with none. I need a heart starter," Todd said, as he watched Vanessa walk down to the kitchen. She looked like she'd been poured into the white jeans she was wearing, and he spent a few seconds that he didn't have, admiring the contours of her butt. Once she was out of sight, he moved quickly. Sure enough, her screen was opened to Virtex and Todd knew where to look. He took out his iPhone and took pics of each of the screens that showed the results. After finishing, he brought up the screen Vanessa had been working on. It took less than a minute, and he was sitting behind his desk when Vanessa brought him his coffee.

It was mid-afternoon when Todd got back to his apartment. He knew that Elliot would call, and he would again be taken to his office. Virtex's results were good, and would most definitely surprise the market to the upside. The company was also forecasting that the good times would continue.

At 7 P.M., the limo pulled up and Ferguson frisked Todd before placing the hood over his head.

Elliot asked many questions about Virtex's results, often repeating himself to ensure Todd's answers were consistent. "You're positive that the market doesn't already have this information?"

Todd shook his head. "I'm certain, outside of senior management and us, no one knows."

"Okay, make sure it doesn't take you as long to get the goods on Philco. I don't know whether we'll even be able to use this," he said, jabbing his index finger on the sheet of paper that he'd jotted Virtex's results on.

Lying bastard, Todd thought. It would be two days before the market had the same information. There was plenty of time to make a killing.

Chapter 20

Despite the US government's efforts, there were still banks in the Caymans where it was possible to open an anonymous bank account. The Cayman National Bank was not one of those banks. However, when it received an application to open an account in the name of U.S. citizen Vanessa Hodge there was no reason to be suspicious. Attached to the application were notarized copies of her driver's license and passport together with her address and a mailbox where she wanted bank statements and correspondence forwarded. The initial deposit of $150,000 was transferred a few days after the opening of the account. It was not an amount that attracted any undue attention.

Brock Borchard was bitterly disappointed. They had cleared nine million on the Pirates game, but he had expected a lot more. He didn't want to admit it, but the problem was that he hadn't known enough about football betting. He'd read somewhere that a hundred million was bet on the Super Bowl and had mistakenly presumed that weekly games would carry the same sort of money. Dirk had told Devlin Cooper that he'd only need to throw one game per season, but that was clearly not enough. It would have to change, and he would need to throw at least two and probably three to make it worthwhile. Borchard had watched the game and was reluctantly forced to admit that Cooper was a class act. He'd taken a brutal pounding to hide what he was doing, and despite the betting plunge, most of the media had bought it. Some commentators said that he'd played with concussion and that Coach Deacon had made a big mistake by not replacing him. Borchard had never considered this but it didn't worry him. He reasoned that Cooper was too smart to allow himself to get badly hurt.

Todd arrived at the office early on Monday morning but had no idea how he was going to get Philco's results. He did know they would come from Vanessa's computer, so he made his way to her cubicle on his usual pretext that he had a query about Hallstrom's. For once she wasn't her vibrant self, and Todd asked her what was wrong.

"I'm out at Philco for the next couple of days," she said, "and it's not a happy place. Profits are significantly down, and senior management is playing the blame game. It's very political and not a pleasant place to be."

"That's a surprise. The financial media's always going on about their pipeline of new drugs."

"That's true, but most are in their early stages of testing. A study was just completed on Philflox, the most advanced of their cancer drugs, and it found there was no significant improvement in overall progression-free survival. Their chemists, scientists, and doctors are under severe pressure. As far as they're concerned, we're just nuisances wasting their time."

Todd said a silent prayer of thanks. He didn't need to know what the sales or results were. The information that Vanessa had provided was more than enough, and it was obvious what its impact would be. "The plight of the auditor." Todd laughed. "Aren't you glad all clients aren't like that?"

"I suppose so. What is it you wanted to see me about?"

"It's unimportant," Todd said.

Phillip Cromwell hadn't expected the irate phone call from the mayor's office. One of the firm's young auditors had been asking questions and even suggested that funds from The Disabled Children's Fund had been channeled into the mayor's reelection campaign. Cromwell had been quick to assure the mayor's office that it was only the action of a young, overzealous employee and that she would be replaced by someone more experienced and worldly. He put his elbows on his desk and rested his head in his hands. Then he shouted for Gary Jenner, the audit manager responsible for the Fund. He was beyond angry. By the end of the day, there wasn't an employee or partner of Montgomery Hastings & Pierce, who hadn't heard about the bawling out that Cromwell had given Jenner. The following morning, a bitter Garry Jenner called and tendered his resignation.

Vulture Inc. indirectly controlled numerous companies in Switzerland (through firms of accountants and lawyers) and those companies had opened and traded eight CFD accounts with different Swiss CFD providers for about three months. Virtex Software's stock was trading at eighty dollars when Dermott Becker issued instructions to his subordinates in Switzerland to acquire five hundred thousand Virtex Software CFDs for four dollars per CFD. The two million dollar order was the equivalent of buying stock to the value of forty million dollars. The subordinates spread the order over the eight CFD providers, and the order sizes were consistent with the previous trading. After Virtex had announced its December results the stock climbed to ninety-six dollars and the CFDs were worth ten million. Becker closed all positions for a profit of eight million.

Philco's stock was trading at sixty dollars when Becker got the news that the company's result was far less than market expectations. He was quick to take a short position selling one million Philco CFDs at three dollars for a total outlay of three million dollars. When Philco announced an abysmal result, its stock sold off rapidly and fell to forty dollars. Again, Becker acted quickly closing the CFD positions for a profit of twenty million.

Todd Hansen's five hundred thousand betting loss had produced a profit for Vulture Inc. of twenty-eight million in just four days.

Becker was pleased with Vulture's first foray into insider trading using CFDS. His only disappointment was that while Virtex and Philco were significant companies, Vulture's CFD positions had had to be small so that they wouldn't attract unwanted attention from the authorities. He salivated about doing the same thing with huge companies like Apple and Microsoft where Vulture could take CFD positions in excess of a hundred million dollars while barely creating a ripple.

The last instruction Becker issued to his Swiss subordinates was to ensure that the proceeds received from the CFD providers disappeared into the labyrinth of Vulture controlled bank accounts.

Chapter 21

The board meeting of Vulture Inc. should have been a celebration. ACME Investments Inc. had acquired the assets and businesses of Webb Transport Inc., Fillwell Axles Inc., and Superior Spares Inc. at rock bottom prices and far less than net asset value. Instead, it was a tense affair. Harry O'Brien was still sulking about the twenty million charged to his loan account. Worse, he was nursing his wounds, knowing that the others were trying to get rid of him.

Arthur Ridgeway, looking to ease the tension, said to Borchard, "Nice little killing with Devlin Cooper, Brock."

"Crap! Nine million? I was expecting a lot more. We're gonna have to do it again before the season's over. Maybe in the playoffs?" Borchard said.

"Did you see the pounding Cooper took to make it look like he was trying?" Lydia asked. "Even so, there were some in the media who still thought it stunk. We agreed one game per season and even thinking about the playoffs is crazy. Fifteen seasons at ten mil a season is far better than doing it twice in one season and getting caught."

"I'm with Lydia," Becker said.

"Me too," Ridgeway agreed.

"What do you think, Harry?" Becker asked.

"He's Brock's asset," O'Brien said. "Why don't we just let Brock manage him?"

"Yeah," Borchard said. "Harry's right. He's my asset. I set the whole thing up. It's nobody else's business what I do."

"No, Brock, he's not your asset. He's our asset. What Harry said was churlish and stupid," Becker said. "Let's put it to a vote. All those in favor of exploiting the asset more than once per season."

Two hands rose.

"All those against."

Three hands went up.

"That resolves that," Becker said. "Be patient, Brock, next season will come around soon enough."

Borchard didn't like being told what to do and was more surly than usual. "Dermott," he said, "you told us we'd make a fifty mil out of the insider trading scam. We didn't even make thirty. What went wrong? What happened?"

"We were conservative and kept our positions small," Becker said. "I was particularly anxious to ensure we didn't tip the authorities off. The last thing I wanted was to have our accounts frozen. We could've made fifty, but I didn't know how the CFD providers were going to hedge their positions. Any large stock purchases by them might've tipped the SEC off."

"So ya were exaggerating," Borchard persisted.

"No, I wasn't. We'll make far more than a hundred mil out of our auditor friend before we're finished. We now know the CFD model works."

"Have you paid the hundred and fifty thousand into the girl's account?" Ridgeway asked.

"What? What are you talking about?" Borchard asked.

"We opened up a bank account in her name in the Caymans. Forged identification and signature," Becker replied.

"It's cheap insurance," Ridgeway said. "We don't think we'll have any problems with the authorities. However, if they do get suspicious, we want to protect our asset. If it looks like he's in the firing line, we'll leak details of the bank account to the SEC. That'll soon refocus them on the girl."

Borchard didn't like any of his co-directors but every meeting he learned something new. They were so devious. "Very clever," he said.

"On another matter," Becker said, "our Philadelphia financial controller has been talking. He's okay when he's sober, but he's an alcoholic. Our people in Atlantic City said he was in the casino, incoherent and mumbling about gangsters and insider trading."

"Shit! That's all we need," Lydia said.

"No one took any notice of him," Becker said.

"That's not true," Borchard said. "Our people did. They could just as easily have been FBI and SEC investigators. I can send Dirk in disguise to keep an eye on him. He'll get close enough to find out how bad his blabberin' is?"

"No!" Ridgeway growled. "Every time that thug watches someone, they end up dead."

"Hang on, Arty," Becker said. "I wouldn't mind Dirk running a backup check and letting us know what he's saying and whether anyone's listening."

"I don't want anyone else getting killed," Ridgeway said.

"Me neither," Becker replied. "Brock, get Dirk to head to Atlantic City on Saturday night, but he's not to lay a hand on Carroll."

"Fine." Borchard sneered.

BOOK 2

Chapter 22

It was 7:45 P.M. on Wednesday when the white van pulled up out the front of Vanessa Hodge's apartment building. Five minutes later, Vanessa and her girlfriend, headed off for their kickboxing class. It didn't take long for Ferguson and Fraser to enter Vanessa's apartment. Ferguson carefully lifted the set of drawers next to her bed while Fraser taped the two mailbox keys underneath the bottom drawer.

Dirk Vaughan disguised himself as an old man with long gray hair, a mustache and horn-rimmed glasses. He wore black pants and shoes and an overcoat that was purposely one size too large. His Star City player card created in a false name by one of his lackeys earlier in the week had $2,000 on it. The undernourished, pasty faced Les Carroll entered the casino at 7:30 P.M. like he had on every other Saturday night for the past three years. Vaughan watched Carroll go to the cashier's window and then take a seat in front of a $100 poker machine. There weren't all that many customers who played the $100 machines and those who did were well looked after. As Carroll sat down, a long-legged brunette, who he apparently knew took his complimentary drinks order, and he settled in for the night. Vaughan strained his eyes but couldn't see what Carroll's starting credits were.

It wasn't often that Vaughan was intrigued by human behavior, but Carroll was the financial controller of a large corporation. Despite this, he was playing a game that he had to know was impossible to win. Vaughan understood drug addiction but didn't understand how anyone could be addicted to losing money on poker machines. After about three hours, Carroll had consumed at least a dozen drinks and had a guy of a similar age on his left and a plump, obviously talkative woman on his right. The machine on the other side of the woman was not being used, and Vaughan hobbled over to it and sat down.

Carroll played at a rapid pace barely waiting for the reels to stop spinning before sending them on their way again. The more he drank, the more frenetic the pace, and Vaughan knew that this was what the casino and the drinks waitress wanted. No sooner had he finished one drink than the waitress was there with a fresh one ensuring he remained lubricated. Even though it wasn't Vaughan's money, he played slowly in keeping with his age and sipped orange juice. Carroll and the plump woman engaged in a lively inebriated discussion mainly about their bad luck and near misses on huge jackpots. It was only when the woman said something about losing ten thousand in one night a few weeks earlier that the conversation changed.

"Thas nothing," Carroll slurred, "I've dropped more than a hundred on some nights. I wass playing the $1,000 machines, but I weaned myself off them."

"Wow, you must be loaded."

"I wass." Carroll laughed scornfully. "They gave me credit and nex thing ya know I wass doing things I never shoulda done."

Vaughan's ears perked up and even though Carroll's words were garbled he knew what was coming.

"Like what?" the woman asked.

"I had no choice. I hadda ta give 'em inside information. They said it wass my only way out," Carroll said, specks of saliva coming from his mouth.

The woman drew back on her chair and started playing her machine again. It was clear to Dirk that she didn't like being spit on or listening to the ramblings of a drunk.

"I hadda to tell 'em about me company. Hadda to give 'em inshide information." Carroll moaned. "They made millions. Said I'd only hafta to do it once but they recorded me. Gangstas thas what they are."

The woman wasn't listening. "I'm having no luck," she said. "I'm going to find another machine."

Vaughan had heard more than enough and a few minutes later called Borchard and told him what Carroll had said.

"What do you want me to do, boss?"

"How drunk is he?" Borchard asked.

"Staggering and he's getting worse."

"It'd be opportune if he had an accident. But it has to be just that. An accident. If the opportunity arises, take it, but if it doesn't, let him go. We can wait."

It was 1:30 A.M. when Carroll stumbled out of Star City and took a cab on the three minute trip to the railway station. Vaughan quickly jumped into the next cab. After the 1:53 to Philadelphia departed it would be another five hours before the next train to Philly. The station was swarming with late-night revelers heading home. Carroll was swaying in the front row of a crowd about five deep in the middle of the station. Vaughan nonchalantly worked his way among the crowd until he was standing at the back of two commuters who were directly behind the unsteady Carroll. There were plenty of revelers in a similar condition, and no one paid Carroll any attention. As the train pulled into the station, the driver sounded its horn to warn those on the station to get back. While it was still sounding, Carroll appeared to lose his balance and fall in front of the train. Pandemonium broke loose, and one woman let out a dreadful shriek while men pushed to the front of the platform in a vain attempt to see if they could help. Vaughan watched as the ashen-faced driver leaped from the cabin and ran along the platform to where Carroll's crushed and mangled body lay. One man who knelt down and saw the body put his hand over his mouth but couldn't stop the vomit squeezing through his fingers. Vaughan worked his way to the back of the crowd and slowly hobbled from the station.

FBI agent Chas Grinich had become aware of the death of company director, Richard Frampton when he had been investigating share transactions in companies in which Frampton had been a director. Something about Frampton's sex-related death didn't ring true to Grinich.

The stock transactions just prior to releasing price-sensitive announcements in Miami based high-tech public company Xenex Inc. were near identical to those that had taken place with the companies associated with Frampton. Grinich had been increasingly wary when investigating Xenex, and when he found out that Valerie Gibson had died in suspicious circumstances his instincts told him that it was more than just coincidence.

Two months after Les Carroll's death, Grinich was searching his database looking for companies where senior executives had met their death in suspicious circumstances. Les Carroll's name was one of those that appeared. Carroll had been an addicted gambler with heavy debts in Atlantic City. An easy mark. Grinich was almost sure that he would find dubious stock trading in the company that had employed Carroll. He wasn't wrong, and Carroll's demise proved beyond any doubt that someone was running a massive insider share trading scam.

The pattern of trading and the death of the apparent source in each of the three corporations were nearly identical. The scam was clever and the transactions through many brokers were singularly not enough to raise suspicion. Grinich threw his legs up on his desk and put his hands behind his head. He wondered how many other company executives were leaking inside information about their employers. He knew there had been stock manipulation and also suspected murder.

Chapter 23

Aaron Lord had just turned thirty but was already one of SEC's most senior and talented investigators. Qualified in law and finance he was a securities expert but that wasn't the reason he had progressed so rapidly in the SEC. That was because he had an almost religious fervor about him when it came to prosecuting white collar criminals for what he saw as their sins against society. He had short cropped blonde hair, piercing green eyes, and an almost perfectly square head that sat atop a bull neck. He looked and was tough.

The Securities and Exchange Commission would not normally have any interest in CFDs over US stocks traded on international markets. However, the increased activity in the volume of stock traded in Virtex and Philco during the week they announced their results to the market was flagged as excessive.

Lord was initially puzzled by what he found, but the haze soon lifted. After he and his team had spent a week specifically looking at the larger stock orders, they discovered that they had emanated out of Switzerland. More damningly they had been placed by CFD providers in the forty-eight hours prior to the companies announcing to the market. It was obvious that the Swiss had hedged their CFD positions.

It appeared to Lord that someone had had inside information about the two companies' results. Rather than drawing attention to themselves by buying and shorting the stocks on the NYSE, the insiders had taken the same positions via CFDs in Switzerland. If some of the Swiss CFD providers had not chosen to hedge their positions, the SEC would've been none the wiser.

By the time Lord's preliminary investigation was completed he had discovered that five CFD providers based in Switzerland had bought stock in Virtex and short sold stock in Philco. Clearly someone with inside information had been behind the trading. He had called each of the CFD providers seeking further information. They had been polite but guarded about the information they provided, and he had learned very little. Lord knew that the only way he'd get the answers he was seeking was by direct interrogation. The Swiss CFD providers were reluctant to meet with him, but he had been very persuasive, suggesting that the U.S. government would be very disgruntled if they refused to cooperate.

SR 23 departed JFK at 7:25 P.M. on Sunday and landed in Geneva eight hours later at 9:25 A.M. on Monday. Lord and his assistant, Ben Drucker, took a taxi from the airport to the Hotel Warwick in the city. Lord knew the hotel well having stayed there many times before. They checked in and twenty minutes later were back in another cab heading for his first appointment at JHM Brokers on Rue du Simplon. They took an elevator to the eleventh floor of an old brick building where they entered a lobby and were greeted by a young lady. "Aaron Lord and Ben Drucker from the SEC. We have an 11:30 appointment."

"Good morning, Mr. Lord," she said. "Monsieur Paul Bossard is expecting you. Please follow me."

She led them to a meeting room where they met a tall, slim man with a goatee. He was immaculately dressed in a three-piece, navy blue, pinstriped stripe suit. He had a thin folder sitting in front of him. "I fear you might have had a long trip for nothing, gentlemen," he said. "Would you like something to drink?"

"Nothing, thank you. We're running short of time," Lord replied, pulling out his diary. "You took a significant long position in Virtex Software on the 17th January. Who were you acting for?"

"It was a proprietary position, and we were hedging a CFD position," Bossard replied, handing the file that had been in front of him to Lord. "You'll find everything in here."

Lord quickly thumbed through the file. It included a complete summary of the Virtex transactions and copies of all documents including emails from a firm of lawyers based in Geneva instructing JHM to open and close the position on behalf of their client, Citadel Investments. "How long has the account been open?"

"About three months," Bossard replied.

"Can we have a history of transactions?" Lord asked.

"Not without a court order, Mr. Lord. With respect, many of the transactions have nothing to do with your jurisdiction. I can say there was nothing untoward or unusual about the position in Virtex." Bossard paused then laughed. "Other than the profit that is."

"Is the account still open?" Lord asked.

"Yes, but there are no active positions. As far as we're concerned we were dealing with a Swiss-registered company. We were surprised to find that the SEC was interested in the transactions. The transactions, while profitable, were relatively small. What is your concern?"

Lord picked up his briefcase, put the file under his arm and stood up. He was sure that Bossard knew more than he was letting on but equally sure that he wasn't going to find out more than what was in the folder. "It could be nothing. I need to check with the firm of lawyers who instructed you. Thank you."

Their second appointment was on Rue du Rhone, and as they climbed into the taxi, Lord handed the file to Drucker. "Call the lawyers. Tell them we want to see them tomorrow. Don't take any bullshit. Let them know they can deal with us or the Justice Department."

It was 6 P.M. when Lord and Drucker got back to their hotel having had meetings with four other CFD providers that had each provided a file with details not dissimilar to that provided by JHM. The Swiss were incredibly polite but not very cooperative and quite secretive. They sat in the bar, Lord nursing a whiskey and the younger man sipping a mineral water. "Five companies, three firms of lawyers and two firms of accountants," Drucker said. "Someone went to an awful lot of trouble to hide what they were doing. All for sixteen million."

"Sixteen million we know about," Lord replied. "What about the CFD providers who didn't hedge or hedged with other CFD providers in the UK or Australia? I think the profit was a lot more than sixteen million."

The offices of Marshall & Associates, International, Commercial, and Finance Lawyers, were in an older building above a cluster of retail shops on Rue des Alpes. It was just after 9 A.M. when Lord and Drucker were shown to a large conference room, the walls of which were surrounded by legal tomes. A portly man with rapidly receding hair got out of a large leather chair and said, "I am Jurg Aberle, and this is my partner, Lars Gonthier. Please be seated, gentlemen, and let us know how we might help you. Before we start, can I offer you anything to drink?"

"Thank you, no," Lord responded taking the file that JHM Brokers had given him from his briefcase. "You act for a corporation, Citadel Investments. Can you tell me the capacity in which you act?"

Aberle pushed himself back into his chair, put his hands on his stomach and looked over the top of his spectacles. "I'm sorry," he said, "Citadel Investments is not an American company and does not have American directors or shareholders. How does it fall under your jurisdiction?"

Lord had been expecting this. "We suspect that your client engaged in insider trading."

"Our client has never bought or sold U.S. stocks." Gonthier smiled. "There must be some mistake."

The hawk-like Gonthier was smirking infuriatingly, and Lord chose his words carefully. "As you are well aware, your client took a sizable long CFD position with JHM over the stock of Virtex Software Inc. JHM subsequently bought stock in Virtex to hedge their position. I want to know who instructed you to buy CFDs on behalf of Citadel Investments. And before you answer, I know that you have many clients that operate in the U.S. that would find it very disruptive if we were to investigate their operations."

"Are you threatening us?" Aberle asked.

"Not yet," Lord replied, "and I hope that I don't have to."

Aberle leaned over and whispered something to Gonthier before asking, "What is it you want to know? We want to cooperate with you. If we can help without breaching client-attorney confidentiality, we will."

"Who instructed you to acquire CFDs in Virtex?" Lord asked.

Without answering, Gonthier slid a copy of an email over to Lord. It was from a firm of lawyers in the Caymans instructing Marshall &

Associates to acquire CFDs in Virtex on behalf of Citadel Investments. A second email contained instructions when to sell.

"Why did you comply with those instructions?" Lord asked.

"They were the instructing lawyers who asked us to form Citadel Investments and to act on their behalf," Gonthier replied.

"And if we go to the Caymans we'll find the instructing lawyers are acting under the instructions of another firm of lawyers operating out of a tax haven. What happened to the money?"

"After we made deductions for our expenses and income tax, we remitted the balance to the Royal Bank of Canada in the Caymans," Gonthier said, sliding a copy of the transfer to Lord. "With respect, Mr. Lord, we don't think the SEC has any jurisdiction in this matter. After all, CFDs over stocks are illegal in the U.S. so I'm not sure how you have the authority to police them."

Lord had pondered this himself, but the hedge positions had been taken over U.S. stocks, and there was no doubt in his mind that these trades had impacted the integrity of the market. "Thank you," he said, as he rose to leave.

As they stared at the watches in the jewelry retailer's window, Drucker said, "Aaron, do you think the funds are still in the Caymans?"

Lord laughed. "No way. They could be in Ireland, Liechtenstein, Hong Kong or God knows where. They'll have been through so many international banks that tracing them will be impossible. Smart bastards!"

"Maybe we'll get lucky with the other appointments."

"You're an optimist, Ben. We've found all we're going to find, but we might as well go through the motions."

Chapter 24

SR 22 departed Geneva at 11:45 A.M. on Wednesday and Ben Drucker looked at Aaron Lord and said, "Well that was a waste of time. Fucking Swiss!"

"Not necessarily," Lord responded. "We know that someone traded on inside information, we know they made at least sixteen million and probably a lot more, and we know they're very smart. I've got a gut feeling it's the same people who Chas Grinich is looking for. I wouldn't call it a waste of time."

"Are we going to go after the auditors when we get back?"

"We'll talk to them, but don't forget, company directors talk to each other. We need to look at both boards too. Then there are senior managers and their PAs. The leak could've come from anywhere."

"My money is on the auditors, Aaron. It's just too pat. Right now they're the only common link we have between the two companies."

When Todd answered his prepaid cell phone, he said, "We're all square now. I've repaid the debt. I'm getting rid of this phone. I never want to hear from you again."

"Todd, that's not a nice way to talk to me. Don't forget, if it hadn't been for me, you might be pushing up daisies. I need to see you," Elliot said.

"Why? Our business is over. I don't ever want to see you again."

"I thought you'd want to tear your note up. Who knows what might happen if it fell into the wrong hands. You might get called on to pay it again." Elliot said.

"You can tear it up."

"You trust me?" Elliot laughed.

Todd paused. "All right," he said, "but I won't be staying. Have the note ready. Where?"

"There's a coffee shop in Chinatown. I'll text you the address. Eight o'clock tomorrow night. I'll order a latte for you."

"Don't bother," Todd said, terminating the call.

Devlin Cooper missed the next two games with the Cougars while his ribs healed, and his body recovered. There was still a lot of conjecture about his game against the Pirates and for many fans he was no longer their golden boy. His replacement, Jeff Sweeny, had seized his opportunity, and the Cougars had had two good wins. However, there was no disputing Cooper's place on the team. Once he'd recuperated he would again be an automatic selection.

Cooper was young and in great physical condition, so it was no surprise that he recovered quickly. His mental condition was something else, though. In all his life, he had never suffered a day's depression, but now he was in constant conflict with his conscience. He found it almost impossible to sleep and when he did drift off, he would awaken after a few hours with a start and in a cold sweat. He had never been booed by fans before, shunned and questioned by teammates, or been taken to task by some in the media. Worse, for the first time in his life, he suspected that his father was no longer proud of him. The bourbon helped him get through the nights, but the mornings were hellish. Devlin Cooper's life was unraveling, and there was nothing he could do about it.

Phillip Cromwell's appointment book for Thursday was full but when the man from the SEC had called he had been insistent, almost demanding, about seeing him. Cromwell had reluctantly agreed to meet with him at 7:30 A.M. However, when he asked Aaron Lord what it was about, the SEC man had said that it was something he didn't care to discuss over the phone.

Cromwell eyed the young man sitting opposite him and thought he looked more like a marine than an investigator. He had little time for public servants and said, "I can give you thirty minutes, Mr. Lord. I'm sorry it's too early for my secretary. I can't offer you coffee."

"That's fine. Your firm audits Virtex Software and Philco Laboratories. Your partner, Douglas Lechte, signed the audit reports on both companies. How long has Mr. Lechte been with the firm?"

Suddenly Cromwell was very interested. "What's this about?"

"We have reason to believe that their results were leaked before being released to the market."

"There was insider trading?"

"We believe so."

"Why do you suspect us?"

"We don't. It's a process of elimination. Your firm audits the accounts of both companies. That piqued our interest. Now, how long has Mr. Lechte been a partner of the firm?"

"Doug has been with us for twenty years, the last twelve as a partner."

"It's unlikely that he would've leaked any information then," Lord said.

Cromwell paused, put his hand under his chin and finally said, "Yes, I suppose you're right."

"That's hardly a vote of confidence."

"Mr. Lord, I don't know Doug's personal circumstances so I can hardly make a judgment about his actions or what might motivate him."

"That's a strange comment. Does Mr. Lechte have any financial problems that you're aware of?"

Cromwell paused again. "No...none that I know of anyhow."

"Did any other partners or employees have access to the results?"

"I don't know. Doug assigns the audit teams. Would you like to talk to him?" Cromwell said. "I'll get him down here."

"I thought you had another appointment," Lord said, looking at his watch.

"Mr. Lord, this matter is of grave importance. Like you, I'd like to get to the bottom of it," Cromwell said, picking up the phone.

"Doug, please come down to my office now. Something urgent as arisen."

There was a lengthy pause. "Yes, yes! It is important. I wouldn't have asked otherwise."

Doug Lechte barged through the door and was about to let loose on Cromwell when he saw Aaron Lord. "What's this about, Phillip?"

Cromwell made the introduction and then told Lechte the reason for the SEC investigator's visit.

Without looking at Lord, Lechte said, "Well, I hope you told him the leaks didn't emanate from this firm."

"Mr. Lechte, I didn't make any accusations. I'm sure you'd appreciate this is a process of elimination," Lord said.

"Good! You can start by eliminating this firm."

"I'd be happy to. I do have a few questions, though. Besides you, do any of your employees work on the accounts of both companies?"

"Yes, Vanessa Hodge. She's one of my senior audit managers," Lechte replied. "Some of her team would've also worked on both audits."

"Ah hah," Cromwell exclaimed.

"What's that supposed to mean? What are you inferring? Vanessa's as honest as the day is long. She's beyond reproach," Lechte said through tightly gritted teeth.

"The leaks came from somewhere," Cromwell said.

"They didn't come from this firm! It could've been the directors, managers, suppliers or customers. Christ, it could've been anyone. Isn't that right, Mr. Lord?" Lechte asked.

"Yes. That's true. However, we may need to talk to Ms. Hodge."

"She out on an assignment, but she'll be happy to talk to you. Is that all?" Lechte said, standing and extending his hand.

It was 9 A.M. when Cromwell's secretary showed Aaron Lord out. He could hear loud, angry voices behind him. He stepped into the elevator thinking what a contrast. Cromwell's handshake had been limp. He hadn't defended Lechte and almost appeared pleased when Vanessa Hodge's name was raised. Lechte had a bone crushing grip and had vigorously defended the firm and his manager. What was blindingly obvious was the two men's disdain for each other. The only opinion Lord had formed was that Phillip Cromwell would be very easy to dislike.

Chapter 25

It was midday when Vanessa Hodge knocked on Doug Lechte's door. He looked up, grim-faced. "Take a seat. I'm sorry, I have some bad news."

Five minutes later Vanessa said, "That's ridiculous. I never discuss clients' business with anyone. Why would Mr. Cromwell want to suspend me? Why does he hate me so much?"

"It's not you that he hates," Lechte replied. "It's his way of attacking me. He spent the morning lobbying the other partners and as usual the Catholic bloc voted with him. I told them that suspending you was stupid, but Cromwell had the numbers. Are you sure you didn't inadvertently discuss the results with anyone? A friend, someone from your family?"

"God, even you think it was me."

"Vanessa, I trust and will defend you with all my being. I just wanted to cover the possibility of you making a slip. You know, you say something to someone you know, and they, not realizing the importance of the information, accidentally pass it onto someone else who acts on it. You know how it works."

"Yes, I do. That's why I'd never breathe a word to anyone." A tear ran down Vanessa's cheek. "It's so unfair."

"Yes, it is. I made sure you're on full pay. You've been working long hours. Why don't you try and get some rest? It won't take long for the SEC to absolve you."

"I'll never be absolved," Vanessa said. "This will stick to me for the rest of my life. Other firms will soon find out. I'll never make partner anywhere. I'll be suspected of breaching client confidentiality. It'll always be on my CV."

Lechte knew that everything Vanessa said was true. "Look, I know how stupid it is and how vindictive Phillip Cromwell is. Don't get disheartened. I'll always support you, and I guarantee you will make partner here."

"I don't know whether I still want to be a partner." Vanessa sniffled as she fought back tears.

Lechte came around from behind his desk and sat next to her, putting his hand on her arm. "Trust me, Vanessa. It'll blow over, and when it does, I'll make Cromwell pay."

Devlin Cooper's return performance was passable rather than brilliant in the Cougars comfortable win over the Marauders. The following day he was awoken by the ringing of his prepaid cell. "Good morning, Devlin," the accented voice said. "You did a good job against the Pirates. We were very pleased. We want you to do it again in the playoffs."

"I won't do it. I won't let my teammates down. Jeez, every camera in America will be on me. It can't be done."

"Yes, it can, and, yes, you will."

"That wasn't what you said. You said you'd only ask me to do it once."

"I lied."

"If I do it again, I'll be finished for life."

"No, you won't. You'll just have to be more convincing. Take a few more hits."

"I can't do it."

"If you don't we'll make you and Mrs. Deacon the best-known porn stars in the country," the voice hissed. "I'll be in touch again before the playoffs. Don't cross me."

Cooper lay in bed staring at the ceiling and for what must have been the thousandth time cursed himself. He was trapped. There was no escaping the mess. He pulled the blankets up around his neck. He had no reason to get out of bed.

Todd Hansen was returning from lunch when he bumped into Vanessa at the elevators. Her eyes were red and swollen. "What's wrong?" he asked.

"You'll find out soon enough. I've been suspended."

"Suspended? Suspended? What for?"

"An SEC investigator was in seeing Cromwell this morning. The SEC suspect there was insider trading in the stock of Virtex Software and Philco Laboratories immediately prior to the release of their results to the market. They suspect the leak came from the firm. Phillip Cromwell thinks it was me."

"That's crazy," Todd said, relieved that Vanessa was staring at the floor. "You'll soon be cleared."

"I'll never be cleared." Vanessa looked up and smiled bitterly. "Some of the mud will stick forever."

"Is there anything I can do?"

"Thanks for asking. You're a good friend, Todd, but, no, there's nothing anyone can do. I have to go." Vanessa sniffled, as she stepped into an elevator.

Todd could barely walk. His feet seemed glued to the carpet, and he felt his lunch surging up in his throat. He stumbled down to the rest rooms and was violently ill. He splashed cold water on his face and tried to regain composure.

Chapter 26

As Todd walked down the poorly lit alley to the coffee shop in Chinatown, a hand reached out and dragged him into a doorway.

"Hello, Todd." Ferguson grinned. "I've just gotta make sure you're clean before you meet the boss. Turn around."

"I'm hardly likely to be wearing a wire. It's my last meeting. I can't wait to see the last of him and you."

"Your last meeting, huh? I didn't know that. That's not a nice way to talk to someone who looked after you. Have you forgotten what happened to Giovani?" Ferguson asked as he shoved Todd back into the alley. "You better get a move on. The boss doesn't like being kept waiting."

Elliot was sitting at a table in the corner and at the back of the near empty coffee shop. He was nursing a short black, and there was a latte sitting opposite him.

"Take a seat, kid."

"I told you I wasn't staying," Todd replied, "but I do want to talk to you. The SEC were in our offices yesterday, and the firm suspended the woman responsible for the audits. You said that no one would ever know about the trades. Did the fools who you work for get too greedy?"

Elliot's demeanor didn't change. "The SEC's got nothing. Don't worry, it'll blow over. You're in the clear. Here's your note. You're off the hook as far as owing anyone anything goes."

Todd wadded it up and pushed it deep into his pants pocket. He hadn't touched the coffee. "I'm going," he said. "I can't say it's been a pleasure, and I hope I never set eyes on you again."

"Not so fast," Elliot said, pulling a Dictaphone out of his pocket. "You might like to listen to this."

Todd felt sick. Even before he heard the first word, he knew what it was. He listened as he heard his voice quoting Virtex Software's results in detail.

"You bastard. You low bastard! You went through the bullshit of searching me every time we met while you were recording everything I said."

"Would you like to hear what you told us about Philco?" Elliot smirked. "Your coffee's getting cold, Todd."

"I won't help you again. I'll go to the police before I ever do it again. I'm warning you."

Elliot laughed. "You're warning us? Here's what will happen if you go to the police. You'll get at least seven years, you'll disgrace yourself and your precious family, and you'll never work in a position of trust again. We own you."

"The seven years might be better than having to deal with you. Besides, if I go to the police, I'll make certain I've got you for company in prison."

"You stupid, little fool. We know every move you make. We know you've been looking for a cheaper apartment. We know everything. We've even got our people on the force. Keep that in mind when you're spilling your guts to your friendly, local cop. He might be one of ours. And if that's not enough, think about what Ferguson did to Giovani and just imagine that little Italian squealer was your mother."

Todd involuntarily reached out for the coffee. It was cold. He downed it in one gulp. "You low life bastard," he said getting to his feet.

"Todd, Todd." Elliot smiled. "Stay and have another coffee with me. We're even prepared to pay the rent on your apartment. We don't want you wasting your time looking at other apartments and going through the hassle of shifting. You deserve a comfortable place."

"Fuck you," Todd said as he stumbled toward the door.

"We'll be in touch. Now you have a good night."

Elliot's laugh echoed around Todd's head as he shuffled down the alley. *Could life be worse?*

Elliot waited for Todd to disappear before calling Dermott Becker. "The SEC are investigating those transactions."

"Is our boy safe?" Becker asked.

"He's not under suspicion. Montgomery Hastings & Pierce have suspended the manager pending the outcome of the SEC's investigation."

"Just as well we covered ourselves. Give the SEC the woman and ease up on Hansen. Let's give him six months or so before asking for another favor."

Vanessa Hodge loved her large family and the support it afforded her, but one disadvantage was the total lack of privacy. She moped around her apartment totally bored. Music didn't work, television didn't work, reading didn't work and the countless sympathetic phone calls, some sincere, others not, did nothing for her. She had never suffered down days, mainly because she was so incredibly busy. Brooding gave her time to reflect on the unfairness of her situation. She was still in her nightgown and hadn't showered. Why would she? It wasn't as if she was going anywhere. She flopped down on the sofa and rested her chin in her hands. She would have loved to visit her mom, but she knew the grilling about why she wasn't working would be intense. Worse, this would lead to a flood of calls from sisters, brothers, cousins, aunties and uncles. She resolved that sulking by herself was the better of the two options. Doug Lechte had assured her that it would take no time at all for the SEC to clear her and that she'd most likely be back at work within the week. She already knew that, but it was comforting knowing she had his unconditional support.

It was an overcast Sunday afternoon, and Devlin Cooper would have rather been anywhere than at a family barbecue, but his parents had insisted. As usual, he was surrounded by cousins, uncles and friends all asking questions about the Cougars when his fifteen-year-old nephew, Jason, laughed and said, "You had a real shocker against the Pirates. It looked like you were tanking."

A few others in the group chuckled.

Without warning Devlin's demeanor changed. "What the fuck is that supposed to mean?" he shouted. "Where do you get off talking shit like that?"

Jason looked like he was going to burst into tears. In all his life, his hero had never spoken to him like that before. "I-I-I'm sorry," he said, "I-I was joking."

Devlin's sister, Marci, who had been standing near the pool, rushed to comfort her son. "What's wrong with you, Devlin? Don't you have a sense of humor? Are you starting to believe that media rubbish about you being the golden boy? Oh, and I watched you against the Pirates. You stunk! Now apologize to Jason."

There were close to a hundred friends and relatives around the pool and barbecue, but there was dead silence.

"Fuck you!" Devlin yelled and stormed across the lawn and out the back gate.

"Devlin! Devlin, get back here," his father shouted.

Devlin didn't look around. He jumped in the Ferrari and screeched off down the street. Thirty minutes later he sat in the driveway of his palatial home and sobbed uncontrollably. His world was falling apart.

Chapter 27

Aaron Lord held the plain white self-sealing envelope up to the light looking for any clue it might reveal. In bold black typed letters, it had been addressed, *Private and Confidential, Mr. Aaron Lord, SEC, 3 World Financial Center - Sandy Hook #400, New York, NY.* It had contained a note that said, *Vanessa Hodge, The Cayman National Bank, Account number 1197:03561.*

Lord had called the bank and with a minimum of pressure had confirmed the existence of the newly created account opened with a deposit of $150,000. For Lord, it was all too easy and had a distinct smell about it. However, Montgomery Hastings & Pierce had suspended Vanessa Hodge on the mere mention of an SEC investigation. Her boss, Doug Lechte, had gone to pains to say that if there had been a leak it could've come from any one of numerous sources. Despite this, Montgomery Hastings & Pierce had suspended her. Were they hiding something? And who had forwarded the envelope? Was it a co-worker or perhaps even a partner?

Lord could have obtained the answers he was after by interrogation and subpoena but a faster way of obtaining it was by seeking the help of the FBI. When Grinich had heard about Virtex and Philco, he'd drawn the same conclusion as Lord. He was more than pleased to be given the chance to participate in the investigation"Aaron, from what you've told me it sure looks like your Miss Hodge is the insider," Grinich said. "What do you want us to do?"

"Warrants to search her mailbox, her apartment, her desk, cell phone, files and computer would sure speed up the investigation."

"Consider it done. We're gonna be charging her with some serious offenses."

It was 6 A.M. when Vanessa was awoken by loud banging on her door and a man shouting, "FBI, open the door, or we'll smash it down."

Vanessa threw on a robe and opened the door. There were half a dozen burly men standing there, one with a sledgehammer in his hand.

"Wha-what's this ab–?" she asked.

The man at the front pushed a piece of paper into her hand and shoved her out of the way, and the others followed. "We have a warrant to search your premises."

"It-it mus-must be a mis-mistake."

"It's no mistake, lady," one of the men said as they threw her mattress on the floor.

The clothes in her closet were strewn everywhere, and they went through her handbag, purse, and drawers. They found her cell phone and laptop and put them in a tie-up bag. They made no attempt to tone down the noise, and soon neighbors were in the hallway trying to find out what was going on. The agent at Vanessa's door said, "FBI, don't worry. Go back to your apartments."

Vanessa was stunned. She couldn't hear herself think. She couldn't phone anyone, and the FBI agents ignored anything she tried to say. She felt defiled and utterly degraded by these obnoxious brutes.

Then one of the agents shouted, "What's this we have here?"

He had overturned the set of drawers next to her bed, and there was a set of keys taped underneath the bottom drawer. The agent who'd shoved the warrant into her hands said, "What are these for, Miss? Why are you hiding them?"

"I-I-I've nev-never seen them be-before."

"You're not a very convincing liar," the agent said. "You're going away for a long, long time."

The FBI search had taken less than ten minutes. Vanessa, now alone, knelt down and plugged the landline back into the wall. Deep in shock she pushed some clothes off a chair and sat down. Her tiny apartment looked like a hurricane had gone through it. As the realization of what had occurred dawned on her, she wept. Tears ran down her cheeks, and she gasped for air.

The FBI were no more subtle when they searched Vanessa's cubicle at Montgomery Hastings & Pierce. Staff were shocked, and partners were dismayed. Doug Lechte had tried to intervene but had been told to butt out in no uncertain manner. Phillip Cromwell could barely contain his delight. With luck, this would give him the means to finally get rid of Lechte.

When Aaron Lord called Vanessa Hodge and asked her to come in and see him, she had been angry and defiant. He had suggested that she bring a lawyer with her, but she had said that only guilty people needed lawyers. When she entered his office, he was taken aback by her beauty despite the contempt written all over her face. She wore a gray knee-length business suit, a white blouse, and black shoes. Lord extended his hand, but she kept her hands folded in front of her. "Take a seat, Miss Hodge," he said. "You know why you're here."

"No, I don't! Why am I here? Why did you trash my apartment? How dare you."

"It'll save a lot of time if you drop the aggrieved act, Miss Hodge," Lord said pushing a Cayman National Bank statement toward her. "I suppose the $150,000 materialized out of thin air?"

Vanessa looked at the statement in amazement. "I've never had an account with this bank. It's not my account."

"We'll progress a lot faster if you start telling the truth. Are these notarized copies of your driver's license and passport?"

"Ye-yes. Where-where did you ge-get them from?"

"They were attached to this," Lord said, sliding an account application with The Cayman National Bank across the desk. "Is that your signature?"

Vanessa felt sick. "Ye-yes, bu-but it must be a for-forgery. I nev-never signed that application. I don't have an account with tha-that bank."

"So someone forged an application and deposited $150,000 in your account and you know nothing about it. Do I look like a fool?"

"Somebody framed me!" Vanessa said, with some of her earlier defiance.

Lord laughed. "Why would anyone do that?"

"I don't know," Vanessa replied staring at the bank statement. "It has a mailbox address. I don't have a mailbox!"

"Stop it," Lord shouted, shoving the PS 1583 form at her. "This is what you gave UPS. Stop lying. We know what you did. Are you going to try and tell me that signature's a forgery too? It's your signature! We've checked it."

Vanessa reached out and held the edge of Lord's desk. She was shaking. "I–I ne-never fill-filled that form in," she said. "I-I've ne-never seen it before."

"I don't suppose you know what these are either," Lord said, jangling two distinctive keys in his hand.

"I-I saw them for the fir-first time this morn-morning when the FBI was trash-trashing my apartment."

"You're not a good liar. They're the keys to your mailbox."

Vanessa felt as if the whole world was closing in on her. She had been so confident when she had entered the SEC investigator's office. Someone had framed her, but she had no idea why. "I-I don't have-have a mailbox. Tho-those keys mus-must've been plan-planted."

"So you have a $150,000 in a bank account that you never opened. The statements are going to a mailbox that you never opened. And before today you've never seen the keys to the mailbox that were found hidden in your apartment. And you know nothing? I told you I'm not a fool, Miss Hodge. You're going to jail, but I can help you if you tell me who else was involved. If you know what's good for you, you'll start cooperating. Who'd you leak the Virtex and Philco results to?"

"I did-didn't breathe a word to anyone ab-about those res-results. It's a frame-up."

"Why?" Lord smirked.

"I-I don't know," Vanessa said and then paused. "To con-conceal the real cul-culprit."

"That's funny. Look, the evidence is damning. You need to come clean. I can tell you that dealing with me is going to be a lot more pleasant than dealing with the FBI, and they're your next port of call. Now tell me, who did you inform about the results of those companies?"

"No one."

Lord sighed. "Miss Hodge, I'm going to ask you one last time. Tell me the names of those who put you up to this and we'll go a lot easier on you. If you cooperate, I'll do my best to make sure you get a reduced sentence. You could be out in two years."

A shiver went up Vanessa's spine. "I-I've told you every-everything I know. If there's nothing el-else. I-I'm going."

Lord sat at his desk looking at the evidence. It was overwhelming. Despite this, a small part of him believed what the young woman had said. She had never paused or faltered and had been adamant about her innocence. As he picked up the phone, he felt sorry for her. He hadn't lied about the FBI and the interrogation she was about to undergo was going to be brutal. Chas Grinich answered his phone on the second ring.

"She didn't talk," Lord said.

"In the face of all of that evidence. Aaron, I gotta to say I'm surprised. You're not losing your touch, are you?"

"She says it's a frame-up."

"Yeah, and three pigs just flew past my window. You're too soft; that's your problem. We'll bring her in. A copy of her confession will be on your desk within twenty-four hours."

"Good luck."

"Luck's got nothing to do with it," Grinich replied. "I'll be in touch."

Chapter 28

The third page of *The Wall Street Journal* carried a small article about a senior audit manager in a blue chip accounting firm facing numerous insider trading charges. The information about the Caymans bank account was disclosed and had obviously been leaked by the SEC or FBI.

Doug Lechte had been quick to call an emergency early morning meeting of Montgomery Hastings & Pierce's thirty-eight New York partners. The mood in the conference room was tense and several partners who traditionally supported Lechte refused to make eye contact. "My partners and friends," he said, "you will have heard that Vanessa Hodge is being arraigned in the Manhattan federal court later today on insider trading charges. I've spoken to Vanessa at length about the charges that relate to Virtex Software and Philco Laboratories. She swears that she did not breathe a word to anyone about the results of these companies and that she is not the source."

"She's lying," Cromwell interjected, "and if you believe her, you're a fool. I spoke to the lead SEC investigator last night, and the evidence against her is damning. They even found a bank account in her name in the Caymans with $150,000 in it. I might add, deposited within two weeks of the results being announced. She's as guilty as sin."

"You'll have your chance to speak after I've finished," Lechte said, his face flushed. "Don't interrupt me again. I believe Vanessa. She's honest, trustworthy and a major asset of this firm. She called me last night. She's been interrogated by the SEC and FBI, and understandably, is severely stressed. She's very concerned about the cost of legal representation. I told her not to worry. The firm will cover her legal fees and if necessary her bail."

"You what?" Cromwell asked. "Haven't you heard of bail bondsmen?

Anyhow, from what I know bail won't be a problem. The assistant district attorney is going to oppose it. The judge will remand her in custody."

"I told you not to interrupt, Phillip," Lechte said. "Her family doesn't have the cash or assets to put up as security. Vanessa said that someone framed her. I don't doubt her in the slightest. We have to support her."

Tax partner Sandra Bishop, normally a supporter of Lechte's said, "She not only opened a Caymans bank account. She opened a mailbox to hide her actions and the FBI found the keys hidden in her apartment."

"How do you know that?" Lechte asked.

"I briefed partners about the seriousness of the situation," Cromwell said.

"More like lobbied," Lechte muttered.

"You had no right to commit the firm to paying her legal expenses or helping with bail," Cromwell said. "She deserves everything that the law throws at her. The firm needs representation but only to distance ourselves from her. We might be facing a large claim against our professional indemnity policy. If that occurs, we'll be facing significant increases in the cost of the cover. We don't want that."

Murmured assents echoed around the table.

"She's not guilty," Lechte said.

"In the unlikely case that that turns out to be true, we'll reimburse her legal expenses," Cromwell said. "We can't be fairer than that."

"Bullshit! You know she hasn't got the money to pay for a decent defense. And if she can't meet bail she'll be incarcerated. You're going to hang her out to dry," Lechte said, his lips drawn in a thin line.

"There's no need for vile language, Doug," Cromwell responded. "My fellow partners, as you know, Doug has been lobbying to make this woman a partner for the past two years. It's bad enough that she's a senior manager but imagine where we would be had we admitted her to the partnership. We should think ourselves lucky."

Dennis Morton, one of the Catholic bloc partners, said, "You're too modest, Phillip. If it hadn't been for you, she would most likely be a partner. The firm owes you a debt of gratitude."

Hear, hears went around the table.

"We cannot be seen to be helping this woman. We must distance ourselves from her and her actions. Doug, because you gave an undertaking on behalf of the firm, we will honor it in respect of today's hearing, but after today, she pays her own legal fees. Surely her family can't be that poor." Cromwell smirked.

"Damn you. That's so unfair," Lechte said.

"I didn't interrupt you," Cromwell said. "Please give me the same courtesy. We need to consider your role in this unsavory affair, Doug. You're the partner responsible for this woman. A woman you have been promoting for partnership. I think you need to look at your position within the partnership. The honorable thing to do would be to resign."

"As much as you'd like that, Phillip, it isn't happening." Lechte laughed.

"You've made a parlous error of judgment about this woman and the companies you assigned her to, yet you refuse to accept responsibility for your actions. You may not know this, but a two-thirds majority of the partners have the power to remove a delinquent partner. I think if I put it to the vote you'll be clearing your office out today."

"I do know about that clause," Lechte said. "In the long and illustrious history of this firm it's never been used. However, thirty days' notice is required, and the partner in question has the right to have a written representation circulated to all partners prior to the meeting."

"I thought you'd resign," Cromwell said. "Don't you have any pride? You're just delaying the inevitable. I'll have a notice circulated before the day is out."

Lechte cast his eyes around the table. Most of the partners had their heads hung or were pretending to jot on their notepads. Phillip Cromwell beamed. He knew he had the numbers.

Despite the protestations of the assistant district attorney, the judge hearing the arraignment of Vanessa Hodge set bail. Unfortunately for Vanessa, the sum was five million dollars, and the judge might just as well have remanded her in custody. Her lawyers promised to appeal the amount, but she would be spending the weekend in Richter's cells.

Todd Hansen was feeling sick with guilt when his prepaid cell phone rang. "Coffee shop, 7:30 tonight," Elliot said and hung up before Todd could reply.

Ferguson was waiting in the alley, and Todd lifted his hands above his head while the thug patted him down. Elliot was sitting at his usual table and smiled broadly at Todd. "Hello, kid."

"What do you want?"

"That's no way to talk to a friend. I wanted to let you know; you don't need to worry. You're not suspected. We're taking care of you."

"You're no friend, and I know what you've done to Vanessa. If the idiots you work for hadn't of got greedy, the SEC would've been none the wiser. Why did you frame her? They would've never traced the leaks to me."

"Jeez, you're not very grateful. We did it to protect you. We just didn't want to run the risk that you might get caught. We were looking after you."

"Liar! You wanted to make sure I'd be around to help you in the future. You've put a good person in jail. I feel sick."

"Not that sick that you'd exchange places with her, though." Elliot grinned. "I just wanted to remind you to keep your head down. There's nothing you can do to help the girl. I know you feel guilty but don't do anything stupid. That way you and your precious parents will stay healthy."

"The partner I report to knows it wasn't Vanessa. He spent the afternoon questioning the employees who report to her. It's only a matter of time before he gets to me. Oh, and he's briefed a firm of private investigators."

"From what I hear he's not going to be a partner for much longer." Elliot sneered. "The only way he can find anything out is if you do something stupid. When he or his gumshoes question you, just make sure you say nothing. He hasn't got a clue. Remember, relieving your conscience will put your parents in a coffin. That's guaranteed."

"If that's all you wanted to see me about, I'm out of here," Todd said. "I don't like the stench."

Todd sat in the cab on the way back to his apartment racked with shame. He couldn't stop thinking about Vanessa. Was she in a cell by herself or were there twenty other women with her as was so often depicted in *Law & Order?* How was she being treated? Was she distressed? How was her family coping? It was so unfair. Todd was no longer worried about himself and had an overwhelming desire to confess and free Vanessa. Only his concern for his parents and the image of what had happened to Giovani stopped him.

Chapter 29

Devlin Cooper had been dreading this day. At 6:30 A.M. his prepaid cell phone rang, and a menacing, ethnic voice said, "You'll either have the Bulldogs or the Devils in the second week of the playoffs. You know what you have to do."

"I told you, I can't. Not in the playoffs. It's too obvious. Too many people will know."

"And I told you what to do last time we talked. You just have to take a bigger beating. You're a tough guy. You can handle it."

"You don't understand the game," Cooper said. "My ribs got broken against the Pirates, but I played on. What happens if I get sacked and break an arm or leg? Have you thought about that?"

There was a long pause. "No, I haven't, smartass. Why don't you tell me what happens?"

"They carry me off and replacement quarterback Jeff Sweeny will replace me. He played while my ribs were healing. The Cougars didn't lose a game. If I get seriously hurt, and Sweeny replaces me, the Cougars will still win."

There was a longer pause. "I'll get back to you."

Cooper put the cell phone back in his pocket and sighed. He'd lost twelve pounds, wasn't sleeping and was irritable. He had no patience left. He was playing poorly, and Sweeny was putting huge pressure on him. His family still hadn't forgiven him for the tantrum he had thrown at the barbecue. Worst of all, Coach Tom Deacon had told him that he knew something was wrong, and he should share his problem.

Well, it's like this, coach, I was fucking your wife, and some low-life filmed me and now I'm being blackmailed.

Cooper felt himself start to color. Tom Deacon had been like a father to him and didn't deserve thoughts like that. He sat on the edge of his bed, his head between his knees and wept. What was he going to do? There was no way out. He desperately needed a drink.

It took less than five minutes for the judge to dismiss Vanessa Hodge's lawyers' appeal against the five million dollar bail. They had appealed to the judge, saying that it might be up to a year before the case got to trial and that it was unfair to imprison Vanessa. The judge responded by saying he was very busy with more than a hundred cases on his docket and that he hadn't imprisoned her. It wasn't his problem if she couldn't raise the bail.

Todd Hansen had had a dreadful weekend and had been unable to block Vanessa from his mind. He had awoken from a restless sleep on Monday morning praying that the judge would reduce her bail to a manageable sum. When he heard that Vanessa had been taken back to the cells at Richter's, he had gone to the bathroom and vomited again. Tears filled his eyes.

When Todd got back to his cubicle, Doug Lechte's PA was waiting for him. "Mr. Lechte wants to see you," she said.

"I'll be down in a few minutes," Todd said, knowing he'd need a few minutes to compose himself.

"Now! If it wasn't urgent, I wouldn't be here."

The door to Lechte's office was closed. "Does he have someone with him?" Todd asked.

"No, go in."

Lechte's shirt was rolled up to the elbows; his collar was undone, and the knot in his tie sat a few inches below it. His eyes were red, and it didn't look like he had slept. There were no smiles or greetings, and he just nodded to a chair. "I was at the Giants/Cowboys game a few weeks back with Max Lustig. He told me that I wasn't paying you enough because he saw you coming out of a pawn shop in Chinatown."

"I–I–"

Lechte held his hand up. "I'm not finished. Max said it could've been worse because it's a front for an illegal betting parlor. He said he couldn't think of a worse combination than an accountant and a betting parlor. I laughed and told him he'd made a mistake. Max got a little feisty with me and said that there was nothing wrong with his eyes. I was sure he was wrong, but I didn't argue and just forgot about it. It was you, wasn't it?"

"Yes, but–"

Again Lechte raised his hand. His eyes were slits, his face was red, his lips compressed and he was flexing his meaty forearms. "You weren't at the pawn shop. You were at the betting parlor, and when you walked out, you were in the hole for more than half a million dollars."

"How-how do you know?"

"The investigators I'm using have some of New York's former finest on their payroll. They can be very persuasive. It was you, wasn't it, Todd? It was you who leaked those results. How could you let Vanessa take the fall?" Lechte asked in a menacing whisper.

Todd was drained. His face was stark white, and he was trembling. "I-I had to," he said. "They said they'd kill my parents."

"They were bluffing," Lechte said.

"No, no, I saw them kill someone." Todd gulped.

"Why don't you tell me about your involvement? Don't leave anything out."

Half an hour later Todd was exhausted but felt the best he had in months.

"You should have come to me when you needed the money," Lechte said shaking his head. "You're going to go to prison. I'm going to call the SEC investigator, Aaron Lord. He can take your confession, and we can free Vanessa."

"I-I-I'm sorry, I can't confess. You can tell Lord what you've discovered. That should be more than enough to free Vanessa, but I can't admit anything. I can't breathe a word. They'll kill my parents."

"They'll already know that we're on to you. That little weasel at the betting parlor will have tipped them off. Let's get Aaron Lord to come in," Lechte said, "three heads are better than one, and he might have some ideas."

Lord listened in silence as Todd repeated his story and after he was finished said, "You're going to jail for a long, long time."

"I told him that," Lechte said.

"Tell me about Elliot, Ferguson and Fraser again," Lord said.

After Todd had finished, Lord asked, "Did they ever mention anyone else? Did they say who their bosses were?"

"No," Todd replied.

"They set you up from the start," Lord said. "They're just lackeys, and the guy from the betting parlor is probably in with them. The people they work for are very smart. I'd give my eyeteeth to know who they are. What was Giovani's surname?"

"They never said."

"Think," Lord said, "they must have said something."

"No, no, nothing. Wait! When Elliot saw him, he called him the fucking stockbroker."

"Good, good. Anything else you can remember. Scars, birthmarks, limps…anything different?"

"Yes," Todd said, "tiny tattoos on the inside of his wrists. Dollar bills."

Lechte hadn't said anything for a few minutes. "Aaron, Todd might be able to give you the big fish you're after. Maybe you could cut him a deal."

"No," Todd said, "you can charge me but I'm not confessing, and I can't help you. If my mom or dad get killed because of me, I'll never be able to live with myself."

"What type of deal?" Lord asked.

"Mutually beneficial of course." Lechte smiled grimly.

Karen Deacon's text message had been short. *Coffee shop tomorrow. Same time as last.*

Cooper was ten minutes early and hidden behind a copy of *USA Today* when he heard, "Knock, knock," and looked up to see Karen.

"Hi." He smiled. "I've ordered. I told the waiter to bring the coffees as soon as my friend arrived."

"My friend. Oh, wouldn't that be wonderful if it was true," Karen said. "Devlin, I haven't been able to stop thinking about our situation. I'm leaving Tom. I don't want to, but I don't have a choice."

"I don't understand. You said you were going to stay. You said that you were too old to move in with me."

Karen gave a feeble laugh. "Devlin, didn't I teach you anything? No woman would ever say she was too old. I said you were too young. There is a huge difference. Oh, and I'm not looking to move in with you."

"Why, then?"

"It's only a matter of time before that CD goes public. It might be six months, it might be five years, it might even be ten but in the end the whole world's going to see it. I can't be sharing a bed with Tom when that happens. He doesn't deserve that. I thought about leaving the kids with him, but I can't. I love them too much. I'm selfish."

"I don't know what to say."

"You need to think about your own circumstances. You're going to take some terrible beatings, and if you get exposed, you'll never play again. Worse, you'll almost certainly go to jail."

"Don't think I haven't thought about it. It sounds like you're telling me not to tank. You know what that will mean."

"I do. I think we're both just delaying the inevitable."

"I'm sorry. I still don't understand. It's going to be far worse for you. Your kids are going to go through hell. Why did you feel the need to tell me that you're leaving Tom?"

"Oh, Devlin, you're so young," Karen said, putting her hand on his forearm. "You said so long as you did what they told you to, they'd honor their word. They won't! That's what I needed to tell you. Think about it. It might be better if you tell them to go to hell now, rather than ruining the rest of your life."

"You're leaving Tom to give me that option."

"That sounds very noble, but I'm not just doing it for you. It's better for everyone. I'm going now. I don't think we should meet again."

After Karen had gone, Devlin pushed his empty cup from hand to hand. His mind was made up. He couldn't stand the thought of seeing his family dishonored.

Chapter 30

After four nights in Richter's, Vanessa Hodge was freed on Tuesday morning when the ADA dropped all charges against her. She looked tired and drawn as her jubilant family hugged and kissed her. She saw Doug Lechte standing on the outskirts and pushed her way toward him.

"Thank you," she said, fighting back tears. "Thank you for believing in me. How-how did you get me out?"

"It's a long story," he said. "I'll tell you when we have more time. Right now, you should be with your family. Like you, they've been through hell."

"Yes, yes," she said, disentangling her arms from around Lechte's waist. "Will I come in tomorrow?"

"Next Monday will be okay. You have to put your apartment back together, and I know your family wants to spoil you. It'd be nice if you let them."

"You seem to be always convening emergency partners' meetings, Doug," Cromwell said. "Out of the fat and into the frying pan I'd say."

"My fellow partners," Lechte said, ignoring Cromwell's comments. "Most of you will know about Vanessa Hodge's release from Richter's this morning. All charges against her were dropped."

"Yes," Cromwell said, "and another member of Doug's team, Todd Hansen, has been charged with multiple insider trading offenses. They were working together on some assignments, and it wouldn't surprise me if they colluded."

Lechte sighed in exasperation. "The SEC and FBI have exonerated Vanessa and acknowledged that they should have believed her. She is innocent and what Phillip just said is errant rubbish."

"Hasn't Hansen been charged?" Cromwell asked.

"Yes, but I caution partners from making any judgment while this matter is before the courts. Many of you were prepared to convict Vanessa without any foundation. Let's not make the same mistake with Todd. I've told Vanessa to take the rest of the week off."

"Take the rest of the week off?" Cromwell said. "I'm not sure we should be re-employing her. After all, she was suspected by the SEC and FBI, and she now has a reputation that precedes her. Not a flattering one, I might add."

"You're a slimy piece of shit, Phillip," Lechte said, joining his hands together and flexing his forearms. "We're not re-employing her; she never left. More to the point, I'll be nominating Vanessa for admission to the partnership. Many of you still don't realize it, but she's smarter than anyone sitting around this table."

"Don't you talk to me that way!" Cromwell said. "And how dare you talk about nominating partners. After our meeting at the end of the month, you won't be a partner, so you'll hardly be in a position to nominate others."

"Drop it, Phillip," Sandra Bishop said, "you don't have the numbers. If we'd removed Doug because of the purported misdemeanors of Vanessa, where would we be now? Staring at a lawsuit and the unwanted publicity that goes with it."

"Hear, hear," chorused several other partners.

"You get to remain a partner for a little longer," Cromwell said. "When Hansen's convicted I'll be seeking your resignation."

Lechte grinned. "I've told Todd we'll pick up his legal fees."

"No, no," Cromwell shouted. "It's not our problem. If a manager or, dare I say, even a partner makes a major mistake or is guilty of an offense, then it's that person's problem. It's not up to the firm to pay their legal expenses or bail them out. The only legal costs that we should bear are those relating to protecting the firm. Let's have a show of hands. All those opposed to paying the legal expenses of Todd Hansen."

More than twenty hands went up.

Cromwell smiled smugly. "Let Mr. Hansen know he'll be paying his own legal expenses."

"And you call yourself a Christian." Lechte sneered.

At the instruction of the SEC and FBI, the assistant district attorney did no more than make a show of opposing bail for Todd Hansen, which was set at a generous five hundred thousand. Doug Lechte had no problem arranging bail through a bondsman.

It had taken all of Aaron Lord's persuasive powers to convince the FBI and Chas Grinich that there was merit to Doug Lechte's plan. Grinich studied Todd closely as the young accountant recounted everything that had occurred from his gambling until Jack Elliot had bought his debt from the betting parlor. Grinich didn't like handling crooks with kid gloves but found himself feeling sorry for Todd. "Tell me again how they killed Giovani?"

"They executed him. Ferguson made him kneel down in front of the car and put two bullets into his head."

"Did you see any blood?"

"No, no. I was in the car and then I vomited, but I know what I saw. They even had a truck equipped with a water pump to wash away the blood. Why do you keep asking the same questions?"

"We've identified Ferguson and Fraser from the identikits that you helped us put together. They're con men. They're not heavies, thugs or killers. They'd run from anything involving violence."

"What? What are you saying?"

"We think they conned you." Grinich grinned. "We're still looking for Giovani, but his family isn't being very helpful. You know they never even reported that he was missing. Don't you think that's strange?"

"I know what I saw," Todd said defiantly.

"No, you saw what they wanted you to see. I don't think Giovani was in that coffee shop by accident. I think it was a setup."

"But why? Why would they do that?"

"Why? Why are you frightened about what might happen to your family? They wanted to scare you from doing anything. They did a good job."

"What did Elliot's identikit reveal?" Todd asked.

"Nothing. He appears to be clean," Grinich said. "We've got you on CCTV going to the coffee shop in downtown Manhattan, but we've got nothing on him. Likewise, the room at the Hyatt was booked by Ferguson and in the footage we have of Elliot, he's wearing a cap that covers his upper face and a scarf that covers his lower. Mr. Elliot is a very careful man."

"You've got nothing," Todd said.

"We've got a start," Grinich said. "You're a betting man, Todd. I'll bet you by the time we've finished checking Giovani's parents' and siblings' phone records, we'll find him alive and well."

"I was tricked." Todd grimaced. "They weren't dangerous."

"Yeah, you were tricked all right, and Ferguson and Fraser aren't dangerous but that's not to say Elliot's not," Grinich said. "Don't beat yourself up. It's too late now. We'll know a lot more by the time you get out of jail."

Dirk Vaughan had taken a severe tongue lashing from Borchard, and when he called Cooper, he repeated what his boss had said. "Don't bullshit, Cooper! You can fake it without getting badly hurt. Release the ball as soon as you get hit."

"You still don't understand. If I do, my offensive line won't protect me. They'll feed me to the opposition. I'll get killed, and when they replace me with Sweeny, you're gonna lose your money. Do you want to take that risk?"

"Crap! You can disguise it, so no one knows. If you don't, we might just have to release the CD. Do you want to take that risk?"

"No, no," Cooper muttered.

"Good, I'm glad we have an understanding," Vaughan said, ending the call.

It was midnight when Devlin Cooper reversed the canary yellow Lamborghini out onto the street. It was only a leisurely half hour drive to I-290, and he drove slowly. The last thing he wanted was to be caught speeding before he reached his destination. He felt sick. He hadn't had a drink all day and prayed for courage. He took a ramp off I-290 and drove along the secluded, heavily treed Dalton Road. The pot–holed road was in a state of disrepair, and its shoulders were crumbling. As a boy, he had camped in the area with his family and knew it well. He unclipped his seatbelt, and the Lamborghini's electronics screamed at him to put it back on.

The engine roared as Devlin pressed the accelerator to the floor, and he moved the paddle shift out of neutral. He said a silent prayer and begged for forgiveness. In less than seven seconds, the Lamborghini was traveling at more than hundred miles per hour. At fifteen seconds, the speedometer went through one hundred and fifty. At twenty seconds, Devlin closed his eyes and took his hands off the wheel. The car flew off the road at nearly two hundred miles per hour plunging ten feet before cutting a swathe through the trees. Airbags deployed when the Lamborghini struck its first small tree, and it plowed on another eighty yards before disintegrating into the trunk of a massive old oak tree.

It was late afternoon the following day when a group of trekkers stumbled on the mangled wreck of the Lamborghini. There was no sign of the driver. The trekkers didn't need CSI to know that no one could've survived and immediately called Chicago PD. Even in Chicago, Lamborghinis weren't written off every day, and after the police had run its license plates, the matter took on a sense of urgency. Three blue and whites and ten officers converged on the scene of the accident.

The wreckage was just visible from the road, and one of the policemen said, "You can see where it veered off the road, but it's strange."

"How so?" His offsider asked.

"There are no skid marks. Whoever was driving didn't brake. I don't get it."

One of the airbags was still behind the steering wheel, but the others had exploded, ripped apart. The trekkers and police formed a line about forty yards long and methodically moved forward from the wreck. The area was dense with foliage and progress was slow. Dusk was falling, and the police shone their flashlights on the ground as they slowly advanced. More than an hour had elapsed, and the searchers pushed aside waist-high foliage as the retraced their steps. They were about fifty yards from the wreck when one of the trekkers screamed, "I've found something."

The jeans and black sweater were barely visible under the dense brush. Two of the policemen pulled back the shrubbery while another crawled under in on his hands and knees. A few minutes later he shouted, "It's him. It's Devlin Cooper."

His face had a few small cuts, but he was virtually unmarked. He was, however, dead, very dead.

That night, news of the tragedy was carried by all of Chicago's television and radio stations. The police had determined that the accident had taken place between 12:30 A.M. and 1 A.M. and Cooper's Rolex had stopped at exactly 12:46 A.M. While Chicago and the nation mourned, hard-nosed reporters were already asking what was Cooper doing out on the secluded Dalton Road at that hour? Why was he driving at more than one and hundred and fifty miles an hour on an unsafe road? And most intriguingly why didn't he brake?

Borchard was furious and ranted at Vaughan. "I told you not to push him to suicide. You put too much pressure on him. You've cost me two hundred million."

"It was your idea to force him into tanking in the playoffs. I told you he was stressed, and you said I was weak," Vaughan retorted.

"Don't tell me it was my fault," Borchard shouted. "You mishandled him. I should've done it myself. Next time I will."

Vaughan didn't respond. His face disclosed nothing, but he was seething. He wasn't scared of Borchard and never had been. If Borchard didn't watch out, he'd find himself in the same condition as Cooper.

Karen Deacon cried and cried as grief completely enveloped her. Then she cried again in anger. She knew what had happened and why Devlin had taken his life. She regained some control and thought about when he had called her *noble*. Noble? *I seduced a boy fourteen years my junior. Real noble!* She wept again and wished that their affair had never occurred.

She also knew that the blackmailers would know what had happened and that with Devlin gone, they would be coming for her.

Chapter 31

As soon as news of Devlin Cooper's death broke, Dermott Becker hastily convened a meeting of the board of Vulture Inc. The tension and anger in the room were palpable and directed at one man, Brock Borchard, who was on time for once.

"What happened to Cooper, Brock?" Becker asked.

"It looks like suicide."

"Tell us something we don't know," Arthur Ridgeway said. "What did you do that drove him over the edge? You couldn't have been stupid enough to tell him to tank in the playoffs. Tell me you didn't."

Borchard glowered. No one spoke to him like that, least wise not some shit kicking, crooked accountant. He was about to respond when Lydia Coe said, "We told you at the last meeting, one game per season, and we'd pull in nearly two hundred million. What did you do?"

Borchard crossed his arms over his chest. "Do ya want your ten cent's worth, Harry?" he asked. "Or I can answer without one of youse buttin' in?"

"Go for it, Brock. I've got no hassles with you," O'Brien replied.

"I've got no idea why he killed himself. I didn't apply any pressure to get him to throw another game and had I, it wouldn't have been the playoffs," Borchard said.

"Is that right?" Ridgeway smirked. "I wish I could believe you."

"Are you calling me a liar?" Borchard asked, his eyes narrowed.

"No, he's not," Becker said. "We're all just annoyed that we only got one game out of him. One payoff. You must feel the same, Brock."

"One payoff? You seem to have forgotten there are two people on that CD and one of them, Karen Deacon, is still alive. We called and let her know the facts of life. We told her she could have the CD and all the copies for five million. After she pays, I've got a buyer for the CD. He's offered five mil but I think I can double that."

"You're blackmailing her," Lydia Coe gasped.

"I don't like it," Becker said. "Releasing that CD while he was alive is one thing. Cooper's near a saint now, and if it gets released, there'll be those who'll move heaven and earth looking for loose ends to find out where it came from. What did the woman say?"

"She was nervous but feisty. She said she'd go to the police and told my man he could go to hell, but it was an opportune call. She said that she knew it was that sleazy little bastard at the Astor who'd videoed them. He was the only link to us."

"Was?" Lydia asked.

"Yes," Borchard said, "he got killed in a nasty hit and run. Police located the car, but it was stolen. They're at a dead end with their investigation."

"You had him hit," Ridgeway said.

"I didn't have anything to do with it," Borchard replied. "It was an accident."

"There'll be plenty of time to see what you can get out of the woman after the frenzy about Cooper has blown over. She'll be distraught and emotional, so don't push her into doing anything stupid like going to the police. Ease up for now," Becker said. "And, Brock, under no circumstances are you to sell that CD. We threaten, we blackmail, and we intimidate, but we never draw unnecessary attention to ourselves. You don't know who the clerk at the Astor spoke to. You have no idea how many loose ends there are. You release that CD and someone will talk; it will lead to you, and then to us."

"What happened to the financial controller?" Lydia asked.

"Jeez. You're not blaming me for that too," Borchard said. "He got drunk and fell under a train. End of story."

"The killing has to stop. We can't condone it," Arthur Ridgeway said.

"So what happened to Giovani? Euthanasia?" Borchard sneered. "Talking about pay-offs, what happened with the auditor and your insider trading scam, Dermott?"

"I don't know. Somehow the SEC found out. Maybe the CFD positions we took were too large, and the providers laid them off on the NYSE. What's important is that we proved the model worked, and we can do it again. Next time we'll aim at one of the big four."

"What are ya gonna do about the auditor?" Borchard asked.

"Nothing! Why should we? I hear that he's going to get at least five years. He's terrified that his parents will be killed if he says anything. He won't breathe a word to the SEC or FBI. See, Brock, you don't need to follow through if the intimidation is potent. Jack Elliot's very convincing," Becker replied.

"Yeah, yeah," Borchard said, loudly cracking his knuckles. "But the risk will always be there. Once he's in prison, we'll be able to fix that."

"What's that mean?" Ridgeway asked.

"Accidents have a way of happening in prisons." Borchard grimaced.

"He's no threat to us," Becker said. "I don't want him harmed."

"Yes," Lydia Coe agreed, "let's not have another Devlin Cooper, Brock."

"We've had a few setbacks," Becker said, "so let's lie low for a while. Before I close, the meeting does anyone have anything else they'd like to raise?"

"Yeah, the Prosser meat contact, the largest single meat cartage contract in the country for hanging and packaged meat is ours for the taking," Borchard said. "I've got a deal with the Consolidated Meat Workers Union where we tender at less than cost. Two months later the union takes their drivers and meatpackers out on strike for higher wages and better conditions. After a brief battle, we cave in and in return the union helps us negotiate new and profitable cartage rates. It's a sweet deal."

"Sounds good," Ridgeway said, getting up from his chair. "You don't need our approval for a deal like that. Just get it done."

"Hold on," Becker said, "who's got the existing contract?"

"Countywide Frozen Meats." Borchard grinned.

"We'll pass," Becker said, "we've got enough trouble without pouring oil on flames. Countrywide is one of Max Lustig's companies, and we don't want to go head to head with him."

"Sorry, Dermott," Ridgeway said, "I should have asked the same question. Forget it, Brock."

"Fuck! What is it with this guy? He's not Meyer Lansky or Bugsy Siegel." Borchard sneered.

BOOK 3

Chapter 32

Six months had elapsed since Todd Hansen's arraignment, but his trial was mercifully quick. Found guilty of six counts of insider trading, Todd hung his head and waited for Judge Dessau to pronounce her sentence.

"It is critical that the financial markets are free of the type of secret manipulation in which you engaged. You have been totally uncooperative, Mr. Hansen. You were prepared to commit crimes that you thought would go undetected. Worse, when they were, you were willing to let a fellow employee spend four nights in jail, and no doubt would have been happy had she been charged and convicted. You have failed to reveal who you leaked the sensitive information to. You have been evasive, and, quite frankly, much of your evidence was not believable. Had you confessed to your crimes or incriminated those who were involved with you, I may have been more lenient. As it is, you leave me no room for leniency. When a person in a position of trust breaches that trust, violates the law and commits financial crimes, a significant prison term is warranted. Please rise, Mr. Hansen," Judge Dessau ordered.

Todd got to his feet in a daze. He hadn't expected such a severe lambasting. He glanced around the court and saw Vanessa sitting next to Doug Lechte. She had been sympathetic and smiled encouragingly. She knew that he had not come forward because he feared for his parent's lives and she displayed no malice toward him. His mother and father were a few rows further back. His mother had been crying, but his father was stoic, jaw thrust out and eyes fixed on the judge. There had been no sympathy from him and nor would there be.

"You come from a highly respected family and have been given every opportunity in life," Judge Dessau said. "Your employer said you showed great promise. You are intelligent and talented. It is a shame that you chose to use that talent in the pursuit of crime that was no doubt greed based. I hope that when you get out of prison you will realize the promise shown earlier in your career. However, because of your lack of cooperation and for the other reasons stated I sentence you to nine years in Castlebrough Penitentiary being eighteen months on each of the six charges."

Todd's mother gasped loudly, and his sister started to sob. Lechte caught Todd's eye and winked.

After the judge had left the courtroom, two court officers led Todd away. He displayed no emotion, but his innards were churning.

Lechte was angry and herded Grinich and Lord into a small room next to the courtroom. "You said you could protect him," he said. "Christ, she's put him in Castlebrough. How are you going to protect him in there?"

"We've got people who'll look after him," Grinich replied.

"Bullshit! Castlebrough's the toughest and worst prison in the state. White collar criminals never get sent there. What was the judge thinking? You can't protect him."

"We're as upset as you," Lord said. "We just never thought Castlebrough. We could've looked after him just about anywhere else, but Castlebrough…"

"Chas," Lechte said staring at the FBI man, "you're going to want him to help you in a few months' time. He's going to be no good to you dead or so fucked up in the head that he can't string two words together. What are you going to do?"

Grinich looked at Lord who was shaking his head. "I've got guards that can keep an eye on him, but I can't guarantee his safety."

"But that was part of the deal," Lechte shouted. "He would've never gone along with you without that guarantee."

"Doug, with respect, he was going to prison, deal or no deal," Lord said. "If he pulls this off, he'll do four months of a nine-year sentence, so don't make out that the benefit's all ours."

"Yeah, and he'll be risking his life. You want the big boys? He can give them to you, but only if he's capable of walking and thinking. You have to do something. Get him into a less violent prison."

"I don't know whether we can," Grinich said, "and even if we could, it'll take time."

"Fuck!" Lechte yelled. "We don't have time. He could be dead or out of his mind in a week." Then he paused. "The FBI and SEC can't look after him, but I might have a way."

"What are you up to?" Lord asked.

"You're an accountant," Grinich said. "What can you do? Stay with what you know. Don't get into something over your head."

"I know someone, and unlike you, he has real power," Lechte said pushing the door open. "I have to go."

Twenty minutes later Lechte was in his office calling Max Lustig. The transport tycoon listened patiently as Lechte related the court's decision and its ramifications.

"He's a good kid, Doug. I like him. He did a very thorough job with that business we bought in New Jersey. I understand your fears about what might happen to him in Castlebrough. It's full of murderers, rapists, degenerates and sickos. What would you like me to do?"

"Can you get someone to look after him? He's young and innocent. There are going to be plenty of nutcases in there who'll want a piece of him. I'm worried that by the time he gets out, that's if he's still alive, he'll be emotionally wrecked. Can you help him?"

There was a long pause.

"Max, Max, are you there?"

"Yeah, I can help him. I was just wondering who to use. If you want his safety guaranteed, we'll have to use the services of Frank Arturo."

"The mob boss?"

"Yeah."

"How do you know him, Max?"

Lustig laughed. "That's something you don't need to know. Consider the kid safe, though. He'll be the second most powerful inmate in Castlebrough after Arturo. Word travels quickly, and it won't take long for the other cons to find out."

"How much do I owe you?"

"It's a favor," Lustig replied. "You'll owe me one."

"I'd rather pay."

"Doug, you insult me. You think I'm going to ask you to do something illegal in the future. I'd never do it. I have too much respect for you, and I've got more than enough of those favors stored up."

"Sorry. Do you know who was pulling Todd's strings?"

"No, but if you tell me everything the FBI and SEC have, I'll soon find out."

"I can't, Max. I swore I wouldn't breathe a word. They'll make it worse for Todd if I do."

"I understand. Give me a call if there's anything else I can do."

At 5 P.M. Todd was shackled with twenty other prisoners for the bus trip to Castlebrough. He'd known this day would eventually come, but nothing could have prepared him for the misery he was now experiencing. Talking was forbidden, and half a dozen guards paced up and down the bus's aisle smacking truncheons into their hands. Anyone talking was struck with force and Todd was petrified. The old guy next to him whispered, "First time, kid?"

Todd was too scared to reply.

"Don't worry, you'll get used to it. How long are you in for?"

Todd felt the blow striking the old guy's head and recoiled. "No talking," the guard shouted.

Two hours later, out of the darkness, a massive, sinister structure appeared lit up like the Atlantic City boardwalk on a hot summer night. Razor wire ran across the top of the towering bluestone walls of the ninety-year-old Castlebrough Penitentiary. The bus stopped at heavy steel doors which slowly opened to a vacant enclosure. There was a second wall thirty yards further on with an electrified grid on top it. The bus crept toward a steel roller door that didn't start to open until the doors behind it closed. The prisoners, still manacled, were led from the bus out into a small enclosed yard, overlooked by cells of the three level prison. Prisoners in the cells yelled and screamed insults at the new inmates.

The deputy warden told them how they would be processed and read the prison rules. The main one being that prisoners were to address guards as *Sir* and only speak when spoken to. One of the prisoners raised his hand, "Sir."

The crack of truncheon on skull bone was like a bullet shot, and the prisoner slumped to the concrete, blood trickling from his forehead.

Ten minutes later, Todd was in a shower room with the other prisoners while the guards sprayed high-pressure hoses on them. Then they were doused with a delousing mix from large plastic containers. Rough towels were hanging on the hooks behind the guards, and prisoners were given a brief time to dry themselves.

The prisoners were then marched naked to the adjoining room where neatly packaged black and white striped coveralls, underwear, and black sneakers were handed to them. "You'll get dressed in your cells," one of the guards shouted. "Do not, I repeat, do not put your coveralls on now. Move it out."

Todd was a little slow to move, and a small, cruel looking guard hit him across the bare buttocks with his truncheon. The sting was excruciating, and Todd gulped and fought back tears. He wasn't sure he could even walk, and the guard raised his truncheon again but before he could swing it another guard grabbed his arm and whispered something. The smaller guard's face visibly changed, and he said to Todd, "I'm sorry, I didn't mean to hit you that hard. I'll give you a few minutes to recover."

A few of the other prisoners glanced at Todd, puzzled looks on their faces.

The guards led the new inmates past overcrowded cells on the first level. Todd could barely think, but he couldn't block the yells out. "Your ass is mine, white boy," a prisoner shouted and Todd looked up to see a huge, toothless African American grinning at him. He was in a tiny cell with five other inmates.

By the time they climbed the stairs to the second level, there were only eight new inmates left in the group. Todd tried to block out the lewd comments, but he was sick with fear. He'd read enough books and seen enough movies to know that prison sickos preyed on young men. The cells on the second level were also overcrowded, and Todd knew what was going to happen once he was locked up. He resolved to fight to his last breath reckoning that death was better than the alternative.

Chapter 33

Todd was the only inmate who hadn't been shoved in a cell when the two remaining guards pushed him toward the stairs to the third level. He was confused. Why was he the only new inmate being placed in a cell on the third level? The cells were no larger than those on the other two levels but slightly less crowded. The guards led Todd along a walkway until they got to two large cells. The first one looked like it had been two cells converted into one and the adjoining cell comprised three cells with the walls removed. There was one man in the larger cell sitting in a chair watching television. Todd was more confused than ever and wondered whether he was hallucinating. The other cell also only had one prisoner. He was lying on a bunk, a cigarette hanging out of his mouth, reading a newspaper. The guards opened the door and pushed Todd in.

Todd stood in the cell trying to use the bundle of coveralls to cover himself. He didn't know what was going on but whatever it was he didn't like it. The man on the bunk looked over the top of his newspaper and said, "I'm Tony Lombardi, Todd. Welcome to Castlebrough. You've got nothing to worry about. That's your bunk over there. Why don't you get dressed? You look like you're freezing."

"How do you know my name?"

"You'd be surprised what I know. When you've settled in, we'll have a little talk."

There were three blankets on the bunk and while Todd didn't know it, that was two more than most inmates got. He hastily pulled the coveralls and sneakers on while Lombardi remained immersed in his newspaper. Todd sat on the end of the bunk and looked around the cell. It had a sink, a stainless steel toilet, and two open metal cabinets positioned next to the bunks. Lombardi's contained newspapers, books and a radio. The cell was cold, and Todd felt wretched. Why had he bet so heavily? Why had he wasted his life trying to make a quick buck? Why had he shamed his family? He hadn't eaten since midday, but food was the last thing on his mind. He felt nauseous, and a level of depression that he'd never experienced before threatened to engulf him.

Lombardi was sitting on his bunk looking at Todd, his sleeves rolled up. There was a cobra tattooed on each of his arms. He was about six foot, wiry with shoulder length black hair and a neatly trimmed mustache. "It's not that bad, kid," he said. "You could be in a cell of six, but someone pulled some mighty big strings to get you up here. You should think yourself lucky."

"I-I don't know any-anyone."

"Well someone knows you and is making sure you're being looked after," Lombardi said. "Have you heard of Frank Arturo?"

"Ye-yeah, he's the mob boss. What's he got to do with it?"

"Mr. Arturo runs the prison. Nothing happens without his say-so. Yeah, there are gangs in here. The Mexicans, the African-Americans, the Hispanics and of course us but there's only one boss. Mr. Arturo's in the adjoining cell."

"I don't understand why you're telling me this. I don't know him."

Lombardi grinned. "I didn't think you did, but you have a friend who knows him. Mr. Arturo has made it known that you're under his protection. I'm one of his captains. I've been commissioned to look after you."

The only person Todd could think it might be was Elliot. Maybe he was being looked after because he hadn't given Elliot up at his trial.

"That doesn't mean that some dumb fuck isn't going to try and hurt or maybe kill you. I'm guessing that someone will attack you in the mess hall or try to fuck you in the showers or maybe get to you in the yard," Lombardi said. "I was thirty when I got locked up. Luckily for you, I've got six months of a ten-year stretch to go. I've seen more than a dozen inmates killed."

Todd was stark white. "So even though Mr. Arturo's looking after me, I'm still not safe."

"You're safer than Fort Knox." Lombardi laughed. "The faster some stupid prick tries to get to you the better. Then we'll send a message to the other four thousand fuckers in here. It'll guarantee your safety and reinforce Mr. Arturo's authority, not that it needs reinforcing."

"I don't understand."

"You don't need to. Lights are out in fifteen minutes at ten o'clock. Breakfast's at 6:30 and I'll introduce you to some more friends who you can trust. Don't worry, you're in here eighteen hours a day and for the other six hours there'll always be someone nearby. Try and get a good night's sleep. Oh, and one last thing. Mr. Arturo might invite you to play chess or cards with him. Unless he says otherwise, you address him as Mr. Arturo and make damn sure you don't win."

Todd didn't sleep. How could he? There was crying and whimpering all through the night accompanied by yelling from inmates angry that they couldn't sleep. Then there was the sound of metal scraping across steel bars. Guards added to the cacophony when they walked the floors shouting for silence. For a few minutes after there was quiet, but it didn't last. Todd looked at Lombardi, and he was sleeping like a baby.

Phillip Cromwell knew what day the court would bring down judgment on Todd, and had convened a partners' meeting five weeks earlier. There was only one item on the agenda. The removal of Douglas Lechte as a partner of the firm. Cromwell rose and put a measured argument to the partners why Lechte should go. He did not claim that Lechte had been dishonest, but that he had been negligent, and as a result of such negligence, the firm had been subject to unwanted and unsavory attention from the media. Lechte had failed to adequately supervise his direct report, Todd Hansen, who had brought the firm into disrepute by his criminal actions. Cromwell thumped the desk, saying that if Lechte had any honor, he would've fallen on his sword and resigned, and that it was reprehensible that he had not. He finished by asking the partners to use their powers under the deed of partnership to remove Lechte. He reminded them that to carry the motion, a two-thirds majority of those present and voting was required.

Doug Lechte got slowly to his feet. "My fellow partners," he said. "There is some truth in what Phillip says. However, can any of you tell me what your direct reports are doing right now? Can you be positive that their work is flawless and will not lead to litigation? Are each and every one of you prepared to accept responsibility for all of the actions of those responsible to you? I ask you–"

"Of course we have to take responsibility for those who report to us," Cromwell interrupted. "The prestige this firm enjoys is because we have managed to remain out of the eye of the media. Our clients like the privacy that we afford them. We simply cannot and should not tolerate anyone or anything that results in adverse publicity for the firm. If you had any honor, Doug, you'd resign."

"Please refrain from interrupting me again," Lechte said, staring angrily at Cromwell. "I was about to say that that provision of the partnership deed has not been exercised in more than one hundred years. I'm asking you not to exercise it now. It's time for unity, and no good can come from dividing the firm. Please, I implore you, vote this motion down."

Both men had lobbied furiously in the weeks leading up to the meeting, and Lechte knew that the vote was going to be very close. The last thing he wanted to do was to exercise his own vote to save himself.

"Enough, enough," Cromwell said. "By a show of hands, all those in favor of the motion."

Lechte did a quick count. There were twenty-five in favor. If one of the remaining partners abstained from voting, he was out.

"All those against," Cromwell said.

Half a dozen hands went up immediately, and others slowly followed until the count was eleven.

"The motion is carry–"

"Not so fast, Phillip. I'm torn by the harm Todd Hansen has caused and my loyalty to Doug. I came to this meeting hoping I wouldn't have to vote," Sandra Bishop said, "but now I have no choice. I cannot in all conscience support the motion."

"It makes no difference," Cromwell said. "There's still a two-thirds majority in favor."

"No, there's not," Lechte said, raising his hand.

Cromwell was purple with rage. "You-you would use your vote to save yourself when there are twenty-five partners sitting in this room who don't want you. Have you no pride? Resign and salvage what little honor you have left."

"I'm staying, Phillip," Lechte said, standing and picking up his papers.

Todd's first morning in Castlebrough saw him lining up for breakfast in the mess hall with Lombardi directly behind him and an associate of Lombardi in front of him. Breakfast was oatmeal porridge, milk, two slices of bread, margarine, jam and orange juice. Two thousand inmates could be seated at ten-stool built-in tables, and there were two breakfast shifts. Mess halls are the most dangerous places in prisons and heavily armed prison guards patrolled the surrounding gantry walkways. The noise was deafening, and Todd could hardly hear himself think. Lombardi directed him to the middle of a table at the rear of the room and took the stool next to him.

"Todd," Lombardi said, "look around the table. You can trust these men. They'll be looking after you."

As Todd glanced at the swarthy group, some nodded or raised their hands while others ignored him. One thing struck Todd. They nearly all carried scars on their faces and arms.

"What table is Mr. Arturo at?" Todd asked.

There were a few sideways glances before Lombardi said, "Mr. Arturo eats in his cell. Occasionally he comes down here, but only when he wants to."

When they got back to their cell, Todd asked, "What are you in here for?"

"Manslaughter," Lombardi replied, "I was unlucky. I was persuading a member of another gang to get out of our territory with a baseball bat. I kneecapped him, and the jamook flatlined in the hospital. Seems he had a weak heart. How fucking unlucky can a guy get?"

"The guys you've got looking after me are a tough-looking bunch. The face of that guy sitting at the end of the table was a complete mess."

"Look at me," Lombardi said. "Do you see any scars?"

"No," Todd replied.

"Enzo let his guard down, and the stupid prick was glassed. There's nothing tough about scars, Todd. You want to be wary of the guys who caused them, not the ones bearing them. We've got three hours in the yard at nine o'clock. Stay near me."

"Don't they make us work?"

"There's a machine shop, laundry, library, and hospital. Maybe work for three hundred. Nah, we don't work."

Two days later Todd was in the communal shower with about fifty inmates. Lombardi was next to him. Two guards were on a gantry overlooking the showers. Another three guards were just inside the entrance. Todd heard a scream come from the showers furthest away from the entrance and saw a young, slim Hispanic man fighting to get away from three white guys. The guards at the entrance turned their backs and the ones on the gantry looked straight ahead. "Why isn't anyone helping him? Why aren't the guards stopping them?" Todd gasped.

One of the white guys pushed the Hispanic kid into the wall face first while the others tried to force his legs open. The biggest of the white guys was trying to shove his erect cock up the young man's ass. He was fighting and squirming when one of the others punched him in the head with all his force. The young man slumped forward unconscious, and the big white guy drove his penis deep into him.

"Fucking queers," Lombardi said. "They must've paid the guards to set the kid up. There's nothing you can't buy or get in here."

"The guards set it up?" Todd asked, open-mouthed.

"Yeah, let's get outta here. They're gonna gang bang the poor bastard."

"The three of them?"

"If he's real lucky it'll only be three. Come on, dry yourself off. It makes me sick to watch this shit. Fucking animals."

The Hispanic kid started to come around and screamed in agony as strong hands pinned him to the wall. There were now five sickos lined up waiting their turn.

"Why don't you stop them?" Todd asked.

"It's not my fight. Let's go."

Three of the guards remained while the other two marched the rest of the prisoners back to their cells.

Todd slumped on his bunk with his head in his hands and sobbed. Castlebrough had to be the worst place on the planet. "Tha-that could-could've be-been me," he managed to blurt out.

"No, it couldn't," Lombardi said. "I would've killed them before they got to you."

"How-how? You-you didn't have any weapons."

"I don't need weapons, but that's not the point. There's no way those guards would cross Mr. Arturo. After he got locked up, a deputy warden and two guards tried to bring him down a notch. They roughed him up so badly, they had to rush him to the prison hospital. In the following week, the deputy warden's wife and young child disappeared and haven't been seen since. One of the guards was run down in a hit and run, and the other one got bashed to within an inch of his life. The deputy warden supposedly took his own life with a bullet to the head. Mr. Arturo and the mob sent the prison administration a message. Like I told you, nothing happens in here unless he says it's okay. The guards know he's looking after you, and they're not stupid."

"But if it wasn't for him I'd be like that Hispanic boy?"

"Yeah, you would, and there's still stupid bastards who might try for a piece of you. I wish they would."

"I don't understand."

"There'll only ever be one try." Lombardi smirked.

The cell door opened, and a guard looked at Lombardi and said, "Tony, Mr. Arturo wants to see the kid."

Chapter 34

Todd was shocked. The man standing in front of him was fifty-ish, no more than 5' 6" and 140 pounds. *How can this guy be so feared? How come he's the mob boss?* The cell was warm, and a fifty-inch television with the sound muted was showing the Patriots versus Broncos. There was a chessboard set up on a table, a chair on either side of it.

"I understand you play chess," Arturo said.

"Yes, I do, Mr. Arturo."

"Are you a good player?"

"I was the champion of my college," Todd replied, carefully examining the small man. He had oily, black, thinning hair, sunken eyes, and a pockmarked face. *How did he ever get to be so powerful?*

"Let's play then," Arturo said through tightly pursed lips.

Todd was surprised by Arturo's skill and after three hours and four games of nearly silent chess the score was two games all. Todd could have won all four games but was cognizant of Lombardi's warning.

"You're a good player," Arturo said. "I hadn't lost a game for five years up until today. I've enjoyed your challenge, but we only have time for one more game."

"Thank you, Mr. Arturo. You too are a skilled player."

"Frank, call me Frank. We're going to have many sessions like this while you're my guest. If there is anything you want, anything, just tell Tony, and I'll make sure you have it. He mentioned that you're still worried about being attacked. Don't be! I'll have the man or men who try to harm you permanently looked after. Now, come on, let's see who Castlebrough's chess champion is."

Todd was relieved that Arturo seemed to like him, but his little speech, delivered without emotion or passion, had made Todd uncomfortable. Arturo had spoken about killing with the same dispassion that normal people talked about going out to lunch. Fifty minutes later Todd looked up and said, "Check." He had left one move for Arturo and knew that he was smart enough not to miss it.

Arturo stared at the board for what seemed like an eternity before he deftly moved his king and trapped Todd in the corner with a rook holding check and a knight securing mate."

"Good move. Well played," Todd said as he stood up.

"We must play again. Soon," Arturo said, his face still as impassive as it had been when they first met. "Thank you, Todd."

After four weeks of imprisonment, Todd had experienced no trouble in the showers or the yard. The prison population knew that he was being protected by the mob, and any attempt to harm him would result in fearful retribution. When the attack occurred, it was spontaneous in the mess hall. Todd was in line and had just been served his porridge and bread when he bumped into the guy who had led the rape of the Hispanic kid. The big mutt's tray crashed to the floor. Porridge and orange juice spilled all over the floor.

"You fucking idiot," he shouted and charged at Todd.

The big guy had moved no more than a yard when he seemed to freeze in slow motion, a blue plastic shank hanging out of his ear. It erupted in a bloody volcano, and he crashed to the ground. Whistles blew, and guards came from everywhere as prisoners scattered to their tables.

"Come on," Lombardi said, as he grabbed Todd's elbow and propelled him toward the table.

"You-you did-didn't have to do that."

"Do what? I didn't do anything," Lombardi said, taking a mouthful of bread spread with margarine and jam. "Eat up. Your porridge is getting cold."

"Is he… is he dead?"

"I fucking hope so." Lombardi smirked. "I've been waiting for this day. They know you're protected. Now they know what's gonna happen to 'em if they try and hurt you. Don't be upset, kid. I just guaranteed your safety and mine. If I let anything happen to Mr. Arturo's favorite inmate, I'd be dead. Fuck, I've known him for fifteen years, and I still don't get to call him Frank."

The guards were questioning prisoners at the tables closest to where the big guy was lying. Todd saw one of the guards take a towel and place it over his face. There was a lot of head shaking, and it was obvious the guards weren't getting very far.

"What'll you do if they find out it was you?"

Lombardi laughed. "They won't. You're the only one who saw anything, and you're not even sure what you saw."

Todd thought about it. Lombardi was right. The speed with which he had moved had been blinding, and Todd had seen nothing in his hand. It was only when the big guy had frozen that Todd had seen the shank protruding from his ear.

"Won't there be an investigation?"

"For a turd like him?" Lombardi said, and then paused. "Yeah, maybe. It won't go for long. Perhaps two days. The administration's not too worried about pricks like that. Just make sure you keep your mouth closed and don't breathe a word about what you saw."

"What I saw? I didn't see anything."

Lombardi grinned. "You're coming along nicely, kid. I'll make an associate out of you yet."

The grounds put forward by Todd's lawyers on appeal were hardly convincing. They did not seek to exonerate him or introduce new evidence but argued that CFDs over U.S. stocks traded in international markets did not come under the jurisdiction of the U.S. security laws. They claimed the judge had misinterpreted the law at the first trial and that this was grounds for a new trial. It was a spurious argument that the assistant district attorney opposed. Strangely, she did not register any disapproval or disappointment when the judge ruled in Todd's favor.

The morning of his release Todd had a visitor claiming to be one of his lawyers.

"You're looking surprisingly well, Todd," Aaron Lord said.

"Yeah, no thanks to you."

"I told you, we never anticipated the judge putting you in here. Anyhow, that's water under the bridge. If you don't want to do another eight years, you know what you have to do."

"Yeah, and in case I forgot you came to remind me."

"You'd do well to get rid of the chip on your shoulder. You got yourself into this mess. No one else is to blame. Maybe you ought to think about that."

"Yeah, yeah."

"You'll be pleased to know that we located a suntanned Giovani alive and well in Hawaii," Lord said.

"So he did trick me and was in with them. I never had to worry about my parents being killed. I feel like such a fool. Jack Elliot played me for a chump."

"Yeah, it's true Elliot played you for a sucker, but you were right to be concerned."

"I don't understand?"

"Giovani was working for a firm of stockbrokers that handled initial public offerings for small companies and raised seed capital for start-ups. He got involved with Elliot and provided him with some highly confidential information. Elliot paid him a million for the info and invested heavily in the biotech companies. They were all failures, and Elliot lost millions."

"Shit. What did he do?"

"Needless to say he wasn't very happy but Giovani had blown his million in the same biotech companies, so Elliot knew he'd hadn't been conned. He read the riot act to Giovani and tried to get the million back to no avail. After that, they had no contact for several months."

"Get to the point," Todd said.

"Settle down. It gets interesting. Elliot contacted Giovani and told him that if he didn't get out of New York, he was dead. It seems that one of Elliot's bosses is particularly violent and doesn't like losing millions. That's when Elliot came up with the idea of apparently killing Giovani in front of you. He could then tell this violent individual that Giovani was dead and that you, having witnessed his murder, were scared shitless. Worked well, didn't it? Giovani was on a plane to Hawaii the following day, and you agreed to do what Elliot wanted."

"Who are Elliot's bosses?"

"We still don't know," Lord replied

"Are you going to charge Giovani? Have you brought him back to the mainland?"

"He's small fry and doesn't know much. He's safe where he is but if we charge Elliot, we'll bring him back as a witness. Our office in Hawaii grilled him and, like you, he has no idea who's pulling Elliot's strings. They're the crooks we want to get our hands on, and you're going to help us do it."

"What an idiot I was."

"Don't beat up on yourself. You were right to be worried about your parents. Giovani said that he sensed even Elliot was scared. His fear infected Giovani, and he couldn't get on a plane fast enough." Lord smiled grimly.

"That doesn't make me feel any better."

"Let's forget about Giovani and talk about you. We've arranged for you to stay at the New York Hostel in Upper West Side for three nights after you get out. Then you're moving into a room above a delicatessen in Chinatown," Lord said sliding five hundred dollars and a piece of paper across the table. "Memorize the address. It's cheap and nasty. Rent's payable weekly, and it's all you can afford. There'll be an ad in *The New York Times* in two days. It's being held for you."

"How am I gonna call?"

"You'll get your cell phone back when you're released. It's paid for thirty days. You'll have to start looking for a job in a hurry. You won't get one, but you have to try. When you've been rejected everywhere, you'll walk past Sammy's Fine Cuisine on Canal Street, and there'll be a sign in the window looking for waiters. You'll apply and get an immediate start. Welcome back to the workforce." Lord grinned.

"Thanks." Todd sneered. "How am I gonna contact you?"

"Vanessa Hodge has agreed to help. She made it clear at your trial that she supported you and bore no grudges. It's natural that you'd stay friends with her. It's perfect."

"Fuck! Did you tell her how dangerous it'll be? They'll be watching her like a hawk. How's she gonna contact you? I don't like it. I don't like it one little bit. Who else knows of her involvement?"

"She knows the risks. You may not believe this, but she wants to help you. Your old boss knows what's happening and no one else. Don't worry, we're going to be looking after her."

"Yeah, just like you were gonna look after me in prison." Todd sneered.

"You know what you have to do, Todd. We didn't put you in this position. You should be grateful that we're giving you a way out."

"Grateful? Jesus! I could end up dead. Yeah, I'm real grateful all right."

Lord shook his head as he got to his feet. "I'll be seeing you."

After four months, three days and seventeen hours, Todd finished packing his meager belongings and prepared to leave Castlebrough. He was one of the very few young inmates who would leave in the same condition that he'd been in when imprisoned.

He thanked Tony Lombardi, but he'd never really got a handle on him. Lombardi smiled with his mouth, but his eyes were always cold, and Todd knew he was a cold-blooded killer.

For the first time, Frank Arturo displayed some emotion but it was not sadness. He told Todd he was disappointed that he would not have anyone of Todd's caliber to play chess and cards with. He had challenged Todd to one final game of chess and Todd had briefly toyed with the notion of winning before sanity prevailed. It had been a hard-fought game of over fifty moves, and when it was over, Arturo said, "I'll miss our games, Todd. You've made the time go faster."

"I can't thank you enough for looking after me, Frank, and I too have enjoyed playing against you."

"I got paid," Arturo said, "but if you find yourself back in here after your retrial, I'll take care of you for nothing. That should make you feel a little better if you lose."

"Did Jack Elliot pay you?"

"I'm not saying who paid me, but I will say that it was a sizeable amount. It's nice to have friends like that, but it's better to have friends like me," Arturo said, handing Todd a small piece of paper with a phone number scribbled on it. "Memorize this and if you get into trouble call it. You are one of the very few to have it."

For the first time, Todd shook the wiry, little mobster's hand and was surprised by the strength of his grasp. "Thank you, Frank."

Chapter 35

Dermott Becker had taken numerous calls from Brock Borchard about Todd Hansen, and they'd become more frequent when he'd found that Todd was about to be released.

"How come he's getting out? What's the appeal about, Dermott? What new evidence does he have?"

Becker sighed. "There's no new evidence. It's an appeal to the Federal Court challenging the law."

"I tell you, I don't like it. He's a loose end who could point the finger right at Jack Elliot and then where will we be? Why run the risk?"

"You're overreacting, Brock. He hasn't breathed a word, and he's not going to."

There was a long pause. "You haven't been able to tell me why he was protected in Castlebrough. Who arranged it? The FBI or the SEC?"

Becker laughed. "I can't imagine Frank Arturo getting into bed with government authorities. It wasn't them. Why? Did you try and have him wacked?"

"No, I toed the party line, but that doesn't mean I liked it. You tell me why the kid had such a powerful protector?"

"I've wondered about that myself. The kid's former boss is a close friend of Max Lustig and Lustig's connected. Perhaps he arranged the kid's protection?"

"Fuck Lustig! I'm getting sick of hearing his name. Anyhow, we don't have to worry about Arturo now that the kid's out. I've got a bad feeling about him. I think we should arrange for him to meet with an accident."

"No! There's no point. If he was going to talk, he would've have done it by now. Don't worry, we're watching him. He's not your concern, Brock. You make sure you don't do anything that we'll live to regret."

The hostel was on Amsterdam Avenue, and Todd was shown to a dormitory with six double bunk beds. He put his bag in the locker allocated to him and went to the community bathroom and had a shower and shave. There were three guys lounging around the dormitory and Todd wanting privacy, took a ten-minute walk to Central Park.

He sat down on a vacant bench and as he'd been instructed, called Doug Lechte. He asked him if there was any chance of a job with the firm or any of its clients. He knew what the answer would be. Then he got on the internet and started looking for employment agencies and job websites. He was only interested in agencies or companies that he could call and make appointments to see. Two hours later, he'd managed to set up eight appointments in the next two days for accounting and administration positions. It was late afternoon, and he was feeling hungry when he started to make his way back to the hostel. Stopping at a hamburger shop he took a seat at the window facing the street and ordered two burgers with everything and a chocolate shake. He didn't lift his eyes but noticed the unobtrusive dark haired man sit down in a cubicle, order coffee and bury his head in *The New York Times*.

It was 8:30 when Todd got back to the hostel, and there were nine men in the dormitory. Some were talking while others were reading. All the bottom bunks were taken which didn't worry Todd. He nodded to a few of the men and climbed the ladder to the comparative safety that an upper bunk provided. It was noisy, and the lights were on but compared to Castlebrough it was a haven. Five minutes later, he was asleep.

The following morning Todd showered before seven o'clock and dressed in the only suit he had with him. It was only a short walk to the Manhattan business district, and he stopped for a light breakfast and coffee. His first appointment was with a firm of employment consultants where he was handed an application form to complete before the interview. In his employment history, he left the last four months blank. One of the first questions the consultant asked him was what he'd been doing during that period. When Todd replied that he had been wrongly imprisoned and that he was out on appeal, the consultant's face collapsed. Ten minutes later, he was shown out of the consultant's offices with the assurance that they would submit his application to the client and would let him know if he was successful. The three other appointments that day were nearly identical, and Todd knew they'd be no different the following day.

The call was brief. "You're having trouble getting a job, kid. Do you need any money?" Elliot asked.

"I wouldn't take money from you if you were the last person on earth," Todd replied.

"You say that now. Wait until you find out that no one's going to employ you. You're a convict, and there's a good chance you're going back in."

"Why do you want to help me?"

"You never said a word. You never gave me up. That's why."

"You would've killed my parents," Todd said, and then paused. "I should thank you for having me looked after in Castlebrough, but I'm not going to. I never should've been in there, and if it weren't for you, I wouldn't have been."

"Have it your way, kid," Elliot said, and Todd heard dial tone.

Todd smiled. Grinich had told him that if Elliot was still interested he'd make contact within seventy-two hours of being released.

The apartment above the delicatessen was a grimy studio with a tiny kitchen and sink. There was a rusted fridge, a kettle and a few knives and forks. The bathroom defied physics but somehow comprised a shower, toilet, mirror and basin in a space that you couldn't swing a cat. There was mold on the walls and tiles and the shower curtain was falling apart. The single bed was hard but when Todd pulled the covers back the sheets were clean, and he breathed a sigh of relief. There was a small three drawer wooden cabinet next to the bed. The once green carpet was threadbare, and the old television didn't look to be any larger than twelve inches. The smell of chicken, ham and other meats permeated the sparsely furnished room. Todd tore a page from the pad in his suitcase and using the cabinet as a desk, started to jot down his expenses and work out how much he needed to earn. He grimaced and wondered if he could sink any lower.

The food in Sammy's Fine Cuisine was anything but fine. Sammy was an overweight, boisterous Italian, who loved shouting at his beleaguered employees. Todd filled in a simple one-page application form, and Sammy spent less than five minutes interviewing him at the back of the kitchen.

"Here's the thing," Sammy shouted. "You wanna work or not? Yo, ya wastin' my time here."

"I've never waited tables before, but yes, I'll work hard," Todd said. "I need this job."

"Okay, you can unofficially start tonight. Learn the ropes," Sammy said. "Then you can officially start tomorrow night. Hours are from five until two, Monday to Saturday. You'll be on four bucks an hour and ya get to keep your tips. There's none of this splitting and sharing bullshit. In a good week, ya can make six hundred bucks."

Sammy looked around the kitchen before spotting a tall, gray-haired man. "Jimmy," he shouted, "get over here. Meet Chad; he's our new waiter. Show him the ropes."

"Todd, my name's Todd," Todd said. He had the answer to his rhetorical question about whether he could sink any lower.

The meeting to consider partnership admission nominations in Montgomery Hastings & Pierce was normally a sedate, formal affair. It was unusual for any partner to nominate more than one manager or senior associate. It was only after the nominations were in that the lobbying began.

Doug Lechte nominated Vanessa as he'd done in meetings in the two previous years. Two other partners nominated managers responsible to them and then Phillip Cromwell rose and said, "I have three outstanding nominees. They are hardworking, diligent, and their families are highly respected. I can confidently say, they will never bring the firm into disrepute."

"Three?" Lechte said. "You can't nominate three and what do their families being respected have to do with making partner? Vanessa's not seeking membership at your yacht club." Lechte knew what

Cromwell was doing. He was attempting to change the balance of partners ensuring that he'd control a two-thirds majority.

"There's nothing in the deed of partnership that precludes me from nominating multiple partners. My nominees are outstanding and will enhance the reputation of the firm."

"Hear, hear," one of Cromwell's acolyte's said.

"My fellow partners," Cromwell said, "I would also like to advise that we have been successful in winning the auditing and consulting work for Strauss Robinson. As you know, they are one of the largest and most rapidly expanding legal firms in the country."

"Well done, Phillip," one of the partners said.

Another asked, "How did you manage to win their business?"

"I had a little help," Cromwell said. "As you know, the mayor and I are good friends, and he's been actively singing the firm's praises. He knows the principals of Strauss Robinson and put in a good word for us. I told you that the gratis audit of The Disabled Children's Fund for the mayor's wife would be beneficial."

"Wasn't Strauss Robinson recently sued for sex discrimination? Weren't some of the female partners harassed and derided?" Lechte asked. "I'm not sure this is the type of client we should associate with."

"That's just sour grapes, Doug. They settled the matter out of court to the satisfaction of all parties. The mayor has personally used Strauss Robinson and here you are seeking to belittle them. You're very churlish," Cromwell said.

Numerous hear-hears echoed around the table.

Phillip Cromwell smiled. With the admission of his new partners, he would have the numbers to rid himself of the irksome Lechte and his favorite employee, Vanessa Hodge.

Chapter 36

Nearly a year had elapsed since the death of Devlin Cooper, and Karen Deacon hadn't heard another word from the blackmailers. The funeral had been huge, the church overflowing. Thousands of mourners listened in silence as the service was piped out into the street. Karen had wept uncontrollably as had many others. The speeches were long, heartfelt and passionate. Tom Deacon spoke about his love for the young man with the bionic arm and how he felt that he'd lost a son. Devlin's father broke down at the microphone having said that his son had barely tasted life.

Half a dozen of Chicago's finest attended the funeral hoping to find out what Devlin Cooper had been doing on a desolate road in the middle of the night. Rumors abounded that he had wanted to test the speed of the Lamborghini, and things had gone horribly wrong. The police had dismissed this theory and leaned to suicide, largely because of the absence of skid marks. Some in the media discussed the Pirates game but were respectful and discreet. No one wanted to speak ill of the recently deceased.

After the service was over the funeral procession had slowly wended its way through the city. Flags flew at half-mast, and the sidewalks were crammed with grim-faced mourners trying to catch a glimpse of the flower encompassed coffin. Others hung their heads or signed the cross.

Karen had felt terrible about leaving Tom, and the kids missed him terribly. He didn't understand why she'd left and promised that if she returned, he would be more attentive and would cut down his work hours. He called regularly, and while Karen listened and felt sorry for him, she knew she could not go back. She didn't know when the CD was going to raise its ugly head again but did know that it was only a matter of time. When it was finally made public it would be unbelievably painful for Tom and the kids, but far more so if they were living together.

Todd had never worked so hard in all his life and felt sorry for every waiter or waitress he'd abused or told to hurry up. In the first two days, he'd messed up orders, tried to carry three plates and dropped one, and had burned his forearm when he'd rested it on a hot plate. Sammy seemed to be everywhere and loved shouting at his hapless employees. Every mistake Todd made, Sammy shouted, "That's a deduction," meaning it was coming out of Todd's paycheck. Amazingly, by the end of the second week, Todd could carry five plates and work a dozen tables without missing a beat. He had even resorted to shouting at the kitchen staff when they were slow in preparing meals. Sammy's prices were cheap, and the restaurant was busy, but in quiet times, Todd found himself washing dishes or sweeping floors. Sammy was a hard taskmaster who wanted his pound of flesh. Including tips, Todd made the princely sum of two hundred and sixty dollars in his first week but doubled it in the second. Finally, he had enough to pay the freight and storage costs on three suitcases that had been in storage since his imprisonment.

It had been over a year since Todd had last entered the betting parlor, but nothing had changed. It was the third Saturday he'd been out of prison, and punters were lined up six deep at every window. He didn't have an iPad or a system, but he did have a form guide and an undertaking that the SEC and FBI would pick up his losses. He took a position at the back of the shortest line and when he got to the window said, "Belmont Park, race three, a hundred the win, number seven."

Ronny Conroy glanced at the battery of cameras adjacent to his desk and grinned. The kid was back. He was sitting at a table by himself passing a betting ticket from hand to hand. A few minutes later Ronny took a seat at Todd's table.

"What are you doing here?"

"Hello, Ronny. I wanted a bet," Todd said. "Don't you want my business?"

"Yeah, of course, I do. I meant how come you're out?"

"My lawyers were granted leave to appeal on a technicality. I've been released pending the outcome. I don't fully understand it. It's complex, but the lawyers are challenging the law."

"So you could go back in again?"

"Unfortunately, yes."

"When's the appeal going to be heard?" Conroy asked.

"Hold on just a second, Ronny," Todd said looking at one of the monitors.

The commentator shouted, "Miami Princess takes the lead with a furlong to go and is careering away for the easiest of wins."

"You got a win?" Conroy asked.

"Four hundred bucks." Todd grinned. "I don't know when the appeal's being heard. It could be next month; it could be a year."

"Who's paying your legal fees?"

"That's none of your business," Todd said a little too sharply as the stressed face of his mother flashed before him. "Sorry, Ronny, that's personal."

"That's okay. Are you working?"

"Yes, I have a job."

"What are you doing?"

"I'm in restaurant administration. I wouldn't mind working here as a teller if a vacancy arises."

"I don't have anything right now. I'll keep you in mind, though. You still have the same cell phone number?"

"Yes. Ronny, sorry I have to be rude, but I need to get another bet on."

"I'll get out of your way. I don't want to cost myself business." Conroy laughed.

Three hours later Todd left the betting parlor. He'd won just over a thousand dollars.

On the way to his apartment, he called Vanessa and arranged to meet her on Sunday evening for coffee. It was the first time they had spoken since before his trial. She had been surprisingly friendly, and Todd wondered how he would feel about someone who had wrongfully put him in jail for four nights.

After talking to Todd, Conroy had gone straight back to his office and called Jack Elliot relating the conversation.

"Say that again," Elliot said.

"He's got a job in restaurant administration," Conroy replied, "but he still asked me for a job as a teller."

"Restaurant administration? He's a proud little shit. I'll say that for him." Elliot laughed. "He's waiting tables and washing dishes in a cheap food dive. And the place he's living in is not fit for dogs. When he comes in again see what else you can find out."

"Don't you mean *if?*"

"Ronny, he'll be back. He's hooked on the horses. Did he have his iPad? Was he inputting details of the race results?"

"Nah, all he had was a form guide."

"No matter. He's a gambler. He wouldn't have come back if he wasn't."

When Todd got back to his room, the smell of freshly cooked chicken mingled with other meats and cheeses was nauseating. He forced a window open, knowing that the street noise was the lesser of two annoyances. He sat on the edge of his bed thinking about his thousand dollar win. It had lifted his spirits, and he picked up his notepad from the cabinet to make some changes to his budget. As he removed the single sheet, he grimaced. He always kept work papers behind the third blank page of his notepads. He was anal about it. His budget was immediately behind the first page. Someone had been in his room. Aaron Lord had said that this would occur, but Todd hadn't expected it to happen so quickly. They were watching him.

He couldn't worry about it. He needed to get cleaned up and off to work. As he rinsed his face, his cell phone rang. There was no caller identification and Todd tentatively said, "Hello."

"Todd, it's Tony Lombardi, I'm getting out in two weeks."

"That's great news, Tony. Do you want me to grab a cab and pick you up?"

"Nah." Lombardi laughed. "That's all arranged. I wanted to let you know that Mr. Arturo is very disappointed. He hasn't said anything, but I know. He misses the chess. You've been out for nearly four weeks and haven't visited. He likes you, Todd and let me tell you, he's the best friend you've got in New York."

"I-I'm working six nights a week, Tony. Jeez, I never thought he'd want to see me. It never entered my mind."

"If I were you, I'd make some time this Sunday. You know how it works. Phone administration and let 'em know what time you'll be there."

"Sure, sure, Tony, I'll do that but you know I won't be able to play chess or cards. We'll just be able to stare at each other through the glass and talk on the phone. And you know Frank's not very talkative."

"Didn't you learn anything in here? Those rules don't apply to Frank Arturo. You make the call, and they'll set up a private room, chess board and all. Make the call, Todd."

"Thanks, Tony. I will. If there's anything I can do for you, just let me know."

Lombardi laughed. "It's a nice thought, kid, but there's nothing you can do for me. Oh, don't tell Mr. Arturo I called. He never would've asked."

Chapter 37

Castlebrough separated visitors from inmates by unbreakable glass and communication was by phone. On the Sunday that Todd visited he was scanned and patted down before being led to a compact room. Frank Arturo was sitting next to a heater and behind a table with a chess board set up on it. He was sipping a cup of coffee. "It's good to see you, Todd. Would you like coffee or a soda?"

Todd knew that he was powerful but was still taken aback by the privileges he received. No other prisoner in Castlebrough got the kid gloves treatment reserved for Frank Arturo. "No, thanks, Frank. I'm fine."

"Let's play then."

Arturo was no more talkative than he'd been when they had been inmates together. His concentration on the game was intense, and they played in near silence. After three hours and four games, scores were even, and Todd was preparing to lose the last game when Arturo said, "We'll have to play the deciding game when you next visit. I need to talk to you."

"What about?"

"I know you've done a deal with the government to get your sentence remitted. You're going to try and infiltrate the gang who put you in here and feed them to the FBI. That's right, isn't it?"

Todd was surprised by how much the mob boss knew and wondered whether Elliot knew too. "I'm sorry, Frank, I can't say anything."

"You're playing a dangerous game. If you get caught, they'll kill you. Have you memorized the phone number I gave you?"

"Yes."

"Good. It's a pity you have to work in that restaurant while you wait for them to make a move. I could've given you a job in one of my enterprises that would've made use of your brains."

There was an abrupt knock on the door.

"Give me another five minutes."

"Yes, Mr. Arturo," a voice replied.

Everything Lombardi had said was true. Frank Arturo did run Castlebrough.

"I know you can't work for me because you've got your deal with the government," Arturo said, "but I'd hate to lose my chess playing partner. Now listen to me. They're going to try and get you to wear a wire. They're gonna say it's for your safety. You wear it, and you're dead. So when the Fibbies put the pressure on you, tell 'em to go to hell. Capiche?"

Todd was amazed. Arturo seemed to know everything. "Yes," Todd replied. "Do you know who set me up?"

Arturo stood up. His face was expressionless, and his lips drawn in a thin line. "I'm ready," he shouted. "When will I see you again, Todd?"

"Is two weeks from today, okay?"

"I'll see you then," the mob boss replied.

The coffee shop on Jane Street, West Village was only a few minutes' walk from Vanessa's apartment, and she got there a few minutes early. She was wearing a stylish padded black coat with a faux fur collar and light blue designer jeans. In the cab ride from Castlebrough Todd wondered whether Vanessa would be cold toward him. She certainly had good reason to be. He need not have worried. When he entered the coffee shop, she stood up and gave him a radiant smile. He kissed her lightly on the cheek. "Given the circumstances, you're looking very well," she said.

"Yes, someone paid to have me protected. I don't know who, but I guess it was that low-life, Jack Elliot, the guy who set me up. It's strange. He called me and when I thanked him he didn't say anything. I don't understand why he'd want to look after me though."

"It wasn't him. I thought you'd know. Doug asked Max Lustig to use his connections to make sure that you came to no harm. Didn't anyone tell you? Todd, if Elliot contacts you again, you should stick to the same story. If he believes that you think he looked after you, he's more likely to give you a job. He might even presume that you harbor feelings of loyalty."

"Good idea. God, Max Lustig. I should have guessed. He's the only man I know who knows those type of people. That was good of Doug. I'll have to pay him back when I get some money."

"Max wouldn't take any money. He said that he liked you and that the crooks had led you astray. I wouldn't be surprised if he offers you a job after this is all over. You have more friends than you think."

A waiter took their order – a latte for Vanessa and a cappuccino for Todd.

"Vanessa, I want to apologize to you again. I'm so sorry I put you through that. I should have owned up. I feel terrible," Todd said.

"Don't think I didn't hate you when I found out what you did. It was after Doug told me that they'd threatened to kill your parents if you said anything that I softened. I still think losing all that money gambling and putting yourself in that position was stupid. What were you thinking? My mom and dad haven't forgiven you. I doubt they ever will."

Todd hung his head. "I'm so, so sorry. Did Grinich and Lord tell you the risks you're going to be taking by acting as my intermediary? You'll be risking your life. Why did you say you would?"

Vanessa took a long sip of her latte. "I think I'll be all right. You'll be the one dealing with the gangsters. I'm doing it because I like you, and it will reduce your sentence. I'm also doing it for Doug. Montgomery Hastings & Pierce are about to admit three new partners all sponsored by Cromwell. According to Doug, Cromwell will then have numbers to remove him."

"From the partnership? I can't believe it. Doug's the rainmaker. They'll lose too many clients if they remove him. What will happen to you if he's not there?"

"Cromwell hates me. If Doug hadn't supported me, I would've been sacked a long time ago," Vanessa said, taking a napkin and wiping the froth from the corners of Todd's mouth.

Her gesture was totally unexpected, and Todd felt himself turning red.

"Oh, I'm sorry. I didn't mean to embarrass you. Todd, there is one thing we have to discuss. Our cover is going to be that we're an item and in public that's what we'll be, but I want to let you know that's as far as it goes. You're a nice guy, but I don't have time for a relationship. It's just a façade and once the reason for it's over we'll go back to our normal lives."

Todd tried to pick up some nonexistent froth from the bottom of his cup. He looked up. Vanessa's hair hung loosely on her shoulders, and her big brown eyes seemed to say *do you understand?* "Wow! That's pretty definitive." Todd grinned. "Don't worry. I owe you so much. I'd never do anything to upset you."

"I know," Vanessa said, putting her hand over Todd's. "I just thought we should sort the rules out from the start."

"You know nothing may come of this. There's only a small chance that Elliot will offer me a job. I think I know how to play him, but I might be wrong. I'm going to hang around the betting parlor and keep asking Ronny for a job. I'm sure he's in cahoots with Elliot."

"I understand but if he does offer you something, it will look better if we're in a relationship now rather than after. You can start by walking me home."

As they left the coffee shop, Vanessa took Todd's hand. Five minutes later at the entrance to her apartment building she said, "Kiss me."

Todd had been wanting to kiss those voluptuous lips since the first time he had laid eyes on Vanessa but had lacked the courage to ask her out, and now he was nervous about kissing her. He put his arms around her bulky coat and gently kissed her but she leaned forward, and he felt the warmth and savored the fullness of her lips. It was everything he had imagined it would be. After about a minute, she drew away from him and said, "Goodnight, Todd. Let's have dinner on Friday night. We're going to have to do some serious dating to ensure our relationship is seen as genuine."

As Todd walked along the street, he was still breathing heavily.

It was midday on Wednesday when Todd entered the betting parlor. It was quiet, and only ten or so patrons were looking at the monitors and betting boards. Todd was disappointed. He had hoped that Elliot might be there. Perhaps he wasn't going to take the bait. Perhaps Ronny hadn't even contacted him. There were only two tellers operating and Todd placed a hundred dollars for the win on The Phantom in the first at Hialeah Park. He ordered a mineral water and took a chair at one of the vacant tables.

The Phantom ran into interference at the top of the stretch and then flashed home to finish third. "A good thing beaten," the race caller screamed. Todd tore up his ticket and buried his head in the form guide.

"You were unlucky then," Ronny said, taking a chair opposite Todd.

"I'll get it back." Todd smiled, pleased that Ronny was taking such an interest in his small bets.

"Sure you will. How come you're not working?"

"I work at nights. It's good. I can spend more time here."

"Oh yeah, you're in restaurant administration, aren't you?" Ronny laughed derisively.

"Yes, that's right. What's so funny?"

"Nothing. I just wondered, if it's such a good job, why do you want to work for me?"

"I never said it was a good job. I'd far prefer to work in a place like this where I can use my numerical skills."

"Yeah, I thought about it but I'd have to be a fool to employ you. I'll teach you the business and in six months' time you'll be back in Castlebrough. How sure are you that your appeal's going to be successful?"

"I'll level with you, Ronny. I'm not. My lawyers say I've got a twenty percent chance, and I think they're optimistic. I'm going to make the most of the time I've got. Sorry, I have another bet I want to put on."

"How come you're not using your system?"

"There's a lot of work in it. If I knew I wasn't going back in, I would be," Todd said as he stood up.

By the time Todd left the betting parlor, he had lost three hundred dollars.

Chapter 38

It had been almost a year since Karen Deacon received the call offering to sell the CDs for ten million and in the meantime she hadn't heard a word. Despite this, she had never relaxed, knowing it was only a matter of time before the blackmailers approached her again. After returning home from dropping the kids off at school, she checked her mailbox. She sorted through the envelopes knowing that they were either bills or junk mail until she came to a slightly larger plain envelope. Details of the sender were blank and as she tore it open, a photo fell out. She picked it up and a wave of nausea almost overcame her. It was a disgusting pic and the date in the right-hand corner was the day that she had spent the afternoon at the Astor Motel with Devlin.

The call from Dermott Becker was opportune, and Elliot said, "The easiest way to keep an eye on the kid is to give him a job in the club. Besides, I could use some help keeping the books. He might even be able to help with collections."

"How do you know you can trust him," Becker asked.

"I don't, but he didn't breathe a word at his trial because he's in fear of what we might do to his folks. He tried to get a job with his old firm and got shut down. He's tried employment agencies and got nowhere. He's washing dishes and sweeping floors in some fast food joint in Chinatown. He's desperate for a half decent job. And get this, he thinks that I arranged to have him protected in Castlebrough."

"Jack, I'm not worried about him. He knows you, Ferguson and Fraser, and he thinks he saw a murder that never happened. He doesn't know much at all. Employing him might be a risk because he'll see and learn things that he might use as leverage to get his sentence reduced."

Elliot paused. "I can keep an eye on him. He's desperate and thinks he's going back inside. If he snaps, there's a bigger risk of him cutting a deal with the FBI and giving them identikits of Ferguson, Fraser and me. Ferguson's weak, and it wouldn't take long for the Fibbies to break him down. He'd give me up in the blink of an eye and might even blab about Giovani. Besides, do you want that nutcase, Borchard, knowing you didn't get rid of him?"

"He didn't talk at his trial and if he's as scared as what you say he is he's not going to go snap."

"I don't understand your concern, Dermott. Nearly everyone who works for you is an ex-con. What makes the kid different?"

"He was in prison, but he's not a criminal. We set him up. The others all committed crimes of their own volition. There's a big difference," Becker said. "Look, if you think you can control him by giving him a job, then do it. But, Jack, I want you to watch him like a hawk. If anything goes wrong, it'll be on your head."

Sammy's was packed, and Sammy was screaming. He ran the restaurant on a very simple philosophy that so long as customers were spending, they could stay all night. It could be food, booze or coffee so long as it is involved dollars coming out their pockets and into his. He loved nights like tonight when customers were lined up waiting for tables. However, he hated what he called the nuff nuffs who'd finished their meals, weren't spending and were just sitting at their tables talking.

"Did you enjoy your meals?" he'd shout. "Can I get you anything else? No? Well, I'll just get your coats so you can be on your way." There was nothing subtle about Sammy.

Todd's proficiency as a waiter improved every day and besides carrying five plates he could now memorize the meals for all of the tables that he was waiting on. He was friendly, efficient, and the customers liked him. The previous week he had earned nearly seven hundred dollars with tips, making him Sammy's highest paid waiter. Todd hadn't noticed the two men in the line until one of them said, "Hello, Todd, how about getting us a table? I'm a generous tipper."

"What do you want? What are you doing here?"

"I thought your manners might have improved after your stint in the joint," Ferguson said.

"Todd, Todd," Sammy shouted while he wiped down a table. "Bring 'em over here."

As Todd showed them to their table, Fraser smirked and said, "So this is restaurant administration, is it? Looks like you've got plenty of room to climb the ladder."

Ferguson guffawed loudly. "What part's administration? The writing down of the orders."

"What do you want?" Todd asked.

"Two T-bones, well done, with fries, and a Jim Beam Black for me and a Budweiser for my friend," Ferguson said. "Oh, and the boss wants to see you at midday on Saturday."

"Well, I don't want to see him."

"Kid, we know you asked Ronny for a job, and he said no. The boss said he might have something for you," Fraser said.

"That's if you can drag yourself away from restaurant administration," Ferguson said, and both men roared with laughter.

"He might even pay you enough so that you can afford to leave those palatial digs you're staying in." Fraser grinned.

"Yeah, you could hardly take that hot little girlfriend back to that dive," Ferguson added.

"I'll get your meals underway," Todd said, hurrying back to the kitchen. Elliot had taken the bait.

Hillary Rodham High School had just finished for the day and Sally Deacon stood at the entrance waiting for her mom to pick her up. A woman got out of her SUV and walked over to the front gates saying, "Hello, Sally, can you give this to your mom?"

Sally didn't recognize the woman but guessed she was one of her mom's many friends. "Sure," she said, taking the small, plain envelope.

There were always circulars and notices coming from the school, and Karen gave no thought to the envelope as she threw it into her bag. It was only as she was going to bed that she remembered it. As she tore the envelope open, she fought back a gasp when she saw Devlin Cooper's photo bearing his signature and the message, *good luck.* There was no note, just the photo, but its intent was clear. Karen knew that the next envelope might be for Sally.

Karen had been steeling herself for when the blackmailers would raise their ugly heads again and had been firm in her resolve to resist them. As she looked at the photo of Devlin, she knew that she was helpless. The thought of her kids ever seeing pics of she and Devlin was too much. She glanced in the mirror. Her eyes were puffy, and she had lines that hadn't been there a year ago. She slipped between the sheets and turned the lights off knowing that there was no way she would be able to sleep.

Chapter 39

Todd was purposely late for his appointment with Elliot and did not arrive at the betting parlor until 12:30. A smoky haze permeated the crowded room, and Elliot was standing in front of a monitor talking to two swarthy looking goons wearing ill-fitting suits. All the tellers were working, and Todd got in line and placed a bet on the first at Aqueduct. When he turned around from the window, Elliot said, "Where's the iPad? Don't tell me you're betting without your system?"

"Your thugs said that you wanted to see me. I'm sure it wasn't about my betting system."

"I thought you might have lost your smart mouth in the joint."

"I might have if you hadn't had me looked after. I don't know why you did it. It must be one of few decent things you've ever done. I'd thank you if you hadn't of been the one who me put in there."

There was a huge roar followed by "yeah, yeah," and a group of men high-fived and patted each other on the back.

"Let's go out the back where it's quiet," Elliot said.

Todd looked up at a screen as the horses were being led into the gates. "That's my race. Hang on, I want to watch it."

"Who are you on?"

"Glistening Jewel."

Two minutes later Elliot said, "Well done, kid."

Todd's demeanor didn't change, but the five hundred he had just won would come in very handy.

Ronny was in his office, and Todd nodded to him as Elliot made himself comfortable in the adjoining office.

"Do you own this place?" Todd asked.

"No. We do some business with Ronny, and he helps us out when he can."

"Yeah, I know. Setting up stooges like me."

"What we do with Ronny doesn't concern you. I know you're doing it hard, and I want to help you. Even if you get off the insider trading charges, which you won't, you're never going to get a job with a reputable business again. The minute you went inside Castlebrough the chances of ever getting honest employment disappeared."

"I've got an honest job now."

"Yeah, washing dishes, sweeping floors and jumping to the screams of that lunatic Sammy. Some job. You're never going to get a job in accounting. For that, you have to be trusted, and no one's gonna trust an ex-con. I'm different, though. I know you're honest and just caught a bad break."

"A bad break." Todd sneered. "Is that what you call it? You have a real way with words."

"Kid, I'm starting to have second thoughts. Do you want to hear what I have to say or are you going to be a smartass? If it's the latter, you can fuck off now."

Todd hung his head. "Sorry," he said. "I owe you for what you did for me in prison. Go on."

"That's better." Elliot smiled. "I've got a club in Queens. Strictly legit on the surface. However, it's also the front for a sweet coke operation and small finance business."

"The place I was taken to blindfolded?"

"Yeah, that's right."

"What makes you think I won't go straight to the cops and give you up?"

"You didn't at your trial, and you won't now, not unless you want to attend your folk's funeral, that is. And–"

"Leave my parents out of it!"

"The mouse that roared. Okay, okay. Here's the deal. You don't realize it, but you need me far more than I need you."

Todd laughed. "I'm not going to sell drugs for you or get into loan sharking. I'd rather wash dishes."

"Hear me out," Elliot said. "You won't be directly involved. The books are a bit of a mess. You'd keep the records and maybe help out with collections. I think the club's carrying too much booze in stock. You could look at that, too. You know, streamline operations."

"You want me to collect loans from druggies? No way. I'm not getting bashed or worse by some lunatic."

"Kid, look at yourself. A decent wind would blow you over. I wouldn't send you out to collect debts without protection. It's just that you have a nice way about you, and you might be able to collect without the normal grief. Heavying customers is bad for business."

"If I say yes, what's in it for me?"

"Ah, now you're talking. I want you nearby so part of the deal is a two bedroom, fully furnished apartment about two hundred yards from the club. Somewhere you'd be proud to take that girlfriend of yours. Oh, how come she forgave you?"

"She knew I didn't set her up, and she thinks gambling is a sickness just like drug addiction or cancer. She thinks the victim has no control over his actions."

"Jeez, you got lucky with her. In addition to the apartment, I'll pay you eight hundred bucks cash a week. Before you bullshit me, I know Sammy's paying you about two hundred after tax, and you're living off tips. If you want, you can have all your meals at the club on the house. What do you say?"

"If you make it a thousand, it's a deal."

"You've sure got chutzpah, kid, but I'm not negotiating. Take it or leave it."

"You're so charming, Jack. How can I refuse?"

Elliot stood up and extended his hand. "For the last time, lose the smart mouth. There are a lot of guys at the club who aren't as patient as me. When can you start?"

Todd paused. "Monday of next week. I'll finish at Sammy's this Friday. I don't want to let him down. After all, he was the only one who'd give me a job."

"That's fine," Elliot said, throwing Todd a set of keys. "You can move in whenever you like. It'll be like a palace compared to the shithole you're in now."

"I'll stay where I am until I finish at Sammy's. One question. How well do you know Frank Arturo?"

"Did he say we were friends?"

"No, I asked him if it was you who paid him, and he told me it was none of my business."

"He was right," Elliot replied. "It's none of your business."

The partners of Montgomery Hastings & Pierce, again voted against the nomination of Vanessa as a new partner and instead admitted Phillip Cromwell's three nominees. After one retirement, the firm now had forty partners. The new partners had barely made their acceptance speeches before Cromwell prepared a notice seeking Doug Lechte's removal for conduct that had brought the firm into disrepute.

More particularly his failure to adequately supervise Todd Hansen. With the new partners' votes, Cromwell knew he had the numbers and in a month's time, he would see the last of Lechte. With Lechte gone and a new audit partner taking his place, there would no longer be a position for Vanessa Hodge. Cromwell signed the notice with a flourish before asking his assistant to circulate it immediately.

Chapter 40

Karen Deacon had been home for ten minutes after taking the kids to school when she received the call that she had been dreading.

"I thought you were going to be late for school this morning when you got stuck in that traffic," the slightly accented voice said. "Did you enjoy the photos? Do you realize how easy it would've been to put that photo of you in the envelope we gave your daughter? If we had, we would have been sure not to seal it."

Karen peered out of the kitchen window looking for anything suspicious. "What do you want?"

"You know. Five million and you'll never hear from me again. You get the CDs and your life returns to normal."

"I don't have it."

"Don't lie to me. You have stocks and bonds, plus the house must be worth at least four million. You can raise it."

"If I could believe you, I'd pay, but I don't. I think you're a liar who'll bleed me for the rest of my life."

Vaughan silently cursed. Borchard had blamed him for pushing Devlin Cooper too far and for his death. He had also told Vaughan that he had to get the five million to redeem himself.

"Would you like me to put one or two photos on the internet to prove that I'm serious?"

"No, no. I can't get that much in cash."

"We don't want cash. The next time I call I'll give you a bank account number."

"A bank account?" Karen said with a tinge of hope.

"We're not fools, Mrs. Deacon. The account was set up fraudulently. We'll move the funds out over the internet, and you'll never trace them. Nor will you ever trace me. Sorry to get your hopes up."

There was a long pause.

"Mrs. Deacon? Mrs. Deacon, are you still there?"

"Yes, I've made a decision. I'm not paying. Put your filth on the internet. I'll tough it out," Karen shouted.

Vanessa sat opposite a worried Doug Lechte. She had never seen him like this before. "Cromwell's got the numbers and this time there's nothing I can do about it," he said.

"That means I'll be out five minutes after you," Vanessa said, "and it'll make contacting the FBI and SEC all the riskier. Can't you explain that to Phillip and ask him to hold off?"

"I can't breathe a word about what we're doing. Besides, he couldn't care less about Todd, and he's hell-bent on getting rid of me."

"God, and Todd's just got in with them. He starts next Monday. We're going to the movies tomorrow night."

"We might have to get you out. So long as you could pass information onto me you had some protection. If we're not working together, and you have to report to the FBI, you'll be putting yourself at significant risk. You can't do it."

"It's going to put you and Todd at risk, too. Seriously, what reason does he have for remaining in contact with you, Doug? None. At least with me there's the cover of a relationship. I can't understand why Phillip is out to get you."

"He's bombastic, and I can't reason with him. All I can do is keep lobbying the partners and hope that I can get at least four to change their mind."

"How do you know it's that bad?"

"Vanessa, the votes against your admission to the partnership were thirty and those in favor ten. I expect the vote to remove me will be the same," Lechte said, shaking his head.

It had been two months since the last directors meeting of Vulture Inc., and an uncomfortable silence permeated the room. Borchard took up his customary position at the end of the board table directly facing Dermott Becker.

"I don't know why we have these meetings," Arthur Ridgeway said. "We tell Brock not to lay a hand on Les Carroll and what happens? He's dead!"

"It had nothing to do with me." Borchard sneered

Lydia Coe rolled her eyes, and Dermott Becker yawned.

"What? You don't believe me?" Borchard asked. "I'm telling you it was an accident."

"You're a dangerous man, Brock," Ridgeway persisted. "People seem to get killed when you're around. You overplayed your hand with Devlin Cooper and look what happened."

"You're blaming me for Cooper's suicide?"

"You pushed him too hard," Becker said. "You got greedy and killed off a nice little earner."

"No, I didn't. Anyhow, it's not over yet," Borchard said. "I waited like you told me to. Now it's time for the woman to pay and as soon as she does I'm selling the CDs to the highest bidder."

"You're going to tarnish the reputation of a national hero and what are you going to get? A few million if you're lucky." Lydia Coe said.

"I didn't think you'd be worried about his reputation, Lydia."

"I'm not," she replied. "I'm worried about the media and the cops. They're going to be all over it. They're going to track it to the Astor and then they'll find the clerk's disappeared. Then they're going to start relentlessly digging. If they find Dirk, they'll find you, and if they find you, there's a good chance they'll find us. It's not worth it. Get as much out of Karen Deacon as you can and then drop it. Forget about selling the CDs. They'll be more trouble than they're worth."

"Hear, hear," Ridgeway said.

"Yeah," O'Brien agreed.

"Lydia's right," Becker said. "Have you thought about using Jack Elliot rather than Dirk? Jack's a salesman, and he can be very persuasive. With all due respect, I'd have more confidence in Jack getting the five mil than Dirk."

"I'll think about it," Borchard said.

"I'm happy to send him to Chicago,' Becker persisted.

"Why? All he needs is her phone number," Borchard replied.

"Do we need a resolution that we're not going to sell the CDs?" Ridgeway asked.

Borchard glared around the table. He was seething. How dare they tell him what to do? "No!" He snarled.

"What else have you got?" Becker asked.

"You'll be pleased to know that your friend Max Lustig won the contract to carry hanging meat that was ours for the taking," Borchard said disparagingly.

"Don't worry about it. There'll be plenty of other contracts in the future, and it's good sense to stay away from Lustig. There are easier fish to catch than him," Becker said. "Is that all, Brock?"

"No. I've got a huge shipment of coke coming in from Colombia. I've bought it extremely well. It'll take a few days to cut, but then I'll need to move it. I might need you to increase the size of your orders."

"Don't worry," Becker replied, "I'll take all the additional. My guys in Queens and the Bronx can't keep up with demand. It's insane."

"How's it coming in?" O'Brien asked.

"Small plane."

"That's risky," O'Brien said.

"Not for us," Borchard replied. "Until it's landed and been sampled the Colombians don't see a cent."

"How's the auditor working out at the club?" Ridgeway asked.

"He's only been there three days," Becker replied. "He'll be fine."

"What? What's this about?" Borchard snarled.

"He couldn't get a job anywhere," Becker replied. "Jack suggested that we give him a job at the club so we could keep a handle on him. He's almost certainly going back inside after his appeal's quashed."

"Are you fucking crazy?" Borchard said, thumping the table. "What if he's a plant for the Fibbies or the SEC? You wouldn't have to worry about keeping an eye on him if he just mysteriously disappeared."

"Sorry, Brock, but we can't kill the whole of New York," Ridgeway said sarcastically.

"Jack's accepted total responsibility for him. I don't think we've got much to worry about," Becker said. "You know who he visited for nearly four hours on Sunday? Frank Arturo. I hardly think he's going to be cozying up to the cops."

"What is it with him and Arturo?" O'Brien asked. "Who paid Arturo to look after him?"

"My mail is that Arturo likes him. It's that simple. I don't know who paid. I thought it was Lustig, but now I'm not sure. Maybe it was his mom. She's paying his legal bills. Anyhow, the kid doesn't know either but, get this, he thinks it was Jack. It's created a warped loyalty."

"How would his mother contact Arturo?" Borchard said. "It wasn't her."

"I'll tell you how," Becker said. "She's rich, so that helps. She contacts a PI, who knows someone who knows someone and when the chain finishes there's Frank Arturo. The last thing a mother wants to think about is her son getting fucked in prison every night. If I had to guess, I'd say she arranged it."

"It would've been faster and safer if he'd had an accident," Borchard growled.

"Perhaps not," Becker replied. "If Arturo likes him, I'd hate to be the one who arranged the accident. And Brock, we all know you're a tough guy, but let me tell you, the Serbian Mafia's no match for the real Mafia."

Nervous laughs came from around the table.

"Arturo's got thousands of soldiers on the streets. He probably doesn't even know we exist. Let's keep it that way," Becker said.

"It's noon," O'Brien said looking at his watch. "I didn't get any breakfast on the plane. Can we adjourn for an hour while we have something to eat?"

Chapter 41

Todd's last night at Sammy's was little different from the first. Friday was one the busiest nights of the week and Sammy was in full flight shouting at the chefs and serving staff. Just before midnight, he beckoned Todd and said, "There's someone in my office who wants to see you. Take five."

Sammy's office was small and frugally furnished with a tattered swivel chair, and an old desk. In front of the desk were three wooden chairs where Sammy seated suppliers while screwing their prices down. Chas Grinich stood up from one of the chairs and locked the office door. For additional security, he kicked a wooden wedge between the worn linoleum and the door. He was wearing a chef's apron and toque.

"What are you doing here?" Todd said trying not to shout. "If they see you I'm as good as dead."

"Other than Sammy, no one knows I'm here. I was in the back of a truck that reversed up to the doors. I'll be leaving the same way. I heard they gave you a job. Well done."

"I thought my contact was Vanessa," Todd persisted. "What are you doing here?"

"I wanted to warn you. Since Vanessa told us about the club, we've been able to do some more checking. There are some truly evil guys hanging there. Some of them would kill you as soon as look at you. You need to be careful. Very careful. They'll be watching you closely in the early weeks so don't take any risks. Bide your time. Try to become accepted. With time, they'll drop their defenses and then you can move."

"What did you find out about Elliot?"

"He's an Australian though you'd never know it. Ex-commando who fought with our boys in Afghanistan and then became a mercenary for hire in Africa. He has no criminal record and has been living here for the past twenty years."

"He's a killer?"

"Yeah, he's killed before both as a soldier and a mercenary, but he's never been suspected of murder. He's clean and he's smart. He doesn't have a rap sheet, not even a parking ticket."

"Is there anything else?"

"Yeah. There's going to be times we need to bypass Vanessa and talk to you. Don't worry, we'll be very careful. You're still going to have appointments with your lawyers pending the hearing of your appeal, and I see you're still visiting Frank Arturo. There'll be times and places where it's safe. We'll get word to Vanessa when we want to see you. Oh, and what is it with you and Arturo?"

"He likes me, and he likes playing chess. Is that all?"

Grinich grinned. "It's far better that he likes you than the alternative. How do you find him?"

"I don't know him. We hardly talk. He keeps to himself."

"Well don't get too close to him. He's personally responsible for at least twenty murders and only God knows how many he's ordered."

"I know what he's like, but he's been good to me."

"He's not a worry where he is," Grinich said, "but Elliot and his cohorts are. They'll have almost certainly bugged your new apartment. There might even be cameras. Don't look for them. Just act naturally and don't talk about anything you're doing with us while you're in the apartment. Not to Vanessa, not to Lechte and not to me. Do you understand?"

"Yeah," Todd said, standing up. "I better get back to waiting tables."

As Grinich removed the wedge and unlocked the door, he said, "Good luck, Todd."

By the time, Brock Borchard's flight landed at O'Hare he had made his decision. Before leaving the terminal, he reluctantly called Becker.

"Dermott," he said, "you may be right. Let's use Jack Elliot to try and extract the cash from Karen Deacon. I'll call you with her number."

"A wise decision," Becker replied. "I'm sure Jack will have some creative ideas."

On Saturday morning, Todd packed his three suitcases and one carry bag and said goodbye to the tiny, smelly apartment that had been his home since getting out of Castlebrough. As he crammed his luggage into the cab, he thought it ironic that he was moving from one Chinatown to another Chinatown. Twenty-five minutes later they pulled up in front of an old, three-story, gray stone building in Gable Street, Flushing. Todd told the taxi driver he'd tip him twenty if he helped get the suitcases up one flight of stairs. He opened the door to #204 and was immediately struck by the extravagance. His shoes sunk into the plush beige carpet and his eyes went straight to the fifty-inch flat screen television built into the wall. Smaller televisions were in each of the bedrooms, and there was a large teak dining table in the living/dining area surrounded by eight brown suede chairs. The kitchen contained a double width stainless steel refrigerator and Miele appliances including an oven, steamer, and microwave. There was a phone in the kitchen and another on the coffee table in the living/dining area. The thermostat was set to seventy-two and the apartment bordered on luxurious. Todd went into the main bedroom, jumped on the king-sized bed, put his hands behind his head and said, "How good is this!"

After Todd finished unpacking he took a walk along Gable Street to Jack Elliot's appropriately named Bandits nightclub. It was a two story, seedy looking brown brick building with double entrance doors and two small, smoked glass windows on the lower level. The upper level was more conventional with large windows running across the width of the building. It looked like it had started life as a warehouse with offices above it before being converted to a nightclub. There was an alley adjacent to the building and Todd made his way along it until he came to another alley that crossed it and ran at the rear of the club. It was a dead end, and he could see a loading bay for deliveries of alcohol and food.

Todd strolled back to the front and entered the club through its heavy timber doors. He was greeted by lush, dark carpet and small, coffee tables surrounded by sofas and recliners spread around a large room. Two pool tables were set back from the carpet on tan colored tiles. There was a long, polished wooden bar directly in front of him stocked with a variety of spirits. To the left of the bar, he could see the stainless steel doors of the kitchen. On the right was a small dance floor with psychedelic lighting above it. There was a young, attractive girl dressed in a low-cut dress behind the bar and perhaps ten patrons lounging in recliners, drinking and smoking. A thickset man stood up and walked over to Todd. "We're not open until six o'clock, dude. Why don't you come back then?"

"I'm not looking for a drink. I start work here on Monday, and I just wanted to check the place out. I won't stay."

"Ah, you're Todd, the accountant," the man said thrusting his hand out. "I'm Jed Buckley. I manage the place. I hope you're gonna help me clean up this mess."

Buckley had meaty hands and a powerful grip. He was only about 5' 9" but looked like he weighed more than two hundred pounds. He was smiling, but he was like many of the inmates Todd had met. His mouth turned up, and he flashed his pearly whites, but there was no mirth in his eyes. This and his Grecian nose gave him a cruel appearance.

"Good to meet you, Jed. Do I report to you on Monday?"

"Shit no! To the boss. He'll want to show you your office and get you started. Do you feel like a drink? I can introduce you to the boys," Buckley said running his hand over his nearly bald head.

"Thanks, but I can't. I've got a date. I'll see you on Monday."

"Lucky man," Buckley said.

Todd turned to leave and could feel Buckley's eyes boring into his back. He was sure that Buckley was going to be watching him intently and knew that a mistake could prove fatal.

As Todd left the club, he called Vanessa on his cell to warn her that he'd be calling her from his apartment and that she shouldn't mention anything about the FBI or the SEC.

A few minutes later, Vanessa answered, "Hi honey. Have you finished unpacking? What's the apartment like?"

Todd smiled. She was a far better actor than he was. "I didn't have much to unpack." He laughed. "The apartment's way cool. Even better than what I had in Manhattan. I can't wait for you to see it."

"That good?"

"Yeah, it sure is. After the hostel, and the smell of the delicatessen, it's like paradise. God, I hope my lawyers get me off. I could get used to living here."

"I've got my fingers crossed for you, hon. Are we going to catch a movie tonight?"

"Sure. Why don't I head to your place now? We'll grab something to eat and then go and see that new Angelina Jolie movie."

"Fine. She's beautiful, isn't she?" Vanessa said.

"Not as beautiful as you."

Vanessa laughed. "You're wearing rose colored glasses."

"No, I'm not," Todd said.

"I'll see you soon."

Todd hung up the phone. Perfect show.

Karen Deacon was sitting in front of her computer when someone she didn't know Skyped her.

"Who is this?" she asked.

"Never mind that Mrs. Deacon, I know you have some problems. I'm going to help you."

"How did you get my Skype address? Who are you?"

"All you need to know is that I know about the CD, and I can get hold of it and the copies."

"What do you want?"

"I told you. I'm a white knight. I want to help you."

"Do you know who the people are that are blackmailing me?"

There was a long pause. "Mrs. Deacon, they are extremely dangerous people who won't hesitate to kill you or those close to you if they don't get their way. You and your family are far safer dealing with me."

"I'll ask you again, what do you want?"

"I just wanted to make contact, Mrs. Deacon. I'll be in touch again, soon."

Chapter 42

Todd arrived at the club just before 9 A.M. on Monday morning and was greeted by a small, nasty looking man who roughly patted him down. The wiry, dark-haired man then barked at another thug telling him to take Todd upstairs to Elliot's office.

"Good morning, kid. Do you like your new accommodation?" Elliot asked.

"It's okay," Todd replied as he looked around Elliot's timber paneled office.

"Don't fall over yourself with gratitude. I hear you met Jed this weekend. You can start by sorting out his paperwork. I'm sure it'll keep you out of trouble for a few weeks. Oh, and I'm the only one who uses a computer and only for communications. All our systems are manual, and anything you introduce will be too. You won't' be emailing any files. Understand?"

"Who would I email them to?" Todd smirked.

"That's something I'll never have to worry about, because everything will be in books, on paper, or in my head. Now I'll ask you again. Do you understand?"

"Yeah, of course."

"Good, I've set up an office for you. Come on, you might as well get started."

The office was two doors down from Elliot's, and Todd could still see a trace of sawdust on the carpet. They had removed the door from its hinges and replaced the timber wall with a large pane of glass. Todd smiled. There were no filing cabinets and no drawers in the desk. Two open metal cabinets, not unlike the ones at Castlebrough sat behind his desk. Every document and action would be visible, and there would be no such thing as working behind closed doors. On the plus side, there was a window on the other side of the office that let natural light in and overlooked the alley.

The small man came up the stairs, and Elliot introduced him as Amon McEvoy, one of Jed's assistants, who would be helping out with the paperwork. This time McEvoy extended his hand, and as Todd shook it, he asked. "Are you an accountant too?"

Before he could reply, Elliot said, "No, he's not. Amon handles security. We wouldn't want anything to happen to you. Amon will make certain it doesn't."

Todd looked at the little man. Tattoos covered his arms, and there was an ugly scar on his neck. He had the hard look that Todd had become so used to seeing in Castlebrough.

"Amon, before Todd gets settled in, why don't you show him around?" Elliot said.

Todd was surprised by the size of the building. It had been a large warehouse. Jed Buckley's office was between Elliot's and Todd's and housed a large steel safe. On the other side of Elliot's, there were two vacant offices and quite a few closed doors. Amon explained that they were sleeping quarters and there were always at least half a dozen "employees" on the premises. Downstairs, Todd was impressed with the all-stainless steel kitchen and the expensive Gaggenau equipment. The receiving store was untidy and overflowing with spirits and food. Todd ran his eye over some of the use by dates and saw that much of the food needed to be thrown out. Adjacent to the store was a large, cool room carrying an abundance of poorly arranged stock. As Todd went down the steps to the cellar, he knew that there was no purchasing or stock control, and that hundreds of thousands of dollars were unnecessarily tied up carrying stock. There were forty kegs of beer in the cellar, some empty and some full, and a long refrigerator stretching down one wall that was full of white wines. An equally large temperature controlled cabinet ran the length of the opposite wall, and it contained some fine red wines. Todd took out a bottle of Scarecrow Cab Sav and read the label. "Hell, you wouldn't get any change out of five thousand for this."

"I wouldn't know," McEvoy grunted. "Are you nearly finished?"

Todd was about to make a smart remark when he remembered Elliot's warning. "Yeah, thanks for showing me around, Amon. Are you going to be working in my office?"

McEvoy laughed. "Not feckin' likely. Don't worry, though, I'll be watching you."

In twenty-four days' Phillip Cromwell would be rid of Doug Lechte, and he was counting them down. He could barely wait for the partners' meeting. Initially, he'd been annoyed that Lechte hadn't resigned, but now he was glad. He was going to enjoy seeing Lechte degraded in front of his peers. He had already arranged for security guards to escort him from the building. Cromwell's position had gone from strength to strength. His photo had been on the front page of the *New York Times* with the mayor and the senior partner of Strauss Robinson after they'd enjoyed a game of golf at the exclusive Redwood Hills. Cromwell asked his secretary to obtain the photograph and have it framed so that he could hang it in his office.

The second Skype call Karen Deacon received from Elliot was little different to the first. He professed to be only interested in helping her and made no mention or demand for monies. His manner was charming and friendly, but Karen sensed there was another side to this unknown caller. Five minutes into the third call the caller said, "You really should deal with me. I can guarantee you that that CD will never see the light of the day if you pay me."

"That's a lie," Karen said. "You don't know how many copies there are. How can you make that guarantee?"

"That's where you're wrong. There's an original and two copies."

"Did your foreign partner tell you to tell me that?"

"I don't have any partners. I'm just an intermediary trying to help you."

His English was far better than his partner's, and he wasn't as volatile, but Karen suspected that it was all an act.

"I think you're a liar," she said. "Yes, I'd pay five million to make sure the CD's never shown on the internet but there's no way you can guarantee that it won't. I'm not paying."

"Mrs. Deacon, I'm warning you," Elliot said, his voice raised. "I'm trying to help you. I'd hate to see your children given copies. They might open them on their school's computers. Can you imagine their embarrassment when all their school friends see it? And what about your ex-husband and the Cougars' players. If you pay, you remove those possibilities."

"That's what your partner said," Karen laughed scornfully even though the butterflies in her stomach were running rampant. "I know what you're going to do. You're going to take my money and then sell the CD to the sleaze who pays the highest price. You might even make multiple sales. I'm not paying a cent."

"I'm going to give you a little time to sleep on it. The next time I Skype you'd better have changed your mind. If you haven't, your kids are going to be devastated, and you're going to be the biggest porn star in America."

"Go to hell," Karen said, ending the call. Then she broke down and wept.

BOOK 4

Chapter 43

After two weeks, Todd had managed to get the club's paperwork in order and set up a ledger of what was owing to it. The thugs that lived at or hung around Bandits seemed to have got used to him and didn't pat him down every day anymore. They were a surly lot when he was around, and their dislike for him was obvious. When they were together, they laughed a lot, usually at the expense of someone they had kneecapped or beaten up. Amon McEvoy hardly spoke to Todd but was never far away, and Todd thought the Irishman would slit his throat as soon as look at him. Twice McEvoy had come into his office and told him to get lost. The first time he had misunderstood. McEvoy had said, "Take fifteen minutes and go get yourself a cup of coffee, kid."

Todd had replied, "Thanks, but I'm okay I'll grab one later."

McEvoy had shouted, "Get the feck out of here. Disappear! I don't want to see your face for fifteen minutes."

The second time, Todd had left instantly. There was a coffee shop across the street, and he had sat at the window and watched the same small, unmarked, white van drive down the alley on each occasion. Todd had little doubt the van was delivering drugs destined for Jed Buckley's safe. Other than this, nothing out of the ordinary had occurred. Elliot worked with his door closed, and his office was too far away for Todd to hear his conversations unless he was shouting, which he frequently did. Despite this, Todd could still only pick up the occasional word. He heard Ronny's name being used disparagingly many times and guessed it was Ronny Conroy. The only other name he consistently heard was Mrs. Deacon, usually after hearing the unique Skype call sound.

On the taxi ride to Castlebrough, all Todd could think about was Vanessa's concern about Lechte being removed as a partner of

Montgomery Hastings & Pierce, and she losing her job. If that occurred he would have no indirect contacts to the FBI and SEC and the danger in what he was doing would multiply twentyfold.

As he emptied his pockets at the visitors entrance, Todd wondered whether he was destined to visit Frank Arturo every second Sunday for the rest of his life. He was shown to the same room as last time, except this time there was a pack of cards on the table, and Arturo was watching a fight on a small flat screen television. His eyes never left the screen, and he held his hand up for silence, but as the guard went to leave, he said, "Hang on, Joe."

Todd and the guard stood there until the round and fight were over. "Mayweather's a bum, but he can sure box," Arturo said. "I love watching the guy."

"He's a great fighter, Mr. Arturo," Joe replied.

"Jeez, don't you know anything? He's not a fighter's bootlace. He's a boxer. He's a master of the art of self-defense. Pacquiao's a fighter and when they eventually meet the master of self-defense will win easily. Put your house on it, Joe."

"Yes, Mr. Arturo."

"Joe, get me a latte. Todd, would you like anything?"

Todd pinched himself again in amazement at the power of the man now shuffling the cards. "I'd like a mineral water if you've got it, please."

"If he hasn't, he'll get it. Won't you, Joe?"

"Sure, Mr. Arturo," the guard replied, nervously opening the door.

"Gin today, Todd. I want to talk and don't want to have to concentrate."

Arturo was a seriously good gin player, and Todd grinned knowing that he wouldn't need to fake losing. "Thanks for the compliment," he replied. It was the first cheeky comment he had ever made to the mob boss.

"Face it. It's not your game. If I wanted fierce competition, we'd be playing chess. You're a passable gin player, but that's all." Arturo smiled.

It was the first time Todd had ever seen Arturo genuinely smile.

"Have you found out anything?"

"Nothing."

"And the Irishman is watching you like a hawk."

"How do you know about McEvoy?" Todd gasped.

Arturo smiled but this time it was just a thin line.

"Do you know who Elliot's bosses are?" Todd asked.

"No, but it would only take me five minutes to find out."

"How?"

"Some of my people could persuade Elliot to tell me."

"No, no, I don't want that. I'd be no better than him if I did that."

"Or me," Arturo said.

"I'm sorry, Frank. I didn't mean it that way."

"Yes, you did. Don't apologize. We live in vastly different worlds. Let's leave it at that. I'm happy to help you, but I won't ask again. Now concentrate on your cards. You're playing worse than what you usually do. Is there anything else worrying you?"

"I have some contacts in my old firm. They're about to be removed. It's going to make what I'm doing far more difficult without them."

"Don't worry. Nothing's going to happen to them. That trouble making managing partner's going to get some bad news, while the young lady posing as your girlfriend is in for a pleasant surprise," Arturo said. "I don't have anything else to say. Let's play cards."

In his third week at the club, Todd reorganized the store and got rid of all the old inventory. When he asked Jed Buckley if he could help with the buying, the thug had fallen over himself saying yes. Buckley hated anything to do with paperwork. Now when he sold drugs, charged interest or collected cash, he just told Todd and left him to record the transaction.

Elliot called Todd into his office at the end of the week to tell him how pleased he was.

"Thanks," Todd said. "I can streamline operations even further by putting the inventory on computer."

"If I ever see a computer here, besides mine, I'll throw it and the idiot who brought it in out the window. Understand?"

"Don't get your panties in a wad, Jack. I was only saying."

"Well, fucking don't. I want you to do the same in the cool room as you did with the store. Get rid of the old stuff. I gotta tell you it's a relief that you're gonna be doing the buying. Jed wouldn't have a clue what he's doing."

One of the five cell phones on Elliot's desk rang. He picked it up and said, "Hello, Dermott," before looking at Todd and saying, "I'll talk to you after. Piss off."

As Todd went back to his office, he thought about the cell phones. He was nearly sure they were all prepaid, but the one Elliot had answered had a blue cover to separate it from the other four which had black covers. Perhaps the cell with the blue cover was for Elliot's bosses to contact him and who was Dermott?

Vanessa, for the first time, made the short trip to Flushing to have dinner and see a movie. Most of the night she was withdrawn and over dinner said, "I'm stressed. I feel sorry for Doug, I'm worried about you, and I probably won't have a job by Wednesday."

Todd toyed with telling her what Arturo had said but didn't because he doubted what the mob boss had said. Instead he said, "I have a hunch that everything's going to work out."

"Hunches mean nothing," Vanessa replied. "Come on. Let's go and see this movie. I like Sandra Bullock, and I could sure use a laugh. Maybe I'll feel better if it's funny."

Nearly three hours later they left the theater and strolled down the street toward Todd's apartment. He purposely walked on the opposite side of the road from the club as he didn't want to run into any of the thugs.

"You know we're not doing anything," Vanessa said.

"Of course. It's going to look a bit strange, though. After all, we're meant to be a couple."

"We'll pet on the couch, and then you'll ask me to come into the bedroom, and I'll say it's that time of the month. Problem solved."

"Feel free to change your mind." Todd grinned. "I'm joking. I do want to show you the apartment. It's so cool. Feel free to be suitably impressed."

At the same time, Todd was showing Vanessa his apartment, Doug

Lechte was sitting in front of his television, beer in hand, watching the Knicks and the Lakers. He had lobbied hard on Friday but at the end of the day could muster only ten votes. Cromwell had outflanked him and as managing partner could make promises that Lechte couldn't. At least three other partners were lobbying for Cromwell and the campaign they had run had been relentless; Lechte had brought the firm's reputation into disrepute and had to go.

Only long-serving tax partner Sandra Bishop had lobbied for Lechte. He wasn't worried for himself. He was more than comfortable. However, he was worried about Vanessa and in his farewell speech he intended to do everything he could to save her. Todd Hansen was another matter. There was nothing Lechte could do to help him, and any contact that Todd had with Grinich and Lord would have to be direct. The meeting wasn't until Wednesday, but Lechte had cleared his personal items from his office on Friday. A few more days lobbying wouldn't change anything.

Chapter 44

Phillip Cromwell's phone rang just after 5:30 A.M. on Monday morning and he answered it with a terse yes.

"Mr. Cromwell, it's Connie Burgess from WABC. Do you have anything to say about the mayor and The Disabled Children's Fund?"

"What are you talking about?" Cromwell said, rubbing the sleep from his eyes.

"Have you seen today's *Wall Street Journal?*"

"It's five o'clock." Cromwell snapped. "Of course not. Get to the point."

"Reporters for the Journal claim that more than ten million dollars of funds from The Disabled Children's Fund were channeled into the mayor's reelection campaign. Did you know that the Fund paid six million dollars to the Muslim community in Brooklyn to help with the building of a hospital for underprivileged and disabled children? The article alleges that more than half the monies donated were spent on advertising for Mayor Johnson and buying the Muslim vote. It further alleges that many functions paid for by the Fund had nothing to do with disabled children and everything to do with getting the mayor reelected. The FBI have just concluded an extensive investigation and are about to lay charges. Do you have anything to say about the alleged misappropriations?"

Cromwell let out an involuntary gasp. "I don't know what you're talking about. Why don't you ask the mayor?"

"We spoke to the mayor's wife. She said that the Fund's audited by your firm, and everything must be kosher. Would you like to comment?"

Cromwell could hear his cell phone ringing. "No," he said. "I have to go." As he hung up, the phone started to ring again.

"What's happening?" Mary asked. "What's wrong?"

"Nothing," Cromwell said testily. "Leave the phone off the hook and go back to sleep. I'm going out to buy a paper."

Ten minutes later, Cromwell spread *The Wall Street Journal* across the dining room table and read the article in detail. The reporters had interviewed the senior partner of Strauss Robinson, who acknowledged that they had drawn up the Fund's trust deed. However, like the mayor's wife, he denied having anything to do with compliance, saying, "That's why the Fund appoints auditors."

Cromwell called the mayor on his private line and got the busy signal and when he called the mayor's wife on her cell phone his call went straight through to voicemail.

When Cromwell arrived at the offices just after 8 A.M. television crews and a horde of reporters were in the foyer waiting for him. The cameramen closed in and reporters shoved microphones in his face. He shouted, "Get out of my way," and then, "No comment, no comment," as he tried to push through them.

"It's claimed that there's more than eight million missing from the Fund. A Fund set up to help underprivileged, disabled children. Your firm was the watchdog appointed to protect the assets of the Fund. What happened? Did you go to sleep?" An aggressive young female reporter asked.

"That's not the role of an audit–"

"Is it true that these misappropriations were reported to you, and after the mayor complained, you severely reprimanded the employee who brought them to your attention?" another reporter asked.

"Get out of my way," Cromwell shouted, throwing his arms in the air while the cameras continued to roll.

Despite the early hour, the phones were ringing incessantly, and most partners were already in their offices. Cromwell shoved the door to his office open then slammed it closed in one motion. There was a memo on his desk from Sandra Bishop convening an emergency meeting of partners for 11 A.M. today. His first reaction was to buzz her on the intercom and ask what she thought she was doing. He didn't though. Instead, he paused. She was the firm's oldest and longest-serving partner. In his current position, it would be a mistake to disrespect her and besides it was better that she had convened the meeting rather than Lechte. He called the mayor again but got the busy signal and then tried the senior partner of Strauss Robinson, but his assistant said that he was out of the office for the day. The rats were running for cover.

When Sandra Bishop rose to address the partners, she looked more like a stern school principal than the senior tax partner in one of the most prestigious accounting firms in the world. She had a yellow notepad in her hand and was wearing a black suit and white blouse. Even with her gray hair pulled up in a bun she was barely 5' tall but her height belied her presence.

"You all know why you're here," she said.

"Don't you think you should have spoken to me before you convened this meeting?" Cromwell demanded.

"No! We're on every television and radio station. Twitter and Facebook have gone into meltdown. We're on the front page of *The Wall Street Journal*. Clients are jamming our switchboard, and my cell phone hasn't stopped ringing all morning. I guess I'm not alone in that," Sandra said.

Murmured assents went around the room.

"We're under siege," Sandra said, looking at her notes. "Phillip, Gary Jenner is being interviewed by *Sixty Minutes* this afternoon. What's he going to say? He resigned straight after you tore him apart because of the concerns that his young employee raised about the audit of The Disabled Children's Fund. What were those concerns? Why were you so critical of Gary? What is he going to say?"

"I'm not on trial here. I resent your attitude."

"You can resent all you like," Sandra said. "Did you know that the leaders of Brooklyn's Muslim community have no knowledge of a hospital for underprivileged and disabled children? And yet The Disabled Children's Fund supposedly donated six million dollars in respect of that hospital. At best, we're staring at a significant claim on our professional indemnity policy, at the worst, Phillip, you may be looking at criminal charges. One of the television stations was speculating, given your relationship with the mayor, that you may have colluded with him."

One of the other partners said, "Then there are the lavish functions and golf days paid for by the Fund that were clearly part of the mayor's reelection campaign. It's terrible. We're going to lose some major clients over this. We have to go into damage control."

Phillip Cromwell had lost some but not all of his bluster. "It's just media speculation," he said. "If there's legal action brought against us, we'll instruct our lawyers to defend it vigorously."

"Don't you mean your lawyers, Phillip?" Sandra said, picking up her notepad and reading from the top page. "Didn't you say, 'If a manager or, dare I say, even a partner makes a major mistake or is guilty of an offense, then it's that person's problem. It's not up to the firm to pay their legal expenses or bail them out. The only legal costs that we should bear are those relating to protecting the firm.' Isn't that right?"

Cromwell turned bright red. He had never anticipated his edicts being thrown back in his face. "I-I didn't mean for–"

Before Cromwell could finish, Doug Lechte stood up and said, "It was poor policy when first raised. It's still poor policy. Now is the time to unite and show solidarity. Phillip is managing partner, and we must stand by him. The firm is bigger than all of us."

Muted gasps went around the room. Most partners had been surprised that Lechte had remained quiet for so long, and now they were stunned to see him supporting his nemesis.

Cromwell ignored Lechte and said, "I will review the audit files in detail over the next two days. It may well be just a media beat up. I'll report to the partners when we consider Doug's future with the firm on Wednesday."

"No, you won't," Sandra said. "We will appoint a four partner committee today who have had nothing to do with the Fund or the mayor to review the audit files. The committee will report back to a full meeting of partners in seven days' time. Does anyone have any objections?"

Cromwell started to say something and then thought better of it. The rest of the partners remained silent.

"Good. Now I want to dispense with this rubbish about Doug. We may need him as managing partner while Phillip fights the charges that I'm sure the FBI will bring. In a worst case scenario, Phillip may be imprisoned. Accordingly, the meeting scheduled for Wednesday is canceled."

"No," Cromwell shouted.

Sandra folded her arms and looked over the top of her severe spectacles slowly casting her eyes around the room. "Does anyone else have any objections?"

No one said a word, and some of the partners started to stand thinking that the meeting was over.

"The meeting's not over," Sandra said, and the partners scrambled back to their chairs. "I want to move a motion that Vanessa Hodge be invited to join the firm as a full partner."

"I'll second that." Lechte grinned.

"No, no," Cromwell shouted. "The firm's constitution provides that in the absence of a vacancy, new partners can only be admitted on an annual basis."

"I have been a partner of this firm for thirty-two years," Sandra said. "I need a rest. Accordingly, I'm announcing my retirement from the firm conditional on Vanessa Hodge's appointment. You have your vacancy, Phillip."

"No," Cromwell said, hanging his head.

"All those in favor of appointing Vanessa Hodge," Sandra said.

Thirty-five hands went up.

"All those against."

Five hands including Cromwell's were raised.

"I declare the motion carried," Sandra said. "This meeting is adjourned."

As the partners filed out of the meeting room, Doug Lechte caught up with Sandra Bishop.

"I don't know how to thank you," he said.

"Thanks are not required. I merely did what was right."

"I've never seen you like that before."

"Sometimes age and being a woman have certain benefits. I knew that Phillip couldn't attack me without being seen to be a bully. In his condition, that was too big of a risk for him to take. He's a good administrator, but he's naïve. It's obvious that the mayor and his cronies played him for a sucker. Unlike you, he's got no street smarts. I was going to nominate you as managing partner until you gave that noble little speech. What was that about?"

"Thank God you didn't. I couldn't stand the thought of managing forty disparate partners. It's a time where we have to unite. Any sign of divisiveness will be picked up by our staff and clients with disastrous consequences. Phillip's the right person to be managing partner, but we have to narrow his role to the administration of the firm. He has no idea how to relate to clients."

"It's more than that. We need to limit his influence on the appointment of new partners or we'll just end up with a firm of clones like him. What am I doing saying *we* when I'm about to leave?" Sandra laughed.

"That was an incredibly selfless gesture nominating Vanessa and then standing down for her. She will be delighted and eternally grateful."

"Oh, it wasn't selfless. I meant what I said. I'm tired. I'm looking forward to traveling around Europe for the next year. I'll think of you while I'm enjoying coffee on the Amalfi coast." Sandra smiled.

Chapter 45

Todd hadn't expected Vanessa to call on Wednesday night, and she could barely contain herself. The firm had finally admitted her to the partnership, and Doug Lechte's position was no longer in jeopardy. Cromwell was in serious trouble, and while Lechte hadn't sought the role, the other partners had gravitated toward him and he was the de facto managing partner. Vanessa said that she was staying back for drinks with some of the partners and was celebrating with her family tomorrow night. Then she invited Todd to her apartment the following night saying that she wanted to prepare a special celebration dinner. Todd had immediately said that he would take her out to a fancy restaurant and that she didn't need to cook, but Vanessa wouldn't hear of it. He was pleased.

When Todd put the phone down he thought about what Frank Arturo had said and how right he had been. He felt squeamish. The mob boss loved playing games, and Todd wondered whether this was just another game for him.

"Do we have anything to be concerned about, Amon?" Elliot asked, as he threw his legs onto the desk and pushed himself deep into his swivel chair.

"On the surface, nothing," Amon replied. "The only people he calls or who call him are the girl, his mom and his lawyers. Oh, he called his old boss last week and asked if he'd reconsider his decision not to re-employ him. It seems there was a coup at the firm, and his boss is now the main man and the girlfriend is a partner. Anyhow, the boss shot him down. He said he was happy to help where he could, but that would never extend to a job. He told the kid that even if he his appeal was successful, it was common knowledge that he'd committed the offenses and that he'd never work for the top end of town again."

"Ungrateful little shit." Elliot laughed. "I give him a job and a great apartment, and he still wants to work in Manhattan."

"He has an appointment with his lawyers next Wednesday afternoon. His mom's gonna be there."

"That's to be expected. She's bankrolling the legal fees. How are he and the girlfriend getting along?"

"Everything seems fine. He asked her to move in with him, but she said that it was too early. He was pissed off, but it didn't last long," Amon replied. "Oh, I nearly forgot. He visits Frank Arturo every second Sunday."

"Now there's a strange relationship." Elliot laughed. "One thing we can count on though is never having to worry about Arturo cooperating with the government."

"I've got someone listening to every conversation. Do you want me to continue or are you happy for me to listen to the recording in the morning? Most nights he only makes one call, and that's to the girlfriend."

"What about his cell?"

"In the two weeks we've been recording he's hardly made a call. He's called you, me, the girl and Castlebrough and that's it," Amon replied.

"I think he's okay," Elliot said. "I don't think we need to be listening to every call. Just make sure you listen to the recording in the mornings."

Vanessa was wearing a white V-neck blouse and black skinny jeans with matching flat shoes when she opened the door. She kissed Todd lightly on the lips.

"Congratulations," he said, "you look stunning."

"Thank you. It was a fantastic surprise. Sandra was so selfless, and I think Doug's as happy as I am. Can I get you a drink?"

"I'm right for now. Is there anything I can do to help you? Peel the potatoes? Grate the cheese? Anything?" Todd said, looking around the small apartment. There was a sparkling white tablecloth on the small table and gleaming cutlery and crockery. Strangely, there was a laptop flickering at one end of the table.

"No, thanks. We're having grilled salmon and salad. Very healthy. Followed by white chocolate pannacotta with coffee syrup. Yummy but not so healthy." Vanessa laughed while beckoning Todd to the laptop.

The Word document on the screen read;

Detective Grinich thinks my apartment and phones might be bugged. If you have anything to tell me, call me at work and ask me if I feel like coffee or a drink. He wants to see you. He wants you to leave thirty minutes earlier than usual when you next go to see Arturo. Walk along Mount Street. It's a one way. Hail a cab to take you to Castlebrough at 12:25 P.M. Grinich will be driving it.

Todd nodded, and Vanessa deleted the message.

"Sounds fabulous," Todd said.

"I have a superb Pinot Noir that I've been saving just for this occasion. Can you open it?"

While they were eating, Vanessa bubbled on about being made a partner and went over what Lechte had told her about the meeting in great detail.

Todd grinned. "Hmmm, Phillip Cromwell might be in the same boat as me. We might be sharing cells in six months."

"That's not funny, Todd. Please don't spoil the night," Vanessa said taking a long sip of her wine.

"I'm sorry, that was a silly thing to say," Todd said, scooping up the last of the coffee syrup from his plate. "God, that was good."

"I'm glad you liked it. Let's watch some television. Bring your wine with you," Vanessa said with the slightest of slurs, as she kicked her shoes off and curled her feet under her on the sofa.

As Todd sat down next to her, he said, "I don't think I've ever seen you so happy."

"There were times I never thought it would happen and I wondered whether all those hours would be worth it. My first resolution is that I won't be working Sundays anymore." Vanessa laughed.

The wine had relaxed Todd, and he sensed it had the same effect on Vanessa. He put his arm around her and drew her toward him. He was surprised when she responded so enthusiastically. They lay on the sofa kissing, and Todd unbuttoned her blouse and ran his hands over her silky skin. He was breathing heavily when she said, "Oh that's good, real good," before whispering, "I think it'd be a good idea if you stayed the night."

Todd smiled. "I'd love to."

"I'll make up the sofa for you," she murmured. "If they're watching, they'll be expecting you to stay."

"Oh, that's what you mean," Todd said, unable to mask his disappointment.

"You're growing on me," Vanessa mouthed. "I do like you, but we have to remain focused."

"Let's stay on the sofa for a few more minutes," Todd mouthed back with a big grin.

Todd walked briskly along Gable Street for about half a mile before turning into Mount Street and heading south. There were few cabs using the street, and he glanced at his watch before turning around and hailing a yellow cab about two hundred yards away. He climbed in the front and said, "Castlebrough Penitentiary."

The driver was wearing a New York Yankees cap, sunglasses and was heavy with facial hair.

"Hello, Todd," Grinich said, "you're looking good."

"What do you want?" Todd replied. "This is dangerous."

"No, it's not. They never follow you when you go to see Arturo. Even if they did, there's nothing untoward. You're taking a cab like you always do. We've been disappointed. It's over four weeks, and you haven't passed anything on to Vanessa."

"If I had anything I would've have got it to you. They're careful about what they say in front of me and Elliot keeps his door closed. You're going to have to be patient."

"You must have seen or heard something," Grinich persisted. "Come on, think."

"I know the club gets a sizeable drug delivery each week. They make sure they get rid of me before unloading. It's delivered in an unmarked van, but it's random. There's no fixed day or time."

"Jeez, you've got to have more than that." Grinich groaned.

"I think Elliot's boss's name is Dermott. He always gets rid of me when Dermott calls."

"Dermott? Dermott who? God, there's a million Dermott's."

"I haven't heard a second name."

"You've got to have more. Who else does Elliot talk to?"

"I wouldn't say talk. He shouts at a woman named Mrs. Deacon on Skype. I think he's trying to intimidate her the way he did with me. I don't know how old she is, but I'm fairly sure he called her a cougar in one of their calls. He's a very nasty piece of work."

"Interesting. What else did you hear about her?"

"Nothing. That's it."

"Okay, tell me about the club. It's layout, offices and security. Don't leave anything out."

For the next ten minutes, Todd provided as much detail about the club as he could recall while Grinich prodded and prompted him.

"Tell me about Elliot's phones again," Grinich said.

"They're Samsung throwaways, four of them are black, and one of them is blue. When Dermott calls it's always on the blue phone and Elliot uses it more than the other phones."

"Does he call Mrs. Deacon on the blue phone?"

"I don't know. I've only heard calls to her on Skype."

"I'd love to get ahold of what's on those SIM cards. You know you could copy them."

"Forget it. That takes time, and they're watching me far too closely. Besides, I'd be so nervous I'd most likely mess it up."

Grinich sighed. "Can you at least get a photo of the phones?"

"I'll try. Why can't you just tap them?"

"We can when he uses them outside the club and in public, but you say that's hardly ever. We have problems with the law tapping phones in private places. Are they still searching you?"

"Yeah, but not as much as they were. About once a week now. They're becoming more comfortable with me."

"How do you feel about wearing a wire?"

"Are you fucking stupid," Todd responded. "Didn't you hear what I just said? They find a wire on me, and I'm dead. Besides, I haven't heard anything remotely worth taping."

"Perhaps when you become more accepted?"

"Grinich, listen to this. I'm never wearing a wire. Not ever. Don't ask me again."

"Jesus, settle down," Grinich said, as the ugly structure that was Castlebrough appeared on the horizon. "Same time, same place in two weeks."

Chapter 46

Dermott Becker was surprised and disappointed when Elliot had been unable to extract the five million from the woman. She had proved tougher than Becker had anticipated, and if it were not for Borchard, who was calling every day, he would have called the operation off.

"I'm sick of waiting, Dermott. Let's just sell the CD and then see how smart the bitch is then."

Becker hated this. He saw himself as a businessman. When a deal went sour, he cut his losses early and moved on. Borchard was the exact opposite, driven by malice and the urge to inflict pain just for the sake of it.

"That will cause us more trouble than it's worth," Becker replied. "If you're lucky you might get two mil. It's peanuts in the bigger scheme of things. If it's just the money, I'll buy it."

There was a long pause. Becker knew what his vindictive partner in Chicago was thinking. He wasn't interested in the money. He just wanted to hurt Karen Deacon.

"I've put Dirk back on the job. I don't want you to call Jack off. Maybe she'll crack under the pressure of the pair of them. She hasn't seen the CD yet. I'm going to make sure she does. It might motivate her to change her mind."

"Not according to Jack. He said that she's convinced the CD's going to end up on the net no matter what she does. She's tougher than Cooper and hasn't got a fifteen-year career in the big league under threat."

"She'll crack," Borchard said without conviction. "And Dermott, if she doesn't, I'm going to flood the net with copies."

"You can't. You were at the board meeting that resolved that under no circumstances would we sell the CD."

"Yeah, and I'm sticking to the resolution. I'm not selling it. I'm putting it on for nothing. Then we'll see how tough the bitch is," Borchard said, terminating the call.

Becker didn't move for five minutes. It had been a mistake bringing Borchard into the operation. Now the question was *how to get him out?*

Aaron Lord listened in silence but when Grinich had finished briefing him, he said, "It sounds like Elliot is blackmailing this woman. I'll run a check on all female senior executives of listed companies and see if Deacon comes up. I wonder what the significance of calling her a cougar is. Maybe she's an older woman with a much younger boyfriend. Todd didn't get much, did he?"

"Nah, and he says they're watching him like a hawk at the club. I didn't tell him it wasn't just the club. The only time they don't follow him is when he goes to visit Arturo."

"It's disappointing, isn't it?"

"Yeah, a little, but if we can find out where those drugs are coming from we might be able to make a sizeable dent in their operations."

"That's good, but unless this Mrs. Deacon is a source of inside information, he hasn't found anything that'll help me."

"I think if we can get ahold of the details on that blue cell phone's SIM card we'll be able to speed up the investigation. I have an idea, but it's risky and the kid might not buy into it. He got angry when I asked him to wear a wire."

"I don't blame him," Lord replied. "Don't push him, Chas. Time is on our side."

The ice cream van parked on Gable Street about two hundred yards south of the club stayed there all of Monday. It was gone on Tuesday when a plumber's van appeared about three hundred yards to the north on the opposite side of the street. For two weeks, FBI agents inside a variety of different signed vans parked in various locations near the club videoing every vehicle entering or leaving the alley. They paid particular attention to the arrival of a plain white van that coincided with Todd leaving the club for the coffee shop. In the third week, a cyclist rode in front of the van as it came down Gable Street causing it to brake sharply. The driver was too busy abusing the cyclist to see the pedestrian, who in one quick movement affixed a tracker under the rear of the van. Grinich cursed the time that he had wasted securing a warrant. His life had been a lot easier before the bleeding heart lawyers had come to prominence.

Elliot sat back in his swivel chair, legs on the desk and grinned. "You're doing a good job, kid. I'd almost forgotten that it was still possible to make an honest dollar."

"It could be more profitable. If you got rid of those thugs sitting around the bar, it'd be a lot better. Customers come in, have one drink and then can't get out the place fast enough."

"They're my salesmen," Elliot said, and then as an afterthought, "and my debt collectors. If you filled the club, got the prices right and had everything running flawlessly you still wouldn't make as much as just one of those guys."

"Drug dealers, loan sharks and standover men." Todd sneered.

"Don't get too precious; they're paying your wages. When you've got the club ship-shape, your next job's going to be to help with collections," Elliot replied. "I gotta take a leak."

Todd started to stand.

"Sit down. I'll only be a minute."

Todd quickly glanced around looking for Amon. He was nowhere to be seen. Todd quickly took two pics of the phones on Elliot's desk and another three of his office. By the time Elliot returned Todd's cell phone was back in his pocket.

"As I said the place looks good, and you might as well finish the job. How long do you think you'll need to straighten out the store and re-price the menus?"

"A week, but I don't like the idea of collecting drug monies."

"What you like is of no account. We'll talk again next Monday." Elliot smirked. "Keep up the good work."

Todd froze as he sorted out the mess in the cool room. The first day was hell, and he barely scratched the surface. Some of the food was over five years old, and there was no semblance of a system. The drinks menu was way out of date, and the prices of many white wines were less than replacement cost. Todd wondered how profitable the drugs were. The volumes and margins had to be huge to make up for the underpricing and cost excesses elsewhere in the club. Amon was still keeping a close eye on him and had a nasty habit of appearing when least expected. Todd wasn't worried. He wasn't doing anything that might cause the thug to become suspicious.

By Friday, Todd was sick with a cold but he'd finally finished the job. Desperate for warmth he went back to his office. He was surprised that Elliot's door was open and as he walked past he could see him talking on Skype. Todd was in the corner of his office on top of a strip heater trying to get his hands warm when he heard Elliot shout, "Mrs. Deacon; this is the last warning I'll give you. If you're wise, you'll transfer the money, and all this will go away. I promise you'll never hear from us again, and your worries will be over."

Todd could hear the woman's voice but couldn't make out what she was saying. Then he heard Elliot, straining to control himself, say in a loud voice. "I didn't put that CD in your mailbox. I know nothing about it. It shows you how dangerous those people are. I can stop them. Just transfer the money."

This time Todd could make out at least one of the woman's words, *no,* which she used repeatedly. "You're stupid." Elliot hissed. "How do you think your husband's going to feel when his players see the CDs? They'll know about your antics and the poor bastard who's the father of your children will be none the wiser. Your husband's a public figure, and these people aren't just going to degrade you, they're going to degrade him too. He doesn't deserve it, and you can make it all go away. Don't, don't you dare end this call."

A few minutes later Todd heard Elliot say, "Dermott, it's me. Those stupid Serbian bastards in Chicago sent her a copy of the CD and she's more determined than ever not to pay."

On the way to his apartment, Todd called Vanessa and asked her if she felt like coffee or a drink.

Chapter 47

Todd was surprised when Vanessa chose to go to a noisy, crowded bar near her apartment rather than a coffee shop. He was more surprised and a little annoyed when she asked for a mineral water. It took nearly five minutes of being pushed and jostled to get to the bar. All the seats were taken, but there was a little space in the corner of the room and Todd handed Vanessa her drink, put his free arm around her waist and steered her in that direction. At the other end of the room, there was a jukebox blasting out hits from the nineties and a small dance floor that was overflowing. With his face only inches away from Vanessa's he shouted, "Why did you want to come here?"

Vanessa put her mouth next to his ear and said, "Grinich said that they're watching us and might be using listening devices. He said if the equipment's sophisticated they'll be able to hear us through windows and from more than two hundred yards away. They're not going to hear anything in here."

"Fuck! I never thought of that," Todd said, pulling her toward him and kissing her.

"What was that about?" Vanessa laughed, her face still close to Todd's.

"Realism," he replied, cuddling into her. "Now listen carefully, I have a lot for you to pass on, and I need to come up to your apartment after. I have some pics to download to your laptop."

Five minutes later they were on the crowded dance floor dancing body to body. Todd knew that she could feel his arousal, but she didn't pull away. He had always wondered if you could be scared and horny at the same time. Now he knew the answer.

For three weeks, the FBI tracked the white, unmarked, refrigerated van. Based in the yard of a small logistics company on the outskirts of Brooklyn, it made very few deliveries. The few it did make were always to the same locations in the Bronx, Manhattan, Staten Island, and Bandits in Queens. Each week, refrigerated trailers from Chicago were quickly unloaded by the logistics company. Within an hour, the unmarked, refrigerated van was on the road to its four locations. It was impossible to track the refrigerated trailers' movements prior to their departure from Chicago. When Aaron Lord tried to trace the ownership of the logistics company, he came up against a maze of companies controlled by lawyers and accountants. The directors of the logistics company did not reside at the addresses they had disclosed in corporate filings and were untraceable.

Grinich had taken all of ten minutes to decipher the information that Todd had provided to work out that Mrs. Deacon was Karen Deacon, estranged wife of super coach, Tom Deacon. He toyed with letting the Chicago office handle the initial contact but sensed it was the breakthrough he'd been waiting for. Within forty-eight hours, he was on a flight to Chicago.

The Chicago office had arranged a small Ram CV van signed in the livery of Lakes Gas Company for Grinich. He changed into blue coveralls and a cap bearing the company's logo. After driving for thirty minutes, he stopped at the entrance to the driveway of Karen Deacon's grand home and got out. Oscillating cameras on brick pillars supporting steel gates focused on him as he pressed the button on the intercom system.

"Yes."

"Lakes Gas Company, ma'am. We've had a pipe rupture, and I need to check your connections to make sure they're safe."

"Couldn't you have called? I'm going out soon. How long are you going to be?"

"Ma'am, if it wasn't an emergency, I wouldn't be here. I'll finish within half an hour, and then you'll be able to rest easy."

"All right, but please hurry," Karen said, as the gates clanked open, and Grinich drove up a long flower lined driveway to the rear of the house.

He took a tool box and pad from the van and got out as Karen came out the back door. He strode over toward her saying, "I just need to get your signature before I start." He handed her a pen and opened the pad to a page that had written on it, *FBI. Don't act surprised. Remain calm and sign the page.*

When Karen looked up, Grinich was holding his FBI badge. She looked both scared and relieved.

"I'll check the connections on the barbecue first and then the pool and sauna," Grinich said. "I don't want to talk in the house. It might be bugged. Now tell me who's blackmailing you and why."

Grinich had worried about whether Karen would talk, but his concerns proved ill-founded as she related all that had had happened. Twice she broke down in tears, and her voice quavered frequently. When she finished, she said, "Thi-this is the bes-best I've felt since the whole sor-sordid business began. Do-do you thin-think I'm terrible?"

"I don't judge people unless I think they've broken the law," Grinich replied. "I'm glad you feel better."

"Wha-what are you going to do?" Karen asked, wiping her eyes as she fought to regain composure.

"I'm going to catch these low-lifes and put them in jail. Logon to the cell phone they gave you and let me have it."

Grinich jotted down the number before scanning the recent calls and asking, "You only ever receive calls from one person?"

"Yes, on the phone and the screen always says private caller. You're not going to be able to get his number. The other one Skypes me."

Grinich laughed. "That part's easy. The carrier will have the number, but that probably won't help because it'll be a prepaid cell. However, I'll soon find the locations from where the calls originated. If we can't get him from that, we'll get him the next time he calls. We know the one who's contacting you by Skype but proving it might be difficult."

"What would you do if you were me?"

"I've been thinking about that," Grinich replied. "I think you should tell your husband, your kids, and Devlin Cooper's parents. After you've done that you should find an interviewer you can trust and tell her everything that you've just told me. There'll be outrage, but there'll be sympathy too and time does heal everything. No matter what you do, the CD is going to make it onto the net. I'm betting that there are many copies."

"God, I'd been thinking of telling those close to me, and you're right I should tell Devlin's parents. I never thought of telling the whole world on television, though," Karen said, turning red.

"It'll be better if you get your side out there before your friends and neighbors see it on the net. You'll remove some of the heat. If you don't, and it just comes out of left field, the media will drive you insane. They still might, but it won't be as bad."

"What if I do and the CD's never shown?"

Grinich shook his head. "Mrs. Deacon, we both know there's no possibility of that."

"Whe-when should I do-do it?" Karen asked, the very thought making her feel squeamish.

"Not until we know where the guy with the foreign accent is calling from."

"How will you contact me?"

Grinich handed Karen his card. "Buy yourself a prepaid cell tomorrow. Text me the number and then delete the text. Don't use it in the house and turn the ringtone off. Put it on vibrate and if you need to call me, do it from around the pool. It's not visible from the street. If you're out, go to a busy coffee shop or bar. If it vibrates, it'll be me. No one else will have the number."

"When are you going back to New York?" Karen asked.

"I don't know. Not before I find out who's calling you."

Chapter 48

Just two days after Grinich's visit Karen received another threatening call from the blackmailer with the foreign accent. "Mrs. Deacon," Vaughan said, "we're sick of waiting. Transfer the money or we'll download the CD to your children's school computers. Don't think we don't have the expertise to do it."

"You low-life. You're going to download it no matter what I do. We've been over this before. Why are you still wasting my time?"

Vaughan softened his tone. "I'm trying to help you. I give you my word that if you pay you'll never have to worry about your dirty little secret coming out."

Karen laughed derisively. "You're not a good liar. There's not a bone of sincerity in your voice. Your partner's far more believable than you. He told me that you were dangerous and that I should deal with him."

"I don't have a partner!"

"Oh, so he's just someone brought into help because you've failed," Karen taunted. "I wish Devlin had told you to go to hell, you bastard. You murdered him as surely as if you'd shot him."

"Yeah, I know," Vaughan replied, "the spoilt, rich boy couldn't take the pressure so he took the easy way out. Gutless bastard!"

"Don't you dare say that! He had more courage in his little finger than you have in your entire body. You're slime."

"You've had your say, Mrs. Deacon. You've got seventy-two hours to transfer the money. If you don't, you're gonna be a world famous porn star by the weekend and your husband, kids and friends are gonna die of shame."

"You're not getting a cent, scumbag."

"I was looking at the CD last night with a few of my friends," Vaughan goaded. "You're a contortionist. Oh, and my friends asked me to find out if your tits are real. Are they?"

"You make me sick."

"Really? You're hardly the one to be taking the moral high ground. Save yourself a lot of pain, lady. Make the transfer."

There was a long pause.

"Are you still there?" Vaughan asked.

"I've got nothing more to say," Karen replied, glancing down at her watch. "Don't call me again."

Grinich was elated. Finally, the blocks were starting to fall into place. The FBI had pinpointed the call to Karen Deacon to a warehouse in one of the poorer industrial areas of Chicago. Grinich was confident that the warehouse housed the blackmailer and was also the source of the drugs coming into Brooklyn. He immediately put it under twenty-four-hour surveillance recording all movements. Aaron Lord returned his call to tell him that the property was owned by a corporation, but its real ownership was hidden in a maze of trusts and other corporations.

There were twenty-three men who regularly frequented the warehouse, and it had been easy to determine who the boss was. Like clockwork, a black limousine was driven through the gates at 8 A.M. every morning by one of three different drivers. The swarthy looking Brock Borchard had no criminal record but had been a prime suspect in at least two murders and associated with drug-running, prostitution and loan sharking. His three drivers were the same ethnicity and like Borchard, none of them had criminal records.

Grinich watched fascinated as the forklifts and other lifting equipment in the warehouse's yard were barely used. Clearly the huge trailers that frequented the yard were already close to fully loaded, or empty, and on their way to pick up a load. Whatever goods they picked up or that were being dispatched were capable of being manually loaded and unloaded. Grinich had no doubt they were drugs and that he was looking at a major distribution center. In the space of the first two weeks surveillance, four of the refrigerated trailers that left the warehouse made deliveries to the logistics company in Brooklyn.

Grinich didn't know how Borchard fit in with the insider share trading but was sure that he was witnessing organized crime on a major scale. He was equally convinced that the warehouse contained a huge stash of drugs. With this in mind, he decided to launch an early Monday morning raid on the warehouse. Once Borchard and his cronies were in custody, Grinich would be able to grill them about the drugs, the blackmail, the other members of the group and their nefarious activities. He knew that he would need more men and called a contact in the Chicago PD and arranged to brief him on the operation.

Brock Borchard carried three cell phones, one of which hardly ever rang, but when it did, it was answered with unusual alacrity.

"Yeah, what is it?"

There was a long pause and as Borchard listened his face clouded over.

"You're sure it's 8:05 on Monday morning?"

This time the pause was brief.

"Thanks, two days is more than enough. Oh, I'm putting a hundred thousand in your Hong Kong bank account this afternoon. It's a bonus."

Around midday on Saturday a refrigerated trailer backed up to one of the warehouse's loading bays, and two of the forklifts sprang into action. One of the two FBI agents manning the cameras said, "That's unusual. I can't remember them using two forklifts before."

The other agent laughed. "I wouldn't worry. It must be a genuine load."

"Yeah, you're probably right," the first agent said, "they're loading pallets."

As Todd walked along Mount Street, he glanced over his shoulder and saw the yellow cab. He climbed in and started laughing. "I couldn't believe it when Vanessa told me you'd be my taxi driver today, Aaron."

"Chas's away and he thought you'd prefer me rather than an agent you've never dealt with before," Lord replied.

"Has it got anything to do with what I passed onto him?"

"I can't say. Just keep your wits about you."

"So it has. What's it about? The woman or the drugs?"

"I told you I can't say. Stay alert and you'll be fine. Chas expects to make some arrests that might bust this thing wide open. With luck, we might not need you for much longer."

"That's encouraging news."

"Yeah, I thought you'd be pleased. Todd, what is it with you and Frank Arturo?"

"Why?" Todd asked. "If you're thinking about asking me to spy on him about his mob you can forget about it. Besides, in all the time I've spent with him, he's never breathed a word about what he does. He doesn't need to. Everyone in prison lives in fear of him. Guards included."

"I wasn't going to ask. I can't imagine him being involved in securities fraud. I'm just intrigued. You visit him every fortnight. What is it with you and him?"

"I don't know. He likes me I suppose and for that I am grateful. You and your mates at the FBI promised to protect me and couldn't deliver. He did."

"Yeah, but you're out now. You know he's a cold-blooded killer, don't you? You don't want to get too close to him."

Todd laughed derisively. "A friend of his got word to me that it'd be wise if I visited him. What would you do?"

Lord didn't answer. "Are they still searching you?"

"Fuck! I told Grinich I was never wearing a wire. Don't you guys know what never means?"

"Jeez, settle down. I wasn't going to ask you to wear a wire. Do you remember seeing this phone before?" Lord asked, passing Todd a blue Samsung Galaxy.

"You know the answer. It's the same as the one on Elliot's desk," Todd said apprehensively.

"You said you couldn't get the number, and you didn't want to run the risk of downloading the SIM card. How do you feel about switching phones?"

"Do I look stupid? None of his saved contacts will be on the phone and his password won't work."

"Any password will work." Lord laughed. "And the phone will crash when he tries to use it."

"So his login's fine but when he tries to make a call the phone will fail?"

"His contacts won't be available and nor will the keypad."

"Okay, humor me. He takes his cell phone to the local dealer and asks him to take the SIM card out of the old phone and put it in a replacement. After the dealer does it, Elliot's saved contacts no longer exist. He doesn't need to be a Rhodes Scholar to work out what happened, and I'm dead. I'm not doing it."

"What if the dealer says he can't get his contacts because the SIM card's corrupted?" Lord smiled.

"Can a SIM card be corrupted?" Todd asked, not trying to hide his skepticism.

"I'm not going to say it's common, but it can."

"I'd rather run the risk of carrying two phones rather than wearing a wire. They only pat me down at random now, and I'm not sure that any of them, except Elliot, would be suspicious."

"So you'll do it?"

"I'll take it with me and think about it. I'm not promising anything."

"Todd, if you do it, make sure you turn Elliot's cell phone off as soon as you make the switch. I'd hate for it to ring while it was in your pocket."

"That's the first thing that crossed my mind. You guys come up with the fancy ideas, but it's not your life on the line."

As they neared the entrance to Castlebrough Lord said, "Enjoy your visit with Arturo. Who would've thought a year ago that you'd be friends with the most powerful Mafia boss in the country?"

Chapter 49

It was a gloomy Chicago morning, and a light drizzle was falling as two carloads of Fibbies drove through the gates signed Refrigerated, Chilled & General Storage Inc. A wagon with two of Chicago's finest and their German shepherds followed them. Police had blocked the surrounding streets. Grinich was taking no chances. He leaped from the leading vehicle and strode toward the lobby's double glass doors, warrant in hand. Surprisingly, a man he knew to be Brock Borchard was sipping coffee in one of the visitors' chairs. He was flanked by two gigantic men while a smaller man sat at the receptionist's desk. Grinich pushed the warrant into Borchard's hands who said, "Terrible weather, isn't it? Would you like coffee?"

"This isn't a social visit." Grinich snarled, as agents shoved open the door to the corridor leading to the offices. "Read the warrant."

"After," Borchard said, yawning. "Don't let us hold you up. If you need anything, just ask. We're here to help."

Grinich took the door to the warehouse where the two German shepherds were barking and straining to get off their leashes. Four of his agents and the two police officers were searching a sparsely filled warehouse. "What have you found?" he asked one of the officers.

"Nothing yet, but the dogs never get this excited unless they're sniffing cocaine," the officer said, bending to let them off their leashes. "Don't worry, they'll find it."

"Keep one on its leash," Grinich said. "Let's see if there's anything in the offices."

The dog strained and pulled to get to the boardroom, but there was nothing in it. The imprints of two cabinets were still in the carpet, and the dog stood over them and yelped. The officer led the dog to Borchard's office where there was a small combination safe. The dog put its paws on it and whined.

"Mr. Borchard," Grinich shouted, "please open the safe or we'll have to destroy it."

"Sure," Borchard grinned, dialing in the combination and opening the door.

The dog went crazy barking and whining while trying to put its head in the empty safe.

Grinich looked at Borchard's smirking face and knew the raid had been leaked. They weren't going to find anything. "Why hasn't the safe got anything in it?" he asked.

"It was here when I bought the place. I don't use it," Borchard replied.

"Yet you had no trouble remembering the combination," Grinich said. "Funny. Real funny."

Borchard laughed. "I've got a good memory for numbers."

"So have I," Grinich said, glancing at one of his agents. "Get Mr. Borchard's three helpers and bring them to the boardroom."

"What's this about?" Borchard asked as Grinich pushed him into the boardroom.

"Empty your pockets and put the contents on the table in front of you," Grinich said to Borchard and his men.

"I said what's this about?" Borchard said.

Again Grinich ignored him. "Turn your cell phones on," he said. "Don't worry about logging on."

"Are they on?" Grinich asked two of the agents who were helping him.

They nodded and Grinich took his cell phone out and punched in a number. The phone in front of Dirk Vaughan began to ring, and his face dropped. Borchard's smirk disappeared.

"Handcuff him and read him his rights," Grinich said.

"What is this?" Borchard demanded.

"Mr. Vaughan is going to be charged with attempted blackmail. What do you know about it, Mr. Borchard?"

"Nothing. Why would I?" Borchard blustered.

"He's your employee, isn't he? Was he acting on your instructions?"

"For what? I don't know what you're talking about," Borchard said.

As the agents marched Vaughan out the door, Grinich looked over his shoulder. Borchard's smirk was gone, and his face was black with rage.

Dermott Becker was in the Hamptons watching his wife play tennis when Borchard called and told him what had happened.

"Don't worry about Dirk," Becker said. "Without the CD they've got nothing. You realize there's no way you can release it now?"

"Yeah, but when Dirk's out and the heat dies down I'm going to fix the bitch."

"Don't lose your cool. I'll call Jack Elliot off. The pressure must have driven her to the FBI. Let's not make it any worse than it is."

"It's more than that. The Fibbies knew about the drugs as well. They didn't find out about them from her."

Becker put the phone down as his young wife bounced across the court and cracked a booming forehand down the line. The mistake he had made bringing Borchard into the business was starting to hurt. The key to their success was that they had always flown under the radar, but the thug from Chicago was drawing unwanted attention to himself. Becker knew that unless something was done it was only a matter of time before Borchard would lead the FBI to Vulture Inc.

On Sunday night, Todd rationalized that the risk of being caught with the blue Samsung Galaxy was remote. Rarely was he patted down and even if he was, it was no certainty that the second cell phone would arouse any suspicion.

Monday morning was entirely different. It was a cool morning, but the underarms of his shirt were wet, and his jacket was confining. As he entered the club, he saw the thugs around the snooker tables. Amon looked up and shouted, "Hold on."

Todd's heart pulsated as the nasty, little Irishman ambled toward him. "You're looking stressed," he said. "What's wrong?"

"I overslept. I didn't even have time to shower. I sprinted to get here on time."

For the first time since Todd had met him, Amon broke out into genuine laughter. "You think we give a feck if you're late? You're not working for that fecking posh Manhattan accounting firm anymore."

"I-I didn't know."

"Well, you do now. The boss won't be in today, but he wants you to calculate the vig on all the outstanding loans and prepare a list of all of the delinquents. You and me are gonna be doing some debt collection this week. If I see you lift your head from the desk today I'll break your kneecaps," Amon said, and then laughed at his joke.

Todd watched as Amon rejoined the men around the pool tables, and they started laughing and looking in his direction. He took the stairs two at a time. The phone in his jacket felt like it weighed a ton and the thought of bringing it in again tomorrow made him sick. There was nowhere in his office where he could hide it, though. He had stupidly thought that Elliot would be in today and that he would get the opportunity to make the switch. Now as he sat behind his desk reflecting, he realized that it might be days, even weeks before an opportunity to make the switch arose. Where could he hide the phone? Then it hit him. He grabbed a roll of masking tape and headed toward the cellar. Once there, he looked around to make sure McEvoy hadn't followed him before kneeling and securely taping the cell phone under the lowest rack. As he walked back up the stairs, he breathed a deep sigh of relief.

Chapter 50

After Karen Deacon told Chas Grinich what had occurred she felt that a burden had been lifted from her shoulders. Soon after she called prominent sportscaster, Libby Mansfield, who was also a friend of Tom's and hers. The following day Karen sat in Libby's office looking at the late thirties, blonde woman dressed in a black suit, black shoes and wearing matching thick framed black spectacles. If she was trying to create the impression of power she had succeeded in spades. After Libby had listened to Karen's story, she said, "This is a story that would be better covered by news and current affairs."

"I want you to do the interview."

"I understand. I'm just not sure my bosses will go along with it."

"Libby, I hate saying this, but you're not the only friend I have in the media. I'd like you to handle it but if not I will find someone else who I'm sure will help me."

"And you want me to go over all the questions with you so that you can approve them and get your answers down pat?" Libby asked.

"Yes."

"It won't work. The audience will see straight through it. I can lead you through the early questions, but I'm also going to ask you some that are out of left field."

Karen frowned. "I'm not sure I like that."

"Karen, listen to me. If you answer my questions with the same sincerity you've just shown, you have nothing to worry about. I'm not going to try and tear you down or make a fool of you."

Karen recalled that Grinich had said something similar. "Okay, when will we do it?"

"I still have to get the all-clear from my bosses. If they say yes, I think we should do it on *Your Nation* this Sunday night. How does that sound?"

"The quicker, the better," Karen replied.

Karen had no idea how Tom would react, so she arranged to meet him in a small city restaurant for lunch. They ordered drinks and then she said, "I don't know whether you'll want to eat after you hear what I have to say."

For the next thirty minutes, she related everything that had occurred. The pain on her husband's face was almost too much to bear.

When she had finished, he was white and wringing his hands. "Why?" he whispered.

Karen thought about saying *because you neglected me*, but Tom was hurting enough without having to listen to feeble excuses. "Animal magnetism," she said, shaking her head. "We knew it was wrong, and we tried to stop, but the attraction was too strong. Devlin took his life because of it."

"I don't know what to say," he said. "I feel like a three hundred pound linebacker just hit me."

"I'm sorry, Tom. I'm really sorry."

"Do you think telling the kids, Devlin's parents and going on national television is going to help?"

"I know it's going to hurt you," Karen said, "but it's the only way of partially defusing the impact of that CD when it hits the net."

Tom groaned and then stood up. "I'm going to skip lunch," he said. "I need time to think. What you did was terrible but no one deserves to go through what you have. I hope the FBI gets those bastards."

"I know you're angry. Later, if you feel better, can we talk?"

"I'm not angry, Karen. I'm sad. Sad for a great, young football player who lost his life far too early. Sad for you. Sad for the kids. And sad for me."

Telling the kids wasn't any easier, particularly the eldest, Sally, who was nearly fourteen. After her mom had appeared on television, Sally knew that she would be the butt of taunts and cruel jokes at school.

"I have to do it," Karen said. "It's the only way I can stop the blackmailers."

"You said they're still going to release that CD. Just don't pay them.

You don't have to go on television and tell the world what you've done," Sally said. "How could you have done that to dad? I hate you."

"What's a blackmailer?" asked six-year-old Tom junior.

"Sally, you'll understand when you get older," Karen said, instantly wishing she hadn't.

"I'll never understand," Sally shouted, wiping tears from her eyes as she stomped out the door. "I'm going to my room."

"Will dad be coming home now?" asked nine-year-old Brett.

"I don't know." Karen sighed.

As expected, Devlin's parents proved the most difficult. At first they had been warm and welcoming but as Karen told them what had occurred, they became cold. Karen had not expected sympathy or forgiveness, and she was not surprised by the Coopers' reaction. When she had finished, there were no questions. Instead, Mrs. Cooper looked at her with hate-filled eyes and said, "Is that all?"

"I-I-I'm sorry."

"Yes, for yourself." Mrs. Cooper hissed. "If there's nothing else, please leave."

"Get out of our sight," Mr. Cooper said, as he strode to the front door and held it open.

Amon McEvoy was dressed in a full-length black coat as he climbed behind the wheel of the dark blue Chevy Impala. "Have you got the list?" he asked.

"Yes," Todd replied, locking his seatbelt.

They drove for ten minutes without a word before stopping at the front of a seedy apartment building. Todd watched as McEvoy took a baseball bat from the backseat and put it under his coat. "How much does the prick in #214 owe?"

"Four thousand," Todd said.

"Let's go."

The concrete stairs were cracked, and the steel railing was rusted. The paint was flaking, and the smell of mold and dampness was in the air. Todd knocked on the door of #214 and a fat, bald guy about forty with his arms covered in tattoos and wearing a dirty white singlet answered.

Despite the tattoos, the track marks were clearly visible. "Mr. Martin," Todd said, "I'm here to collect the four thousand you owe Bandits."

"What is this? I only owe twenty-five hundred!"

"You forgot the interest, sir. Here, let me show you," Todd said, sensing the little Irishman moving behind him.

For more than five minutes, Todd went over the calculations, explaining that interest kicked in at ten percent per month on the first of every month no matter when the money's borrowed. "If you borrow in the first week and pay back in full in the last week, you won't pay any interest, sir."

The man grimaced. "I don't have any control of that. Hold on."

When he returned, he had a handful of cash in all denominations. "Count it," he said, "it's all there."

As they got back in the car, McEvoy said, "Maybe the boss is right. You might make a good collector."

The scenario was repeated three more times. In each instance, Todd was respectful and helpful.

"We'll see how good you are in here," McEvoy smirked as they stopped on a street that looked like a ghetto.

Todd glanced at McEvoy and saw him rest his hand on a bulge under his coat at chest level. This time the apartment was on the ground level and when Todd knocked the door was opened by an African American at least 6'6" and three hundred pounds. His eyes were yellow, and spit was coming from the side of his mouth. "Whaddya want, white boy?" he shouted.

"You owe-" was all Todd got out before two huge hands in the middle of his chest sent him crashing into the opposite wall.

As the man moved forward, McEvoy swung the baseball bat with all his force. It cracked into the big man's kneecap, and a look of shock came across his face as he toppled to the floor. In an instant, McEvoy had the barrel of his gun hard up against the man's head. "Listen, motherfecker, I'm going to count to ten, and if you haven't told me where I can find five gorillas, your brains are going to be splattered all over the wall. One, two-"

A woman came to the door and screamed, "No, no. Don't hurt him anymore. I'll give you your money."

"You better hurry, sister," McEvoy said, "three, four, five, six, seven-"

"Here, here," she said. Todd got to his feet and quickly counted the five one thousand dollar rolls of cash."

"It's all there," Todd said. "Let's go."

As McEvoy reached down to pick up the baseball bat, the man said, "The next time I see you, you're dead."

"Is that right?" McEvoy said, and then without warning smashed the bat into the man's head. As he lay unconscious on his back, McEvoy raised the bat again and slammed it into the man's other kneecap. "You'll find that mighty hard, motherfecker when you can't even walk."

The woman was screaming, but McEvoy acted like he had all the time in the world.

"Let's go," Todd said, the panic in his voice palpable.

"Don't worry. The cops never come here, and there ain't anyone else around who wants to tangle with this," McEvoy said, patting the bulge under his coat.

Todd sat ashen-faced in the car. "I don't care what you do," he said. "I'm never debt collecting again."

McEvoy sneered. "I told the boss you were spineless. You sure proved that. Weak bastard!"

Chapter 51

Karen Deacon pushed herself back in the recliner as the makeup artist did some final touchups. The lights above her were hot and uncomfortable but looking at Libby Mansfield, sitting opposite, you would have never guessed it. She was cool, calm and in control.

One of the production staff shouted, "Ten, nine, eight...we're on."

"Tonight we're going to bring you a tragic story of infidelity, lust, blackmail and the apparent suicide of one of the nation's greatest young sportsman. With me is Karen Deacon, wife of Cougars coach Tom Deacon who entered into an illicit affair with Devlin Cooper, an affair that led to his death," Libby said. "Karen Deacon, why don't you tell us how the affair got started?"

"There had always been a mutual attraction," Karen said. "One day we bumped into each other in the city, and I gave Devlin a lift home."

"And that's when the affair started?"

"No. All we did was kiss, but it sowed the seeds for the future."

"You must have realized that no good could come of it. You were a married woman with three children, nearly fourteen years older than Devlin. Why didn't you just stop it before it got started?"

"I didn't see him for another three months. Like me, he too knew that it was wrong, and we purposely avoided each other."

"What happened?"

"He came to my home to pick some documents up."

"And that's when it started?"

"Yes."

"And it continued for nearly a year?"

"Yes."

"Mainly at seedy out of the way motels?"

"Yes."

"Then what happened?"

"Someone videotaped us and began blackmailing Devlin."

"How did they blackmail him?"

"They wanted him to lose games and said that if he didn't they'd put the video on the internet," Karen said dabbing a tear away.

"That's why he threw so badly in the Pirates game?"

"Yes."

"But that wasn't enough for them?"

"No. They wanted him to tank in the playoffs. That's the reason he took his life."

"But you can't be sure of that. He never told you that he was contemplating suicide, did he? It could have been an accident?"

"No. He never said anything but I know. I just know."

"Then what happened?"

"They contacted me on numerous occasions saying that if I wanted to stop the CD from being shown I'd have to pay them five million dollars."

"Let's backtrack," Libby said. "Did you love Devlin?"

Karen put her hand under her chin and took a long time to answer. "Yes," she said, "and I think he loved me."

"Why do you say that?"

"After the blackmailing started he offered to move in with me, to help bring up my kids. He said that if we were living together it would take a lot of the heat out of the CD."

"What did you say?"

"I told him he was too young and that both our families would be terribly upset. I regret saying that now. Maybe if I hadn't, he'd still be here now."

"So was your relationship founded on love?"

"I like to say yes, but that would be a lie. It began because of lust and physical attraction. The love came after."

"What's on the CD?"

Again Karen paused. "Everything that consenting adults do in private."

"Nothing kinky?"

"No, but not anything you'd want the world to see."

"Had you ever been unfaithful to your husband before?"

"No."

"Why should we believe you?" Libby asked staring over the top of her spectacles.

"Because I've never been drawn to another man like I was to Devlin. I was weak. I couldn't fight the attraction."

"Why didn't he go to the police when the blackmailers first contacted him?"

"There were many reasons." Karen sighed. "The shame he felt he'd brought upon his family. His concern for me and my children. His worries about his career."

"That wasn't all, though, was it?"

"No. The blackmailers told him that they owned the Chicago PD, and he believed them. There was nowhere to go."

"Is that why you went to the FBI?"

"I didn't go–," Karen said and then stopped. "Well, yes there was no one else to turn to."

"And they've already caught one of the blackmailers?"

"Yes, I identified his voice. I'll never forget it." Karen grimaced.

"We have to go to a station break," Libby said. "We'll be right back."

Chas Grinich thought that Karen was a pretty gutsy woman who'd handled some tough questioning extremely well. He hadn't told her that her identification of Vaughan's voice wouldn't stand up in court. Vaughan's lawyers were the best money could buy, and they'd find half a dozen men with voices near identical to him and Karen wouldn't be able to tell them apart. Vaughan was a tough customer and hadn't admitted anything. Unfortunately, he would be released in the morning.

Todd Hansen watched the interview in astonishment. Karen Deacon was obviously the Mrs. Deacon whom Elliot had been trying to heavy.

Dermott Becker cracked his knuckles hard as he watched Karen answer her interrogator's questions. She came across as being honest, truthful and remorseful, and Becker reasoned that the consensus would be sympathetic to her and furious with the blackmailers. There wasn't enough evidence to hold or charge Vaughan, but the Fibbies would know that Borchard was behind it, and they'd be closely watching him. The key to Vulture's success was that it was unobtrusive and low key. That was starting to unravel, and Becker was far from happy.

Borchard watched and recorded the interview in silent fury. If only Dirk hadn't pushed Devlin Cooper over the edge, they would have never had to deal with the Deacon woman. One part of the interview particularly caught his attention when the interviewer asked her about going to the FBI, and she had said *I didn't go* and then changed her answer. It looked to Borchard like she had been going to say *I didn't go to the FBI,* and if that was the case, it meant someone had leaked. The FBI had undoubtedly tracked Dirk through the woman's cell phone but why had the warrant been to search for drugs?

Chapter 52

Todd was more on edge than ever now that he knew what McEvoy was capable of. He told Elliot that he was never debt collecting again and if that meant losing his job and apartment, then too bad. Elliot hadn't objected. Instead, he had broken out in raucous laughter. Todd wondered whether McEvoy's little performance had been to scare him about what might happen if he crossed them. If so, it had worked. Todd was very nervous.

In nearly two weeks, Todd had not had one opportunity to switch the cell phones. Elliot had only left his office unattended on one occasion for about thirty minutes, but McEvoy had been skulking around, and Todd had been too scared to retrieve the hidden cell phone. The opening, when it came, was totally unexpected. Todd was just about to go to lunch when two of the gang got into a noisy fight in the bar over a game of pool. Elliot bounded out of his office, and Todd immediately followed him down the stairs bypassing the bar. He quickly retrieved the cell phone from the store and scampered back up the stairs. On the way back he saw Elliot, in the bar, with McEvoy next to him, reading the riot act to the two protagonists. Todd looked around the corridor before entering Elliot's office and making the switch. He paused to turn Elliot's phone off, and then took off downstairs to the store again. It had taken less than three minutes but for Todd it seemed like hours. After making sure, there was no loose masking tape lying around he made his way back to his office. Elliot's booming voice was still echoing around the bar. Todd got back to his office and set up a date to see Vanessa for dinner that night. He thought that with a little luck, Elliot may not even try to use the phone for the rest of the day.

It was late in the afternoon when Elliot shouted, "What's wrong with this bloody phone. Todd, come in here."

"What's up?"

"My phone won't work. See if you can fix it?"

"You've got another four phones. Why don't you use one of them?"

"I need this one," Elliot replied.

"What's wrong with it?"

"It lets me logon, but after that I get squiggly lines. Look," Elliot said, prodding the screen with his forefinger.

"I'll take the battery out and reinsert it. Sometimes that works. What's your password?"

"Give it to me," Elliot said and entered his password. "Shit, there's still squiggly lines! What other ideas do you have, genius?"

"I'll try taking out and reinserting the SIM card. That might work."

As Todd reinserted the tiny card, Elliot, who'd been watching closely, grabbed the phone. "A lot of fucking help you are."

"There's a shop on the corner of Mount that sells and fixes phones," Todd said. "Do you want me to take it down there?"

Elliot looked at Todd slyly before saying, "Nah, don't worry about it, I'll get Jed to take care of it."

As the partners of Montgomery Hastings & Pierce filed into the conference room it was evident they already knew the outcome of the preliminary investigation into the audit of The Disabled Children's Fund. The mood in the room was somber as the committee of four delivered their findings. At least nine million had been misappropriated from the fund and applied to the mayor's reelection campaign. Worse, the young auditor who had been questioning the Fund's employees had suspected defalcation, and it was only Phillip Cromwell's intervention that had circumvented her.

Sandra Bishop asked, "Are you saying that had this line of audit been pursued we would probably not be in this position?"

"Yes," replied one of the committee members.

"Do we know who the trustees are going to sue?" Lechte asked.

"No, but clearly the fund manager and its directors," the committee member said.

"They'll sue us, too," Lechte said. "I'll talk to our PI insurers. It's in our interests to settle as fast as we can. The publicity of a long drawn out civil action can only be detrimental. That's the last thing we need."

Phillip Cromwell took his hands from behind his head and looked defiantly around the room. "As managing partner I think I'm best placed to handle negotiations with the trustee. I certainly don't believe we should settle."

"Phillip, you're managing partner in name alone," Sandra Bishop retorted. "You got us into this mess, and you're not going to make it worse than it already is."

"For someone's who's resigned the partnership and won't be here in two months you have an awful lot to say," Cromwell said.

Sandra ignored Cromwell and instead said, "Can I have a show of hands of all of those who would like Phillip to handle negotiations with the trustee and our insurers."

Even Cromwell's closest supporters hung their heads, and not a hand went up.

"It would not be a good look for our clients and the media if it appeared that Phillip was no longer managing partner," Sandra said. "However, internally Doug will continue to assume that role until the matter with The Disabled Children's Fund is resolved."

Cromwell glowered but knew it was pointless saying anything. Doug Lechte wasn't happy either. He hated managing the firm, listening to the other partners' gripes, holding them accountable and taking responsibility for decisions they should be making. He was always short of time, his meetings with the government officials were starting to take their toll and he was having sleepless nights worrying about Vanessa. He regretted getting her involved and knew that if Todd was detected things could go very badly for her.

Todd shivered and dug his hands deep into his overcoat pockets while he waited at the front of Botticelli's. It was an inexpensive busy Italian restaurant only two blocks from Vanessa's apartment. The cab pulled up, and Todd held the door open and as Vanessa got out, he put his arm tightly around her.

"Sorry I'm late. I got held up at work with Doug," she said, kissing him lightly on the lips.

They waited a few minutes before being shown to a small table set against the wall that afforded them privacy.

"This is very cozy." Todd grinned, as their feet touched under their table.

Surprisingly Vanessa did not return his smile and instead put her hand to her mouth and said, "Doug's worried about me. He said it's taking longer than he thought and that my involvement's very dangerous. He suggested I back out while I still can."

"He's right. I've been thinking the same."

"But then you won't be able to pass messages on."

"I'll find a way. I can always do it every second Sunday on my way to visit Arturo. They never follow me on those days."

"What if something urgent comes up like today?" Vanessa asked.

"I don't know," Todd replied without confidence. "I'll find a way."

"I told him that I appreciated his concern, but I was going to keep seeing you." Vanessa smiled. "I've grown fond of you, Todd Hansen, and I'd never forgive myself if something happened to you because of me. We're in this together."

Todd felt his heart start to pound. He hadn't expected that response, and as he stared into Vanessa's deep brown eyes, he was overcome with emotion.

"Me too," he said, "but that's all the more reason for you to cease your involvement. We can stage a breakup argument, and you'll be in the clear. If you still feel the same way after we can pick up where we left off."

An overworked waiter interrupted the conversation to take their orders for spaghetti Bolognese and risotto marinara.

"Didn't you hear what I said? We're in this together. The faster we put these crooks away the safer we'll be."

"Bu–"

"No buts."

Twenty minutes later, as they were leaving the restaurant, Vanessa took a tissue from her bag and carefully wiped a small spot of Bolognese sauce from Todd's shirt. He fought back an overwhelming desire to kiss her. If anything the weather had become more bitter, and as they hurried to her apartment she said, "What messages do you have for me?"

"None," Todd said, slipping his hand into her coat pocket. "I got the cell phone that Grinich is so desperate to get. I just put it in your pocket. I'm staying at your place tonight. Don't worry, I'll be on the sofa."

"I know what you're doing. You're sweet," Vanessa replied, squeezing his hand.

As she opened the door to her apartment, Todd swung her around and kissed her passionately. "I've been dying to do that."

"Don't worry about the sofa," she whispered, "but you have to be quiet. I don't think the apartment's bugged, but I'd hate for them to be listening."

Todd had dreamed of this night and as Vanessa turned the bedside light off he drew her to him. Her lips were warm and moist, and her tongue darted inside his mouth as he fought to control his breathing. She ran her hands up and down his chest while he gently fondled her breasts. He felt her tremble with pleasure, and he slowly moved his hand to her thigh and began exploring. He had read all the books about great lovers and how gentle they were, so he was surprised when, with a sense of urgency, she whispered, "Honey, I'm not made of glass."

It had been years since she had been with a man, and she was eager, excited, and sick of waiting. Todd didn't need to be told twice, and he was almost out of control with desire. Sixty seconds later he let out an almighty yell and Vanessa half whispered, half giggled, "I told you no noise."

Chapter 53

The newspapers and talkback radio were evenly divided about Karen Deacon. Some were sympathetic, and some were downright nasty. Her kids had been the subject of some vicious teasing and when she picked up Brett from school he was sporting a black eye. Someone had called his mom a *ho*, and while he hadn't known what it meant, he knew it wasn't good. Sally fared worse when some of the girls said that her mom was a slut and had killed Devlin Cooper. Tom Deacon had recovered from his initial shock, and while he wasn't happy, he had supported Karen and even asked her to move back in with him. His players were sympathetic, and some of them felt terrible about the way they had treated Devlin after the Pirates game. Karen knew that the first two weeks would be the worst, but the relief she felt from being free of the blackmailers was cleansing. It was too late now, but she and Devlin should've come out when the blackmailers first contacted him.

Chas Grinich was not surprised when forensics told him that all calls made to and from Elliot's cell phone were private. Further examination revealed that calls were only ever made to and received from one number. The cell phone was a prepaid, and its present location was a mansion in the Hamptons. The majority of calls were made from a high-rise office building, an apartment in Manhattan, the house in the Hamptons and locations between those buildings while traveling. When Aaron Lord checked the ownership of the house, he found that it was owned by a corporation, owned by other corporations, a structure now all too familiar. It concealed the ownership of the property but indicated that the real owners were the same people who had blackmailed Todd Hansen and engaged in insider trading. Old fashioned surveillance of the property soon confirmed that disgraced former lawyer and now mega-wealthy investor, Dermott Becker, and his much younger wife were the occupants of the Hamptons mansion. By 11 A.M., Becker's prepaid cell phone had either been destroyed or the battery had been removed because it could no longer be tracked. It made little difference as the link between Borchard, Elliot and Becker had been established.

Agents followed Becker to the Truman Building and watched him take a private elevator from the parking garage to the offices of ACME Investments Inc on the fiftieth floor. That night they attached a tiny camera to a concrete roof beam engulfed in shadows. Anyone using the private elevator would be caught on disk. Grinich was encouraged by the progress the agency was making.

When Todd entered the club the following morning, he was greeted by guffaws and smartass comments.

"Have a night out did ya, Todd?" Jed asked.

"Were you on the nest all night, Red?" Another thug laughed.

"Nothing like the taste of hot chocolate," McEvoy chipped in.

Todd felt the color race to his face. Was Vanessa's apartment bugged or were they just keeping close tabs on him? He was about to say something when Elliot said, "Knock it off, you bloody hyenas."

As they walked up the stairs, Elliot showed Todd a red Samsung cell phone. "No wonder you couldn't fix the other one. It died," he said.

Todd silently breathed a sigh of relief. There was nothing in Elliot's demeanor to suggest that he knew anything.

Brock Borchard knew that he was being watched. He didn't see any agents, nor did he notice any cars following the limo but his gut instincts were on high alert. He knew that he couldn't fly to New York undetected. It was nearly midnight when Ahmet dropped him at the Rialto Towers like he did almost every night. Borchard took the elevator to his penthouse on the 40th level, turned on all the lights and poured himself a Glen Fiddich. Twenty minutes later he pulled a Chicago Bears cap down over his forehead and left the penthouse without switching the lights off. He took the stairs to the parking garage two at a time before climbing behind the wheel of an unobtrusive, blue Toyota Camry with heavily tinted windows. Ten minutes later, he pulled up on a dark street behind a silver Cadillac limo. As he got out, one of his warehouse employees jumped in the Camry and took off down the road. Farik was behind the wheel of the limo and Ahmet was next to him. Dirk was sitting in the back.

"Don't speed or do anything to attract attention, Farik," Borchard said. "Drive for six hours and then switch with Ahmet."

"We should be in New York just after midday," Vaughan said.

"That's right. We'll get settled into the hotel, and Farik and Ahmet can pick up the Camrys from the rental places. I don't want anything drawing attention to us. We'll start work the following day."

"Have you got false licenses and cash with you?" Vaughan asked.

"We're not stupid," Ahmet scornfully replied.

Chas Grinich was fuming. His agents had lost Borchard and his gang. They appeared to have vanished. The agents had watched Borchard get dropped at his apartment building and had followed the black limo to Ahmet's house where he'd driven into his garage. Since then there had been no sign of life at the house and the limo remained parked in the garage. Borchard was dangerous, and while he had never been convicted, Grinich knew that he had committed at least five murders and probably more.

Chapter 54

Vaughan drove the dark blue Camry down the alley and behind the club. There appeared to be no one else in it, but Borchard was lying across the back seat. Vaughan parked hard on the curb, opened the rear door, and Borchard slipped into the club.

Todd had his head down calculating the vig on the outstanding loans when he felt someone looking at him. He looked up, and a dark, swarthy, heavyset man in his mid-thirties was standing in the corridor just outside his office. There was something unsettling and intimidating about the man. McEvoy was standing directly behind the man with another swarthy looking character who wasn't much bigger than McEvoy.

"What is this?" Todd asked.

The heavyset man ignored him and instead said to the other two, "I'll see Elliot by myself. Wait downstairs."

Dermott Becker had been angry when he called Elliot to say Borchard would be visiting via the entrance to the store. Becker had cursed and ranted about Borchard interfering in matters that didn't concern him before relenting. Elliot sensed that Becker was wary of upsetting the Serbian. Without saying a word, Borchard sat down opposite Elliot and slowly put a cigarette in his mouth. He was a master of turning up the pressure even though Elliot appeared unfazed.

"Tell me about the accountant," Borchard said, blowing a perfect smoke ring. "How much does he know about the drugs?"

"What's this about?" Elliot asked.

"Someone leaked to the FBI. I suspect it was him."

"It's not. I have him tagged twenty-four hours a day. I know he hasn't seen anyone from the government. You're barking up the wrong tree."

"Really? What about the girlfriend? Why couldn't he be passin' information on to her?"

"Because I've had her watched as well, that's why."

Losing patience, Borchard snarled. "Answer my question. What does he know about the drugs?"

"Virtually nothing," Elliot replied. "We get rid of him every time we get a delivery. He would've seen some of the guys making sales, and he helped with some collections last week."

"Get rid of him?"

"He's never here. We send him out for lunch, coffee or whatever."

"So he could be watchin' from across the road?"

"Watching a white van drive down an alley. It could be delivering anything."

"Didn't you say he was smart?" Borchard sneered. "Tell me about the woman."

"The woman?"

"Jesus! You were calling the Deacon woman. Where did you call her from? Here?"

Elliot paused. "Yeah, I Skyped her from here, but I always closed my door so he wouldn't have heard anything."

"You never lost your cool? You never shouted at her?"

Again Elliot paused but this time for longer.

"Don't worry about answering," Borchard said. "You already have. So he probably did hear some of your calls. I'm sure the Fibbies traced Dirk from her cell phone. Why do you think they didn't trace you?"

"That's easy. Skype's virtually untraceable, and it's heavily encrypted."

"So the FBI can't crack or trace it?"

"All they'd get is a jumble. It's caller to caller secure."

"Okay. Maybe I'm wrong. I doubt it, though. Have there been any other strange occurrences since he started working for you?"

"Strange? No, other than turning the club from losing a shitload to making a profit." Elliot laughed.

"Nothing else?"

"Nothing."

"My gut's rarely wrong," Borchard said, standing up. "Do you search him every day?"

"Of course," Elliot lied.

"You need to keep a very close eye on him, because if you're wrong, it'll be you who's in the gun. I'll be in touch."

Vaughan brought the Camry up to the store entrance and opened the rear door. His boss slid into the back seat and said, "Head for Manhattan, Dirk. I'll tell you where to go when we get there."

Thirty minutes later Vaughan drove into the parking garage below the Truman Building.

"Stay here," Borchard said, getting out and striding toward the private elevator.

Dermott Becker was sitting in the boardroom by himself. He didn't get up or shake Borchard's hand and instead said, "You're encroaching on my territory, Brock. I hope you've got a damn good reason."

Borchard pulled out the chair nearest to Becker and eyeballed him. "I have. Listen to this."

For the next fifteen minutes, Borchard related his suspicions and finished by saying, "The only reason the Fibbies haven't questioned Elliot is because the kid's a plant. They don't want to rock the boat. I told you to get rid of him. If I hadn't been paying my friends in the Chicago PD, I'd be staring at ten years hard time. Fuck that!"

Without saying anything, Becker reached for one of the phones on his desk.

"What are you doing?"

"I'm calling Jack to tell him to double the watch on the kid and his girlfriend," Becker said, shuffling through some papers in front of him. "He's got a new phone. So do I. I jotted down his number before. I've just got to find it."

"Why the new phones?"

"Something happened to Jack's. A power surge or something. I don't exactly know. All he could get was squiggly lines on the screen, and it was beyond repair. As you know, we always changeover dedicated prepaid cell phones at the same time, so I had to get a new one too."

Borchard's eyes narrowed, and he reached out his hand as Becker punched in Elliot's number. "Cell phones don't crash these days," he said. "My guys have all got cell phones, and I can't ever remember one crashing. Put Jack on speaker mode. Something stinks."

Before Becker could speak, Borchard said, "Jack, we want you to get your old cell phone back pronto. Dermott will give you the name of a telephony expert. I want you to take it to him and find out if it's been tampered with."

"It might've already gone out with the trash."

"Nah," Borchard said, "techies never toss stuff like that out. They always think they might be able to use the parts for something. Get Amon to go get it now. There's no time to waste."

"What's this about?"

"It should be obvious, Jack. I just hope Brock is wrong," Becker said. "I'll phone you with a name within the hour."

Chas Grinich was both relieved and worried when the cameras in the parking garage of the Truman Building picked up Brock Borchard entering the private elevator. What was Borchard doing in New York? What did he know? Did he know about Todd? He hadn't traveled by plane and his gang hadn't been sighted recently, which probably meant they were with him in New York. It was clear that they had known they were being watched and slipped out of Chicago.

Five minutes after Borchard left, Elliot barged into Todd's office. "Stand up and put your hands above your head."

"You're joking," Todd replied, not moving.

"No, I'm not. Now get the fuck up."

Todd got up and slowly put his hands up while Elliot vigorously patted him down. "Unbutton your shirt!"

"What is this?" Todd asked nervously.

Elliot ignored him and started rifling through the papers on his desk. Eventually he said, "Nothing," and left Todd's office without another word.

Todd sat behind his desk taking deep breaths. They hadn't searched him for weeks. He was taking Vanessa to the movies tonight and thoughts of canceling went through his mind. What had that evil, swarthy looking hoodlum told Elliot to make him so suspicious?

Chapter 55

Todd tried to keep calm, but he was nervous and kept glancing over his shoulder as he walked along the sidewalk with Vanessa. It was a cold, windy night; the streets were poorly lit, and it would be two blocks before they reached the restaurant district.

"What's wrong?" Vanessa asked, pulling the collar of her coat up around her face.

Todd quickly related what had occurred. "They want me to work tomorrow morning," he said. "That's never happened before. Elliot wants to look at the outstanding debts."

The wind howled along the street, and flickering streetlights gave off a pantomime of moving shadows.

"Stop looking behind," Vanessa said, walking even faster to keep up with him. "If they were going to do anything, they'd have done it by now. I'm worried about you. I'm going to talk to Doug Lechte in the morning. I think you've done enough. It's time to get out."

"Doug's working on a Saturday?"

"It's a job for Max Lustig and Doug doesn't want to disappoint him. Max said it was a pity you weren't still with the firm because you would've been the best person to handle it."

Todd hardly heard a word Vanessa said. He was still thinking about what she'd said about getting out. He felt better now that he could see the lights of the entertainment district. "They won't let me. They'll want more."

"They had nothing before you told them about Karen Deacon and who knows what they'll get off Elliot's cell phone. You've done more than enough."

"I'm visiting Arturo on Sunday, so I'll talk to Grinich, but I already know what he's going to say."

Todd was as tight as a drum during the movie and when they came out he grabbed a taxi.

"That's only two blocks." The taxi driver growled. "How am I gonna make a buck out of that?"

"I want you to wait and then take me to Flushing."

"Ah, that's better." The taxi driver grinned.

"You're not staying?" Vanessa whispered, obviously disappointed.

"Sorry. I'd be useless and besides you'll be safer without me."

Todd tossed and turned most of the night. Elliot was a gangster, but the swarthy guy and his henchman were something else and positively scary. The usual smell of stale smoke and alcohol greeted Todd as he entered the bar. The thugs were around the pool tables, and McEvoy strode toward him shouting, "Stop right there, kid."

What followed was a search that lasted more than two minutes.

"Early night last night," McEvoy said. "Did you have a fight with the girlfriend or didn't she want to put out? Give us your phone. What's your password?"

McEvoy ran his eyes down the numbers called and received. "Don't you and the girlfriend ever text?" he asked, as he returned Todd's phone.

"No."

"Oh, I nearly forgot. Jack called to say he can't make it. He told me to tell you to go home." McEvoy grinned.

As Todd walked along the street back to his apartment, he knew that Elliot had never wanted him to work. It had been a setup so that McEvoy could search him. He racked his brain trying to think what he'd done that had them so suspicious. His call to Vanessa went through to voicemail, and he said, "Sorry, I'm feeling sick. Can we skip tonight? I'll come by after Castlebrough tomorrow."

Todd was careful not to change his regular Sunday routine, and he left his apartment at precisely 12:30 P.M. His senses were on high alert as he made his way along Gable Street, and he paid close attention to the cars parked on the street. Two taxis passed him, but he kept on walking toward Mount Street where he knew Grinich would pick him up.

Todd paid little heed to the dark blue Chevy parked in a no park-ing area. He was about fifty yards past it when he glanced around to see if anyone was behind him. There was a flash of movement in the Chevy and then there was nothing. He had never been followed on his visits to Castlebrough before, but now he was sure they were watching him. He stopped on the curb, slowly looked around, and hailed the first cab that he saw. Chas Grinich wouldn't be picking up his usual fare today. Todd sat directly behind the driver so that he could look in his side mirror. The Chevy maintained a distance of about three hundred yards from the taxi and was only conspicuous when it changed lanes to pass.

Chas Grinich was surprised and then worried that Todd wasn't walking along Mount Street at the appointed time. He drove slowly around the block and when there was no sign of him he became very concerned. Twenty-five minutes later he was relieved when his office called to let him know that Todd had arrived at Castlebrough at the usual time. Something had made him change his schedule, and Grinich pondered what he should do. He toyed with the idea of lining up on the cab rank in front of the jail, but there was no certainty that he would be at the front of the line when Todd was leaving. He had no idea what had occurred, but it hadn't been serious enough to curtail Todd's visit to Castlebrough. It was clear to Grinich that he should lie low for the time being.

Arturo never changed, and Todd wondered what was behind the veil. The room was set up, and the mobster was anxious to get his chess fix. After two games that he won easily, he stared menacingly at Todd and said, "You're no competition. You're playing like shit. I didn't have to wait two weeks for this. Any asshole in here who can hold a chess piece would put up a better fight than you."

"I'm sorry, Frank."

"What's wrong? Did you go out drinking last night? Are you hungover?"

"I wasn't going to tell you, but I think they're on to me," Todd replied.

"Tell me everything," Arturo demanded.

When Todd had finished Arturo smiled grimly and said, "So the Serbian has returned to New York."

"You know him?"

"Know of him," Arturo corrected.

"Is there anything you can do?"

"I warned you. They're in my backyard, but killing for the sake of killing is bad for business. However, if they break the rules I'll send them a message they won't forget."

"Break the rules?"

"You wouldn't understand. Shuffle the cards. I hope your gin's better than your chess."

As Todd was leaving, Arturo said, "Do you still have that number I gave you?"

"Memorized," Todd replied.

There was a line of taxis waiting at the front of the jail and Todd climbed in the back of the first one. There was a small shopping mall about two miles from Vanessa's apartment, and he told the taxi driver to drop him at the entrance. Within two minutes of being on the highway, Todd looked in the driver's side mirror, and there was the Chevy again. *Why are they watching me so closely? It has to have something to do with switching Elliot's cell phone. What do they know? Are they following Vanessa too?*

When the taxi pulled up at the mall, Todd gave the driver a fifty and took off. It was late in the afternoon, and there were few shoppers as Todd raced to the stairs to the parking garage. Without slowing, he ran through the garage and up the ramp to the street. There was no sign of the Chevy, as he worked his way down back streets to Vanessa's apartment. When he reached her street, he poked his head around an alley. The Chevy wasn't on the street. He sprinted the last two hundred yards, and when she opened the door, he was distressed and breathless. Before he could say anything she put her finger to her lips and said, "Hang on," and plugged her iPhone into the docking station and Beyonce's voice blasting out "Drunk In Love" echoed around the apartment.

Todd collapsed onto the sofa and in gasping breaths related what had happened with the Chevy.

"You look exhausted. You can't go back to Bandits, and you can't go back to your apartment. You'll have to stay here."

"You don't understand. Grinich won't agree and if he doesn't, I'll have to do the remainder of my sentence."

"Isn't that better than being killed?"

"That's just it. I don't think they know anything. If they knew about the phone switch, I'd already be dead. I don't know who that scary guy is but I think he's the reason they're taking so much more interest in me."

"He might be Elliot's boss?"

"No. Elliot didn't defer to him like he does when he talks to Dermott."

"Poor darling," Vanessa said. "Why don't you try and get some sleep? When you wake up, we'll go and get something to eat."

Chapter 56

The manager of Big Apple Mobile laughed when Jed Buckley asked him if he could get Jack Elliot's old phone back. "We've got a recycle bin with thousands of trade-ins and old cell phones in it."

"But it hasn't got thousands of blue Samsung Galaxies in it," Buckley replied. "I'll pay someone to go through it."

"Can't you see how busy we are? I can't spare anyone right now," the manager replied. "Besides there'll be quite a few blue Galaxies that we've binned. We'll have to identify the one you're looking for."

"Fuck! I need someone to start looking now."

"It isn't going to happen. The best I can do is get a couple of my staff to come in early tomorrow morning and then only if you pay. I don't know how long it's going to take though. Why's it so urgent? What do you want it for? There's nothing on it that you can use."

Buckley ignored the questions. "That's not good enough. I need it today. What if I get a few of my guys to help?"

"Can't do it," the manager said. "I'd have no insurance, and they're only going to be able to find the blue Galaxies. They won't be able to identify the phone you're looking for, and I've told you I've got no one I can spare to help them."

"All right, all right," Buckley said. "Call me as soon as you find it."

Elliot had been furious with Buckley and had called the store manager all to no avail. However, he didn't have long to wait and at 10:15 A.M. the following morning got the call he was waiting for. Forty-five minutes later the cell phone was in the hands of Manhattan's foremost telephony expert.

Brock Borchard had never been to Becker's house in the Hamptons before. As he sat in the study overlooking the tennis court he could see himself living in the same style, even in the same house and with Becker's young, well-endowed wife.

"I told you the kid was a plant," he said, "but you never listened to me. You know what your problem is, Dermott? You're getting soft and old. The FBI are probably watching you right now. Luckily I'm here to mop things up for you."

"If they're watching me, they're watching you, too," Becker replied.

"Yeah, but there's a difference. I'm young enough, smart enough and nimble enough to give them the slip. For that you should be grateful 'cause by tomorrow night I'll have made sure the accountant's disappeared. I knew there was something fishy about that phone. I'll get Dirk to take care of Elliot, too. He was the one who gave the kid his job, and has to pay the price for his mistakes. It's the only way the others will learn."

"You like killing, don't you?" Becker said, shaking his head. "You murder the kid and the Fibbies will come down on us like a ton of bricks."

"When I first came here, I learned that without a body it's impossible for the police to get a murder conviction. What a truly marvelous country." Borchard smirked. "That's why I'm here. I need to borrow your cabin cruiser tomorrow night. Don't worry, I promise there'll be no trace of him."

"I don't like it. The yacht club dining room's busy on Sunday night. There will be a lot of members around the jetties."

"Bullshit! We won't be there until after ten o'clock, and it'll be quiet by then. All I need are the keys to the jetty and the boat. Dirk's a master mariner so we won't need any onboard help. I shouldn't have to remind you that the buck should stop with you. It was you who let Elliot have his way and have a look at the shit that's put us in. You should be grateful that I'm bailing you out."

"All right, you can use the boat but make damn certain you don't get caught."

"Oh, I won't get caught. I never have. After this is over, I'm coming back to New York to work with you. Dirk is more than capable of running Chicago, and he won't fuck up like Elliot did."

"What are you talking about? I don't need you."

Borchard sneered. "You will. You won't have Elliot to do your dirty work, and besides, you're getting old and it's time you thought about retiring."

Becker flushed with anger. "You're not even close to being ready to run an organization this size. You might never be."

"I could already run it better than you are." Borchard laughed. "In six months' time you'll be superfluous. You're slipping, Dermott. It's better that you get out now while you still can. I'd hate to see you go the same way as Elliot."

"Are you threatening me?"

"Am I? Call it what you like. You knew this day was always going to come. We'll talk again after I've cleaned your mess up," Borchard said, noisily shoving his chair back as he got up.

Chapter 57

It was a two block walk to the south to the popular restaurants and a one block walk to the north to a greasy hamburger shop. Todd chose the latter, and as they left Vanessa's building, he scanned the street looking for the Chevy, breathing a little easier when there was no sign of it. He was jumpy and walked close to the curb in the beam of car headlights rather than in the shadows of buildings. It was drizzly, and the street was quiet, quieter than Todd liked, and he paused when they reached a short section that was in total darkness. When he saw the headlights of three cars behind them, he said, "Come on," and they walked briskly toward a flickering street light on the other side of the road. It had taken less than five minutes to reach Joe's Burgers but for Todd it seemed like an eternity. It was warm, and the smell of hamburgers and steak on the grill was overpowering. They sat in a cubicle where Todd could see the door and the street. "We should have sent out for pizza," he said.

"You can't hide forever. It's not as if they're going to seize you off the street."

"They're capable of anything. I just wish I knew why they followed me to the prison today. They've never done that before. All I can think of is the phone but how would they have found out?"

Their server introduced herself as Joan and said that the special was rib eye was on special and was excellent. Vanessa ordered it while Todd opted for a cheeseburger.

"One cheeseburger? You're too worried to eat. You've done more than enough," Vanessa said. "The FBI had nothing before your information," Vanessa said, reaching across the table and squeezing his hand. "You can't go back to your apartment."

Todd gave a feeble laugh. "All my clothes are there and without them I'm going to be stinky in a few days' time. Can you live with that?"

"When you tell Chas Grinich that you're out, give him the keys to the apartment, and he can get his men to get your stuff."

"I wish it was that easy." Todd sighed. "Grinich is not going to let me out, and if he doesn't, I'm staring at eight years hard time. Even if he does, and the Mr. Bigs aren't locked up, I'll still be in danger and so will you. I'll stay at your place tonight, but then I'll have to find somewhere else."

"Where?"

"I don't know. Maybe the FBI will put me in a safe house."

"You might as well be in jail. You'll have no freedom."

"I know. I know. Finish your coffee and let's get out of here."

The drizzle had stopped but the sidewalk was still wet, and Todd put his arm tightly around Vanessa's waist. "You know I always dreamed about you," he said, "but was too scared to ask you out. I'm no hero, you know."

"Why?"

"I just thought I was batting out of my league I suppose," Todd said with a weak grin.

"And now?"

"I'm still batting out of my league, but I love you. That's why you've got to take Doug Lechte's advice. It's not your problem, and if they catch you, God knows what they'll do. I'd never forgive myself if anything happened to you."

"Have you ever thought that I might love you?"

"Hoped," Todd replied. "Do you?"

"I don't know. There are times when I think I do. I don't like it when you put yourself down and say things like 'I'm no hero.' What you're doing takes a lot of courage. I don't know why you sell yourself short?"

"I don't want to disillusion you, but I'm doing this because I have no choice. If I wasn't facing eight years, do you think I'd be helping the FBI? No way! I spend half my time at the club living in fear. I'm not selling myself short. It's true. I'm no hero."

"I don't think you know what heroic means," Vanessa said, stopping and looking into Todd's eyes. "It means being scared, in your case terribly scared, but still doing what you have to in spite of the fear."

Todd felt better, but was still alert, glancing over his shoulder and looking for the Chevy while Vanessa was talking. As they neared the small section that was in total darkness, Todd looked around for the headlights of cars. The flickering streetlight on the corner of the alley flashed light every thirty seconds or so, and Todd steered Vanessa toward it. He paid no attention to the black Camry parked on the street and didn't see the dark blue one parked down the alley.

Dirk Vaughan moved out of the alley like greased lighting and held an ether-soaked cloth over Vanessa's mouth. Todd turned to see a mountain of a man before collapsing into unconsciousness. Farik and Ahmet dumped them in the trunk of the dark blue Camry.

"Find their phones," Vaughan said.

"Here," Farik said, passing two phones to Vaughan.

Vaughan then carefully searched Todd and Vanessa again.

"Don't you trust me?" Farik growled.

"You can't be too careful," Vaughan replied, removing the batteries from the phones before giving them and the casings to Ahmet in the black Camry. "Get rid of them in four separate bins."

Borchard hadn't moved from the black Camry. "Dirk," he shouted, "she lost a shoe. Pick it up. Don't leave any trace."

By the time Vaughan got back to the trunk, Vanessa was bound and gagged. "Hurry up, Farik," he said, as the huge man tied Todd's ankles.

"The girl is like something out of *Playboy*." Farik leered.

"In a few hours' time you'll be fucking her." Vaughan grinned. "After me that is."

When Todd came to, he was disoriented but it didn't take long for him to realize he was in the trunk of a moving car. He could feel Vanessa next to him and the only thing he could see was her luminous watch. It was 8:25, thirty-five minutes since they'd left the hamburger shop. He tried to shout, without success and then he felt Vanessa stirring.

The last place that Dermott Becker wanted to be on Sunday night was the Hamptons. As he looked out at the Manhattan skyline from his seventy-fifth story penthouse, he pondered the threats that Borchard had made. The Serbian thug was moving back to New York for one reason, and that was to take over the whole organization. The mistake of letting him in as a shareholder was coming home to roost. He was too violent and what he was doing tonight would bring the full weight of the FBI down on them.

Becker felt exposed and knew that the FBI would have almost certainly tracked him via Jack Elliot's cell phone but what evidence did they have? None! It was only Borchard and his violent actions that were likely to bring him down. The unsophisticated thug had even said that he was going to kill Jack Elliot for making the mistake of employing the accountant. Elliot had made a serious mistake, no doubt about that, but Becker didn't think he deserved to die. Besides, Elliot was only one of only a handful of people that Becker trusted and was vital to the New York operation. Becker picked up the keys to his wife's town car, put the prepaid cell phone that he'd bought the prior day in his jacket pocket and took the private elevator to the parking garage. He would destroy the phone after making just one call and sending one text to a number that very few people had.

Twenty minutes later, Becker stopped in a quiet Brooklyn street and made the call.

"Max Lustig speaking."

"You don't know me, but two of your young friends are in serious trouble."

"Who is this? How'd did you get my number?"

"I don't have much time. Do you want to hear what I have to say?"

"Go on."

Two minutes later Lustig said, "How do you expect anyone to find the boat?"

"It has a GPS tracker that can't be deactivated. I'm texting you the details."

"How do you know all this? Why are you telling me? Why don't you call the police? What do you expect me to do?"

Becker didn't reply. Instead, he laughed and hit the end button. He had avoided competing against Max Lustig for thirty years because he believed the transport tycoon was connected. He was about to find out if he was right.

Chapter 58

It was a moonless night, and the two Camrys stopped in the shadows of the jetty hidden from CCTV. Vaughan flicked open the trunk and held an ether-soaked cloth over Todd and Vanessa's noses. Then he removed their gags and untied their bindings. Ahmet lifted Vanessa from the trunk and put her under his arm like he was helping a drunk to walk. Farik did the same with Todd and a few minutes later they were onboard the Sea Folly.

"Gag and tie them up in the galley," Borchard said. "Farik, drive the car they were in, to a quiet place and set it on fire. Make sure you destroy it. Ahmet, follow him. Don't be long and when you get back, park away from the marina. Dirk, get the boat ready to go. The longer we're here, the more exposed we are."

The Sea Folly was a sixty-five-foot cabin cruiser luxuriously fitted-out with a runabout at the stern. Vaughan removed the moorings, kicked the massive Mercury engines over and raised the anchor. Twenty-five minutes later the two giants, both gasping for breath, climbed aboard, and Vaughan eased the boat away from the jetty. There was a small bar in the galley, some bar stools, a long white four seat sofa, two matching chairs, a built-in dining table and half a dozen padded, wooden dining chairs. Todd and Vanessa hadn't come around and were gagged and bound to two of the dining chairs.

Looking around the luxurious boat, Borchard said, "What a waste," to no one in particular, and then, "Farik, go upstairs and tell Dirk to anchor about four miles out. Then he can join us."

"Do you want me to wake them, boss?" Ahmet asked.

"We've got all the time in the world," Borchard replied, picking up the baseball bat and smacking it into his hand. "You can remove the gags but let 'em sleep. After all, it'll be their last."

The engines cut out, and they heard the anchor being lowered. A few minutes later Vaughan came down the stairs. "Did you check the runabout?" Borchard asked.

"It's fine, and it's got plenty of fuel."

"Good. We'll torch this thing when we've finished. We don't want to leave any evidence."

"You're going to burn this boat? You can't be serious. What's Becker gonna do?" Vaughan asked.

"Don't worry about Becker. He's yesterday's man. We're taking over, and we don't need a boat like this."

"You're the boss."

"Ain't that the truth. Dirk, we're not parked in a shipping lane or anything stupid like that are we?"

"We're moored about three miles offshore," Vaughan replied. "No one's gonna hear or trouble us."

Todd moaned and slowly came around. His arms and wrists were strapped to the arms of a chair, and his ankles were bound to its legs. "Wha-what is this?"

The man he feared was standing in front of him shouting. He had a baseball bat in his right hand that he was smacking into the palm of his left hand.

"Oh, I think you know what it is, kid. It's called getting caught snitching to the cops." Borchard snarled. "Now I want to know who you told and what you told them. You can tell me and I'll put a bullet in your head. You'll die without pain. Or you can fuck me around, and you'll die in agony. Who's your contact at the FBI?"

Vanessa slowly opened her eyes. "Miss America." Borchard sneered. "I promised the boys they could have some fun with you. You're gonna love it."

"Leave her al–"

Todd never got another word out before Borchard's left hand crashed into his cheek nearly knocking the chair over. "Shut the fuck up. I'm gonna ask you again. Who's your contact at the FBI? You know, the one who gave you the phone to switch."

"I-I don't know what you're talking about."

"Dirk, get me the pliers," Borchard said. "Listen to me, kid. They say that having a fingernail pulled out is more painful than having your nuts crushed. Can you believe that? If you don't start talking, you're gonna be able to tell us because you're gonna experience both. What's his name?"

"I don't–"

"Dirk, hold his hand down flat," Borchard said and clamped the pliers around Todd's thumbnail and slowly pulled.

Todd had never experienced pain like it before and mercifully blacked out.

Blood gushed from Todd's thumb, and Vanessa screamed. Tears rolled down her cheeks. "You bastards! You bastards!"

"Wake him up, Dirk," Borchard shouted.

Vaughan started slapping the sides of Todd's face, and he opened his eyes. His thumb was throbbing with excruciating pain and there was blood everywhere.

"Who's your contact?" Borchard asked.

"Chas-Chas Grinich," Todd said through clenched teeth

"Better," Borchard said, the baseball bat back in his right hand. "That wasn't so hard, was it? How did you get the phone?"

"I-I go to Castlebrough ever sec-second Sunday. Grin-Grinich has been driving the taxi."

"Slimy bastard. That's how he did it. How did you get the messages to him in between Sundays?"

"I-I did-didn't. It was only Sun-Sundays."

"Give me the pliers, Dirk."

"You might not need them," Vaughan replied, ripping off Vanessa's blouse. Then he grabbed her bra and stretched it until the clips gave away.

"No, no," Todd shouted, as Vanessa screamed and tried to pull away from Vaughan's groping hands.

"Nice firm tits," Vaughan said, coupling them in his hands. "I'm gonna enjoy doing you."

"I was the contact," Vanessa said fighting back tears.

"Now we're getting somewhere." Borchard grinned. "Well done, Dirk."

Vaughan took his hands off Vanessa's breasts and slid them up to her neck and face. Her head hardly seemed to move as she bit into his fingers with everything she had.

"Bitch!" he yelled, drawing back his fist but before he could bring it down Todd rocked his chair into Vaughan's legs, and they crashed to the ground. The thug was quick to get to his feet, stomping on Todd's head and then breaking his ribs with a vicious kick."

"Get him up," Borchard said.

As Ahmet righted the chair, Borchard drew the baseball bat back as far as he could and smashed it into Todd's knees.

Two of Vaughan's fingers were bleeding, and he was shaking his hand. "When your boyfriend wakes up, I'm gonna spread-eagle you on that sofa in front of him, bitch. When I'm finished, they're gonna be next. Farik's three hundred pounds and he's big. You're gonna wish you'd never been born."

There was a light bump and Borchard said, "What was that, Dirk?"

"Nothing. Probably just a buoy. Don't worry, there's no one else out here."

As Todd's eyes opened, Borchard said, "Did you tell the FBI about the Deacon woman?"

"Yes." Todd gulped.

"You overheard Elliot threatening her?"

"Yes."

"Fuck, and I thought Elliot was smart. He won't be far behind you," Borchard said.

Vaughan stood behind Vanessa's chair cruelly gripping her breasts while ordering Farik to cut away the bindings.

"What are you doing?" Borchard snapped.

"It's time for some fun with Miss America," Vaughan replied, exaggeratedly holding his crotch.

"Not yet," Borchard said. "We need to find some chains or weights first. I want them to disappear forever. That means no bodies floating to the surface. You can have your fun after we're prepared."

"Fuck! Farik, get upstairs and have a look in the storage lockers. If you can't find anything, the larger items will be stored under the deck at the stern. And hurry up. I'm looking forward to getting my hands on hot chocolate," Vaughan said, leering at Vanessa's breasts. "On second thoughts try under the deck first."

Chapter 59

There was no light at the stern of the cruiser and Farik fumbled around with a small flashlight looking for access below the deck. The click was almost imperceptible, but Farik's body thumped to the deck. The suppressor and hollow point bullet had done their job, and Farik's head exploded like a watermelon explodes when hit by a sledgehammer.

"What was that?" Borchard asked.

"Farik thumping around trying to work out how to get below the deck," Vaughan replied. "Fucking idiot. Ahmet, go and help him."

Ahmet could see the beam of the flashlight on the deck and walked toward it saying, "Farik, why are you taking so long? What's wrong?"

He gasped when he saw Farik's headless body but before he could shout the hollow point hit him in the neck just above the spine killing him instantly.

Tony Lombardi, dressed in all black, climbed down from the top of the flybridge and hid behind the bulkhead at the front of the boat. He knew the next man to come up the stairs would be Borchard's right-hand man, Dirk Vaughan, and that he would be far more cautious than the two dead members of his gang. About five minutes had elapsed before Vaughan shouted, "Ahmet, Farik, what are you doing? If this is a joke, I'll have your balls."

Lombardi watched as Vaughan came out on the deck, pistol drawn and edged toward the flashlight at the stern. Lombardi moved like a cat, and as he shoved the barrel of the Glock hard into Vaughan's back, he whispered, "Don't move or you're dead. Pass me your gun and don't get any funny ideas. I'm using hollow points and from this range they'll tear you apart."

"Who are you?" Vaughan asked as Lombardi threw his gun into the sea.

"You don't need to know," Lombardi replied while he patted Vaughan down. "A derringer and a switchblade. You came well prepared."

"Dirk," Borchard shouted, "what's taking you so long? Is everything all right?"

"Answer," Lombardi hissed, "tell him everything's okay."

"It's fine, Brock. We'll be down in a minute," Vaughan replied. He never called Borchard by his first name, always boss.

Lombardi threw the derringer and switchblade overboard and then pushed Vaughan to the stern near Farik's body. "Take a good look at where your man's head's meant to be. That's what a hollow point does. When we go downstairs, you'll have your arms at your sides. Try anything and I'll blow your guts out."

Vaughan edged downstairs with the Glock pressed hard into his back. Lombardi looked over Vaughan's shoulder and saw Borchard standing behind Vanessa with a knife to her throat. She was naked from the waist up and tied to a chair. Todd was in the chair next to her. He looked like he was dead.

"Don't take another step," Borchard said, "or the girl's dead. Who are you?"

"So you tipped him off," Lombardi said, dropping the Glock behind Vaughan's right knee and pulling the trigger.

Vaughan screamed in agony and then blacked out. His leg was just a bloody stump. Lombardi shoved him hard down the stairs, and his head crashed into the floor.

Borchard was hiding behind Vanessa and Lombardi couldn't get a clean shot. "Is the kid still alive?"

"Yes, but he's lost a lot of blood," Vanessa said as tears streamed down her cheeks.

"Shut the fuck up," Borchard said, punching her in the head.

"You're lucky he's still alive. He's the only reason I'm here. He's your one bargaining chip. He dies, you're dead. Oh, you asked me who I was. I'm one of Mr. Arturo's helpers and the kid's one of his friends. Providing he lives, you can still walk off this boat alive."

"I'll kill his girlfriend if you get one step closer," Borchard said, pressing the knife hard into Vanessa's neck. "Now drop the gun or I'll slash her throat."

Lombardi laughed and pointed the Glock directly at Vanessa. "Do you think Mr. Arturo cares about her? He doesn't know her. He couldn't care less. I ought to put a bullet through her myself. You know what it'll do, don't you? It'll still be expanding and releasing energy when it goes through her tiny waist. When it hits your guts, it'll blow it into a thousand pieces. You've got your knife under the wrong throat."

Vanessa's sobbing was the only sound in the cabin. If Borchard didn't kill her, the other man would.

Lombardi appeared to lower his eyes as Vaughan stirred. Borchard saw his opportunity and flung himself the three feet to Todd's chair with his knife outstretched. Lombardi knew a head shot would be too risky, but Borchard's body was an easy target and the bullet hit him in the middle of the chest. Blood and guts spewed from the jagged hole in his back and splattered all over the wall. Vanessa screamed hysterically as blood, and bone fragments sprayed all over her.

Lombardi soaked a towel in water and began gently cleaning Vanessa's body while he spoke soothingly to her. "Miss," he said, "you're safe. I was never going to shoot you, but I had to say something to make Borchard move. Mr. Arturo likes your boyfriend, and he told me I had to rescue both of you."

Vanessa was gasping and struggling to get control. She jumped when Lombardi took off his t-shirt and bent down to pick up the knife.

"Miss, I'm not going to hurt you. I'm going to cut you loose, and you can put this on," he said, dropping his t-shirt on her lap. "Take deep breaths. Try and get control. I know it's not easy. Sit there until you feel like getting up and then do it slowly. I'm going to cut Todd free."

"Who-who are you? How did you get here?"

"Tony Lombardi. I met Todd in Castlebrough. I'm not alone. Neri," he shouted, "it's all clear. See if you can find a stretcher. Tell Bruno to get ready to kick the Zodiac over."

"Oh, you're Tony Lombardi," Vanessa said. "Todd told me about you."

Lombardi carefully cut Todd's bindings away and put two fingers on his neck. "His pulse is feeble, and he's lost a lot of blood. We have to get him to a hospital before it's too late, but the pain of moving him might be more than he can bear. We can't stay here."

"They-they had ether," Vanessa said. "Would that help?"

"Yes," Lombardi replied, patting down Borchard's pockets. "He hasn't got it."

"Maybe they left it in the car," Vanessa said.

"No, I've got it," Lombardi said, pulling a small bottle of ether out of a pocket of Vaughan's jacket before putting his foot on him and rolling him over.

Vaughan groaned, and Vanessa got shakily to her feet and asked, "Are you going to help him?"

"No," Lombardi replied. "Don't worry about him. He'll either bleed out or drown. I don't care which. Get some movement back in your limbs and then see if you can clean Todd up. It'll save the paramedics a few minutes and might be vital. Hopefully, it won't take long for Neri to find a stretcher."

Lombardi bounded up the stairs. Todd was in a far worse way than he had let on to Vanessa. The Zodiac was tied up to the cabin cruiser, and Bruno was waiting. "Bruno, get back to the boat and tell the captain to moor hard against us. Get him to arrange for a hospital helicopter to meet us when we reach shore."

Bruno kicked the oars out of the way, and a moment later the roar of the Zodiac's motor broke the stillness of the night.

There was an extensive medicine cabinet on the flybridge and Neri found a portable stretcher at the bottom of it. Then they rushed down the stairs. Time was not on Todd's side. Vanessa had cleaned him up as best she could, and he was mumbling incoherently. Lombardi unfolded the stretcher on the floor and told Vanessa to soak a cloth with ether and hold it over Todd's nose for five seconds. With great care, Lombardi picked him up in his arms and gently placed him on the stretcher. "Sit down, Miss," he said. "Our boat's going to be tying up soon and we might get quite a thump."

A few minutes later they heard the deep, slow throb of powerful engines and felt a gentle bump. "Our captain's very skilled," Lombardi said. "Miss, you can go up on deck and wait for us. Neri, take the front of the stretcher and be very careful."

Bruno was standing on the deck of a dark blue cabin cruiser. Lombardi and Neri balanced the stretcher on the rails of the two boats and then pushed it over to Bruno and the captain. "Can you climb over, miss, or would you like us to help you?"

"I'll be fine," Vanessa said, scrambling over the rails.

"Bruno," Lombardi shouted, "grab your tool box and join us."

"The young man needs urgent medical attention," the captain said.

"We'll only be a few minutes," Lombardi said. "Come on, Neri, let's get the bodies below deck."

As they dragged Vaughan up the stairs, he groaned, and Neri said, "He's still alive."

"So?"

"Nothing."

"If you want to be merciful and put a bullet in his head, do it," Lombardi said.

Bruno joined them and helped push Vaughan under the deck. "What do you want me to do?" he asked.

"Two charges. Set them to explode in ten minutes. I want minimal or no flame. Just make sure they're powerful enough to sink this thing. I'm going to have one last check before we push off. Neri, tie the runabout up behind our boat."

The galley and the adjoining saloon were a complete mess. Blood and bone fragments covered the floor and walls. Lombardi stared around the room and saw Vanessa's torn blouse and bra on the floor. He left them there. They would fit perfectly with the story she would tell.

Chapter 60

Todd was still on the stretcher on a double bed in one of the cruiser's bedrooms. He hadn't regained consciousness, and Vanessa was holding a damp cloth on his forehead. They were about two miles from the marina when she heard two deep, distinct booms. "What was that?" she asked.

"The sinking of the Sea Folly," Lombardi replied. "Now listen to me. When the FBI questions you, tell them everything that occurred until you lost consciousness."

"I never lost consciousness."

"Yes, you did. You never saw me or my men. You never saw this boat. The captain's just cut the runabout loose. I'm going to tell the helicopter pilot and medics that we found you and Todd in it unconscious and that you haven't regained consciousness."

Vanessa looked puzzled. "I don't understand?"

"I'm sorry. I'm going to have to give you a dose of ether. You'll be out for about fifteen minutes. It's important that your last memory before blacking out is being tortured."

"Bu-but they're going to want to know how we got away. What am I going to say?"

"The same as what Todd says."

"But he doesn't know," Vanessa said, and then, "Oh, I see."

"I can't afford to let anyone see this boat. We're going to have to take the Zodiac," Lombardi said, pouring some ether on a hand towel. "Are you ready?"

"I suppose I have to be."

"Bruno," Lombardi shouted, "get the Zodiac ready. Neri, bring the stretchers down."

Five minutes later the Zodiac motored into the foreshore. The helicopter was in a grass clearing about seventy yards away. Lombardi and Neri carried Todd up the beach where two medics took the stretcher and loaded it on the copter. One of them started attending to Todd immediately. "He's in a bad way," he shouted over the noise of the rotors. "What happened?"

"Dunno," Lombardi shouted back, pulling the captain's hat down over his forehead. "They haven't regained consciousness since we found them floating around in a small boat."

"We'll get the other one," the medic said, signaling the pilot to come and help. "You'll have to make a report to the police you know."

"Of course," Lombardi said.

"They must be important," the medic said. "We were told to drop everything and get down here. They must be rich kids."

"I wouldn't know."

Ten minutes into the flight, Vanessa woke up. She was strapped down, and Todd was next to her. "Where am I?" she asked.

"You're in a medical helicopter, miss. Don't worry, you're in safe hands. What happened to you?"

Vanessa closed her eyes.

"She's drifted off again," the medic said to his partner. "She's got some bruising on the face and cuts and scratches. Compared to the guy she got off light."

"You don't know what trauma she went through," the other medic said. "They were both found unconscious. I don't think she got off lightly."

He's got broken hands and fingers, a thumbnail ripped out, broken ribs, shattered kneecaps and a broken jaw and cheekbones. He'll walk again, but he'll never regain full use of his legs."

"That's if he wakes up."

"What type of animal does something like this?"

There was a helipad on the top of Saint Michael's Mercy Hospital, and doctors and nurses were waiting to rush Todd into the O.R. They wheeled Vanessa into a consulting room where she was given a full examination. "I'm fine," she protested. "I just need a hot shower. When will we know if Todd's going to be all right?"

"You've had a severe blow to your face. It's quite swollen," the doctor said. "There's nothing broken though. Is Todd your boyfriend?"

Vanessa paused. "Yes," she said. "He's very brave. How is he doing?"

"He's in the hands of the finest surgeons. We're going to have to wait until he comes out of the O.R. We have a private room for you where you can a shower and get some sleep."

"No, I'm waiting until the surgery is finished. I need to know that he's okay."

"That won't help anyone," the doctor said. "I'm going to give you a mild sedative to help you sleep."

"What a mess," a young surgeon said, as he hovered over Todd. "What could he have done to deserve this?"

"That's not our worry," the lead surgeon replied as the anesthetist gently inserted a tube into Todd's throat.

The young surgeon made a linear incision over the front of the kneecap and blood erupted. "Swab," he said to the nurse.

"Beethoven's 5th," the lead surgeon said to another nurse, and a moment later the music of the master flooded the operating room.

"It's worse than what we thought," the young surgeon said. "There are a lot of small fragments. I hope we have better luck with the other knee."

Ten hours later Todd was wheeled out of the O.R. and into intensive care. Todd's parents had already questioned and sympathized with Vanessa. She and her parents held back when his father approached the surgeons. The lead surgeon didn't know him but had seen his picture and read his papers in medical magazines. They spoke in hushed tones for a few minutes and then Todd's father rested his hand on the surgeon's shoulder and said, "Thank you, doctor. It was fortunate that the paramedics brought him to Saint Michael's. I know of your work with the reconstruction of faces."

"Please, call me Chris," the doctor said. "His face, hands, and ribs will heal, but he'll need to learn to walk again and God knows what psychological damage he suffered. He's going to be with us for quite some time."

"Thank you, Chris," Todd's mother said. Her eyes were red, and her cheeks were stained.

Vanessa had been standing behind the Hansen's listening. "Doctor," she asked, "when will he recover from the anesthesia? When will I be able to see him?"

"Within the hour I'd expect," he said, "but he's going to be dopey. I'd leave it until tomorrow. He should be out of IC by then."

Vanessa was about to ask another question when they were interrupted by a nurse, "Miss Hodge," she said, "Detective Grinich from the FBI is here. He'd like to see you."

"We'll come with you," her mother said.

"He'll want to see me by myself, mom. Why don't you and dad grab coffee in the cafeteria? I won't be long, and then you can take me home."

Grinich's clothes were rumpled, and it looked like he hadn't slept. "How do you feel, Vanessa? Are you okay?"

She could tell by his tone that he wasn't genuinely interested in her health but was dying to know what had happened. "I'm all right," she said, "but Todd's in a bad way."

"Yeah, I know. I'm sorry. We were up all night trying to find you. What happened after you left that hamburger joint? That's when we lost you."

Vanessa related everything that occurred until she lost consciousness.

"The medics said that two guys brought you to shore in a Zodiac. Do you remember anything about that?"

"No, they told me the same thing. They said that one of the guys said they found us unconscious and floating around in a small boat. I don't understand. Have you spoken to them?"

"The paramedics said that your rescuers were going to file a report with the police, but no one's heard a word from them. Don't you think that's strange?"

"I don't know. Maybe they just didn't want to get involved?"

"Weren't you wearing one of their t-shirts?"

"I guess it must have been, but I have no recollection of putting it on."

"Yeah," Grinich said looking skeptical. "Tell me the names of your kidnappers again."

"As I said I only heard their first names. Brock, Farik, Dirk, and Ahmet. Brock was their leader. Do you know them?"

"Yeah, I know them. They're called the Serbian Mafia. Don't worry, we'll get them and when we do they'll be going away for twenty years. I'm still confused about how you got away. Do you remember getting into that runabout?"

"I've already told you. No, I can't."

"Concentrate! Think! You either got in yourself or someone put you in it. Why would they do that?"

"I don't know. Maybe Todd will be able to tell you after the anesthesia's worn off."

"Yeah, yeah. They won't let me talk to him until tomorrow. Vanessa, I'm sorry about what happened to you, but I promise you we'll get these guys."

No, you won't. "I hope so," Vanessa said.

The following day, Vanessa was at the hospital just after 9 A.M. and was pleased to find that doctors had moved Todd from IC to a private room. The nurses said that he had awoken in the early evening, and while he was incoherent they had managed to get some orange juice and cereal into him. Vanessa entered his room quietly not wanting to disturb him if was asleep. He wasn't and smiled then grimaced in pain when he saw her. His lower face was heavily dressed, and his hands swathed in bandages. "It hurts to smile," he said in a raspy voice. "I've been racking my brain. How did we get away?"

If I tell you, you might slip up with Grinich. "I've been wondering the same thing. I was hoping you might be able to tell me."

"It's a mystery," he said. "I felt so sorry for getting you involved. I was certain they were going to kill us. I wonder why they changed their minds."

I'll tell you what happened when you've healed. "You were heroic. Do you remember throwing your body at that thug to save me from getting hit?"

Todd paused, and his eyes glazed over. "I'm sorry, I don't," he said self-effacingly. "The last thing I remember is them tearing my thumbnail out. I think I blacked out."

"Yes, you did. Don't you remember them smashing your kneecaps?" she asked and immediately regretted it. "I'm sorry."

"No," Todd said, a tear trickling down his cheek. "My knees are full of screws and wires. The surgeon said I'll need extensive physical therapy. How did the bastards do it?"

"You need to rest," Vanessa said, kissing him on the forehead. "There'll be plenty of time to talk when you're feeling better."

Later that afternoon Grinich visited Todd but left not having learned anything.

Chapter 61

On Monday morning, Dermott Becker called Brock Borchard on numerous occasions but his calls went straight to voicemail. He then called the warehouse in Chicago, but no one had seen or heard from Borchard. Becker then asked to speak to Dirk Vaughan and was told that he was with Borchard.

Becker was a cautious man, and his next call was to Jack Elliot to ask if Todd was at the club. He wasn't. Elliot hadn't heard from him. Becker told Elliot to go to Todd's apartment to see if he was there and to find out where the girl was. When Elliot called back, he said that there was no sign of Todd, the girl was not at work and that neither of them were using their cell phones.

On Tuesday morning, there was still no sign of Borchard or Todd and Vanessa. Becker had driven down to the marina, and his cabin cruiser wasn't there. He was frustrated and hated uncertainty. What was Borchard still doing on the boat? Had he killed Todd and Vanessa? Late in the afternoon, Elliot called to say that the girl was at her apartment and that her mother was staying with her. Two hours later, he called to say that he'd had the girl followed to Saint Michael's Mercy Hospital and Todd had been admitted with life-threatening injuries.

Becker knew what had happened and doubted he would ever see the Serbians again. He was pleased. Borchard had been a loose cannon, and with him out of the way there was nothing to connect Vulture Inc. to the blackmailing of Karen Deacon. Of course, the FBI would know that Vulture was behind the insider trading and the bribery of union officials but with Borchard dead, they would be unable to prove anything. Vulture would lose its access to drugs out of Chicago, but Becker wasn't worried. They were making more than enough from the legitimate investments of ACME and perhaps it was time to have a break or even cease their illegal activities. The FBI and the SEC would posture and threaten, but as a former lawyer, Becker knew they didn't have enough evidence to proceed in the courts. He smiled contentedly. He had had a gut feeling about Max Lustig and spent a lifetime being careful not to cross paths with him. His gut had proved to be accurate.

On Wednesday morning, Becker drove down to the marina. A few minutes later, extremely agitated, he called the local police to report that his cabin cruiser, Sea Folly, had been stolen.

By Friday, Todd was feeling better and lying on his ribs was no longer painful but his knees still ached. He was surprised when Vanessa turned up to visit with Doug Lechte and Max Lustig. They chatted for a few minutes and then Lechte said, "You're off the hook. The FBI and the SEC know that your cover is blown. You're no use to them anymore."

"What about the jail time and the appeal? What are they going to do about it?"

"Well, they can't let your appeal succeed," Lechte replied, "because that would create a precedent."

"So I'm going back inside?"

"No." Lechte laughed. "Unfortunately the conviction will remain but a judge in chambers has commuted your sentence to time served. You won't serve another day."

"That's a relief," Todd said, but he looked far from happy. "I'll never get another decent job as long as I live though."

"Todd," Lustig said, "these two brought me along because I told them that they're not going to get anywhere near the accounting fees they've extracted from me in past years."

"Why are you smiling, Doug? I don't understand. What's it got to do with me? Vanessa, why are you so happy? Can someone tell me what's going on?"

"I won't need them, Todd, because I'll have you," Lustig said. "That is of course if you accept my offer. As soon as you're well, I want you to become my group financial controller. I've been coasting the last few years and with your financial expertise and my charm, we're going to embark on a foray of takeovers."

"And as Max's empire grows, we'll get all our accounting fees back and then some. It's a win, win, win." Lechte laughed.

"Oh, I nearly forgot," Lustig said. "Your salary and benefits will be considerably more than what you would have earned as a partner of Montgomery Hastings & Pierce. There's one condition though. If I ever catch you gambling, I'll terminate your employment instantly."

"Max, I'm not a gambler. I never have been. I'm obsessed with systems. I just had to test what I thought was an infallible system. If I was a gambler, I would've bet on the fights, basketball, baseball and football. I never did, and I never have. That's something you won't ever have to worry about."

"I'm pleased to hear that," Lustig said, "we're going to make a great team. Todd, I'm surprised you're not happier. Is there something you don't like about my offer?"

"I'm sorry. I just can't stop thinking about those guys who grabbed Vanessa and me. I don't know how we got away, but they were going to kill us. They're going to try again."

"Oh, I wouldn't worry about them." Lustig smiled grimly. "I think you've seen the last of them."

"You're looking tired, Todd," Lechte said. "We better go. Good luck with the new job."

"Before you go, tell me what's happening with Phillip Cromwell and The Disabled Children's Fund?"

"Our professional indemnity insurers settled the civil claim and significantly increased our annual premium. I can tell you, the partners, including Vanessa, were not happy. The FBI haven't finished their investigation, but the mayor's been charged and it's likely that Phillip will be too."

"Is he still managing partner, Doug?" Todd asked.

"Yes, but he's confined to administrative tasks. He turns sixty next year and the partners have suggested that he retire."

"Will you be the new managing partner?" Todd asked, stifling a yawn.

Lechte laughed. "No, the role holds no interest. Someone will surface. They always do. You're looking tired, son. We better get going before the nurses kick us out."

"I want to have a few minutes with Todd," Vanessa said. "Thanks, Max. I'll see you back at the office, Doug."

"You're a lucky man, Todd." Lustig laughed. "If I was thirty years younger I'd give you a real run for your money."

After they had left, Vanessa said, "You don't have to worry, babe," then explained everything that had happened on the boat.

"God," Todd said, "you must have been terrified. Poor thing. I feel for you."

"Your friend, Tony Lombardi, is a strange man. He's cold, cruel and ruthless and yet not without compassion. He was gentle with me, and it was his t-shirt that I was wearing."

Todd was about to say something and stopped.

"What's wrong?" Vanessa asked. "What are you thinking?"

"Did you tell Max Lustig what you told me?"

"No, of course not. Lombardi told me to tell no one other than you."

Todd smiled. "Max Lustig knows. Why would he tell us not to worry and that we won't see them again if he didn't know? Do you think he was behind our rescue?"

"I don't know, but I do know we have nothing to worry about. I'm going to find out what type of man you are when you're not under stress. It's going to be fun."

Chas Grinich sat opposite Aaron Lord and contemplated what might have been. "Borchard was the weak link, you know. He would've brought their dirty empire down had he lived. They killed him. What was Becker like when you interviewed him?"

"Smug. Sure of himself. Without a worry in the world. They've stopped dealing drugs and loan sharking out of Bandits. They're squeaky clean," Lord replied.

"Yeah, he's smooth all right. What temerity, reporting his boat stolen to the local police and his insurers. From the girl's description, it's the boat they were on. He undoubtedly lent it to Borchard, and when he failed to return, Becker reported it as stolen to cover his ass."

"What do you think happened to it?"

"It wouldn't surprise me if it's on the bottom of the Atlantic," Grinich said.

"Yeah, but if it is, who put it there? The Serbians had a history of violence, so who'd take them on?"

"Someone more violent," Grinich said.

"You're probably right."

"What did you dig up on that crooked L.A. accountant, Ridgeway?" Grinich asked.

"Nothing," Lord replied, "he's supposedly retired and living off his investments. On the surface, the directors of Vulture Inc. are upstanding citizens."

"Bastards! They know we know who they are, and they're lying low. They were behind those murders and the insider trading. If only they hadn't found out about Todd Hansen. If we'd been able to keep him in there for another six months, we would've had enough to nail them all."

"It might've been a mistake to do the phone switch," Lord replied. "Something must have gone wrong. Somehow they found out about Todd."

"Yeah," Grinich said, "maybe you're right. I'm sure he knows what happened to Borchard, and if he doesn't, the girl does. They're playing us."

"And there's nothing we can do about it." Lord sighed.

Five weeks after the surgery, the surgeon removed the plaster but told Todd it would be another year before he removed the metal pins and wire. Physical therapy started immediately to rebuild his wasted muscles, but it would be another two weeks before he attempted to walk again. His face and ribs had healed, and his thumbnail had started to grow, but he was in constant pain with his knees. Doctors were gradually weaning him off painkillers but the pain, particularly in the early hours of the morning, was unbearable. It was outside visiting hours, and he was watching television when he looked up. Tony Lombardi was standing at the door. "You look a lot better than the last time I saw you." He smiled.

"Come in," Todd said, pointing to the chair next to his bed. "I owe you my life. I'll never be able to repay you."

"I told you before that you have some very powerful friends. I was just their instrument."

"I know what you are," Todd said, looking into the professional killer's eyes, "but Vanessa told me how gentle and kind you were. What you did terrified her, but she said you're not all bad."

"I hope you told her not to circulate that opinion." Lombardi grinned. "I'd hate it rumored that I was getting soft."

"We don't talk to anyone about you, and Vanessa will never breathe a word about what she saw on the boat."

"Relax. I was joking. I know you'll never say anything, but I do have a message for you. Mr. Arturo said that he's looking forward to resuming the chess challenge as soon as you're mobile."

Todd frowned and rested his chin in his hand.

"Todd, I know you don't want to mix with us gangsters but without Mr. Arturo you'd be on the ocean floor right now. He won't do anything if you don't show up, and he won't show any disappointment, but if you don't visit him, you'll be making a big mistake."

"Thanks, Tony. Let him know I'll be there as soon as I can walk."

"I wish someone had taught me how to play chess when I was young," Lombardi said. "You don't know how powerful you are. You have more clout than your new boss, and he's very influential."

"Did Max Lustig have a hand in saving us?"

"You ask too many questions," Lombardi said, getting out of the chair. "If I never see you again, have a nice life."

"You too, Tony." Todd grinned.

Epilogue

Nearly a year had elapsed when two scuba divers spearfishing in the bay came across the wreck of the Sea Folly. Excited, they spent the rest of the day exploring the galley, bar, and bedrooms. It was late in the afternoon when they forced the hatch to the under-deck storage open and discovered the skeletons. Shocked and having no idea how many there were, they wasted no time getting to the surface and radioing their find to marina authorities.

Grinich was on the scene the following morning and later that day authorized the salvage of the crime scene. He would have to wait for confirmation of DNA before he could identify the remains, but he had no doubt who they were. When he called Becker, the crooked ex-lawyer appeared to be shocked before saying, "Thank God you've found it. The damn insurance company has been refusing to pay out. Now they'll have to."

"Why would Borchard steal your boat? You were associates."

"You just said you won't know who they are until after DNA testing. However, if you're right, I have no idea. You'll have to work that one out, detective. Excuse me, I have to call my insurers."

Vanessa was also shocked but in Grinich's professional opinion, nowhere near as shocked as she should've been. As she had done all along, she denied knowing what had happened that fateful night. Grinich visited Todd at his Brooklyn office. The young man walked with the aid of a cane and moved like he was seventy. He was more open than his girlfriend, but no more helpful when he said, "Thank you, Detective Grinich. That's the second best news I've heard this year. I hope the DNA confirms your thoughts."

"Second best," Grinich queried.

"Yes, Vanessa and I are getting married in the fall. Nothing could beat that."

"Congratulations."

It had been more than a year since Karen Deacon had heard from Grinich, and she was surprised when he called.

"So the men who were blackmailing me are dead," she said.

"Yes."

"Did you find anything?"

"No, Mrs. Deacon, not yet. I think the CDs might have died with them."

"How?"

"I think they hid them in a place that only they knew about."

"So there's a possibility that someone will eventually stumble over the CD? Besides, it's sure to be on a hard drive somewhere."

"I think it's remote," Grinich said. "We went over their computers and the video wasn't on them."

"Tom wants to get back together again. If only I could be sure they wouldn't surface, I'd say yes. I don't know what to do? What would you do, detective?"

"Life's too short to spend jumping at shadows. I think you should make your decision on the basis that the CDs will never surface."

"Thank you. I'll think about what you said."

"Good-bye, Mrs. Deacon. Good luck with whatever you decide."

Grinich looked at the fat open file in front of him and silently cursed. He had devoted the past year to following and investigating Becker and his cohorts, but they hadn't as much as jaywalked. His gut told him that Borchard and the Serbians had gotten out of control and Becker had set them up. Grinich had been convinced that Jack Elliot was the hit man, but he had had a watertight alibi. He suspected that Todd and Vanessa knew what had occurred, but they were never going to talk. Grinich closed the file and bound it in legal tape. It was time to move on.

Reviews:
Good, bad or indifferent are important for readers and authors alike. The Amazon links are:

U.S. http://a.co/bO3FqKb
U.K. http://amzn.eu/7n88WNS
Canada http://a.co/d8EvLmU
India http://amzn.in/j8XL1AI

Other Books By Peter Ralph

More white collar crime suspense thrillers by Peter Ralph are on the drawing board.

For updates about new releases, as well as exclusive promotions, visit the author's website and sign up for the VIP mailing list at http://www.peterralphbooks.com/

Visit here to get started:
Amazon USA: http://goo.gl/Ya6GB7
Amazon UK: http://goo.gl/Uxc4Iy

FREE DOWNLOAD

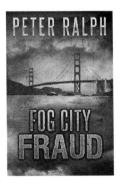

FOG CITY FRAUD

Why is an irate investor holding his advisor's receptionist hostage on the 16th level of a high rise building?
Sign up for Peter Ralph's reader's group and get your free copy of the novella Fog City Fraud: a financial suspense thriller.

Visit here to get started:
http://www.peterralphbooks.com/

Printed in Great Britain
by Amazon